KATERI'S TREASURE

A MATT O'MALLEY ADIRONDACK MYSTERY

THOMAS G. KANE

Galtee Press
Maitland, Florida

<u>**Also by this author:**</u>
Desperate Hours
Desperate Days
These books are available in print at fine bookstores,
online at <u>www.ThomasGKane.com</u>
and are available for Kindle and Nook

ISBN: 978-0-578-14694-2
Published in the United States of America
Galtee Publishing
Maitland, Florida
www.ThomasGKane.com
2 4 6 8 10 9 7 5 3

PRINTED IN THE UNITED STATES OF AMERICA

The cover photograph was taken by Molly Kane
and is used with her permission.
The image was captured from the deck of the
Algonquin Restaurant looking out at Sweetbriar Island.

DEDICATION

I have been told that two of the loneliest jobs in the world are being either a judge or a writer. I cannot speak to the first, but I do not think the second is really true.

This book has been cobbled together thanks to the help of many friends, whom I hope will recognize their contributions throughout this book. Some have unique insights into the history and geography of the Adirondacks, one spent a lifetime of dedicated public service in the State Attorney's Office which gave him encyclopedic knowledge of all the creative ways we human beings have found to end the lives of others in sudden and violent fashion.

Others are just plain smart, and would help me talk through my writer's blocks, and figure out ways to move the story forward, or helped just by being good friends and asking when to expect the new Matt O'Malley adventure, which gave me the encouragement I needed to finish this book. These people are too numerous and too private to list here, but I hope you all know who you are, and I hope you will accept my deepest thanks! I must single out for special thanks, though, Jeanne Klein and Kevin Murray for reading the manuscript and helping find a multitude of mistakes before we printed them!

All the help I received would still not have resulted in the completion of this book without one other irreplaceable person in my life, my wife. Eileen, by her love and encouragement, is the one who keeps me going on my writing projects. She is the one who, by thoughtful reading and analysis of the manuscript, finds the flaws and helps me correct them. She is the one who, by her attention to matters that are beyond my grasp such as spelling and the rules of grammar, has made this book as readable as it is. By her dedication and hard work over too few days and into too many nights, she managed to edit this book in a remarkably short time, made necessary by my procrastination and lack of diligence.

Most important of all were the many probing questions Eileen would ask in order to help pull the story into focus and to keep it from wandering down rabbit holes so that, hopefully, you, the reader, will find the time you spend reading this book enjoyable and exciting.

Tom Kane
July 2014

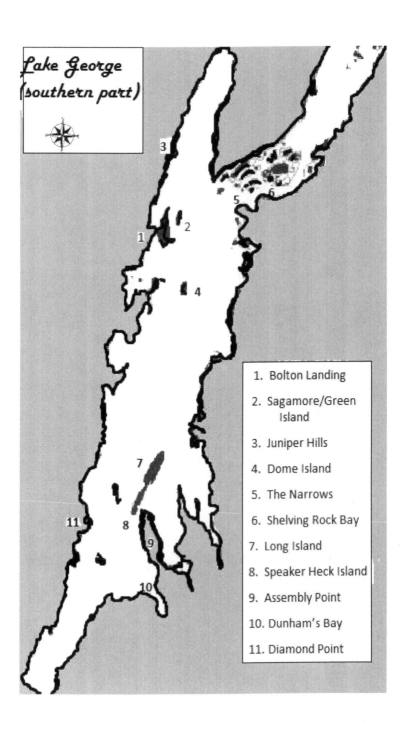

Lake George
(southern part)

1. Bolton Landing
2. Sagamore/Green Island
3. Juniper Hills
4. Dome Island
5. The Narrows
6. Shelving Rock Bay
7. Long Island
8. Speaker Heck Island
9. Assembly Point
10. Dunham's Bay
11. Diamond Point

CHAPTER ONE

Matt O'Malley's wetsuit flooded with the cold water found forty feet below the surface of Lake George. He shivered in the cold and hoped his body would warm the trapped water quickly; but, for a reason he did not quite comprehend, he did not think it would. It was more than the water that was making him cold. It was a noise. It was a noise he had never heard before, and one that seemed strangely out of place.

Moments before, Matt was sitting on the gunwale of Danny Hilman's SeaRay enjoying the warm sun and beautiful sights that surround you when you are on the Queen of American Lakes. This dive into history had been planned for years. Matt was fascinated by the stories of the Lake George bateaux – lumbering old ships designed to be the most fearsome naval platform ever conceived by a Seventeenth Century mind from which to wage war. He had learned everything he could about them.

His last words before rolling backward into the water were directed at Stanislaus Okonski and Danny Hilman, who had elected not to dive with Matt and their friend, Kevin Murphy. "You guys don't know what you're missing. These boats were like Darth Vader and the Death Star, except these were real and just as frightening in their time."

The bateau that O'Malley had come to dive on was a gunship built by the British during the French and Indian War, intentionally sunk in the waters off Wiawaka, near Fort William Henry, in 1757, to keep it out of the hands of the French. The high walls of the vessel slanted back at the top, much like a mansard roof, to provide protection to the gunners who would blast cannons through the tiny portholes. These gunboats reminded those with good imaginations of turtles.

The bateaux struck fear in the hearts of those under attack. They could withstand being struck by shot, and had the capacity to carry and fire a fearsome assortment of artillery, cannon, and mortar designed to reach the enemy no matter where he hid. If Matt had any idea of the amount of death and destruction that would result from this SCUBA dive, he too would have been just as afraid of the bateaux.

Matt hung suspended in the water and concentrated on just listening. Thump ... thump ... thump. There it was again. Matt stopped moving and he stopped breathing. Without the gurgle of the bubbles coming out of his regulator, the water was nearly silent. He could hear the whine of distant powerboat engines and the other normal underwater sounds, but the odd thumping sound was gone. Shaking off a vague and unexplainable sense of dread, he pressed on with the dive. Tilting himself down, he kicked his flippers and headed for where he believed the bateau was located.

He fought to contain his excitement when, for the first time, this link to an age long gone by came into view. The boat was too large to take in all at once, but he could tell the approximate size and configuration of the bateau by what he was able to see. It was then that the thumping noise returned. This time it was just a rhythmic sound, but it was even louder than before.

Matt again suspended voluntary activity and just hung quietly in the water, trying to orient himself and locate the source of the sound. As he floated in the water, he felt one with the lake. He could feel the ebb and flow of its currents and eddies. Completely relaxed, he felt almost hypnotized by the thumping and the gentle motion of his body moving back and forth at the whim of the lake's forces. It slowly occurred to him that his motion had somehow become synchronized with the thumping sound. Was it something he was doing unconsciously? He resolved to do nothing to affect his motion – but he remained synchronized with the thumping sound.

O'Malley turned in the water to signal his dive buddy, Kevin Murphy, to join him. Kevin was a high profile anti-trust lawyer from Miami who was nowhere to be seen. *"Not exactly textbook dive protocol,"* thought O'Malley, but not unexpected with Kevin, whose incredibly active and creative mind often led him off to explore things that others would scarcely notice, let alone find intriguing.

Matt swam closer to the bateau. While most of it was gone, the keel and some of the ribs could clearly be seen. One small portion that remained was the side that gave protection to the artillerymen. Matt's heart was beating faster than normal as he felt he was swimming back into time, and was about to touch and be a part of something that had not been seen or touched, except by a lucky few, in nearly three hundred years.

The roof of this part of the wreck was very efficient at blocking the sunlight from above. Matt had to let his eyes adjust for a moment before he saw a long, dark object float under the roof. It too was moving with the ebb and flow of the lake, just as Matt had, and it was banging into the wall and roof, causing the thumping sound. Matt had a moment of relief and embarrassment when he realized that a submerged log was making the thumping sound. He had allowed his mind to play tricks on him, and had conjured up some scary image based on nothing more than a vivid imagination and an eerie sound.

O'Malley released air from his buoyancy compensator to allow himself to sink below the level of the object on which he had been so focused, and be on what was left of the deck. Then, as he slowly swam up the wall, he examined the portholes where centuries before men, long weary of war, had fought tremendous battles - not to win, but to merely live to go home.

As he went further up the wall, the log came back into sight. He had the horrible revelation that he had been wrong. The object was not a log. The black neoprene wetsuit completely covering the body may have briefly given it the appearance of a log, but eerily white hands floating alongside the body put an end to that belief. The lack of any voluntary movement, combined with the complete and prolonged absence of air bubbles from the diver put an end to any hope that this was something other than a dead body.

As Matt stared, transfixed by the body, it rolled in the water, exposing the face for the first time. Empty dark eyes stared out of a blue-white face. Long black hair floated freely about the face, moving randomly in the gentle eddies. O'Malley jerked away from the body, kicking his legs and waving his arms in a furious effort to put space between himself and the corpse. O'Malley threw up into his regulator. Death had that effect on him.

CHAPTER TWO

Miles Smythe eased back in the leather barstool, tapping the edge of his now empty glass while mouthing the words, "I'll have another," to the extremely attractive young woman manning the bar at The Boathouse Restaurant.

As the name would imply, the restaurant was directly on Lake George and looked like it was, or at least had been, a boathouse. They maintained a system of docks, available for hungry boaters to pull in, tie up and grab a table for a wonderful meal. There was also a small, enclosed area directly under the dining room for more long-term storage of boats. The top floor had been renovated years ago to be a delightful restaurant with a long bar where one could sip a favorite beverage while either gazing east across the lake, or south down the lake towards the Village.

The prime dining spot is off the main dining room. An outdoor hexagon-shaped area accommodates one large table where the lucky al fresco diners can enjoy an outstanding meal and watch the comings and goings on the lake. It was quite easy while sitting there to imagine you were sitting in a gazebo during a more gracious time as you watched the paddleboat Minne-ha-ha steaming slowly north up the lake with its cargo of awed tourists. In the bar, a flat-screen TV was always tuned to whatever sports channel had a game playing. The place was comfortable, cozy and welcoming. It was a favorite dining spot among the locals and the experienced tourists.

The lovely bartender quickly delivered Smythe his third gin and tonic with a warm smile, showing a set of perfect, white teeth that seemed brighter still when contrasted against her deeply tanned face, which, in turn, was framed with long, straight blonde hair. She lingered just a bit longer than was necessary. She was the kind of girl who smiled with her lips and with her eyes, in this case a set of green eyes speckled with gold.

Ordinarily, Smythe would have been intrigued, and he never let a difference in age interfere with his pursuit of a conquest. Why should he mind? They never seemed to mind. The American girls were charmed by his high-toned British accent and clever banter. Though he had passed the five decades mark, he had too much discipline to let his body betray his age, and he certainly was not impaired by any quaint sense of morality that may have restricted his actions towards those he considered to be his lessers.

However, today he had more important matters on his mind – like what to do about the body. When he had killed the Chechen, it had been a matter of necessity. After all, he was a professional and he did not take a life just for sport. Disposing of the body was a problem he would have taken care of earlier in the day when he had returned to the bateau, but that damn SeaRay had been parked over the dive site, flying a red flag with a white diagonal stripe, the universal "Diver Down" flag, and he had to turn back without cleaning up his mess. He would watch carefully, and when the time was right, he would go back for the body. That is, unless the new divers had discovered the body.

Smythe leaned back on the leather barstool that groaned slightly under the torque exerted by his shifting weight. He smiled a little thinking of how he had not panicked when he had seen the SeaRay. He was pleased with himself that he had the presence of mind to write down the bow number of the boat. *"Once an agent, always an agent,"* he thought to himself. He was determined that the owner of NY 8975 MA was about to become his new best friend.

He wondered what they would do when or if they discovered the body. Whatever they do, it will give him insight into how this situation was changing. If they called the police, at least he would know that they were not searching for his prize. However, if they did not call the police, he would know who his competitors were, and they might even provide him with the information he lacked. He was determined to get back and finish his search of the bateau.

The people on the Sea Ray were a minor problem, or perhaps an opportunity. His more pressing problem now was to figure out who had sent the Chechen to interfere with his work. The dead man would cause him few problems. His worries now were how many more like him may be out there, and what they might know of the treasure he sought.

Things were easier when he had worked with MI-5 in one sense. He had a vast array of resources and other agents to help him solve problems like this. One phone call and a clean-up team would have removed every bit of evidence from the scene, not that he left much evidence behind, and the body would just disappear. Still, he preferred the freedom that working independently gave him. Mostly, he liked the idea of not having to answer to superiors who cared more about rules than results; and, of course, he hated the idea of turning over the booty to some faceless bureaucrat. The prize he would find would be his! No matter what his current employer believed.

Even though his firing by the head of MI-5 was years ago, he could still see the smug, merciless face of the Director as he stared over the bar and out into the lake. His tormentor's face was as clear to him now as the day he was made redundant in 2010. The man who fired him sported a cold, meaningless smile under his dead eyes. His bald head was fringed on the sides with dark, short hair, dyed no doubt, and trimmed close to foster his military bearing. Stuffed shirts like Jonathan Evans were more interested in being knighted than in getting results. Evans could cashier him out of the service, but he could not take away his unique skill set, or his burning desire to embarrass MI-5 and the entire British security establishment. *"Revenge was a dish best served cold – and by the rich!"* thought Smythe as he sipped his gin and tonic, savoring the bit of lime pulp that had floated onto his tongue.

It mattered not to Smythe that Evans had retired and that, like his predecessor, had been awarded a minor non-hereditary title. Nevertheless, he had been dragged through the mud by the press and some members of Parliament too queasy to do what was necessary to win an asymmetrical war waged by Middle Easterners or Africans. *"Bollocks on them,"* thought Smythe, *"The pay is so much better when you take it from the bad guys."* This payday might be around twenty five million dollars US, a tidy sum that would let him live a life like a noble even if he did not have a title. He smiled to himself as he did the conversion in his head and realized that it was nearly fifteen million pounds.

The pretty bartender came up to Smythe, again displaying that dazzling smile. "You ready?" she asked.

"What an intriguing enquiry!" replied Smythe with just the hint of a smile. "Am I ready for what?"

He thought he detected an ever so faint blush as the bartender's eyebrows briefly rose, and then she looked down momentarily. When she looked back up she locked eyes with him and, in a steady voice, said, "Why another gin and tonic, of course." There was a pause before the "of course" that Smythe thought lasted meaningfully too long. The creeped-out woman behind the bar hoped that her "of course" had put an end to whatever the customer had been thinking.

"As much as I would delight in passing the evening in your company sipping G&Ts at your bar, I am afraid that duty calls and I must answer."

"Too bad," she replied with just the hint of a pout, not forgetting she worked for tips. "I am here nearly every day, all summer," she said while she thought to herself that if this guy came back he would be getting his drinks served in dirty glasses.

"Useful information," said Smythe as he turned from the bar and strolled toward the exit. He left behind the unpleasant scent of his cologne, peanut shells, broken straws he had been fiddling with, and an empty glass. What he did not leave behind was a tip.

Katie wiped the bar and put the glass into a rack to be taken to the kitchen to be washed. She was expressionless as she efficiently went about her duties. She thought to herself, *"What a jerk!"* When she glanced up, Miles Smythe had disappeared from sight, but not from memory.

CHAPTER THREE

Albany International Airport is a wonderful place to fly into or out of as a passenger. It is large enough to attract major airlines eager to serve the capital of a large state; yet, it is small enough to navigate with ease, and travelers enjoy a friendly and welcoming atmosphere with upscale eateries and a few nice shops. The airport has the same type of security Americans have come to expect in a post 9/11 world, but somehow it just seems a bit more laid back than most airports.

The baggage handling area of Albany International, however, is no better than any other airport, and worse than some. Here there are no pleasant amenities, just dreary, unpainted concrete block walls, the roar of antiquated conveyor belts, and the relentless, backbreaking flow of luggage demanding to be either taken out of the belly of airplanes or to be placed there. It is hot work in the summer, and in the winter, the work is enough to break even a strong man.

The work is so hard that the baggage handlers sweat profusely under their heavy coats and gloves, their jeans wet from their efforts. Yet, it is so cold most days of the winter that when there is a brief respite between the arrivals and departures, the men and women who labor anonymously in the belly of the planes and under the concourses can feel their jeans stiffen as their sweat freezes. It is in those brief moments when most dream of doing something grand someday that would change their lives. Usually, the dream involves winning the lottery, as it often does for the mathematically challenged who cannot begin to understand the daunting odds that this government-backed shell game imposes on them.

It was here that Edgard Onobanjo toiled away in anonymity. He did not mind hard work. When he was a boy in Africa, it was nothing for him to get up before dawn and walk six miles from his village to go to the school the Irish priests had set up. There he learned to do his sums, improved his English, and learned of the Catholic faith. He excelled in his religion classes because he wanted to impress his teachers, but he never understood this religion, nor did he ever avail himself of the opportunity to be baptized. After the long walk home, his father, who did not believe in education, would insist that he still do a complete days work on their subsistence farm. Edgard would dutifully scrape away at the dry earth as he and his family tried desperately to coax a crop from the burned-out land.

Edgard would still be there if his family had belonged to a different tribe. One day, when he was away at school, rebels came onto the poor farm and killed his father, mother, and his two sisters. They were on a mission to kill everyone in the area that did not belong to their tribe. He found his father with his arms hacked off, and his throat slit. His mother and sister had obviously suffered terribly before their death, a death they probably welcomed rather than endure further abuse by the rebels.

Edgard Onobanjo knew what he had to do. He had no future in Somalia. His father had spoken of taking the family to the refugee camps in the Sudan. He did his best to bury his family in the hope of protecting them from the jackals, vultures, and other scavenger animals. He found a small satchel in his father's chambers, which he filled with his only other set of clothes and some canned food and preserves his mother had prepared. He climbed on a chair to reach the small tin where his mother had hidden the family savings. He had stared at the few coins and the filthy bank notes for just a moment, wondering if his mother, who could be extraordinarily stubborn, had given up her life rather than tell the rebels where the savings were hidden.

That very night he began to walk. First, he went back to his school to thank his teachers and the Irish priests who had tried so hard to educate him. They urged him to stay, but he had nothing left in Somalia except bitter memories. The priests warned him of all the treacherous people he would encounter on his journey, but they could not shake his resolve. If only his father could have torn himself from his nearly barren farm and gotten the family to the relative safety of the refugee camp they, at least, would still be alive and together. He would not repeat the mistake.

The priests were successful in convincing him that a trip to even the southern part of the Sudan was too dangerous and too arduous. Instead, they convinced him that Kenya was both closer and a safer journey. The priests' school was located west of Bardere and the journey to a refugee camp near Wajir was a distance of about one hundred and fifteen miles as the crow flies. However, there were few roads and Edgard was not a crow. He could have made the trip faster and easier by rafting the Webi Jabbu River, but he decided to take the priests' advice and avoid the river that was under the control of pirates. The main road connecting the two cities was also ruled out because of the rebels who controlled it and demanded tribute for safe passage. Edgard promised to go overland through the arid deserts. He would shadow the road for guidance but he would not travel on it if possible.

The priest, Father Monahan, when he would get homesick for Erin's Green Isle, always told his students stories of his hometown of Knocklong near the beautiful Glen of Aherlow, and would sing lovely songs of his homeland. He cried as he pressed a piece of paper into Edgard's hand.

"Here, lad, take this. 'Tis the name of a mate of mine from the seminary in Maynooth. Sure, he's a good man, and he's working in the refugee camps. Find him, show him this note, and tell him that I asked him to look out for ye. Will you do that, so?"

Edgard stared at the priest with giant, unblinking eyes sunken into his gaunt face and solemnly nodded that he would, as he stuffed the paper, unread, into his satchel.

He secretly hoped that this friend of Father Monahan's might actually send him to this magically beautiful place called Knocklong, where he could live out his life in peaceful tranquility, gazing on green hills and eating something called a

"99," whatever that was.

Edgard avoided all human contact on his journey since he knew not whom to trust. The meager supplies he had brought from his home were soon gone, as were the supplemental provisions given to him by the priest. Fortunately, they had lasted him long enough to trek through the most arid portion of his trip. He was a resourceful hunter, and, as the landscape gave way to hills and green forests, he was able to snare small animals to eat during the day while he hid out and rested. At night he would walk. He walked for twenty-four nights until he finally found the refugee camp in Wajir. He had avoided the rebels and large animals of prey along the way. He was lost for a while. He was delayed by rivers he could not forge, and by mountains where he could find no passage. Pure determination finally led him to the refugee camp.

He immediately set out to find his protector. However, Father Monahan's seminary classmate could not be found. He had recently fallen ill from the local parasites and had returned to Ireland for treatment and rest.

He did find another man who was impressed by his knowledge of English, his determination to leave the refugee camp, and by his compelling tale of how he happened to arrive at the refugee camp. This man was Arthur "Skip" Mackey, formerly the voice of NASA, and now with the Catholic Relief Services. After a forty year, wildly successful career involved with space exploration, Skip had retired and had volunteered to come to Africa. He felt it was time to do something to improve life on earth. His contacts with various governmental agencies over the years had resulted in quite a database of the private phone numbers for many "Movers" and "Shakers." Skip had decided that the problems in the camp were overwhelming, and that he could not save everyone, but he could make a real difference for a few of these poor lost souls.

Skip took up the cause of Edgard Onobanjo. He wanted to get him out of the squalor of the refugee camp and send him somewhere spectacularly different. It took months of wrangling, emails and phone calls, but eventually Skip got him the needed immigration visa. Edgard was on his way to

America - to Albany, New York specifically, and to a foster family where he could complete his education.

Mackey wanted Edgard to experience what he had experienced as a boy: the belief that life's adventures were limited only by your imagination, the beauty of the Adirondacks, and the thrill of leaping from a cliff into the glorious waters of Lake George. The family that had agreed to accept Edgard, Peter and Mary Ann Winkelman, had a summer cabin in Diamond Point; and, thanks to Mackey, would provide a loving home, safety, and the hope of a new life to Edgard.

However, the world is a small place, and tribal ties are unbreakable. It would only be a few years before Edgard would be called upon to do some favors for the rebels he had tried so hard to avoid on his twenty-four day trek to a new life.

CHAPTER FOUR

Danny Hilman and Stanislaus "Big Oak" Okonski were enjoying the warmth of the summer sun on board the SeaRay. The twenty-two foot boat rocked gently as the lake's waves lapped at its sides. Neither could understand the fascination of Matt and Kevin for suiting up in smelly neoprene and hoisting on weight belts and heavy air tanks to go poking around a nearly three hundred year old wreck in the cold waters at the bottom of Lake George. They were perfectly happy to relax and stretch out on the boat, take in the warm July sun, and enjoy some cold Genny Lights.

While the other two men were diving the wreck of the bateau, Danny and Oak prepared to enjoy an hour or so of peace and quiet, complete with a tasty lunch from their favorite place. Oak was setting up the support for the boat's round dining table while the theme from the movie, *Last of the Mohicans,* played on the boat's stereo system. It was a curiously appropriate selection since they could see the rebuilt Fort William Henry, the scene of the massacre described in the James Fenimore Cooper book, just south of them on the lake. A gentle breeze ruffled through the bimini top, adding to the perfection of the day. Danny was unpacking the Neuffer's Deli chips and sandwiches from the ice chest.

"Hey, Oak, what would you say to a cold beer?" asked Danny.

"Hello, friend!" said Oak, as he extended his arm to catch the Genny Light flying in his direction.

"You had the roast beef on an Everything Bagel, right?" asked Danny.

Before Oak could respond, however, they both turned toward a commotion erupting by the stern of the boat.

"Holy crap! Holy crap!" yelled Matt as he spit the

regulator from his mouth.

Oak and Danny glanced at one another in alarm.

"What's the matter?" asked Danny.

"Where's Kevin?" asked Oak.

"Holy crap! I can't believe it!" was the only reply.

"What?" they both yelled in alarm, just as Kevin popped to the surface about ten yards off the port stern.

"What's going on? Why did you come up so quickly" yelled Kevin as he rolled to his back and began kicking his fins to propel himself toward the boat. By the time he arrived, Matt had already thrown his swim fins on board and had climbed up the ladder.

"I found a body!" gasped Matt as he loosened the buckle on his equipment, shrugged the tanks off his shoulder, and gently lowered them to the deck of the SeaRay.

"You ... WHAT?" asked an incredulous Danny.

"I found a body wedged inside the bateau," said Matt in disbelief.

"I didn't see any body," said Kevin, as he threw his fins on board.

"That's because we got separated! It's like we never heard of the Buddy System," said O'Malley in exasperation.

The wake from a passing boat caused the SeaRay to rock dramatically as Kevin clung to the ladder, waiting for the boat to settle down again before he tried to climb the ladder. His head was forced underwater as the wakes passed and the arm clinging to the ladder jerked at his shoulder as the boat bobbed up and down.

"Oh, no! Not again!" said Danny as he leaned back against the gunwale.

"What do you mean, 'Not again?'" asked Matt with an offended tone.

"What do you think I mean? Every time you show up to visit, the body count in this quiet little burg starts to skyrocket!" said Danny.

"That's just not fair," said Matt. "This is just a drowning victim. I had nothing to do with it."

"What's not fair is that dead people start popping up all

around you, and I get involved," said Danny.

Even though he had been retired from the New Jersey State Police for ten years, Oak's "cop senses" started to tingle. "What makes you think this is a drowning?"

"Where the hell was this body?" asked Kevin, as he finally got on board and flopped, tanks and all, onto the rear settee.

"It was wedged under the gambrel on the bateau. I heard a bumping sound, and when I went to check it out, I found this diver – dead as the proverbial doornail," answered O'Malley.

"I get it," said Oak. "There's a dead body down there. My question is, why do you assume it was a drowning?"

"I don't know. I guess because inexperienced divers drown all the time, and there was nothing to suggest that anything else happened."

"Why do you think the diver was inexperienced?" asked Oak.

O'Malley gave an annoyed look at Oak. He did not like being questioned as if he were the subject of a police inquiry, but then his lawyer's mind clicked in. Years of handling trial and discovery matters in Florida had taught him never to assume anything. He was making a rookie mistake by jumping to the obvious conclusion. Vacations make the mind lazy.

"You're right. I don't know his experience level. I just assumed that because he was diving alone; and experienced divers just don't dive without a buddy."

"You were alone," said Danny.

"Okay, do you know if it was a man or a woman down there?" asked Oak.

"I only got a brief look, but I am ninety-five percent sure it was a man," said O'Malley, more thoughtfully now as he turned other possibilities over in his mind.

"Oak, you've got something on your mind. Spit it out. Why don't you think it was a drowning?"

"I have no way of knowing right now, but it's an unexplained, unattended death. I just think we shouldn't make any assumptions."

"Agreed," nodded O'Malley.

"It is kind of odd," said Kevin.

"What is?" asked Hilman.

"That there are no other boats here. How did that guy get here? It's too far to swim from shore," mused Kevin.

"Should they go back down and retrieve the body so we can bring it to shore?" asked Hilman.

"Nope," said Oak. "This is a crime scene. We need to call the authorities."

"I'll call Reardon," said O'Malley.

Mike Reardon was the former New York State policeman assigned to the security detail of Senator Ted Gleeson. When he retired, his only goal was to do as much fly-fishing as possible. Instead, in need of professionalizing its small force, the town of Bolton Landing snapped him up to be their Police Chief by making him an offer he could not refuse.

Reardon first met O'Malley a few years before when O'Malley had played a role in thwarting a terrorist plot that was unleashed on Lake George. Other circumstances had their paths intersect over the years, and he and Matt had become good friends. Each had come to respect the integrity and skills of the other. Reardon was a complex man. He gave every appearance of being a "strictly by the book" sort of guy, yet he had a strong moral compass that compelled him to exercise the discretionary latitude that is afforded to the "cop on the beat" to decide when to arrest and when to look away. Reardon had looked away when he had observed a crime committed by O'Malley and his friends as they had combated an even more heinous crime just a year before.

"We are out of Mike's jurisdiction down here," said Hilman, who lived in Bolton Landing.

"I know, but these small local departments share resources; and, since I doubt anyone else around here will have Mike's credentials, I suspect he will end up getting involved one way or the other," said Matt.

"You call Reardon," said Oak, "while I get a call into the Lake George Village police."

CHAPTER FIVE

Miles Smythe rolled his eyes as he felt the small phone in his back pocket vibrate. He had never placed a call on this phone, and the only incoming calls were from the man who presumed he was Smythe's employer.

"Is it done?" was the only greeting offered by Fahran Zadran.

"I am offended that you would even feel you have to ask whether such a menial task has been completed," said Smythe in a tone meant to convey humor and good fellowship among colleagues. However, Fahran Zadran was not a man who enjoyed jokes, and he did not consider Smythe a colleague. Zadran had an historical hatred for the British that ran deep in his blood. Smythe was merely a necessary evil he would tolerate, but only for as long as was absolutely necessary.

Zadran failed to respond to the bonhomie, which made Smythe just a touch uncomfortable. Zadran was in a hard business in a hard part of the world, which made him a hard man. You do not become the largest producer of poppies, and the largest exporter of heroin and opium in Afghanistan by being "Mr. Nice Guy."

Zadran fought everyone – the Taliban, the Russians, rival producers, the Karzai government, and, even occasionally, the CIA, which seems to rapidly change its position on the drug trade – sometimes fostering it, and sometimes restricting it. So far, he had always won. He had one inviolate rule – if you take his product, you pay his price.

"Of course! You ordered it, and I did as you wished. The Chechen has decided not to pursue the business opportunity any further," replied Smythe, ever mindful of the powerful algorithms used by the NSA to keep track of criminal and terrorist activity being plotted on telephones.

"Excellent," said Zadran. "Can I assume that his decision will not be revisited?"

"Indeed, you can," said Smythe.

"In your negotiations with him, were you able to get any helpful information?"

"Sadly, he was not interested in sharing his sources," said Smythe. "He may have hoped to sell that information to other interested parties. He had a reputation for being stubborn," said Smythe, as he pictured the Chechen twisting in agony, as he was repeatedly being tazered to encourage him to talk.

"He also was a hard man from a hard part of the world, so he refused to divulge any information."

Clearly, whoever had employed the Chechen had scared him more than either Smythe or Zadran.

"That is unfortunate," said Zadran.

"Not to worry. I have another reliable source, and I expect progress over the next few days." Smythe's jaw was set firmly as he contemplated his source.

"Jambo is going to screw you, but he better not screw with me," he thought.

"I will call back on Thursday. I expect you to have progress that will please me by then," Zadran said in a tone that was more threat than idle conversation.

"Tickety-boo," was the cheerful response from Smythe, who was not as confident as he sounded, but was relieved that the call was going to end before he was asked about how he had disposed of the body.

*　　　*　　　*

Michael Reardon could be identified from quite a distance as he stood ramrod straight at the wheel of the center console Boston Whaler that was plowing through the waves on Lake George. While shorter than "Big Oak" Okonski, Reardon stood well over six feet tall, and was deeply tanned from his time on the boat. Thanks to twenty-seven years of self-imposed discipline and physical training during his career as a law enforcement officer, he remained youthful appearing and flat-bellied. Only the extensive graying of his short-cropped hair hinted at his true age.

He approached the SeaRay at nearly full speed, right up until the last moment when he spun the wheel hard and dropped the engines briefly into neutral, then reverse, and then back to neutral. The Whaler wound up drifting its starboard side gently into the port side of the SeaRay, where Danny had already deployed his oversized bright blue fenders.

"Hi, Mike!" said O'Malley. "Thanks for getting here so fast."

"Are you kidding?" said Reardon. "When you're in town and bodies start popping up, I know my nice, peaceful and tranquil life is coming to an end unless I get control of the situation right away!"

"Great," sighed O'Malley, "Now he's starting in on me as well."

"You know I'm only kidding," said Reardon, "but you have to admit you are a magnet for trouble."

"It's not me," exclaimed O'Malley, "I just happen to be around when other people do bad things."

"I assume that's the body you found," said Reardon, as he nodded toward the Lake George Patrol Boat where a team of divers were struggling to steady the body, and the deck crew was beginning to lift the body, now on a backboard, onto their boat.

"Who is it?" asked Reardon.

"Dunno," said O'Malley.

"What happened to him?" asked Reardon.

"Dunno," replied O'Malley.

"Wow! You're just a bundle of useless information," said Reardon.

"Mike, all I know is I went for a dive on the bateau and I heard a thumping sound. When I went to investigate, I found this guy. That's when I called you."

"And thanks for that," said Reardon, ironically. "You

know I am the Chief of Police of Bolton Landing, not Lake George Village."

"Yeah, yeah, but we both know they will call you in on this, and I figured you might as well be in on the ground floor."

"Maybe, but until I get an official request for assistance you're going to have to deal with them, and I hope you have better answers than you just gave me, " said Reardon.

"Crap on a cracker!" said Hilman.

"What's wrong with you?" asked O'Malley.

"Are you kidding me?" asked an incredulous Hilman. "What are the chances they haven't heard of your past exploits up here. With all that smoke, they are going to assume fire, and we are all in for a rough ride."

The Big Oak smiled broadly and said, "Just think, Danny, in a few days you could be locked up, and someone could buy you for a pack of smokes!"

"You are not helping," said O'Malley.

"Why me?" asked Hilman to no one in particular. "It was you," pointing at the Big Oak, "that shot that guy with the RPG, and nearly burned down a forest; and it was him," pointing at O'Malley, "who they thought was going to blow up a tour boat."

Kevin sat back on the settee laughing to himself and enjoying the show.

"It is what we in law enforcement like to refer to as an accessory before and after," said Oak. "You are going down for hard time."

"No one's going down for any time, hard or otherwise. We found a body and did what good citizens do. We reported it," said O'Malley, just a bit more forcefully than necessary, as he tried to convince Hilman of his lack of concern.

Reardon looked on and tried not to laugh, but finally he could no longer contain himself. Hilman looked at the four other men and realized that he was having his leg pulled.

"Great. I have two friends who are cops and two who are lawyers, and they happen to be the only funny cops and lawyers in existence. I need a better class of friends!"

"That's odd," mused Kevin as he stared at the police

launch while the officers were lifting the basket with the victim onto the swim platform.

"What's odd?" asked O'Malley.

"Didn't you say that the guy you found was a diver?" asked Kevin.

"Yeah, of course," said O'Malley, stretching out the response as he tried to figure out the point that Kevin was about to make.

"The body they are lifting onto the swim platform appears to have no diving equipment on," said Kevin.

"You're crazy! That's impossible!" said O'Malley, sure of what he had seen. A diver was the only thing that made sense.

O'Malley grabbed his digital camera and, zooming in on the body, snapped a picture. Peering at the image on the screen, he enlarged it to get even more details. Exhaling softly, O'Malley spoke under his breath, "I'll be dipped in shit!"

Matt turned to Kevin and confessed, "You're right! There is no tank, no BC, no snorkel, no fins, no facemask. There is a weight belt, but when I saw him he was floating, so the weights had not been calibrated correctly."

Confusion spread across O'Malley's face like a dark cloud on an otherwise clear day. "I guess I just assumed he was a diver. He was in a dive spot and wearing a wetsuit. What else would I think?"

"Maybe the cops removed the equipment underwater to make it easier to retrieve the body?" suggested Danny.

"I doubt that," said Oak. "That would be a clear violation of accepted police investigative practices."

"That's true," agreed Reardon. "Even way up here in the sticks we know better than that. You risk losing important forensic evidence when you start to disrobe a body before it's on the slab and in a controlled environment."

A patrolman from the Village of Lake George came over to the SeaRay on his jet ski, acknowledging Reardon. "Hi, Chief, How's it going?"

"Pretty good, Pete," said Reardon. "Are we just about done here?"

"Yeah," replied Pete. "The detectives are finishing up,

and the county CSI guys are still down on the boat collecting samples and finishing up with the pictures."

"Alright then. Great stuff," said Reardon. "Are these guys free to go?"

"Absolutely, but here's Detective Harp's card. He wants them to come down tomorrow to give their statements."

"Can we do it now and get it over with?" asked O'Malley, turning the card over in his hand as he examined it.

"No, the detective wants to start fresh in the morning. He says it might take some time."

"For a drowning?" asked O'Malley, although he was getting a very uneasy feeling that this was not going to be just an ordinary drowning.

"If that's what it is, it shouldn't take long, sir," answered the young patrolman, noncommittally.

*   *   *

Miles Smythe put the phone back in his pocket before he eased his boat away from the dock at The Boathouse Restaurant. He wanted to head back to the cabin he had rented at the bottom of the hill below where the Juniper Hills condominiums were located, but he knew that he needed to see what was going on at the wreck site where he had spotted the SeaRay earlier in the afternoon flying the "Diver Down" flag. He tried to give the appearance of a tourist on a leisurely shoreline cruise, yet his full attention was directed not at the western shore of the lake he was cruising along, but rather south and east toward Crosbyside and Wiawake, where the sunken bateau was located.

He could feel his tension rising as he strained his eyes trying to find the location. He was still too far away. He resisted an urge just to make a beeline for the wreck site; he was far too smart to risk drawing any attention to himself. The mansions he passed by at Antlers barely merited a glance as he focused his attention southeast. The brightness of the day made him squint, but still he could not pick out the area where the sunken bateau was located.

As he came abreast of Tea Island, he saw, to his left, a marked police boat with the blue lights flashing. His mind raced as he considered the possibilities. Was the officer going to pull over an errant boater, or was he headed for the wreck site to investigate the dead body? Maybe he was just heading to an accident, or to a boater in distress. He considered turning around and heading back to Bolton Landing, but rejected the idea in favor of gathering all the intelligence he could. He would just have to be circumspect as he proceeded. *"Keep Calm and Carry On,"* he thought to himself, picturing the World War II poster, which was rarely seen during the war, but which has become so ubiquitous now that it is familiar to many people not only in London, but across Europe and the States.

He ignored the impressive stonework of Erlowest as he began to nudge his boat in a more easterly heading. He finally was able to see the wreck site across the lake. There were now numerous boats bobbing around the site. Ominously, most had flashing blue lights on them. He continued south for another few minutes to position himself for a better view, and then swung the wheel hard to reverse course and head north. He immediately dropped the boat into neutral and reached for his binoculars. He spun the captain's chair as far as it would go as he trained the binoculars on the wreck site. Slumped down and shaded by the bimini, he was sure that he would attract little notice from passing boaters.

The SeaRay he had discovered earlier was still there, along with four police boats, including the one that had passed by him at Tea Island. It was difficult to make out who was actually on what boat, but he concluded there were at least three, and maybe as many as five, men on the SeaRay,   no women.

They were all white men. It was impossible to estimate their ages, but they were not teenagers, and they were not old men. The boat was dark green with a swim platform, but no other distinguishing markings. He had contacts who could run the bow numbers. He was not worried about finding the owner.

His observations of the activity at the wreck site led Smythe to two conclusions. First, since the interlopers had apparently called the police, they were not competitors for his prize; although he could not discount that they may have come across it by accident. Secondly, he no longer had to worry about repositioning the Chechen. The police would do that for him, and he was quite confident that they would find nothing forensically that would bring them to him. Remembering the spent shell in his pocket, he removed it and tossed it overboard into the deep waters of Lake George.

While he was starting to regret yesterday's decision to bring the dead Chechen with him on the boat, he still felt it would have been too dangerous to leave him behind at the cabin. Had his first dive proved fruitful, he would have left the Chechen wedged in under the bateau's roof and headed for warmer climates before the police or Fahran Zadran could think to look for him. But he had found nothing on the first dive, and the Chechen refused to admit that the package had been hidden there, although he tried many ways to get Smythe to explain why he thought it was on the wreck.

Once they returned to the cabin, the Chechen had proved to be quite resistant to interrogation, and even more resourceful than his reputation had predicted. Somehow, the Chechen, in the early morning hours, while Smythe dozed, had slipped out of the handcuffs Smythe had assumed held him securely to a bed frame in the cabin. He had donned a wetsuit, taken the navigational chart that Smythe had used to locate the wreck off of Wiawaka, and already had the keys to Smythe's boat when Smythe awoke and spotted him creeping down the steps heading to the marina at the bottom of the hill. Without ever verbally confirming it, he obviously believed that the package they both had been so urgently searching for was hidden on the wrecked bateau.

Smythe had grabbed for his 9mm Glock 17. He was something of a traditionalist, and missed the Browning, which had been standard issue for decades for the police and soldiers of the United Kingdom. Her Majesty's forces had converted to the smaller, lighter Glock 17 in recent years, and he recognized its superiority, so he had switched as well even though he had to purchase his own.

Overtaking the Chechen had been no problem. Smythe

knew that, at some point, he would have to kill him just to tidy up, but he had hoped to extract much more information before completing that bit of housekeeping. While the area was heavily wooded and lightly populated, he had not been willing to risk any commotion that might have attracted unwanted attention. As he ran up to the Chechen, he had raised the Glock and struck him in the back of the head.

He had instantly collapsed in a heap, his limp body sliding along the ground for a short distance. He had been so intent on making it to the boat that he had been totally unaware of Smythe as he had raced toward him. Smythe had straddled the crumpled figure on the ground, and then sat down firmly on his back. The moaning man had expelled a gasp of air as Smythe's full weight had pressed suddenly onto his back.

"Off for your daily constitutional so early, mate?" Smythe had said. "Or, maybe you think you can go for a dip on the wreck without me?"

The Chechen had made no reply, but it had not been clear if his silence was an act of defiance or was due to his inability to speak after Smythe had knocked the air out of his lungs.

Smythe had bent down to whisper in his ear, "It's hardly proper to leave without thanking me for my hospitality. That's the problem with the world today. No one knows how to be gracious anymore."

The Chechen had moaned even louder.

"No worries. You can make it up to me. All you have to do is tell me where the package is."

The Chechen had turned his head as far to the left as he could, and tried to rise up from the ground.

"That's it. Come on. All you have to do is tell me what I want to know. I let you go and we part friends and there you go, Bob's your uncle."

The Chechen's face had been set in a grimace as he had tried to spit at Smythe's face.

"Aw, that right there demonstrates a very bad attitude. What, with me trying to be so friendly and all!"

The Chechen had struggled and attempted to turn over. Another firm blow with the base of the Glock's grip put an end to the struggle.

"You are never going to tell me what I want to know, are you, mate?" Smythe had sighed.

"What do you think?" the Chechen had asked contemptuously, enraged that he was under the control of his English captor.

"I think, no, you will not tell me. Too bad. Just when we were starting to get to know one another as colleagues."

While he had been addressing the Chechen, Smythe had slowly raised the Glock 17 to where it was now pointing at a spot at the back of his head. Calmly, Smythe positioned his left hand by the ejection port cut out on the barrel's side as he even more calmly exerted pressure on the trigger.

The Glock performed precisely as designed and discharged the projectile into the back of the Chechen's skull. The barrel first moved backward and then the recoil extracted and ejected the cartridge into the waiting hand of Miles Smythe, who then slipped the spent cartridge into his pants pocket.

The weapon had performed flawlessly and without emotion, as did Miles Smythe. The Chechen's whole body had shuddered from the impact of the bullet and then remained motionless.

CHAPTER SIX

"I got the information you wanted," said a coarse voice.

"Brilliant," said Smythe into his phone. "Give it to me."

"The boat with the bow numbers you gave me is owned by a Daniel Hilman, who lives at 1310 Chinckakook Trail, in a subdivision known as Mohican Heights."

"Where? In what town?" demanded Smythe, as he jotted down the rest of the information.

"Right there in Bolton Landing," replied the voice on the other end of the call, as if it was so obvious that it did not bear mentioning.

"That's super," said Smythe. "I'll look into this today. If it checks out, look in the drop I told you about tomorrow and you will find your money."

"Don't you worry none. It will check out," said the man with the coarse voice, who wondered why he was dealing with someone he had never met in person, and who insisted on making payments for services by hiding money in a hole in a tree behind the rest stop at Exit 22 on I-87. *"No matter, all I need to know is that Zadran wishes me to help this man,"* thought the owner of the pawnshop.

Smythe hung up the phone and went to the small suitcase he customarily traveled with when on business to search for his iPad. The suitcase was small, but it held all the essentials of his profession: a Kershaw Blur knife, his Glock with adequate ammunition, an assortment of phones and IDs, passports from several European and South American countries, brass knuckles, and a garrote. The garrote had sentimental value to him since it was the first lethal weapon he had ever made. It was constructed with a piano wire he had pinched from his grandmother's piano and had handles fashioned from ten-penny nails and electrical tape he had found in his grandfather's tool shed.

The case also contained both his civilian and professional garments. His professional attire consisted of an assortment of tee shirts, socks and pants – all black. The civilian attire varied with location and mission, but could most accurately be described as generic and non-descript. Smythe did not like to draw too much attention to himself.

A safety razor, toothbrush, toothpaste, a comb, and a few other personal items rested in a small shaving kit. Packs of U.S. currency and Euros were nestled into the side compartments where most people stored their socks. There was also a small camera and an assortment of electronic listening devices.

Smythe believed in traveling light and quick, and never carrying anything that might reveal his true identity. Anything else he needed, he would purchase along the way and throw out as soon as he was done with the item. Purchases would be made with the cash he carried, since cash did not register on the computers that dutifully record the date, time, and place of each credit card transaction.

The iPad might be considered a luxury item, but it was invaluable as a way of accessing a wealth of information, and was a reasonably secure way of communicating with his clients. The NSA and Interpol, and even his old friends at MI-5 had become skilled at intercepting emails and phone calls, but he only used burn phones, and he never sent the emails he wrote. He and each of his clients would share email accounts. Messages were prepared but never sent. He could sign in and look at the mail drafts to read a coded message. The system was far from foolproof, but Smythe had no confidence in encryption software. Governments worldwide were demanding to be provided with back doors and keyholes that would allow them to monitor those communications. The very act of sending an encrypted email starts the snoopers snooping.

Using the information provided by his source and the iPad, Smythe was able to quickly locate the address of at least one of the boaters that had interrupted his plans. Google Maps gave him a general idea of the locale. Using street view he was able to get a feel for the neighborhood. A more detailed aerial view was obtained by using the successor to Keyhole.com, the magnificent Google Earth Pro. The 3-D images allowed Smythe to have a clear idea of what challenges he may face in trying to conduct surveillance. It also showed a little used footpath from the town up to the subdivision. He was able to identify a house directly in front of the Hilman residence that might make an excellent perch from which to observe.

Focusing on the nearby house, with a little effort he was able to obtain the owner's name, an Albany address, and telephone numbers for the pretextual calls he would make in order to determine occupancy of the house, if needed. He preferred to conduct his surveillance outside. It allowed more opportunity for plausible explanations if discovered. Going into a strange house upped the ante for potential problems.

Smythe was a cautious man, and he would make no final plan until he had visited the site. It was time for a trip to Mohican Heights, and a little on-the-ground reconnoitering.

*   *   *

Mohican Heights is set high on a hill looking over the town of Bolton Landing, and offers most of the homes a spectacular view of Lake George. The entrance or exit for vehicular traffic is a narrow, one-lane, private road that meanders through the subdivision.

As Smythe drove slowly through the subdivision, he got eyes on the Hilman house, which appeared to be empty with no cars around it. He cruised past Hilman's house a short distance to where the street terminated in a roundabout, with two driveways intersecting the roundabout. One driveway led to the Anniston house next to the Hilman's; the other to a house that offered no strategic advantage to Smythe.

The hillside, as it fell away from Hilman's house, sloped down to the lake. The Albany executive, Robert Anniston, had built his dream summer home down the hill from Danny's place. However, one man's dream can also be his nightmare. Anniston's house was huge and beautifully landscaped, with a summer kitchen and gazebo for entertaining in the yard. The tragedy was that the owner had to work so hard to pay for his dream house that he rarely got to stay there.

The neighborhood was heavily wooded so it would be necessary for Smythe to get very close to observe anything. While the woods would provide him cover, the setup of the subdivision made it virtually impossible to hide his vehicle, and the houses were close enough together to make it difficult to avoid detection if he were there for any length of time. Monstrous mosquitoes buzzing around finally tipped the scale in favor of his breaking into the house just below the Hilman's.

Smythe observed the house carefully before deciding it was safe to pull into the driveway. He slowly went up the gravel drive and stopped in front of the middle garage bay. There was complete privacy at this point, due to the heavy growth of trees that surrounded the front and north sides of the property. To the west was a retaining wall built of locally sourced boulders and a flagstone staircase. Smythe left the car running as he got out and quickly went up the staircase, which put him in the backyard and facing the Hilman house. There was no cover here, but he had observed no cars or any sign of activity at the Hilman's. He put on some gloves, crossed the yard and ducked under the deck attached to the A-frame house. There he placed a small, black UHF transmitter and switched it on. A small red light glowed on the face of the device. Smythe took out a roll of black electrical tape and covered the light while attaching it to the underside of the deck.

He quickly returned to his car. As he reached the car he nearly was tripped by a wire clothes hanger that had been carelessly left behind on the driveway. "Bollocks," he said, as he reached out to brace himself on the car to prevent the fall.

*   *   *

The records from the County Appraisers' office Smythe had reviewed on his iPad were an excellent resource. Not only did they include the names of the owners, the address the tax bill would go to, and a phone number; there was a sketch of the footprint of the house, dates of purchase, square footage and many other particulars that were of no interest to Smythe. There was even a link to the Comptroller's office if he wanted to take a peek at the actual deed. Smythe did not avail himself of anything but the phone number, which he dialed in the hope that there would be an answer. The phone rang five times, and he was about to give up, when he heard the connection being made.

"Hello," said a voice that was both a little winded and a little annoyed to be answering the call.

"Hello. Good afternoon," said Smythe in his best effort at an American accent. "Have I reached the Anniston residence?"

"Yes," said the voice, with growing suspicion and annoyance, "but we aren't interested in buying anything or taking any surveys."

"Oh, no. Oh, no. That's not why I'm calling. This is Scott Turner from FedEx," said Smythe, as he slipped on the new identity as easily as pulling on a favorite robe. "We have been trying to deliver a package, but we've had no luck in finding anyone home."

"I don't know why. I've been here all week with a sick child," said Maria Anniston.

"I'm sorry. I don't think I've made myself clear. I see I've called an Albany exchange. We are trying to deliver a package to your home in Bolton Landing. And, to be clear, am I speaking with Mrs. Robert Anniston?"

"Yes. I am she - and how did you get this phone number?"

"It's on the package," said Smythe without missing a beat.

"Oh," said Mrs. Anniston. "I haven't been to our house in Bolton Landing in quite a while. Who sent us the package?"

"I really am not supposed to say. When do you expect someone will be home to accept delivery?"

"I really couldn't say. I don't go very often. It's just a place my husband goes with our kids or his drinking and fishing buddies."

"Well, actually the package is addressed to Robert

Anniston. Do you expect him up anytime soon?"

"No, he's away on business and I don't expect him back for a few days; and after that, he's usually so backed up at his office that he can't get away for a week or two. Can you forward the package to us in Albany?"

"Hmmm. No. The instructions say not to forward, and it requires a personal signature for proof of delivery," said Smythe.

He did not want her to be looking for a package the next day when nothing was ever going to show up. No sense in getting anyone to start asking questions.

There was a long pause during which he could hear a frustrated sigh on the other end of the line. Smythe realized that people were probably used to FedEx agents being helpful, and he needed to solve the problem for her – and one final issue for himself.

"Well, really, most anyone can sign for the package. It doesn't have to be you or Mr. Anniston. Will there be anyone there in the next few days?"

"No, that big, white elephant sits empty most of the time, generating expenses," said Mrs. Anniston, who clearly had not been in favor of the acquisition.

"Tell you what we can do," Smythe said in his friendliest voice, "the package isn't marked *perishable*. Why don't I just hold it in the office here in Glens Falls until you folks can get by and pick it up?"

"Okay," said Mrs. Anniston. "It won't be me. I'll just let my husband know and he can stop by on his next trip up."

"Perfect. Just tell him to ask for Scott Turner. I am here most days until 4:30."

"Thanks," said Mrs. Anniston.

"No problem. Have a great day," said Smythe, almost choking on the words. God, he hated how, in this country, everyone would instruct him on what kind of a day to have.

As the call disconnected, Smythe was quite happy with himself. Mrs. Anniston had told him everything but her social security number, and perhaps would have divulged that as well if he had asked nicely.

He now knew he had free run of the house. He was also a bit amused, as he hoped for the great serendipity that there might actually be a Scott Turner at the Glens Falls FedEx office. If so, that bloke was in for a bad day when he would have to explain what he had done with Robert Anniston's package.

CHAPTER SEVEN

The sun was beginning its daily journey behind Dixon Hill, Kellum Mountain, and all the topography west of I-87. As the sun sunk lower in the sky, the shadow of Danny Hilman's house in Mohican Heights grew longer, encompassing the deck and backyard in a gathering gloom. Coolness could be felt on the back deck; but, far below on Lake George the beautiful water still reflected back the glory of the setting sun on every random wave and passing boat wake. These leaping flashes of light covered the waters of Lake George like a blanket full of diamonds. The towering exposed cliff face of Shelving Rock on the east side of the lake began to glow a radiant golden color, as if the rocks themselves were about to be permanently altered by the alchemy of the setting sun.

After a long day racing around on the lake, this was O'Malley's favorite time of day. Everything seemed to slow down, and the beauty of the natural surroundings just screamed out, *"Look what God has done here! Pay attention to it! You are one of the privileged few who get to experience this day!"*

O'Malley would have loved to give the wondrous tableau spread before him more attention, yet all his focus was on a more mundane endeavor, Hilman's barbeque grill. He was convinced that it was possessed, and innately evil. At this particular instant, he was concerned that the crotchety old propane gas grill that squatted menacingly in a corner of the deck was either not going to light at all; or, in the alternative, it would light in a monstrous explosion that would consume everything in a one hundred foot diameter of this location. Either way, O'Malley and his friends were going to be denied their dinner.

"Danny, would you take a look at this thing? It won't light," said O'Malley.

"There's nothing wrong with the grill," said Hilman. "You just don't appreciate classic equipment."

"Jimmy Hendrix playing the National Anthem at Woodstock is a classic. A '64 Ford Mustang is a classic. *Animal House* and *Caddyshack* are both classics. This worn out piece of crap is ready for the dump. Why don't you get rid of it before it burns the place down?"

"Have you no sense of history? This was the first grill that featured a sauce burner on the side, dual burner controls, and an electric starter. Besides, I won it in a sales contest, and it has sentimental value to me," said the slightly offended Hilman.

The Big Oak was inside watching the Yankee game on the television, but the bickering was disturbing him, and he was becoming concerned that his dinner might be delayed, something that he considered an intolerable affront. He listened to O'Malley insult the grill a bit longer, sighed, and rolled his eyes as he grabbed Kevin's cigar lighter.

Oak walked out onto the deck and stared at the grill. Bending over, he grabbed the handle on the gas tank and lifted it just enough to decide it was empty. He bent his six foot six inch body over; and, with a practiced efficiency, switched the empty tank out for the full spare tank. Oak wordlessly twisted the valve open; and, without bothering to test for leaks, turned on the right burner. He lifted the grill rack up and stuck the cigar lighter down near the lava rocks. The grill let out a loud *wumph* that vibrated the grill's lid as the flames roared to life, scorching the hair on Oak's right arm. The process was repeated for the left burner.

Oak lowered the lid and turned to Danny.

"I want my steak rare. It should be rare enough that a moderately talented veterinarian could bring it back to life."

With that, he returned to the Yankee game. Due to an aging lineup and a lack of pitching, the Yankees would prove more difficult to fix than the grill.

"Okay, but I can't put the steaks on until Reardon gets here," called out Hilman, as Oak ducked his head to go through the screen door in the converted breezeway.

It had been two days since O'Malley had found the body on the bateau, and other than an unpleasant interrogation, nothing new had been disclosed to him. In fact, he had put the unpleasantness out of his mind as he had enjoyed those days boating on the lake and traveling to Lake Placid to watch the Olympians train. He knew he had done nothing wrong and was merely a witness. He was determined to enjoy the night and the rest of his vacation. Soon enough he would be back in the summer steam bath that was Orlando. He grabbed a beer from the cooler and eased back into an Adirondack chair to admire the cobalt sky with the garishly painted orange and red clouds. He felt great!

He may have felt differently if he knew he was being watched.

*   *   *

The house behind the Hilman house appeared as it did most nights – a dark, empty, soulless McMansion. However, tonight it would not be empty. Tonight it would serve as a perch for Miles Smythe to spy on O'Malley and his friends.

It was close to sunset when Smythe left the cabin he was renting in Juniper Hills. He waited for traffic to clear on 9N before turning south onto the main road through Bolton Landing. The road dropped at a constant rate into the little town until it flattened out in the main business district. He noted a few stragglers left at the public beach, squeezing every bit of summer fun out of the day. People who live in climates where the winters are long and hard tend not to waste a second of summer when it pays its brief visit.

Smythe drove past the landmarks of the small town. The parking lot of the Grand Union finally had some free parking spaces. The nearby nightclub was getting ready for a big night, but the music had not started yet, so the younger tourists had not arrived. In four hours, the place would be hopping, and the band would be loud. He drove past Trees, a shop he had already explored when he first arrived. Everyone who visits Bolton Landing eventually winds up shopping there because it is such a wonderful amalgam of bookstore and gift shop.

Smythe's goal was to get to the south end of town and park behind the Anglican Church. From there he would begin his trek up the hill to Mohican Heights.

He parked, and had to search a bit to find the pathway he had first spotted on Google Earth Pro. The satellite image proved to be quite accurate, and he was able to locate the path with little effort. Once on the path he found the area to be heavily wooded, so it was no problem to proceed undetected up the overgrown, little used, and long forgotten trail.

Smythe paused at the edge of the woods before entering the clear space in front of the Anniston house. Most people had elected xeriscape, but Anniston had gone with boulders and turf. No matter, the house was dark and quiet. It seemed safe, so Smythe slowly approached the front door. If challenged, he was merely a tourist who stumbled upon a trail; and, being something of a birder, he wanted to see where it might take him.

Smythe was not happy when he looked at the door lock. The house must have cost in the millions to build, so they had not scrimped on the high-tech Abloy Protec2 locks securing all the perimeter doors. He had hoped for home store locks that he could open with his bump key, or even his picking tools, but no such luck. Still, he was confident that getting in would prove no challenge.

Given the quality of the door locks, he knew there would be a security system; therefore, the first order of business was to be sure that the alarm would not go off. The telephone junction box was conveniently located on the side of the house, hidden from the neighbors' view. *"How thoughtful,"* thought Smythe, as he put on some gloves, popped off the plastic cover, and quickly unscrewed the terminals disconnecting the telephone line to the house.

Once inside he would have to disable the power source for the alarm in case they had installed an audible local siren. That control panel was his only concern. It is the heart and brain of the security system, and as such should be hidden in a safe room, an attic, or another spot that would make it difficult to find and disable in the twenty to thirty seconds most alarm systems allow for the owner to enter a code to shut the system down.

Smythe was counting on human nature. The installers know where to hide the interior control box to make sure the system is secure, but they also know they will have to come out from time to time to replace batteries and perform service and programming on the system. When balancing customer security with the installer's comfort and convenience, the customer usually loses.

He had noted the three single-car garage doors on the north side of the house during his drive-by earlier in the day. They were aluminum faux carriage house doors with a row of windows in the top panel. He went to them immediately. His near bad fortune earlier in the day when he almost fell would now turn into his good fortune. He quickly found the wire hanger that had nearly sent him "ass over teacups" this afternoon.

Smythe untwisted the neck of the coat hanger and straightened it out, leaving the hanging hook at the end. Standing on an upended log, he easily fished the coat hanger past the flexible weather stripping at the top of the garage door. After a few failed attempts, Smythe snagged the emergency release cord, twisted the hanger, and gave it a good tug. He heard the distinctive *"pop"* as the door disconnected from the lift springs and the electric opener. With nothing to hold it in place, the biggest door in the house easily lifted up, and Smythe was in the garage. He immediately lowered the garage door.

Perimeter breached – no fuss, no muss, and no incriminating signs of forced entry. If all went as planned, he would re-connect the door to the electric opener as he was leaving, restore the control panel, and reconnect the telephone line. No one would ever know he had even been there.

Smythe could not help himself. A sly little smile flashed across his face when he thought about the Albany executive who felt his state-of-the-art security system would keep his house safe and sound.

Anniston had spent thousands of dollars on the system, and it would have taken about twenty-five cents and two minutes to secure the garage door quick release with a small plastic zip tie, like electricians use to bundle wires.

Even more amazing was what he saw hanging on the garage wall. There it was, proudly displaying the bright red and yellow logo of the security company that sold and installed the alarm system – the interior control panel!

The panel was not the only thing he saw that should not have been in the garage. At the far end, in the third bay, a car was parked. Smythe had assumed that an empty house would not have any cars in the garage, so the sight of the Toyota Corolla was a bit disconcerting. He walked over to the door leading into the main portion of the house. He put his ear on the door and listened. He heard ... nothing.

He went over to the car and examined it. He did not want to turn on a light, so he took out a small LED flashlight and swept it over the car. It was not the car of a rich executive. There were clothes strewn across the back seat. An assortment of bikini tops and bottoms were on the back window shelf, presumably thrown there to dry out. There were long-ago expired parking permits for SUNY-Plattsburg on the windows. He looked at the tires and they were probably ten thousand miles past their useful life.

Maybe it was a kid's car, stored here as an extra vehicle for when the family wanted to go in different directions. Maybe it had broken down on the last visit and they just had not had time to retrieve it. Smythe got down on his hands and knees and looked under the car. He saw a small puddle of oil glisten on the floor under where the car's oil pan would be.

"No," thought Smythe. *"This is someone else's car."* It had to be, since he reasoned that the child of a wealthy family would have a car in better repair. Also, if this car had been left behind, the oil puddle would be larger. The garage floor was otherwise fairly clean, so this car was not normally parked here long, nor was it parked here often. Perhaps a housekeeper, he thought, but quickly rejected that idea because it made no sense for a housekeeper to put her car in the garage.

He walked around to the passenger side and put his

upper body in through the opened window. He pulled open what he thought of as the *drop*, and grabbed a handful of whatever was inside. He examined the contents with the flashlight gripped in his mouth to free up his hands. He recovered some of the usual debris found in a car's glove box: tissues, receipts, and the car's manual. He glanced at all of them and let everything drop to the floor until he found what he was actually looking for – the car's registration. The car was owned by Maura Owens Sullivan of 2658 Capital Circle, Apartment 205, Albany, NY.

"*Who is she?*" Smythe asked himself. "*Not an immediate family member based on the name. Is she here?*" Smythe discarded the rest of the glove box's flotsam onto the passenger seat as his mind rapidly sorted through the possible consequences of this new development. None of them seemed positive at this moment. It might be time to abort this mission.

He shone the light into the interior of the car once more and spied what appeared to be a leather purse peeking out from under the driver's seat. After dumping it, he retrieved the wallet and found Maura's driver's license and photo. She was a beautiful blonde, had green eyes and was five foot two inches tall. He checked for her date of birth and did a quick calculation that determined her age to be twenty-eight, soon to be twenty-nine. Based on the little he knew about Mr. Robert Anniston he put his age at about fifty-three, a dangerous age when men get restless and begin questioning the choices they had made in their lives, which often leads to shopping for intriguing new toys. With Mrs. Anniston home caring for a sick child, could this Maura be Robert's new toy?

Smythe stood quietly in the garage next to the Toyota. "*This changes the calculus,*" he thought, as he experienced a moment of indecision. Should he stay or should he go? He really wanted to get closer to the boaters and get some idea of what they were up to. If they had information that could help in his quest for the package, he would have to get it out of them. But, if they did not, approaching and confronting them would not only be a waste of time, it would bring too much attention to him.

"Bobby?" slurred a woman's voice from behind the door

leading to the house.

Smythe's head snapped up at the sound of the voice, and he whipped his eyes in the direction of the door.

"Bobby, I know you're out there," followed by a short burst of giggling.

Smythe made no reply. He slipped the LED flashlight into his right trouser pocket, and allowed his hand to remain there as he struck a casual pose.

"Bobby!" the clearly inebriated woman said again. "I knew that selfie of me would get you up here before Friday!"

There was a brief pause, followed by, "I said get you up!" she said with a giggle that rapidly morphed into a snort.

"You stay right there. I have a surprise for you," she announced, followed by more laughter.

"I'm putting on the gift you sent me. Bobby, I think you should know . . . I've been drinking . . . and you're going to love the new Victoria Secret nightie you bought me . . . and let me tell you . . .," Maura Owens Sullivan slurred as she swung the door open, nearly falling into the garage, ". . . Victoria isn't hiding too many secrets!"

Maura flipped the light switch on and stared in confusion upon seeing Miles Smythe.

"Saaaaaay," she said, slurring the single word out as far as it could possibly go, perhaps as a way to clear her mind while she tried to make sense of what she saw, which certainly was not what she had expected.

"You're not Bobby!" came the vehement accusation from the inebriated young woman.

Smythe's moment of indecision had passed. He smiled and started to walk toward the beautiful young woman.

"I am," a brief pause, "Scott Turner," reincarnating the ever-flexible Mr. Turner. "I work with Bobby, and he sent me here," said Smythe as he extended his right hand, palm down, as if to give a business-like handshake as part of his introduction.

"I know everyone Bobby works with, and I don't know you!" Maura said suspiciously, totally ignoring the fact that he was wearing gloves.

"I am the new guy," said Smythe, his smile widening as he raised his extended right hand out and up to shoulder height. He was much taller than Maura, and even if she had been sober, it would have been unlikely that she would have seen what was hidden in Smythe's right hand.

The flashlight had been traded for another tool of Smythe's trade. Maura was quite drunk and had no chance to see the pocketknife that Smythe was holding in such a fashion that the blade ran down and extended past his index finger by about three quarters of an inch. His right thumb pinned the knife to his right index finger and palm, while the other fingers of his right hand were drawn up and served as a brace to prevent the blade from moving backward on impact, although the Kershaw Blur knife was so well made there was little chance of that happening.

Smythe never changed expression in the brief instant it took him to raise his arm and then slash his arm down and toward Maura's slender and exposed neck. To someone standing behind him it would have looked like a smooth, continuous motion that appeared as if he was just taking a swing at her and missed. But he had not missed. Maura's jugular vein was cut nearly all the way through.

Her heart pumped a few last times, more out of habit than for any useful purpose at this point, and blood spurted far enough through the gash to splash onto the back wall of the garage. She tried to speak, but her esophagus was also opened by the blade, so all that came out was a hissing sound as air pushed through the precise incision across her throat. Maura crumbled to the floor and then made one inexplicable effort to crawl toward Smythe. Was she seeking help? Was she determined to attack her attacker? Was her brain even functioning? Who knows? The effort was short-lived and futile.

Smythe stood still as a statue as he dispassionately watched her brief struggle. He made no effort to back away from her until the pool of blood slowly ebbing from underneath her lifeless body approached his shoes.

Bending down, he lifted the bottom edge of the frilly Victoria Secret top that Maura was wearing and cleaned his blade on it.

"More's the pity. You look like you could have been quite the diversion," Smythe said to the now lifeless body on the floor.

Smythe felt a sudden pang of regret as he stepped past Maura's body. *"I should have kept her alive long enough to find out when the philandering Mr. Anniston was scheduled to arrive, and how long the tryst was scheduled to last,"* he thought.

Oh well, in for a penny, in for a pound. He would deal with Mr. Anniston when and if he had to. At least he had until Friday before his scheduled arrival, and that should be plenty of time for his purposes.

CHAPTER EIGHT

At about the same time that Maura Sullivan's blood was seeping out onto the garage floor of Robert Anniston's summer home, Edgard Onobanjo was finishing up a shift that had begun twelve hours earlier when he was called in to cover for a sick co-worker. Once he finished that shift, he then started his own. He was bone-tired, but grateful for the overtime.

Onobanjo prided himself on being a hard worker. He loved his new country, and he loved the overtime pay he would get this week. Upstate New York was very different from his home in Somalia. While he loved and missed his murdered family members, he was growing to love his new life in America, and reveled in the concept of upward mobility that his new home seemed to promise.

It had not always been so. He had been very lonely at first, until another African came to work at the airport. Lifting baggage all day was heavy work, and it built a sense of camaraderie among the workers. His new friend was also Somalian, and was named in the Somalian tradition that typically consists of three names. An individual's middle name is the father's first name; and the last name is the paternal grandfather's first name. Thus, his friend came to be named Keenadiid Amiin Kuciil. Keenadiid hated his name. Americans could not pronounce it. There were way too many vowels, and he knew he would never blend in this new country with such a name. He assumed an American sounding name. He was simply Kenny. As soon as he had saved enough money for lawyer's fees and the bribes he assumed he would be required to pay, he was going to have his name legally changed to Kenny Ames.

Kenny and Edgard hit it off immediately. Kenny was new at the airport, but he actually had been in America three years longer than Edgard. He knew things that Edgard had yet to discover. He introduced Edgard to a whole African emigrant community that shared some cultural traditions and practices Edgard found to be comfortable, and which reminded him of the happier days at home.

Kenny also introduced Edgard to Nubia Mayardit. She was Sudanese, but her family came from the area formerly known as "Upper Nubia," which was, in modern-day, central Sudan between the Second and Sixth Cataracts of the Nile River. Nubia had fled the country during the civil war and before the partition. She claimed that her family was descended from a royal family of Nubia in some distant time, and that she was somehow related to the President of South Sudan, who she would refer to only as Kiit. She was beautiful, and Edgard spent all his free time with her.

There was a social club in Southwest Albany where the African emigrants would congregate. Edgard was amazed how people from so many different tribes and nations would come to this club, and how they would be friendly and helpful to each other – even if their tribes were at war back in Africa. The common heritage and the common struggle to thrive in this strange new country made the old differences seem unimportant.

It was at the club that Edgard was introduced to Jambo. Jambo had no interest in becoming a success in America. He was already a success in Africa. He was wealthy, not just by African standards, but even by most Americans' standards. His wealth was tainted, but he never gave that a thought. People in the club always smiled at Jambo, but they never sought him out. In fact, they sought to avoid him.

Jambo would disappear for months at a time. Each absence brought the hope that he would never come back. Rumors would fly about what nefarious activity he was involved in, or what tribe had tracked him down and exacted their vengeance. However, the rumors were mostly unfounded, and the hopes were always dashed when he would eventually return to the club.

Edgard had heard the stories of violence that swirled around Jambo. He was afraid of Jambo and sought to avoid him at all costs. It had been a very unpleasant surprise when Jambo came into the club three weeks earlier and, after briefly scanning the room, walked purposefully to the table where he and Nubia were sitting.

"Good evening, Edgard," Jambo had said in his near basso profundo voice, "May I join you and the lovely Nubia?"

Edgard was stunned that Jambo, whom he had never met, knew his name. Worst still was that he wanted to sit with him. Before he could even think of a response, Jambo had taken a seat.

"Good evening," stammered Edgard.

"So, what are we drinking tonight?" Jambo had asked with a wide grin that displayed large, extremely white and powerful looking teeth. Jambo was an imposing figure – about six feet tall, exceptionally dark skin, broad through the chest and shoulders but narrow at the waist. He wore a tailored black suit with a black silk shirt opened at a neck that seemed too big for the head it was supporting. Jambo's hands had scars and deformed knuckles, evidence of a hard-scrambled life, where his skills at street fighting had served him well.

"We," Nubia had said, placing great emphasis on the pronoun, "were just about to leave." She had not returned his smile.

"Ah, just so," Jambo had said, "how fortunate it is that I arrived when I did. I have important business to discuss with Edgard."

Edgard sat completely still, not having a clue what was about to unfold.

"I do not mean to be rude, but the nature of our business is quite confidential, so perhaps you could attend to some personal matter while Edgard and I speak. I am sure we will be done when you return."

"Edgard, I think we should both go, right now!" Nubia had said with urgency.

"You may go now. Edgard will stay and speak with me," said Jambo, all pretense of friendliness having disappeared.

Edgard observed two other men standing by the door that he had not seen before. They began to move toward his table.

"Nubia, please do as the gentleman requests. I will be with you shortly, I am sure," Edgard had said, but with a voice that did not convey the confidence he had attempted to project.

Nubia had stared at Edgard in disbelief. He had made a nearly imperceptible nod of his head, which caused her to look in the direction of the approaching men. She realized what was about to happen, so she abruptly stood up, sniffed "Humph," and strode off to the Ladies Room. The two men had stopped and watched her walk away, and then they began to back up to the shadows from where they had emerged. All three had danced their dance to perfection.

"She is a spirited one," Jambo had said, but Edgard had not been able to tell whether the comment was meant as a compliment or criticism.

"What do you want of me?" Edgard had asked. "I do not even know you."

"Ah, but I know you," Jambo had said. He had reclaimed his smile, yet it still produced no warmth. "I know you, I know your family, and I spoke with your village elders. They told me you are a good boy. You are smart, and you work hard."

Edgard had stared at him. He had not known what to say. His body suddenly was pouring adrenaline into his bloodstream, and it was screaming at him to get up and run. Run far, and run fast. Yet he had remained transfixed, and feeling as if he were belted to the chair in which he was seated.

"Those are excellent traits in an ambitious young man," Jambo had observed. "You are ambitious, are you not?"

Edgard had sat silently, staring at Jambo, sill afraid to speak, and concerned that his fear would be evident in his voice.

"Of course you are," Jambo had said, "or you would not be working so hard at Siena College and at the airport. It must be very difficult for you."

"How, how do you know my school?" Edgard had stammered.

Jambo had chuckled and said, "I make it my business to know everything about the people I trust enough to work with, and I trust you because your village elders told me I could. Even the priests back in Bardere told me you were an exceptional young man."

"Thank you," Edgard had choked out, "but, as you say, I am working very hard now and I do not think I can take on another job."

"You have not even heard what the job is yet. Do you have a problem with me?" Jambo had asked, feigning hurt feelings.

"Oh, no, of course not," Edgard had stammered. "It's just . . .," Edgard's voice had trailed off as Jambo leaned in and put his lips very near Edgard's ear.

"Good," Jambo had said, "Because people who have a problem with me really have problems."

Edgard was so nervous he had just stared straight ahead.

"It would be a shame if anything . . . unpleasant were to happen to your family."

"My family is all dead and buried back in Somalia," Edgard had said, as memories of that horrible night when he found their bodies came rushing back at him, causing tears to form in his eyes.

"I know they are," Jambo had said. "In fact, I knew before you did."

"How . . . how . . . how would you know such a thing?" Edgard had asked while he could feel his fear being replaced by a sudden anger rising in his body. His head was swirling and he had struggled to keep control of himself.

"Unless you were the one who killed them!"

Edgard had reached across the table for a steak knife, but Jambo had seen what was about to happen and had pinned Edgard's wrist to the table. He again spoke in a harsh whisper in Edgard's ear.

"Do not be foolish, Edgard. It was not me who killed your family, but if you do me this little favor, I will tell you who did, and I will pay you enough so that maybe you and Nubia could go on a nice trip together."

"And if I do not do you a favor?" Edgard had asked, "Will you kill me then?"

"Not right away. I would want you to live a while to see the consequences of your decision, because you will experience a terrible loss, something no one should ever have to endure. You will lose a second family. The Winkelmans will go to bed one night, and when they awake in the middle of the night I will be there, and what will happen to them over the following several hours will be . . .," Jambo had paused pretending to search for just the right word, ". . . tragic."

Edgard had stared into the malevolent eyes of Jambo and knew he was not making idle threats. He could not bear the thought of losing another family.

"But why do we speak of such terrible and unnecessary things when I ask so little, and I pay so well?" Jambo had said with a smile.

His rapid changes of demeanor were disconcerting to Edgard, who had never before met a person whose mood could change so rapidly and so completely. It made him wonder whether Jambo was more monster than man.

"What is it you want me to do?" Edgard sighed, knowing he had no choice at this moment but to make a pact with the devil sitting at his table.

"It really is a slight favor," Jambo said. "In a few days a man will call you," he continued conspiratorially. "Listen to him carefully. He will give you the name of an airline and a flight number. Do not write the flight information down, but commit it to memory. Make sure you are one of the baggage handlers who unload that plane. You will find a package that the caller will describe to you. When you find the package, just put it aside and hide it. Soon another man will contact you and you will give the other man the package. So, you see, it is no big deal."

"It is a big deal," Edgard had complained, "I could lose my job."

"You will lose much more if you fail in your task!" Jambo had hissed. "And who is to say you are going to lose your job? You are doing nothing wrong or illegal," he reassured him. "You are merely providing an added level of customer service by providing a convenient way for a man to pick up a package which belongs to him."

"What is in this package?" Edgard had asked. He regretted asking the question as soon as the words left his mouth. It was better to be ignorant of such things.

"There is no need for you to know," Jambo had said. "Just do what you are told."

"How will I know the man who is to receive the package?" Edgard had asked.

"Ahh, there's the rub," Jambo replied. "I don't know who the man is. I only know him as 'The Chechen.' The caller will describe him, and will give you a sign and a countersign to exchange with the man to confirm his identity. Do not surrender the package unless the man can give you the countersign. Do you understand?"

"Oh," Edgard had said, sure that he hated this plan, "Yes."

"Just be sure you give it to the right man," Jambo reminded him.

"To be sure," responded Edgard, who was not sure at all.

"One last thing," Jambo leaned in for emphasis, "and in this you must not fail. As soon as you retrieve the package, you are to call me. No one else but me. Do you understand?"

Jambo intended to be there when the package was delivered, and he would have both the package and the courier.

As Jambo began to walk away, he turned back to Edgard and laughed as he pulled a tube of Chapstick from his front trouser pocket and tossed it toward the still shaken Edgard.

"A small gift for my new friend," he laughed as the tube sailed toward Edgard. "A little balm to help smooth out our rough beginning."

Edgard reached up and caught the tube. He stared in bewilderment at the tube of Chapstick and at Jambo. The confusion on his face seemed to lighten Jambo's mood and he laughed even harder as he strode out of the club and into the

Albany night.

*   *   *

Too many days had passed, and with each passing day, Edgard had become more and more agitated. Finally the call came, just as had been foretold by Jambo. Edgard had the flight information memorized, but he was not supposed to work that day. It took many promises of future favors to get the shift he needed.

Bad weather had delayed flights all over the country, and this incoming flight was no exception. Edgard's stomach was tied in knots by the time the airplane finally arrived.

He was smart; but, more importantly, he was also sensible. He was relieved that the package was supposed to be relatively small, and could be concealed by the windbreaker the airport authority had given him.

He had used the days before the flight's arrival to learn where every surveillance camera in the baggage handling area was located. They were nearly everywhere except for the restrooms and a few blind spots.

He did not know when the Chechen would contact him, so he went about finding a place to hide the package. He was also relieved to find that the package was not too heavy, because he had decided that the best place to hide it was above the suspended ceiling in the men's room.

Everything went well, and once the package was hidden, he began to feel like all his problems were about to be over. All he had to do was wait to be contacted.

And so he waited. And he waited some more, and still the Chechen did not call. As he waited, he was bedeviled by two emotions. Anxiety and curiosity. These were two very dangerous emotions that were in competition with each other. He knew he must fight them. He was anxious for the Chechen to call and get this over with, and at the same time he was curious about what could be in the package that would be worth all this trouble, and all the one hundred dollar bills that had been wound tightly and slipped into the Chapstick tube that he had been given by Jambo.

He would have been more anxious than curious had he been aware of the fate of the Chechen.

CHAPTER NINE

Smythe decided to leave Maura where she fell. He shut off the light she had turned on when she made the fatal decision to enter the garage. Darkness would be cover enough to conceal the body for his purposes tonight. He complimented himself on having worn the surgical gloves from the start, since an investigation would be forthcoming now because of the dead girl.

He was a cautious man, and he decided to go carefully through the entire house to make sure there were no more surprises awaiting him. He felt sure that Robert Anniston's intended tryst with the girl in the garage was meant to be a couples' weekend romp, but one can never be too careful, nor was it ever a good idea to underestimate the absurdities of a middle age man's fantasies.

Smythe went through every room and found no one else hidden away. He found a room with an overnight bag, which led him to believe it was the room Maura Sullivan was occupying. He searched it until he found her cell phone. He slipped the phone into his pocket, figuring it would have her life story on it. Taking it would serve to slow down the police.

He did find other things that made him admire the absent Mr. Anniston, including a humidor with genuine Cuban cigars, presumably obtained during a day trip to Canada.

Smythe's esteem for Robert Anniston rose further when he found the wine cooler. It was stocked with a delightful assortment of some of the finest wines he had seen in a private collection in some time. He needed to keep his wits about him so he could not indulge as much as he wanted. He carefully evaluated his options before selecting a 2006 Chateau de

Beaucastel Chateauneuf-du-Pape. This was one of Smythe's favorite red wines, but it was a pleasure seldom indulged in, due to its cost. A factor that, if everything went well in his current endeavor, he hoped would never again enter into his decision-making in the future.

Delighted with his good fortune in finding both the excellent wine and the Cubans to help ease the tedium of the evening's surveillance, he never gave a thought to the lifeless body of Maura Owens Sullivan in the garage below. He slowly poured the Chateauneuf-du-Pape through a Vinturi aerator and into the whimsical Riedel Crystal Dove decanter he had found in a cabinet near the wine. He would allow it to breathe before sampling it. After all, that was the only civilized way to truly enjoy a fine red wine.

While the wine breathed, he evaluated his listening post options. He settled on a second floor bedroom. There was a small desk placed under a window looking directly out onto the deck of the Hilman residence. He was amazed at how close the deck was to the window, probably no more than fifty feet. He could easily see the men on the deck and them coming in and out of the house, but he could not make out their conversation yet.

He unlocked the window and raised it just high enough to let in a pleasant evening breeze and to insert his UHF receiver on the windowsill. He plugged in a set of headphones and could clearly hear everything that was going on over at the Hilman's deck. He was pleased with himself on his good work with the hidden microphone below the deck, and sat down to listen.

"Danny, would you take a look at this thing? It won't light," said a middle-aged man with a full head of grey hair.

"There's nothing wrong with the grill," said the man Smythe assumed was Hilman. "You just don't appreciate classic equipment."

Smythe observed a very tall man come out of the house, wordlessly go to the grill, and fiddle with it until it lit. He carried himself like a man who was used to taking charge and having his instructions followed. Perhaps he was ex-military, maybe even a cop; but, regardless of what he was or had been,

Smythe decided that if there were ever a confrontation, he would need to eliminate this man first.

Smythe had an odd habit born out of a strong instinct for self-preservation. He assessed how long it would take him to kill every new person he met. Not that he killed everyone he met, but he felt it was always prudent to think ahead, set priorities, and evaluate one's options before critical situations arose – when thinking might not be as clear or as objective. The assessment was never made giving Smythe any unfair advantage like a gun or a knife. It was always done on the most primal level, hand-to-hand combat. The one constant in these mental exercises was that Smythe always won. The only variations were technique and length of the struggle.

Grey Hair might take a minute or two. The same for the man who was not involved in lighting the grill, the one who wore a baseball cap and unlaced shoes, and seemed to watch the goings-on in amusement. Such men were unlikely to put up much of a fight once they were hit hard enough in the balls or in the throat.

Hilman might take a little longer. There was an energy about him, a spring in the step that suggested an athleticism that would make him more difficult to kill. But, Tall Man, who lit the grill – he would be a challenge. It might take nearly five minutes to kill him.

Tall Man began to speak. "I want my steak rare. It should be rare enough that a moderately talented veterinarian could bring it back to life."

"Okay, but I can't put the steaks on until Reardon gets here," called out Hilman as Tall Man ducked his head to go back indoors.

Smythe smiled as he thought about how easy all this had been, and about the Chateauneuf-du-Pape that awaited him. He decided that nothing of substance was going to happen immediately so this would be the perfect time to fetch his wine and cigars before settling in to listen. An embedded 4GB smart stick would record everything anyway.

CHAPTER TEN

Matt, Kevin, Danny and Oak sat on the deck gazing out across the lake at Shelving Rock, which was still glowing with the rays of the setting sun. The sky above was turning indigo and the lake to an inky black, and there was not a cloud in sight.

"Tomorrow, first thing, I have to get the boat down to Dunham's Bay and get that prop checked out," said Danny. "Anyone want to come along?"

"Sure," said O'Malley, "We should all go; and while we're down there we can explore the Southern Basin. We hardly ever get down there. Maybe we can take a dip in Echo Bay."

Everyone nodded in agreement.

"I bet it gets cold tonight without a cloud cover," observed Kevin, as he drained the last of his beer.

"Yeah, but the Milky Way will be spectacular without all the light pollution from the cities," replied Matt. "It will just light up the sky, especially since there is no moon tonight."

"What time is Reardon supposed to be here?" asked Oak. "I'm starting to get hungry. I can't be out on the lake all day and not fed!"

"Reardon will be here soon," said Matt. "He called and said he had some news on the murder."

"Great," said Kevin. "I'd like to hear what is going on with that. I didn't enjoy being interrogated."

"What was the deal with going diving anyway?" asked Hilman. "The surface and the first ten feet of water are beautiful, but it gets really cold after that."

"I just wanted to scratch an itch," said O'Malley. "Kevin and I went to Mass at Blessed Sacrament down on Goodman Avenue in Bolton Landing just before the 4th of July. That priest loves this area, and his sermon on the 4th every year is about the history that can be experienced here. This year was special because we recently have a new American saint that the priest was all excited about. She's the first Native American saint, and she was born nearby. "

"So, who's the new saint?" asked Hilman.

"Kateri Tekakwitha. She was known as the Lily of the Mohawks, although once she converted to Catholicism, her tribe didn't want much to do with her," said O'Malley.

"So, I still don't get how that has you diving on a bateau from the French and Indian War era," said the Big Oak.

"The priest told of an interesting legend," said Kevin. "Kateri Tekakwitha supposedly came into possession of a sacred relic of great value that had belonged to the Catholic priest who supposedly 'discovered' Lake George, Saint Isaac Jogues - except, he called it *Lac du Saint Sacrement.*"

"What was it?" asked Hilman, who had no interest in religion, but had a keen interest in area history and treasures.

Kevin and Matt looked at each other and shrugged.

"Who knows?" said Matt. "The Mohawks killed Isaac Jogues and threw him into the St. Lawrence River. Kateri wasn't even born until about ten years later."

Kevin joined in the narrative. "The speculation is that the Mohawks divided up Isaac Jogue's possessions when they killed him, and that the tribal leaders got the most valuable possessions. Kateri's father was a chief, so it stands to reason that whatever was most valuable would have gone to him and his family; and, apparently, when Kateri converted, she obtained possession of the priest's treasure."

"I'm still not on a bateau," said Hilman.

"After Kateri converted, she left her tribe and lived among the French missionaries. She was a member of the Turtle Clan, and all of her adult life, she supposedly carefully guarded a turtle-shaped box, where, legend has it, she stored Isaac Jogue's treasure," said O'Malley, clearly warming to the story.

"After her death, people started to attribute miracles to her," said Kevin, as he picked up on the narrative. "It's said that the smallpox scars that had ravaged her face all disappeared on her death, and she was a radiant beauty when she was buried. People started to pray to her for intercessions, and claimed to experience miraculous healings."

"That's messed up," said Oak. "Who wants to wait until they're dead to become a hot babe?"

"You are so going to Hell," said O'Malley.

"I'll save you a spot and let all our friends know that you will be by shortly!" Oak jokingly responded.

"Are we ever going to get to the bateau?" asked an impatient Hilman.

"I'd like to get to the bateau right now!" said a loud voice behind the four men, startling them all.

"Bloody Hell," thought Smythe, as he sat up straight in his chair to get a better view of the newcomer. *"At last this might get interesting!"*

CHAPTER ELEVEN

"Damn!" exclaimed O'Malley. "For a big guy you sure don't make much noise!"

Michael Reardon smiled at the four friends gathered on the deck. "It must have been all those years of doing undercover work for the great State of New York. Who do I have to threaten to arrest around here to get a beer?"

"Great idea," said Kevin. "And since it would be a social faux pas to allow you to drink alone, I think I shall have another as well!"

"Kevin?" said Oak, his voice rising as if to turn his friend's name into a one-word question, "We all have beers."

"I can't help it if I don't want our guest to feel at all uncomfortable," said Kevin. "I was brought up to always follow the social conventions."

"I, for one, would be a lot less uncomfortable if someone would finally throw the steaks on the grill," said Oak.

"Let's do it," said Hilman, standing to begin his grill master duties.

"So, what's the news on the guy I found?" asked O'Malley. "Are you here to arrest us?"

"If Detective Harp had his way, he would like to arrest you just on general principles!"

"Why?" asked an astonished O'Malley.

"He doesn't like you," said Reardon.

"That's hard to believe," said Kevin. "I don't think Matt called him an idiot more than four times during his interview."

"Says the guy who spent forty-five minutes being interviewed, and most of that was talking about the Yankees," replied O'Malley.

"It's not my fault that people are drawn to my personality," said Kevin. "I'm a very interesting and amusing conversationalist. Oh, and I don't give off a murderous vibe like some people."

"Let's see how amusing you'd be after a four hour grilling," said O'Malley. "I can't believe he thinks I'm a suspect!"

"I never said he thought you were a suspect," said Reardon. "I just said he doesn't like you."

"I bet it's the way you're always jumping to conclusions," said Oak. Tipping his beer bottle in O'Malley's direction, he continued, "That's very off-putting for a lot of people."

"No, it's his total lack of a sense of humor," added Hilman.

"Have we ever considered Matt's lack of social graces?" asked Kevin.

"I think it might be the way dead bodies seem to pop up wherever he goes," offered Reardon.

"Okay, this is a ton of fun," said O'Malley, "But, I would really like to hear what is going on in the case."

"Me too," thought Smythe from his listening post. *"If they thought dead bodies popped up before, just wait until they find the one downstairs!"*

"Well, I do have some news, but not much that we didn't know before," said Reardon.

"First, you have been eliminated as a person of interest," Reardon said as he nodded his head towards O'Malley.

"Good!"

"Next, the unknown subject doesn't appear in the New York State fingerprint database, nor did we get a hit from the NCIC computer."

"What does that mean?" asked Hilman.

"It means this guy was never in trouble, or he was in trouble outside the United States, and he didn't make it into the FBI's database," said Oak.

"Oak is right," said Reardon.

"So, are we at a dead-end in identifying this guy?" asked O'Malley.

"No," said Reardon. "The Medical Examiner looked at his dental work and concluded that most of it was done in Europe, so they have a request in to Interpol to review the fingerprints."

"Okay," said O'Malley. "Anything else?"

"Yeah, the M.E. could only find an entry wound and concluded that death was caused by a gunshot wound to the head."

"One wound," said O'Malley. "Okay, what did forensics turn up on the bullet?"

"No bullet," said Reardon.

"No bullet?" asked O'Malley. "How can that be? If it went in and there's no exit wound, it must still be there."

"No bullet," said Reardon again.

"Did the killer remove the bullet?" asked Kevin.

"No evidence of that. The M.E. says the entry wound was undisturbed," said Reardon.

"Oh, crap!" said Oak. "Are you trying to tell us that the shooter was using Fiocchi ammo?"

"Ding, ding, ding, no more callers, please. We have a winner," said Reardon, touching his index finger to the tip of his nose and then pointing at Okonski.

"That's not good news!" said Oak.

"No, it isn't good news," said Reardon.

"Huh?" said O'Malley, "Miocchi, Fiocchi . . . whatever. What the hell is that, and why is that such bad news?"

Kevin's practice was devoted primarily to complex price fixing cases that took him all over the country for depositions. He flew so much the flight attendants knew him on sight on his most common flights. He had gold-plated clients who were thankful to have him handle their cases so they never balked when he flew First Class, and he always flew First Class. Being a garrulous sort, he got to meet a lot of pilots who were being shuttled into position for the airline's scheduling needs. He knew immediately what Fiocchi meant.

"This is the Rule of Unintended Consequences coming

into play," said Kevin. "You solve one problem; but, in the process, create a worse problem that you never anticipated."

"I am still in the dark," said O'Malley.

"After the 9/11 attacks, the government and the public were crazy with fear that it would happen again," said Kevin. "The government was determined to restore the flying public's confidence that no one would ever again hijack a plane and crash it into a building, so they set about hijack-proofing the planes. But, no matter what security measures they put in place, there was no way to guarantee that someone could not somehow get into the cockpit and take over the plane."

Kevin paused as he got up to reach into the cooler for another beer.

"In spite of all the ground level security measures before you can get on a plane, and in spite of all their efforts to harden the cockpit entry, the government felt they needed a last line of defense in the air. That's how the armed Sky Marshall program took off."

"Okay, so?" asked Danny.

"I tried to get in that program when I retired from the Jersey troopers," added Oak, "but they felt that at six foot six, I might not be nimble enough to get about an airline cabin in an emergency. They were afraid my first response would be to shoot the bad guys."

"So what?" asked Hilman. "Isn't that what you were there for?"

"The problem with normal ammunition at that close range is that, even if I were to hit the bad guy, the odds are that the round would exit, and either hit an innocent civilian or, worse yet, penetrate the fuselage where the difference in pressure could tear the plane apart."

"That doesn't sound good," said Hilman.

"No, but they came up with a solution," said Oak. "An Italian company, Fiocchi, developed a line of ammunition originally designed to be used in firing ranges. The bullet simply hits a target, and basically turns to dust - no ricochets.

The Sky Marshall program jumped all over that, and made the ammo standard issue for its agents. They can shoot the bad guys and the bullet just breaks up into basically grains of sand before it can exit. It still has the same stopping power as traditional bullets, but the EMB ammunition is safe to use on a plane. You can bring down the bad guys without bringing down the plane."

"What are the unintended consequences?" asked Hilman.

"There's a tiny subset of sociopaths in our society who make their living by killing people," said Oak. "Word got out about the disappearing Fiocchi bullets and it was like Christmas morning for those guys. Imagine being able to do a murder and leave no forensic evidence behind. It was a deal changer."

"So, now all the bad guys have these disappearing bullets?" asked Hilman.

"No, not really," said Reardon. "They're still a little hard to come by, so the gangbangers don't have them, and the impulse murderers haven't planned ahead enough to have that kind of specialized ammo. It's primarily used by contract killers; spooks doing the wet work of various governments around the world; and Sky Marshalls, who, by the way, have never discharged their weapons in the line of duty during the entire history of the program to date."

They all sat silently for a moment as the significance of what they had just learned sunk in.

"Wow," sighed O'Malley. "I think we can eliminate impulse murderers and Sky Marshalls from our list. That leaves us with contract killers and spies!"

"Great!" said Kevin, unhappily. "We're left with the two groups who don't like to leave loose ends, and who knows what to do about them!"

"We're not a loose end. The perp dumped the body and was long gone by the time we got there. How would he even know who we are?"

"I guess you didn't see today's Post-Star," said Reardon.

"No, why?" asked Hilman.

"This isn't New York City. A murder is big news around here. It will keep tongues wagging all summer. You four are on the front page, picture and all," said Reardon. "It says you're being questioned as persons of interest, and that you're cooperating with the authorities, and that the police are running down leads on other boats you saw in the area."

"Crap on a cracker!" said Hilman.

"I suggest you lock your doors at night," said Reardon, "at least until we can run this thing down."

"I suggest we all grab a piece from my trunk!" said Oak.

"Oak, please don't say things like that in front of me. There are things I just don't want to know!" said Reardon, remembering the arsenal that Oak had brought when he and Matt had confronted the Russian Mafia the year before in their effort to rescue a young girl who had been abducted. "I'm still not allowed to use the Piseco airport!"

"The steaks are done!" announced Hilman, as he hefted the large slabs of beef onto a tray. "And, for our vegetarian friend, Kevin, I think you'll find that this potato is baked to perfection, the onions grilled just right, and the garlic bread is strong enough to protect you from vampires!"

"I wish there was something to protect me from lunatic killers!" said Kevin.

*   *   *

Smythe watched as the men picked up the cooler of beer, the grilling tools, and the charred meat, and began to move inside for their feast. He decided he could learn no more tonight, and that it was time to move on.

He took a last puff on the cigar, snuffed it out, and dropped the stub into a Ziploc bag, which he then put into his black cargo pants. He took a final sip of wine, emptying the glass, and then went to the kitchen to wash it thoroughly - first with the bleach he had found in the laundry room, and then with the liquid dish soap he had found on the kitchen sink. The glass was carefully dried and put neatly back into the arrangement of identical wine glasses. He would wait until he exited the house before removing his surgical gloves. He was determined not to leave behind any DNA.

He had hoped that he could get in and out without being

discovered, but the dead body made that unlikely. He elected to leave the UHF transmitter attached to the beam under Hilman's deck. He might need it again, and retrieving it seemed like more risk than it was worth.

This had been a productive evening, and many of his questions had been answered. These four men now had names, and he was relieved to learn that they did not seem to be in competition to find the package. The police had no idea who the victim in the lake was as of yet, but when Interpol responded they would surely know. That knowledge would send their investigation in different directions. Smythe was troubled that the men may have described boats they saw in the area of the wreck to the police. *"Had they spotted him when he saw them?"* he wondered. However, he did not seem to be on their radar at this point.

When the body in the garage was discovered, it would increase pressure on the police to step up their efforts. Interpol would certainly identify the Chechen, and then his task of recovering the package would become more difficult. Thankfully, Interpol was infamous for its inefficiency; and, he surmised, he still had a few days.

He learned something else as well. He knew the men had an interest in the new saint and her treasure. *"Perhaps the foundation for a new friendship,"* Smythe thought to himself. *"It could prove quite helpful to have a conduit to feed me information about the investigation, and these lads seem to be very close to the local constabulary."* This would not be the first time he extracted useful information from a source without the source knowing it was one.

All in all, it was a successful night; yet he was left with a gnawing concern that even on a lake as vast as this one, these four interlopers may have actually described his boat to the authorities. It was time for a new boat, and to perhaps bump into these men and find out what was to be found out. He would need to act quickly, and, fortunately, he knew exactly where they would be first thing in the morning. Dunham's Bay is where he would be as well.

Smythe felt no urgency to leave, at least until the police officer was gone home, so he sat and thought about the events of the past two days. Today had been a good day, and being able to eavesdrop on the chief was certainly an unexpected bonus. Yesterday had not been such a good day, thanks to an early morning meeting with Jambo.

It was Jambo's fault that he had wasted so much time searching that damn wreck for the package that was not there, and probably never had been. Jambo swore it was not his fault, and that he had been misled by Fahran Zadran. That could easily have been a lie by someone who had intended to secure the package for himself while sending his competition to chase red herrings. Unfortunately, it just as easily could have been the truth that Zadran had changed the plan at the last minute.

Zadran had a reputation for not trusting anyone, even his own operatives. He would break missions into small tasks so that no one knew what anyone else was doing. It was maddening. It was this uncertainty, and Smythe's complete lack of other sources, that was keeping Jambo alive, at least for now.

Tomorrow would be another busy day. He would go to Dunham Bay and create an encounter with Hilman and the others so he could resolve in his own mind whether or not they could recognize him from when he had approached in his boat. He had gotten close enough to get their bow number so they may have seen him. He did not like loose ends in a mission.

Afterward, he would go to meet Keenadiid Amiin Kuciil, a/k/a Kenny Ames, a baggage handler who Jambo told him probably got the package off a plane and hid it. Jambo said he was sure that Ames had the package and was holding it for the Chechen to call, except there had been no call. Only Smythe knew that the Chechen was dead, so that part of the story rang true; and it would be consistent with Zadran's S.O.P. to use an African emigrant to intercept the package.

If Jambo's new story turned out to be a lie, he resolved to kill him - not because he wanted to, or, even because it would help him. He would kill Jambo because he had promised Jambo he would. Of course, he would have to find Jambo, which might not be easy.

Hours after their very uncomfortable meeting, Jambo got on a plane for what he was sure was going to be a much more uncomfortable meeting in Cairo.

CHAPTER TWELVE
Cairo, Egypt

Jambo feared no man; yet, Jambo believed with all his heart that Fahran Zadran was more devil than man; and he feared him greatly. He had counseled his superiors back in Africa not to do business with such a man, but their greed had overcome their better judgment and now he had been sent to Cairo to deal with a very angry man.

Jambo sat in the lobby bar of the Fairmont Nile City Cairo Hotel. He sipped some Jameson and stared morosely at the larger-than-life statue of a seated man holding his head as if he were being crushed by his headache. *I would be happy to change places with you,"* thought Jambo, as he awaited the arrival of Zadran, whom he knew would be infuriated at having to travel to Cairo for this meeting. Still, it was better to bear the anger in a highly visible place, on neutral ground, than it would have been for him to go to Afghanistan. Jambo nervously checked his watch, determined to be on the evening flight out to London.

Jambo froze when he felt a powerful grip on his right shoulder.

"You seem like a man with an important appointment to make," said a voice from behind him.

Jambo was startled and jumped a little at the sound. He was disappointed in himself. He had already done what he had vowed not to do; he had displayed weakness. He knew the meeting was off to a bad start.

"Fahran, it is so good to see you," said Jambo, hoping that his mellow basso voice conveyed ease and confidence.

"I hope your next appointment is not more important than me," said Zadran, realizing he had an advantage to press.

"I assure you, nothing is more important than you," insisted Jambo. "I was merely checking my watch to see if I would need to change my flight, to be sure we had enough time."

"Where are you flying to?" asked Zadran.

This did not seem like a time to be completely honest, lest things not go well in the meeting. "I have a flight to Berlin tonight with a connection in the morning to New York."

"Well then, let us speak frankly with one another so that we waste no time. I want you to make your flight, and then I want you to work very diligently to find my diamonds. I think you will find that I am nearly out of patience."

"Yes, yes, of course. I had no idea that there was a problem with delivery."

"No delivery is a problem," said Zadran. "I delivered for you, did I not?" Zadran sat in the club chair next to Jambo, so close that their forearms were touching when Zadran had leaned in to speak.

"Yes, of course, everyone knows you are a man of your word."

Zadran's excessively calm demeanor and uncomfortable proximity were unnerving for Jambo, even though he had used the same techniques to intimidate others in the past. He did not enjoy being the subject of the intimidation.

"Yes, I am. Therefore, when your leader told me that he needed guns, and RPGs, and automatic weapons, and rocket launchers, and I told him I would help him, I helped him. Did I not?"

"Yes, yes you did," said Jambo, conscious that sweat was forming on his forehead, even though the hotel lobby was cooled by the best air conditioning available.

"I shipped all the heroin I promised I would, did I not?"

"Yes, but we did . . ." Jambo was cut off before he could complete the sentence.

"No buts!" said Zadran in a harsh whisper. "I delivered the product; you collected the cash; you purchased your

weapons – but I have not been paid! I have no diamonds!"
Zadran pounded his fist on the arm of the chair as he felt his
anger rise.

Jambo picked up the tumbler of Jameson that he had
been sipping and downed what remained in a single gulp. He
hoped it would steady his nerves.

"We . . . I did exactly as promised. The package was
removed from the plane and was available for the Chechen to
pick up and deliver to you."

"It was never delivered," said Zadran.

"Then he is delayed; but he will pick it up and deliver it.
You have my solemn promise on that," reassured Jambo. "We
have used him before and he has always been very reliable."

"Perhaps he was in the past, but people change. Great
wealth, or at least the promise of great wealth, has a way of
changing people. He will not deliver the package!"

"You cannot know that. It has only been a few days.
Please, be patient. I am sure he will deliver the diamonds,"
implored Jambo.

"He will not deliver the package because he is dead."

Zadran watched closely for any sign that Jambo knew
that the Chechen was dead. He saw none.

"Dead! How could that be?" asked Jambo, although he
knew that he lived and worked in an odd segment of the world
where human life, at least that which was not your own, had no
intrinsic value.   All that mattered was performance.   All
mistakes, all disloyalties were punished harshly as a warning to
others.

"We found out your Chechen was working for people
who wanted to buy my diamonds – at a deep discount. He
thought he could make his own deal. We picked him up. We
asked him where the diamonds were, and he claimed he did not
know."

"What people were trying to buy your diamonds?"
asked Jambo. "I will cut their eyes out!"

"For your purposes, you need not know," replied
Zadran.

"But he must have known!" said Jambo. "You killed the

best lead we had to locate the diamonds!"

"I assure you we can be quite persuasive when we ask questions. I was assured he did not know," said Zadran.

"Then they have the diamonds! He must have given them to these other buyers!"

"I do not think so. The one fact of which we are sure is that we got to the Chechen before he retrieved the diamonds."

Jambo chose not to ask how he could be so sure. He also began to wonder if his bosses had even sent the diamonds. Was he sent here to be the fall guy?

"Remember, I said the Chechen was your man," said Zadran, putting special emphasis on the word *your*. "If your man stole from me, then you stole from me. If your man failed me, then you failed me. You understand I cannot allow that. It would not be good business."

"We are honorable men. You will be paid," said Jambo, trying to sound indignant.

Zadran laughed before leaning in to whisper to Jambo, "Either you are a great fool or you think that I am a great fool. Your people do not have the funds to pay me, and even if they did, do you really think that they would part with twenty-five million dollars to save your sorry ass? I think not!"

"No, no, no! I will call them! I will make them pay!"

"Jambo, you must grasp the reality of your situation. You are totally alone. The only one who can save Jambo is Jambo."

"What do you want? I will do whatever I have to do to make this right with you!"

"You can start by telling me what the process was for securing the diamonds."

"I do not know the full process," said Jambo. "Someone was to make the arrangements and coordinate the delivery to the Chechen."

"Too bad. It seems that Jambo does not want to save Jambo," signed Zadran as he looked up and beckoned to one of his men.

"Wait! Wait! I know who can help!" pleaded Jambo.

Zadran turned his hand up and palm out. His man

stopped immediately.

"I am listening."

"My job was to find someone at the airport in baggage handling who I could intimidate into doing what we wanted. I did that. He was supposed to get a call from someone else. I don't know who, but someone was going to tell him the flight information and how to find the package."

"Yes," said Zadran, who stared deeply into Jambo's eyes to encourage him to tell even more.

"Do you not see, all I have to do is go back to Albany and pressure this boy? He must still have the package! He will talk! I will get it, and I will bring it to you personally!"

"I am starting to like this plan. Does this boy have a name?"

"Yes, yes," said a relieved Jambo, who wanted desperately to believe he had talked himself out of this problem.

"Write it down," said Zadran, handing Jambo his Monte Blanc pen and a napkin from the table, "along with his address and all that you know of him."

Jambo did not like the turn matters were taking. "But, why write it down? I know it, and maybe it will fall into the wrong hands, and they might get to him first, or the authorities could use it as evidence against us."

"Unexpected things happen in this cruel world. You are about to embark on a long journey. If your plane should crash we would be desolate. We would have lost an important ally, a dear friend really, and our only way of contacting the person who holds my diamonds."

"But . . ."

"No, Jambo, it must be this way. I will take no chances," Zadran said sternly.

Then he shifted into a more conciliatory tone, "But, to ease your mind, I assure you that I will keep strict control over the paper, and I shall return it to you, along with a handsome bonus for valuable services rendered, when I receive my diamonds."

"So be it," said Jambo, "as you have said it, so shall it be."

For a fleeting instant Jambo considered the odds. He had an overpowering fear of Zadran, yet his passion to possess the diamonds was driving his every decision. This meeting was going to end in one or two ways. Zadran was going to allow him to go home and fetch the diamonds, or he would kill him when he left the hotel. Either way, Jambo could see no advantage to him in disclosing Edgard's identity.

Zadran waited patiently for Jambo to write down all the information. When he handed him the paper, Zadran read it over slowly to be sure he had no questions.

"It is getting late," said Zadran. "It will not do for you to miss your flight. I very much want you back in America tomorrow, working diligently on finding my diamonds. My men will escort you to the airport."

"I wish not to trouble you further," said Jambo. "I have time, and can easily take a taxi."

"It is no trouble, and I insist. I will not have you out and about in Cairo alone. This city is full of blackguards, cutthroats, and revolutionaries; and all of them are more worthy of trust than the taxi drivers. You will be properly cared for by my men. Do not forget how important you have become to me."

"You are too kind. Thank you," said Jambo, wearing his most sincere smile and shaking Zadran's hand with both of his, willing himself to believe that all was going to be well.

Zadran watched as Jambo walked out of the lobby with his men. Looking down he read the paper in his hand. *"Keenadiid Amiin Kuciil, for your sake I hope you still have my diamonds and are not as foolish as Jambo,"* thought Zadran.

A third man walked up to Zadran and made a slight bow. Zadran grabbed him by the elbow and they both turned and started walking toward the bank of elevators. Zadran loved the rooftop pool of the Fairmont Nile City Cairo Hotel. It had an inspiring view of the city, and the women who sunned themselves on the deck chairs were beautiful beyond the imagination of a man who normally only saw women wrapped up in burqas and hijabs.

He intended to be at that pool in moments, but first he must take care of business. He whispered a few words in the ear of the man next to him. The man made an obsequious gesture as he turned, quickly departing to follow his instructions. Zadran hoped that Jambo had written down accurate information, but twenty-five million dollars or not, only Jambo's death would prevent problems like this from occurring in the future. Payment must be made when due. No excuses. Ever.

*   *   *

Darragh Deering, a standby passenger, was grateful that someone had missed his or her flight to London that night. As Mr. Deering settled into his seat he was happy. His business had concluded early; and now he would get home, surprise his wife and son, and enjoy a long weekend.

The plane took off and gained altitude as it banked over the Nile, giving the lucky traveler a wonderful view of the historic waterway. It never occurred to him, as he gazed out the window, that the missing passenger, whose seat he was occupying, was floating face down in some weeds along a section of the river.

CHAPTER THIRTEEN

In Latham, New York, outside of Albany, Nubia and Edgard were having lunch.

"Edgard, you must tell me. What is troubling you? You have not been the same since that awful Jambo sat with us."

"I am so worried," said Edgard, as he listlessly pushed his red beans and rice around with a fork. "You know I took his money and I did what he asked."

"And now you are fearful. I told you not to get involved with that man. He is pure evil!"

"Nubia, you do not understand. I was told someone would contact me and pick it up, but no one has. He keeps calling me and asking when the package will be picked up, and I keep telling him I do not know, but I do not think he believes me," said a clearly agitated Edgard.

"So what? I am sure they will, eventually."

"But what will happen then? I have been thinking about this and the only thing I can think of is that Jambo wants to know when the man will come for the package because he wants to kill the man, steal the package, and maybe kill me!"

Nubia looked at Edgard, eyes wide in horror and her fingers covering her lips as if to suppress a scream.

"Yes, but what if the package is found by someone else before this Chechen contacts me? There would be an investigation and I could go to jail or be sent back to Africa! I would never see you again, and I cannot stand the thought of that!"

"You may have even bigger problems," said Nubia. "What if someone takes the package and tells no one. When Jambo's person comes, they will think that you stole it!"

"What do you think they would do to me?" asked Edgard querulously.

"You know what they will do. They went to a lot of trouble and paid you a lot of money to take care of the package. Back home they cut off arms of people just for being a member of the wrong tribe. I cannot bear to think how horrible your death, and maybe mine, will be!"

"Yours? Why would they kill you?" Edgard asked.

"You are in America for too short a time to have already forgotten what they do to people in our country who cross them."

Edgard cast his eyes down and nodded.

"They might even kill me first to try to get you to talk. They know I am your girlfriend," said Nubia, her voice rising as her sense of urgency to do something grew. "Maybe even the Winkelmans!" she said with fear in her voice.

"What should we do?" asked Edgard.

"You need to get the package out of the airport and hide it somewhere else, somewhere it cannot be discovered by accident," said Nubia.

"No, it is too dangerous! What if I am caught? No, it is better to leave it where it is and I can check on it every so often," replied Edgard.

"Man, that is pure stupid. You cannot be there all the time. The airport is always open. What if they do maintenance and find the package?"

Edgard looked forlorn as he contemplated his options. "Okay, if I take it out of the airport, what do I do with it? Should I go to a bank and get a safe deposit box?"

"Oh, Lord, no," said Nubia. "That is the worst idea ever. I do not trust banks. They are always so snooty and ask so many personal questions when all you want to do is give them your money. We should be asking them questions if you ask me. Besides, people like us, we do not have safety deposit boxes. If we walk in and ask for one, do you not realize how suspicious they will be? The first thing they will do is call the police. Do you want to have to answer a bunch of questions from the police?"

"Then what am I to do? I cannot leave it at the airport, and I cannot take it out!" said Edgard, sounding more hopeless than ever.

"Buck up, man. You can do anything. Are you not the boy who walked alone across the Horn of Africa? We just need to be smart."

"If I were smart, I would have said no to Jambo and taken my beating then and there," said Edgard.

"Ah, but you did not, so now we must make a plan. Do you know what is in the box?"

"No," said Edgard. "I just grabbed it and hid it in the ceiling."

"Are you not even a little curious?"

"Yes, of course, " but that is the kind of curiosity, like the Americans say, 'killed the cat'!" said Edgard.

"Oh, I do not believe that," said Nubia. "I think ignorance killed the cat and curiosity merely accepted the blame."

"What are you saying?" asked Edgard.

"I think we need to find out what is in that package. It might help us deal with whatever is coming," said Nubia.

"No! Absolutely not! I do not want to know what is in it. I just want to give it to whoever is supposed to get it and be done with this whole thing!"

"There is no sense talking about it. We do not have any package to open as long as it is in the airport waiting for someone else to find it!"

"Okay, okay, you are right. It is better to have it and control it, than to just leave it unguarded. But, how do we get it out? It is in the baggage handler's restroom, and airport security checks us very closely when we leave our area to make sure no one is stealing anything."

"How big is the package?" asked Nubia.

"It is not as long or as tall as a small shoe box," replied Edgard. "It is about like this," he said, gesturing the shape and size with his hands.

"What about when you go on a break, or at meal time? Does security check you then?" asked Nubia.

"Not if we stay in the building," answered Edgard.

"What about if you go up to the gate area to eat? Do they check you then?"

"No, we use a special staircase. The only security checkpoint is at the time clock when we exit."

"I have a plan. See if this works. I will buy the cheapest ticket I can and go through security. You get the package and we will meet at that Italian Kitchen place you like on Concourse B. We can sit close to each other, but we must not talk. We must not let on that we are friends. Remember, there are cameras everywhere. I will have a big carry-on bag, and I will leave the top open. All you have to do is, casually, when no one is looking, slip it into my bag. We can practice at home and then in McDonalds until we do it perfectly."

"Okay," said Edgard, "but then what happens? If you fly away, you will have to fly back and go through security."

"There is no security when passengers leave the gate area. You leave first. Then I will stay and wait for a plane to arrive, and I will just wait for a big group and merge in with them. I'll just be another traveler hurrying to get my baggage, except once I am downstairs, I'll go out across the street and walk into the garage. I can be in my car in less than five minutes."

"Hmmmm, I need to think about this," said Edgard, who thought the plan could work, but was worried about involving Nubia in case anything went wrong.

CHAPTER FOURTEEN

Three things always impressed Matt O'Malley about the operation of the Bell & Langston Marina. The first was the speed at which the boats were retrieved from dry storage and placed into the lake. The next was the size and power of the enormous blue forklift with slick, solid white tires that handled the boats as if they were children's toys, which, of course they were, but for older children. And, finally, was the way Bobby Winthrop, the dock master, commanded the forklift, making it pirouette as gracefully as one of the dancers from the New York City Ballet Company in Saratoga, which is to say it seemed to move effortlessly.

"Danny, I can't really see any damage to the prop," yelled Winthrop over the roar of the forklift. Both men examined the prop before Winthrop gently lowered the long forks into the lake, allowing Hilman's green SeaRay to bob happily in the crystal clear water.

"I can't see anything either," said Danny, "but something feels off. I'm taking it down to Dunham's Bay and letting them check it over. I don't want to screw up the shaft."

"I don't blame you," said Winthrop, as a couple of the college age boat wranglers began to pull the SeaRay toward the end of the one hundred fifty foot pier in order to make room for the next boat to be plopped down.

"Watch your RPMs!" cautioned Winthrop.

"I will, don't worry," said Hilman as he stepped over the gunwale and onto the boat. Oak was carrying an ice chest with food and drinks enough for a full day on the lake.

Danny turned on the blower as each man set about to get the ice chest, towels, cameras, dry bags and noodles stored away properly. The engine roared to life as Matt and Kevin lifted the bimini into place and secured it with the stainless steel pins.

"Okay, boys, just a nice easy cruise down to Dunham's Bay. I can't go all out until I know the prop and shaft are okay."

"Works for me," said Matt, lowering himself into the passenger side captain's chair. "It's a perfect Lake George morning, and I've got nothing better to do than to enjoy the sights."

Oak claimed the rear settee and sat in the middle with his arms stretched out the width of the boat on the top edge of the settee. He extended his legs to their fullest reach, placing his enormous flat feet directly between Matt and Danny. Kevin settled into the seats in the bow, his Hawaiian print shirt flapping in the wind, and his Scranton Wilkes-Barre RailRiders baseball hat pulled down firmly on his head.

As they pulled out of the marina, they could see the pool attendants at the Sagamore opening the market umbrellas and getting ready for the onslaught of guests they would experience on such an ideal day.

Danny set the boat for a leisurely cruise designed to savor the sights. They would glide south, hugging the shoreline so they could admire the mansions along Millionaire's Row, and they would tuck into Huddle Bay to see how busy the Round Table Restaurant was. Danny liked the challenge of threading the needle at the shoals by Clay Island. With Dome Island behind them, they focused their attention on Three Brothers Island to their left. Although Matt had seen it many times before, he was always fascinated by the enormous structure that nearly covered the island, and looked like it had been plucked from the Bavarian forest and dropped onto Lake George.

"Anyone ready for a dip?" asked Danny. However, the sun was still low in the sky and had yet to fully dissipate the night chill that pervades the lake every morning.

"Not yet," said Matt. "Let's get a little further south."

In a half hour, they arrived at the house they knew only as "the waterfall house." It was spectacular, and mind-bogglingly large. The house, which had a distinctive New

England flair to it, sat high above the lake on an outcropping of granite. The owner had done something curious and generous. There was a natural basin at the top of one part of the cliff upon which the house sat. The owner dammed the basin on the lakeside to form a bowl. He then installed a pump that continuously pumps water from the lake into the bowl. The overflow creates a beautiful waterfall that can't even be seen from the house, but which many passing boaters on the lake pause to admire.

The waterfall was positioned at the entry to a small cove in a low speed area. Danny stopped the boat, and before anyone could say a word, he was over the side and into the crisp waters of the southern basin of Lake George.

"Are you kidding me!" he yelled as his head broke the surface. "This is Paradise! Paradise, I am telling you! Come on! Get in!" he called to the others.

Kevin and Matt each grabbed a foam noodle, stepped onto the swim platform, and then took a giant step off and into the lake.

Matt popped up first, spraying the water that he had let into his mouth.

"Out – damn – standing!" said Matt. "This is the best medicine ever for clearing your head and opening your mind!" Oak looked on, but made no indication of any intent to join in.

The three-step ladder made for easy re-entry after a fifteen-minute swim in the calm water.

"I feel so great when I get out of that water!" said O'Malley.

The wet men wrapped themselves in towels and happily dripped all over the deck.

"You know," said Oak, "you never finished telling the Katie Takes It With Her story last night."

"She's a saint, Oak. Get her name right. It's Kateri Tekakwitha," said Kevin. "Come on, man, have a little respect!"

"Whatever. Just finish the damn story."

"Where was I?" asked O'Malley.

"She was a Mohawk, daddy a chief. She had a turtle-shaped box with a treasure from Isaac somebody or the other, and she died and got hot and started healing people - yada, yada, yada," said Oak.

"Wow. I had no idea you were paying such close attention," said Matt sardonically. "There's not a whole lot left to tell."

"Tell it anyway. It will seem like a lot the way you tell it," said Oak.

Kevin chuckled to himself.

Matt gave a disgusted look, but, undeterred, resumed the story. "She would never show anyone the contents of the box. She kept it hidden away. Some people thought it was some sort of magic talisman; others thought it was the Holy Grail; and still others believed it was a block of pure gold."

"What happened to the box when she died?" asked Oak.

"Well, we're talking about something that happened nearly three hundred years ago, so the story is a bit muddled. Most people seem to believe that she knew she was about to die. At the time, there was a company of French soldiers garrisoned in what is now Montreal. One in particular had expressed his hope that he would survive the war and return to France to become a priest. It is that soldier that, legend has it, was entrusted with the turtle box."

"Talk about Mr. Lucky," said Oak.

Danny pushed the throttle forward, turned the boat and began a straight shot east across the lake to Dunham's Bay.

"Not as lucky as Kateri Tekakwitha. She was very sick, but eventually pulled out of it," said O'Malley. "But not before the soldier was shipped out to engage the British at Fort William Henry. Before the battle, some say he hid the box in the back of a cave along the shore of Lake George. Others say he was captured by the Brits and all his possessions confiscated and placed on one of the bateaux, which is ironic, since the bateaux were called *turtle boats*."

"So, you were looking for Kateri's treasure?" said Hilman.

"Not really. The bateau we were on has been well researched, photographed and surveyed by the state. If there was ever anything on it, it would be long gone by now. It was just kind of fun to imagine what it must have been like back then."

"Do you even believe there was a treasure?" asked Hilman.

"I do, but I don't believe it was on a boat."

"Why not?" asked Oak.

"Just think about it," said Kevin, joining in on the conversation. If you're a French soldier about to go into battle with the British in the seventeenth century, the odds of being killed or captured are pretty high. You would want to be at your best for the fight, so why would you carry the extra weight of a box with no military purpose? Besides, if you had pledged on your honor to keep it safe, would you take it into battle?"

"No, probably not, but what would he have done with it?" asked Oak.

"My best guess is that the part of the legend about him hiding it in a cave along the lake makes the most sense. It would be secure and he wouldn't have to carry it into battle."

"I've been coming to this lake since I was five years old," said Danny. "I've swum, paddled and power boated every inch of its thirty-two mile length, and I've never seen or heard of anyone who claims that there's a cave at the water's edge."

"There may not be . . .," said O'Malley, ". . . now."

"What do you mean, now?" asked Oak.

"The lake is always changing. More water comes into the lake by rain, snowmelt and underwater springs than the La Chute River up by Ticonderoga can let out into Lake Champlain. Therefore, the lake level today is about three and a half feet higher than it was during the French and Indian War," replied O'Malley.

"So," said Kevin, "we can assume that the soldier would have looked for a small opening in which to hide his treasure; and we can further assume that if he was executed by the British, which was their normal practice at the time, the spot remained undiscovered, and the treasure is still there."

"Cool, let's go get it!" said Hilman.

"Easy say, hard do," said O'Malley. "We have no idea where to look."

"Actually," said Kevin, "we do. It's fair to assume that he couldn't get far on foot, so wherever he found a cave to hide the treasure must have been close to the redoubt in which they had their encampment. Historical records could help to pinpoint the spot."

"This is starting to sound like a huge waste of time," said Oak. "We'll never find a cave that probably never existed. That's why it's called a legend."

CHAPTER FIFTEEN

The marina at Dunham's Bay was still quiet. Mornings can be overcast and cool in the Adirondacks, so people develop a rhythm to their day that usually doesn't allow for early starts. The days start slow and then take off. Today was bright and beautiful, but people, for the most part, were slow to realize it. The ship's store had only one other customer browsing through the offerings of charts, ropes, nautical-themed souvenirs and a host of bits and pieces necessary to keep a boat working, or the fish nervous.

Danny was out with a mechanic who was test driving the SeaRay. Kevin, Oak and Matt had elected to shop and enjoy the free coffee and rest room privileges afforded customers. None of them took any particular note of the only other customer, an ordinary looking man, who was deliberately affecting a round-shoulder appearance and walking with just the slightest hitch in his step, as if he had a stiff knee.

Smythe took his time sizing up the three men in the store before deciding that the one they called Kevin seemed the most open and ready to talk to a stranger.

"I beg your pardon. Smashing forenoon, eh?" said Smythe.

"Huh?" said Kevin.

"Oh, so sorry, I guess you chaps say 'Good Morning,'" said Smythe.

"We do, and it is," said Kevin with a smile. "Good Morning to you as well."

"Yes, quite," said Smythe. "My name is Myles Smythe, and I wonder if I can ask you some questions," he said, trying to seem as ingratiating as possible.

"I can't think why not," said Kevin. "How can I help you?"

"Well, I was out back a while ago and I saw you chaps come in on a beautiful boat. I was very impressed with the way you were able to dock it. You chaps seem to know a lot about handling a boat."

"You've got the wrong guy," said Kevin. "My job is to stay out of the way and make sure we have enough ice and beer on board. You need to talk to Danny or Matt."

"Hey, Matt!" said Kevin, raising his voice to get O'Malley's attention, "Come over here. There's someone I want you to meet."

Matt put down the bright red fender he was examining and started over toward Kevin.

"So, what kind of questions do you have?" asked Kevin.

"I am interested in buying a used boat, but I don't know much about them," said Smythe.

"You don't sound like you're from around here," said Kevin. "Why would you want to buy a boat?"

Smythe chuckled. "Oh, no. I am not from anywhere around here. I am from London, in the UK."

"Matt O'Malley, this is my new friend, Miles Smythe from London, and he wants advice on buying a used boat."

"A boat! Most people settle for t-shirts. You're never going to fit it under the seat in front of you when you go home," said Matt with a friendly grin as he extended his hand to shake Myles' hand.

"I don't think I shall be returning to the UK with a boat. I just want to use it while I am here."

"Wouldn't it be cheaper to just rent one?"

"Well, I am on an extended holiday so I need it for the entire summer, and it is very expensive to rent. I intended to travel all over, but I have just fallen in love with this area and decided to summer here before I move on to other places in the States."

"Nice life! What do you do that lets you take off so much time?" said O'Malley.

"I am an instructor at Blyth Academy, and I came into a

spot of money when Auntie died and decided to take an extended sabbatical. I am forty-eight years old and I have never had an adventure, unless you consider parent conferences an adventure."

"What do you teach?" asked Kevin.

"It depends on the academic year and what the school needs, but I usually teach the religion and church history courses, sometimes comparative religion."

"The summers here are pretty short," said Matt. "What will you do with the boat at the end of the summer?"

"I thought I'd just sell it. I figure the difference between what I buy it for and what I sell it for will be less than the cost of a rental."

"Maybe, but you're buying at the beginning of summer when the prices are the highest, and selling at the end of summer when no one wants to buy a boat because they don't want to pay to store it all winter."

"I see. Great point. I believe I have found the right chaps to advise me," said Smythe ingratiatingly.

"Another problem is where you're going to keep a boat. Dockage here is very limited and very expensive."

"I am looking to rent someplace for the summer that has a dock," said Smythe, happy he had anticipated most of this conversation ahead of time, and thinking it might be time to move it in another direction.

"I don't want to seem intrusive," said Smythe, "but have we met before?"

"I don't think so," said O'Malley. "Have you ever been to Florida?"

"No, but that is part of my winter plan," said Smythe. He looked intently at Matt, and then at Kevin, and back again to Matt, all the while muttering under his breath, "Florida, Florida."

Suddenly, Smythe's face broke into a wide grin. "That's it! I knew it! I never forget a face," he said, as if relieved that he finally solved a puzzle.

"What's it?" asked Kevin.

"I know why I know you. Well, not know you, but

recognize you. You are the blokes from Florida who found that body. I saw your photos in the paper yesterday. Bad business, that."

"Oh, great, I always wanted to be famous," said O'Malley.

"Well, they let you out, so it must all be good," said Smythe.

"They didn't let us out," said O'Malley. "We were never in. The police just needed information from us because we found the body."

"Of course," said Smythe, "I hope you don't think I was implying anything else."

"No, no, I'm just a little touchy. Sorry," said O'Malley.

"No worries. So, have they caught the perpetrator yet?" asked Smythe.

"Not that I know of," said O'Malley.

"But they have a good idea of who did it, don't they?" said Smythe, hoping for any other information he could get.

"I'm not sure they know who the victim is, let alone who killed him," said Kevin.

Matt shot him a glance that clearly conveyed, *"too much information."*

"You seem very interested in all this," said Matt as he paused and stared, waiting for a response to his statement.

"Oh, my, yes! It is so exciting, so American," said Smythe, hoping a seemingly thoughtless slight to his country might get the suspicious Matt thinking of other things. "Back home, we rarely have a shooting murder. Your CSI shows on the telly are all the rage. Wouldn't miss it. I am sure they will get their man."

"Probably," said O'Malley, not knowing what to make of this odd man.

"What kind of a boat are you looking at?" asked Kevin, sensing the conversation was getting a little tense.

"I am thinking about a Four Winns that they have here. It is eight years old. Is that too old for a boat?"

"No, not really, if it has been looked after properly. How many hours are on the engine?" responded Matt.

"Hours. Of course!" said Smythe, slapping himself on the forehead. "I don't know. I asked the salesman about mileage. He must think I am a pure dolt. I'll never be able to bargain with him now."

"It will be alright. These are pretty good guys here. Ask him if the boat was always used on Lake George. You may not want a boat that's been in salt water a lot; and ask how it was stored in the winter. Inside is better than outside. Winterized and shrink-wrapped is okay if outside. Ask if they did the maintenance here at Dunham Bay, and if they will show you the records. Also ask him if you can have your own mechanic inspect it."

"Super! These are great ideas. Any suggestion of which mechanic I should use?"

"I'm actually not from around here either, but when Danny gets back in, he can tell you."

"Actually, I can't wait. I have an appointment in Glens Falls."

"Oh," said Matt, shrugging.

"I hate to be a bother, but would you mind if I rang you up if I get close to making a decision? Maybe get that information about the mechanic...?"

"Um," Matt hesitated, "well, I guess that would be alright. I'll give you my cell number."

"Thank you. This is just so kind. You must let me take you all for a drink and a ride on my new boat."

"Okay, sounds good," said Matt, hoping that the invitation was the British version of *"let's do lunch."* Something about Mr. Smythe did not sit well with O'Malley.

"What will you do with the boat? Are you a fisherman?" asked Kevin.

Smythe looked from side to side as if to be sure he was not going to be overheard. Leaning in and whispering conspiratorially, he said, "Actually, I am on a bit of a treasure hunt. I don't expect to find anything, but it will be great fun looking."

"What kind of a treasure?" asked Kevin.

"It wouldn't do to tell you too much," said Smythe, "but

if I find it, just let me say, it will be heavenly!"

"Cool," said Matt, as he turned to finish his shopping.

"Cheerio," said Smythe, waving as he headed toward the front door. He thought to himself, *"This could not have gone better. I introduced myself; I know how to contact them; and I have a pretext to call them if the need arises."* The warm sun on his face felt wonderful as he stepped out of the store, not feeling a care in the world.

O'Malley stepped closer to Okonski and asked, "Oak, is it just me or did that guy seem a little off to you? He sure had a lot of questions."

"He was curious," allowed Oak, "but, so what. He's on vacation in a foreign land. But, maybe he's just a squirrely kind of guy."

"He was curious," said O'Malley, "too curious."

CHAPTER SIXTEEN

The cruise down to Dunham's Bay was relaxed on the calm, mirror-like surface of the early morning Lake George. The trip back was the exact opposite. Traffic on the mid-day Lake George had picked up, as had the wind, causing the mirror-like surface to disappear under a jumble of waves, whitecaps and wakes.

The other thing that had changed was Danny Hilman's mindset. Reassured that neither the prop nor the driveshaft was a problem, and all that was needed was a slight adjustment on the idle, Danny was free to resume his preferred piloting method – all out, hell bent for leather. As he relentlessly pushed the SeaRay harder and harder through the rough water on the east side of Lake George, he treated his passengers to a bone-crushing ride as the bow would first soar over a wave and then come crashing down into the trough. Sometimes the boat would momentarily surf the top of a wave, the bow suspended in air, and then, seemingly with even greater force, crash flat-footed into the trough hard enough to loosen teeth.

Some boats are designed to ameliorate the impact of such a ride on the passenger's spine, but not the SeaRay. It would crash down on the lake, sounding like the water had been struck with a flat board, and send a huge spray out in all directions as it displaced the water. The boat would shutter with each impact, yet it held together as if it enjoyed the punishment. The passengers could do nothing but hold on and hope that the ride would slow, and their pain ease, before they developed compression fractures in their vertebrae.

"There are cliff divers on Calf Pen," yelled Hilman. "Should we stop?"

"Absolutely," said O'Malley, who had hoped for some relief at an earlier spot. Hilman had just roared by Echo Bay, not even considering the hoped-for swim and respite from the pounding that O'Malley was craving. He liked watching the divers, but he loved the idea of just floating peacefully for a while.

There are many places to go cliff diving in Lake George, with varying degrees of difficulty – from the novice leap in Paradise Bay to the insane sixty-five foot leap from a triangle of rock with the sheer face known simply as the Big Jump. It is not marked on any navigational charts, probably at the insistence of the Lake George Patrol. It can be found easily by the nutty folks willing to hurl themselves off it, because it is conveniently located near the north end of The Narrows and across from the popular camping spots on St. Sacrament Island, one of the Mother Bunch Islands.

Despite the size of the Big Jump, there is nowhere on the lake that can compare to the jump from Calf Pen for pure terror and technical difficulty. Calf Pen is a deep and narrow v-shape that was carved into an otherwise flat cliff face by retreating glaciers. There is no easy approach to Calf Pen. The diver must approach by boat, swim to shore, and climb up slippery rocks to make an assault on the cliff.

Just getting into position to jump is dangerous enough. No one who does this jump would ever be accused of being sensible, but the least crazy among them climb to a level of about twenty-five feet, which places them on the widest part of the "v" where it intersects with the lake. Jumping from here means you survived the climb, and the plunge back to the lake should be easy and uneventful.

For the more adventurous, there is another jumping platform about eight to ten feet higher. Here the diver must jump further out to avoid jutting rocks at the base of the cliff. Those who make it to this level often hesitate for extended periods while they contemplate the series of bad choices that have led them to this spot.

Truly adventurous jumpers, or truly suicidal, depending on your point of view, aim for the ultimate jump at the top, where the narrowest part of the "v" was cut into the cliff. From here, they must jump blind – unable to see the landing point at takeoff.

Fifty-five feet above the water, the jumper must also back up to get a running start on the jump. Gravity will bring him or her back down to the lake, but momentum is necessary for the jumper to avoid the tree that has somehow gained purchase on the side of the cliff. The cold weather and short growing season have served to keep it a straggly looking tree, but it nonetheless possesses a canopy that requires a mighty leap to clear.

Danny Hilman and his friend, Timmy, have used cliff diving around the lake to foster in their children a sense of confidence, adventure, accomplishment and courage, but even they refuse to let the most important people in their lives jump from the top of Calf Pen.

The SeaRay bobbed and drifted in the current for about twenty minutes as a series of jumpers tested their mettle against this foreboding leap. The payoff for those who jumped was an adrenaline rush, a deep plunge into the colder waters far below the surface, and a sense of exhilaration – or relief – as they swim back up toward the surface, where they are usually greeted with a cacophony of boat horns acknowledging the triumph of peer pressure over good sense.

O'Malley could see this brief respite was over. Danny was getting impatient to get on with the plan he had worked out in his head for the day.

"Anyone want to go in for a dip?" asked Danny.

O'Malley knew this was the precursor to a departure, but the water here was rough, and as appealing as a swim sounded, the difficulty climbing the ladder dissuaded him and the others from going in the water.

"Okay, next stop is Glen Island for a snack and then we hit Paradise Bay," said Danny.

Others may have offered this up as a suggestion, but everyone on the boat knew this plan was already carved in stone. No one minded, however, because it was a good plan and allowed a continuation of a perfect day on the lake. If telepathy was a thing, all their minds were in sync, thinking, *"Are you kidding me? Does it get better than this?"*

*   *   *

Keenadiid Amiin Kuciil had a bad feeling about his day. He did not like the sound of the Englishman on the phone, and he did not trust him. It had not helped that Smythe had laughed at him when he had asked to be called Kenny Ames. The Englishman was pushy, and Kenny did not like that. He said he just wanted some information about a co-worker, but he would not say who that was, and would not discuss it on the phone. Smythe would not come to Albany. He insisted that he would pay Kenny well if he would just come to Glens Falls to talk to him. He had made Kenny very edgy; so edgy that he decided to bring along someone to make sure he stayed safe. He would not have gone at all except that he needed the money.

He was able to convince his friend Tyrone "Mookie" Jones to make the trip. They had gone to school together for a while before they both dropped out. Kenny went to the airport and started unloading planes while Mookie went to a gang and started to unload crack on street corners.

Actually, there were two Mookies - who lived in two very different worlds. Mookie from the 'hood was still everybody's friend, liked to hang and be with his friends, and was sweet and tender in caring for his grandmother. Mookie from the Crips was another story altogether. He was earning a rap sheet that showed a progression of criminal activity and violence that did not bode well for his future, or that of his community.

Mookie was the only person Kenny knew, however, who would put up a fight if things went bad with the Englishman. He was hoping that when he picked Mookie up just before lunch that he was going to get Mookie from the 'hood. Instead, he got the Crips version, who had been sampling his own product, and liked it.

When Kenny arrived at Mookie's house, he saw him sitting on a metal folding chair on the bare dirt where a front lawn should have been, affecting an insouciant attitude as his girlfriend was unmercifully berating him. When he saw Kenny turn into the driveway, he casually flipped the hood of his sweatshirt over the oversized baseball hat he was wearing sidewise and slowly stood up, walking away as if he had been all alone in the yard.

"Don't you be walkin' 'way from me!" she screamed at him. "I am not done with you yet!"

Mookie opened the door, threw in a gym bag, and got in the car, paying the same heed to the woman screaming at him as if he had been born deafer than Helen Keller.

"What's the problem with your baby mama?" asked Kenny.

"Sheeeeet," was the only response Mookie made.

"I do not understand why you put up with her," said Kenny. "I would kick her booty to the curb."

"Bro' do what a bro' gotta do," said Mookie, with a shrug, thinking about the baby mama's brother, Jerome "KilzB" Richardson, who was the leader of his gang – and not a man to be on the wrong side of.

"It is your life," said Kenny. "I am just saying."

Mookie made no reply. He slid down in the seat, crossed his arms over his chest, and leaned against the window to try to sleep. There had been a lot of partying the night before and KilzB had provided some PCP for everyone. Mookie liked his crack, but was still undecided about the benefits of Angel Dust. The PCP made him feel like he was the strongest, meanest son of a bitch in the world - who could beat any dude that might challenge him, but he did not like the unpredictable length of the high, or the rough landing when it was finally over.

"Good idea," said Kenny. "Get some rest." Kenny was already beginning to regret his decision to include Mookie in this trip. "I am going to need you to be on the top of your game when we meet this Smythe dude."

Mookie grunted and turned toward the door. "Don't you be worryin' 'bout me. You be worryin' 'bout you."

Kenny pulled onto I-87 and headed north. As he went, he tried to plan what he would say and do when he met Smythe. The first thing he wanted to know is how the Englishman came to call him. Then he wanted to know how much he was going to be paid. He had been promised that this trip was going to be worth his while. How much money he would insist on would depend on who he had to give up, and what information was needed. He would have to play that by ear.

The miles were being chewed up quickly as Kenny drove north to Glens Falls. He had been given some specific directions, but he had never been there before, so he was watching closely in order not to miss his exit. However, he became so engrossed in the fantasy of how much money he could demand for his information that he almost missed his exit. The swerving and slamming on the brakes as he was trying to get off the interstate woke Mookie.

"Damn, you drive like my grandma!" said Mookie, rubbing his eyes and sitting up straighter in his seat as he was forcing himself to comprehend where he was and what he was doing.

"Oh yeah," he said softly, as he remembered what he was doing in this strange place. Mookie reached into the bag at his feet and pulled out a crack pipe and cigar lighter. He fired up the lighter over the bowl and sucked hard on the pipe. He could feel an almost immediate response by his body to the drug. He liked it.

"You want a drag?" he said, extending the crack pipe over to Kenny.

"No, are you crazy?" said Kenny, as he struggled to drive and read the directions. They had taken exit 18 onto Main Street.

As Main Street turned to Broad Street, Mookie announced, "Boy, you gonna need to pull over."

"Why?" asked Kenny.

"'Cause."

"'Cause? 'Cause why?" asked Kenny. "I have got to meet this Englishman!"

"'Cause I gotta pee, if you gotta know," said Mookie irritably.

As they approached the intersection of Broad and Hudson, Mookie became agitated. He pointed and commanded, "There! There! Pull over there in front of that liquor store."

Kenny swerved to the right and did as he was told.

"They are not going to just let you walk in and pee there," said Kenny. "Let's go. I'll find you a McDonald's."

"I ain't gonna pee in some punk ass old Mickey D's. Looky, that looks like a real nice place," said Mookie.

"Annie King's Fine Wine and Spirits," he said aloud, reading from the sign.

"Look at her on the sign. She a sweet old lady. She ain't gonna turn away a brother in need," said Mookie, his broad grin revealing his elaborate gold grillwork.

Reaching over, Mookie pulled a Glock 42 out of the gym bag at his feet and tucked it into the waistband of his jeans.

"Holy shit!" exclaimed Kenny. "What is that for!"

"Maybe that nice grannie on the sign not be working today. Maybe someone else give me a hard time 'bout peeing," said Mookie, and he laughed as if he had just said the funniest thing ever.

"Please, Mookie!" pleaded Kenny. "You do not need a gun! Just leave it here!"

"Don't be tellin' Mookie what he needs or what he don't need!" said Mookie angrily. "You heard dat bitch at home. Mookie needs to earn; and there's no mo' betta place to earn than someplace where nobodies know who you be!"

All that Kenny had time to say was, "Wait!" before Mookie opened his door. The afternoon sun flashed off the car door window as he exited with the smoothness of a tiger stalking his prey.

Confusion washed over Kenny. Ratting out a friend for money was just business, but this was just plain wrong. He wanted to slam the car into gear and get the hell away, but he knew that if he did, Mookie or one of the other Crips would make him regret the decision for the rest of what would then promise to be a very short life.

Kenny stayed, the car idled, and the world around him seemed to change in ways he could not even imagine. Coming to Glens Falls was proving to be the worst decision of his life.

It would shortly get even worse.

CHAPTER SEVENTEEN

Everything seemed to be falling into place for Miles Smythe as he turned out of the SeaRay parking lot heading south on Ridge Road toward 9N in Lake George Village, where he would get on I-87 and go even further south to Glens Falls. He intended to arrive early for the meeting that was to take place in Crandall Park, near the tennis courts at the corner of Glen Street and Fire Road.

Smythe liked to have such clandestine meetings in open spaces. He had picked it, and would be there first to survey the rendezvous spot. He would be in place when Kenny Ames showed up, and would watch him for at least fifteen minutes before he approached him. That should be enough to be sure Ames had not tried to alter the balance of power at this tête-à-tête. Smythe was a big proponent of the concept of situational awareness. The battle may go to the quickest or the strongest, but he always put his money on the smartest and best informed.

The package he sought was clearly not going to be found on the bateau. Jambo's information on where he could seize the Chechen had been spot on, and he had grabbed him with no trouble; but he had been way off on the hiding spot for the diamonds. Perhaps this suggestion of squeezing the baggage handler would work out better. Certainly, this Kenny would not be as resistant to his interrogation techniques as the Chechen had been. If he had no useful information, Smythe would next squeeze Jambo to make sure he was not just being played for a fool while Jambo recovered the diamonds.

Glens Falls was not really a city. It was at best a big town; yet, in this out of the way place in the world, Glens Falls did offer some comforts for Smythe. The wine he had enjoyed at Robert Anniston's had whetted his appetite for some of the finer things in life, and, he thought, *What is more fine than a good bottle of wine!"* He was growing weary of the rustic Adirondack life and craved the glitter of London, or even New York City.

He had budgeted time to go to a place he had seen advertised in a local magazine, claiming to have the best selection of wine in upstate New York. Smythe did not think it would take much to claim that modest honor, but it was worth checking out Annie King's Fine Wines and Spirits while he was here.

The store was easy to find, and was delightfully surprising in several ways. Annie King certainly knew her wines. While the selection was wide, it tended toward merlots, which was just fine with Smythe. He was surprised that, in addition to the wine, Mrs. King had done a remarkable job with pairings of locally sourced artisanal cheeses.

The best surprise of all was that this was not some corporate shell game. There actually was an Annie King. She had inherited the store from her father, and she and her husband had run it together after her father's death. She was just north of ninety years old, but she still ran the store – by herself now after her husband's death.

She would employ help when she had deliveries coming in, or if she thought the store would be busy, but usually she worked alone – and she liked it that way.

She was able to know all her customers and what they liked best. The customers loved it when she would call to give them a heads up when a special wine became available. Her grandson, Matt, would come in whenever he could to help around the store.

Smythe was thoroughly enjoying chatting up Annie King and wandering up and down the racks and stacks of wine. The store was set up a little like a convenience store, with Annie perched on a stool at the checkout counter, and the center of the store filled with shelving that ran parallel to the counter. The side of the store facing the street was made of fixed, floor to ceiling plate glass. The wall opposite that was lined with walk-in coolers containing refrigerated white wines.

Not all surprises in life are delightful. Smythe's

attention was drawn through the windows, where he saw a late model car swerve to the curb and a young African-American man getting out, wearing a hoodie. Smythe's danger radar was on full alert. Both the movement of the car and the attire of its former passenger seemed out of place. He was wondering why anyone would cover their head and face with a hoodie on such a warm day. Smythe was nothing if not a survivor, and his instincts and MI-5 training were kicking in.

Smythe slowly crouched down next to the pinot noirs, and positioned himself so he could see the front door and the sales counter in a parabolic mirror that hung near the ceiling over the walk-in coolers. He saw the young black man enter the store. It was clear that he was not a typical oenophile as he nervously walked to the back of the store, checking the aisles for other customers. Smythe watched and carefully timed his movements to slide around the end caps so to always keep shelving between himself and the new customer.

Smythe glanced in the direction of Annie King, who had stopped her paperwork and was watching the young man very intently as he strode purposefully toward the front of the store.

"Can I help you find something?" she said coldly.

"Yeah, bitch. You can help me find the cash drawer. This be a hold up," Mookie replied defiantly as he reached into his open hoodie for his weapon.

Without missing a beat, she stood up, brought her hands out from under the counter, and began slapping a Louisville Slugger baseball bat on her outstretched hand as if to prove that she would defend her store to the death.

"I don't think so! Not today! Not in my store!" she said with quiet authority.

Smythe could not believe what he was seeing. *"Bloody hell! She is going to get herself, and worse, me, killed!"* he thought.

Mookie raised his Glock 42 up to shoulder level and with palm down and arm fully extended, waved it at Annie King and screamed, "Bitch, put down dat bat before I pop a cap in your face!"

Smythe was relieved that the thug who was robbing the

store apparently had no real weapons training other than aping what he had seen in the Hollywood movies. They were poor role models for proper weapon handling technique. Smythe could see Annie's eyes widen, and he could see she was either too scared or too determined to put down the bat.

The calculus of survival must be done quickly. Smythe's gun was locked in the trunk of his car. He felt he would have no use for it before the meeting, and he did not want to call attention to himself if it were inadvertently exposed.

The young robber appeared to be high as he bounced on his toes like a boxer, still screaming profanities at Mrs. King, while she stood her ground and continued to slap the bat on her hand.

Normally, Smythe would be inclined to extend a professional courtesy to the robber and mind his own business, but this man was no professional. He was nothing but a street junkie, high, and wound tight as a coiled spring that was about to pop. When he did, Annie would be dead, and so may he, he feared, if this coked-out loser spotted him. It was time to take matters into his own hands.

Fortunately, Mookie was not used to such resistance from little ninety-year old ladies who were not tall enough to ride the Comet roller coaster at Great Escape, so he was focusing all of his attention on her, convinced they were alone in the store.

Smythe knew he had to act quickly and definitively. While he had left his gun in the trunk of the rental car, he always had his Kershaw Blur knife with him. The combination of its crucible steel blade and its SpeedSafe ambidextrous assisted opening system, which allowed for easy one-handed opening, made it the perfect weapon for his purposes. He slipped his knife out of his pocket and carefully opened the surgical steel blade. His training took over at this point.

He was a David taking on a Goliath that he was confident he could defeat. He acted without thought or fear. He had an objective and a plan to meet that objective. All that was necessary was carrying out the plan with speed, precision, and, most importantly, merciless efficiency.

Thinking about what he was about to do served no

purpose at this point except to allow fear and indecision to divert his attention from a simple plan, and hamper his finely honed skills. Emotions were the enemy, and through discipline and training, all emotion had been banished from within him, and replaced with well-practiced, yet instinctive reactions.

The blade was hidden along his index finger, just as he had done with Maura Owens Sullivan. The positioning was just second nature to him. Maura Sullivan, however, was weak and drunk when he attacked her. It was hardly a contest. He did not know Mookie's name, but he felt like he knew everything he need to know about him. He knew how big he was; he knew what weapons he had; and he could smell the fear coming off his target. Smythe knew he could approach the robber from behind and, with luck, remain undetected. At worst, he calculated, this would be a forty-five second kill.

Mookie continued to bounce on the balls of his feet as he glanced nervously around, first at Annie King and then at the entrance. Smythe knew the robber was nearing the end of his endurance for waiting. Fear that another customer would stroll in, dramatically increasing his problems, was gnawing at him. He was not thinking with his brain. Emotions were driving him. The robber would shoot, and Smythe calculated he would shoot in the next fifteen to twenty seconds.

The robber's gun was becoming a burden to him. Smythe could see he was finding it more and more difficult to hold the gun up with his arm fully extended, so it was slowly and unconsciously drifting down. He had already switched the gun from his right hand to his left. When he let it drop to the level of his waist, Smythe calculated, he would probably decide he must act - at which point he would most likely decide to shoot Annie King.

Knowing time was running out, Smythe braced the blade, which extended beyond his index finger, with the other fingers of his right hand, and pinned it to his palm with his thumb. Smythe stood and began walking toward the robber. He closed the distance with remarkable speed and stealth.

The robber was still spewing spit and profanities when he felt his head snap back, and the sharp blade slice his neck. He had no idea he had been fatally wounded. He spun to see what it was, and for the first time he was face to face with Smythe. Mookie's eyes went wide with amazement as blood spurted in front of him. Clutching his throat, he could not believe that there had been someone else in the store; and he could not understand where all the blood he felt was coming from.

The fight or flight mechanism had clicked in and Mookie decided this was the time for flight. He tried to run, but he found that his legs were in revolt with his brain, and they were operating on their own, and without supervision. Left to their own devices, his legs could not agree on a single course of action, so each leg started in a different direction. Mookie never made it to the door. His collapse resulted in the destruction of a display of Bordeaux, which, as it turned out, were mourned longer than Mookie was.

Annie King surveyed the damage. Still holding her Louisville Slugger, she came from around the counter and walked over to Smythe.

"Thanks, mister. I guess I owe you some wine!"

Smythe smiled and said, "You are too kind. Perhaps this La Crema." He picked up two bottles and headed for the door.

"Wait!" yelled Annie King. "I have to call the police. They will want to talk to you."

The last thing in the world Smythe intended to do was talk to the police.

"Oh, that will be such a bother. I am sure you can fill them in on all the details. Cheerio!"

Annie King had led a long life. She had a wealth of experience, but nothing could compare to the last few minutes. The bells over the door made a little tinkling sound as it closed after Smythe's departure. It reminded Annie of the Christmas movie with Jimmy Stewart. She wondered if the sound of ringing bells really did mean an angel had earned his wings, because she thought an angel had just left her store - an angel who had just saved her life.

Smythe walked smartly, but not fast enough to draw attention to himself. He would pause briefly to feign interest in a window display, but, in reality, he wasted no time waiting around to see what would happen, because he knew what would happen. The police and EMTs would arrive. The robber would be declared dead. People would gather in gaggles, and stare and chat. Multitudes of photographs would be taken, and everyone close-by would be interviewed and try to be helpful, but they would each give wildly varying versions of the events. Uniformed patrolmen would block off the scene, and detectives would fill out reports. In the end, no one would care that a young black man with high levels of illegal drugs in his system was killed while trying to rob a respected local business. The detectives would go through the motions of the investigative process, and, in the end, other matters would have greater priority and this would end up as a cold case.

*   *   *

Kenny Ames also left the scene. He, however, could not pull it off with the aplomb displayed by Miles Smythe. Kenny was nearly in a full-blown panic attack as he waited for Mookie to return. Each minute seemed like an hour. He resolved to leave three times, and three times the fear of retribution caused his resolve to falter. The fourth time, however, was the trick. Once Kenny heard the sirens, he knew it was time to get out of there.

He backed the car up, intending to blow the horn and wave at Mookie to get him to leave. What he saw horrified him. There was Mookie's lifeless body lying in front of the checkout counter. Kenny could see blood everywhere. An old lady and a white man stood over the body, appearing to be chatting, until suddenly the white man picked up two bottles of wine and gave the little old lady a wave and a smile as he pushed the door open and started to stroll down the street.

All this was too much for Kenny. He was sure that Mookie was dead. The tires on his car squealed as he made a u-turn from the curb, causing an approaching motorist to have to take emergency evasive actions to avoid a collision. Kenny did not care. All Kenny could think about was getting to I-87 and back to Albany.

CHAPTER EIGHTEEN

The day had flown by and Danny had pulled out all the stops. There was a picnic on an island, too many swims to count, and even a stop at Bass Island, where, several years before, Matt had been shot at by a fanatical Fundamentalist Muslim intent on killing him and perpetrating a terror attack on Lake George. Matt was not fond of the memories and did all he could to push those desperate hours out of his mind, even as Danny re-enacted the jump off West Dollar Island where Matt had escaped the terrorist.

During the day, they met up with Timmy Lufwick and his family and friends as they were racing about in his deep blue Cobalt bow rider. Timmy's wife, Sybil, always the perfect hostess, broke up the party so that she could be returned home to prepare dinner for their guests. Plans were made for the next day, since weekend days required much more planning than weekdays because of the influx of boaters.

Everyone knew that a perfect day on the lake was nearly over as they slowly cruised along Green Island. They were passing by the Pavilion, a double-decked outdoor restaurant at the Sagamore that was built over the lake and offered incredible views of Dome Island, when they first heard the sirens.

"Is it just me, or does it sound like there's something going on in Bolton Landing?" said Danny.

"Sounds like every cop car in town is going somewhere," said O'Malley.

"Wow, both of them," added Kevin with pretextual irony.

Oak was sitting up straight and listening intensely.

"Something's going on. And, those are not just police cars. Can't you hear the ambulance?" asked Oak.

By now, they were in front of the Sagamore. Danny had begun to drop the canvas and they all were storing gear and getting ready for the giant forklift to put their boat on the shelf for the night.

Once the SeaRay was shipshape, Danny nudged the throttle forward, pulled the boat in at just over idle speed, hugging close to a row of cigarette boats before turning hard, and approached the dock, bow first. Kevin was positioned in the bow with a rope that he tossed to one of the boat wranglers. Oak was at the stern, and once the wrangler fended the boat off the dock with his sneaker and pushed it just a bit in a counter-clockwise direction, Oak tossed the stern line to a pretty college-age girl, who tugged the back of the boat close to the dock.

The men grabbed the wet towels and a few gear bags and stepped onto the dock. Bobby Winthrop was sitting on a lawn chair watching a television perched precariously on another lawn chair near the entrance to the boat barn. As they approached Bobby, he nodded his greeting to them.

"So, how're the Yankees doing?" asked Hilman, confident that Bobby had the game on.

"Not great," said Winthrop. "They got this Masahiro Tanaka pitching."

"They have to," said Kevin. "They spent one hundred and fifty-five million dollars on him."

"What a waste," sniffed Winthrop, waving at the TV.

"He was supposed to have been a great strike-out pitcher in Japan," said O'Malley. "He had a really strong start of the season. I think he went eight for nine through June."

"Trouble is, Toronto ain't got no Japanese players. They got American players who are just killing this guy."

"What's going on with all the sirens?" asked Oak.

"Beats me. I've been here all day," replied Winthrop.

"We heard them as we were coming around Green Island," said Kevin.

"They have been going off for a couple of hours. They

should be going down and arresting the blockhead who decided to pay this stiff a hundred and fifty-five mil, if you ask me," said Winthrop.

CHAPTER NINETEEN

After a brief stop at the Grand Union for KC Barbeque sauce and some chicken, the group drove through town and up Mohican Road, turning at the top and heading for Mohican Heights - where they found the road blocked off with yellow crime scene tape. Guarding the entrance was Dave Lurman, a patrolman with the Bolton Landing Police Department.

Hilman put his car in park, got out, and approached Lurman.

"Hey, Dave! What's going on?"

"The road is closed for an investigation," said Lurman.

"I can see that," said Hilman. "What's going on?"

"Can't say," said Lurman. "My job is to keep anyone from going in or going out. Sorry."

"You know I live here, right?"

"Chief says to keep everyone out, so I keep everyone out."

"Great," said Hilman, sarcastically.

"I am calling Mike now," said O'Malley, gesturing to Hilman that his phone was ringing. "Hey, Mike, it's Matt O'Malley."

"I should've known you'd be calling me," said Reardon.

"What's that supposed to mean?" asked O'Malley.

"Just that I've got another dead body."

"Oh, no," said O'Malley.

"Who is with you?" asked Reardon.

"Danny, Kevin and the Big Oak."

"Okay, come on down. I need to talk to you," said Reardon.

"Lurman won't let us in," said O'Malley.

"Give him your phone," signed Reardon.

O'Malley passed the phone over to Lurman, saying, "Chief wants to talk to you."

Lurman took the phone and listened for a while. He returned the phone to O'Malley and told him to go in and go directly to the Anniston house.

"Why?" asked Oak.

"You'll find out when you get there," responded Lurman.

Oak shrugged and thought, *"So much for professional courtesy."*

All four men got back into Hilman's car and rode the short distance down the hill, passing Danny's house and parking on the circle by the Anniston residence. An officer told them to wait where they were for the Chief, who they could now see exiting the garage.

"Mike, what's happened? Is it one of the Annistons?" asked Hilman, concern evident in his voice.

Reardon did not answer the question.

"Matt, come walk with me for just a little bit."

O'Malley could tell from the tone that this was not a request. He looked at each of his friends and shrugged as he walked up the driveway. The garage doors were up and Matt could see a sheet that was obviously covering a body. Blood, nearly brown in color, spread out from under the edge of the sheet. Reardon steered Matt away from the garage and the two went and sat on the front porch.

"So, where have you been all day?" asked Reardon.

"Are you freaking kidding me?" asked Matt. "Are you going to treat me like a suspect? Are you going to read me my rights?"

"You know the drill as well as I do. Everyone who hasn't been eliminated as a suspect is a suspect. Now stop busting my balls and just tell me where you were today."

Matt was clearly disgusted at the question, but responded nonetheless. He proceeded to run down the day and the contacts he had at Dunham's Bay, Glen Island, and the other spots who could verify his story. Three other cops were going through the same process with Kevin, Danny, and Oak.

"How about yesterday. What were your activities?" Again, giving as much detail as he could, Matt outlined the goings on of the previous day. Reardon frequently stopped him to get more details, to clarify the timeline of events, and to take copious notes on a steno pad.

"How much time did you spend on the deck last night?" asked Reardon.

"I don't know, couple hours maybe," replied O'Malley. "We went in when the food was cooked and the mosquitoes were coming out. But you already know that. You were there, remember?"

"I remember, but I left and you guys were still there. Did you hear anything unusual?"

"No."

"Have you seen any strangers hanging around?"

"No, nothing like that. You barely see the neighbors around here, which begs the question - if there was no one around, how did you ever find the body?" asked O'Malley.

"We didn't. A gardener by the name of Bill Bell came by to work on the property. Skinny guy; always wears broad brimmed hats; talks to himself a lot; and you never see him without his dog, Bailey. Used to be a big hospital executive; now he runs a landscape business to keep himself busy during his retirement."

"Sounds like an interesting character," said O'Malley.

"He is. Great guy, actually. He can sing just like Leon Redbone. Anyway, he showed up to do some work, and Bailey went crazy scratching and barking at the garage door. Bill Bell looked in, saw Sullivan on the garage floor, and called us right away."

"Wow! Talk about a bad day at the office," said O'Malley.

"Yeah, he was pretty shook up. How about Mr. Anniston. Do you know him?"

"Not really. I have seen him in the backyard once in a while. I know him enough to wave at him."

"Any indications that his marriage was in any trouble?"

"We don't talk. We barely wave at each other. He seemed like an okay guy, but it's not like we spent any time together. Do you think he had something to do with this? Is it his wife in the garage?"

"No, she's in Albany. At least she was when we called her. She claims her husband is out of town at a convention in Orlando. Do you have any idea what kind of a car he drives?"

Matt thought for a moment and then said, "No, I can't ever recall seeing a car. His driveway is blocked from view by that little guest house, and I think they were in the habit of putting the cars in the garage anyway."

"Matt, just do me a favor and stay put for a minute while I talk with my officers."

Matt thought about making a wisecrack about how he was sure they had the same story, because they had spent all day rehearsing it, but for once in his life the editor in his brain had control and, instead of saying what he wanted, he just said, "Sure."

In a short while Reardon re-appeared.

"Matt, I know this is a crappy thing to ask you to do, but I want to try to verify the I.D. of the victim before we start contacting families. Would you mind looking at the body?"

Matt stood up, put both of his hands in the small of his back, and stretched. "I guess somebody has to do it, but I doubt I'll know who it is."

"Just give me a minute for the photographer to finish up and I'll get all four of you guys in together," said Reardon.

Matt started to walk toward the other three men who were gathering again near the foot of the driveway.

"Well, that was a ton of fun!" said Hilman. "They wanted to know everything we've done for the last two days except how many times I belched."

"That would be nearly impossible to calculate," said Oak, trying to relieve the tension.

"Why all the questions to us?" asked Kevin.

"It's just standard police practice," said Oak. "Don't get your panties all up in a wad. They're just doing their job. They have to canvas the area and speak to anyone they can find. We may know something that we don't even know we know."

"What do you think they are after?" asked Hilman.

"They are trying to figure out who the bad guy is," said Oak, the ex-cop, looking at him in amazement for asking such a dumb question.

"Sounded to me like they think this happened in the last twenty four to thirty six hours, and Mike was real curious about Robert Anniston and what kind of a car he drives," said O'Malley.

"I told them about Bob's car. He has a dark green Jaguar. What was weird was they kept asking me if Bob ever spoke about any military or Special Forces training, and they wanted to know what kind of a temper he had, and how he was getting along with his wife," said Hilman.

"What did you tell them?" asked Oak.

"Nothing. I have no idea if he was ever in the military and I thought he and the wife got along okay."

"This isn't my first rodeo," said Oak. "I dealt with a lot of dead bodies when I was a trooper. If this body has been lying in a closed up garage for a day or more, this isn't going to be pleasant. The stink will overwhelm you. If you have a handkerchief you'd better get it out and put it over your nose and mouth."

"Good advice," said Reardon, as he approached the group. "We're ready for you - if you're ready."

Reardon and the four men walked toward the garage. Someone from the medical examiner's office for Washington County was standing near the body wearing what looked like a full hazmat suit.

"Pull it back," said Reardon.

Maura Owens Sullivan, her hopes, her dreams, the sparkle in her eyes, the lilt of her laugh, the flirty way she used to glance over her shoulder, the sum and the substance of all the experiences and quirks that made her a unique and wonderful individual were gone, gone entirely. What was left was a bloated, eerily white lump. The only hints of color came from the red polish on her toes and fingernails, and the wide gash across her throat. Kevin, Danny and Matt were repulsed at the sight, and struggled to control the contents of their respective stomachs. They were positive that they did not know whomever this had been.

Oak took a step closer and, without asking for permission, pulled on a surgical glove from a dispensing box that was on the floor near the body. Using two fingers, he lifted her hands and examined the fingers. He pressed the flesh of her stomach, and he ran one finger along the wound on her neck.

"What do you think?" asked Reardon.

"I'm no expert, but, based on the swelling and the rigor she has been here a while, no more than two days. She was killed here and not moved, since there are no marks anywhere to indicate she was dragged. The blood splatter patterns also confirm she was killed standing close to here, and she basically dropped to this spot when she was killed. She either knew who killed her, or she was not expecting it. There are no defensive wounds, and her hands don't seem to have anything under the nails to indicate a struggle. My guess is that whoever killed her knew what he was doing, and was a trained killer."

"We are seeing the same things," said Reardon, "but why do you think that the killer was trained? She's all dressed down for a party. Maybe it was a lover's squabble that got out of hand."

"Maybe," said Oak, "but I don't think so. That wound on her neck is wide and distorted now, but look at the edge of it – it is perfectly smooth, like someone trained to kill with a knife did it in one overpowering, slashing blow, with a very sharp blade. An amateur will hesitate, be overcome with emotion. Cutting someone is a very up close and personal act. It's not like shooting. An amateur would hack. He would stab first, and it would be a mess. No, this was done with skill and dispassionately by someone who had a purpose and was confident in his skills," said Oak.

"You keep saying it was a man. What makes you think that?" asked Reardon.

"Just playing the odds."

"You will be happy to know that our M.E. agrees with

your assessment of the wound," said Reardon.

"So, have you found Anniston yet?" asked Oak.

"No, but we will. I already have a request out to the local police in Orlando to see if he is registered at the hotel for the convention, but who knows how long that will take. I got the impression that it wasn't going to be a high priority item with them. Have a BOLO out for his dark green Jag."

"What hotel is the convention at?" asked O'Malley. "I might be able to save you some time."

"It's at a place called the Marriott World Center."

"Cool," said O'Malley, "my sister works in HR there. What was the group?"

"The Convention was the annual meeting of the National Association of Manufacturer's Representatives," said Reardon, after flipping back through his steno pad.

"Okay, let me call her," said O'Malley, taking his phone out and stepping away from the group.

"Not to seem like a naysayer, but I have known Bob Anniston for a few years now, and he just doesn't seem like the type. He can be a little pushy, but what salesman worth his salt isn't. He's never seemed violent," said Hilman.

"There's always a first time. You say you've never seen this woman before," said Reardon, "yet here she is. You have to admit that a young woman alone in this place seems suspicious. Add in the sexy outfit and it becomes almost textbook."

"Maybe it's a relative they loaned the place to," suggested Hilman.

"We found her purse opened on the front seat of that car with the contents all strewn about," said Reardon.

"Maybe it was a robbery?" offered Hilman.

"The money and credit cards were still in her wallet. The driver's license is for a Maura Owens Sullivan. Mrs. Anniston denied knowing who that was."

"Okay, so she's not a relative getting a free weekend. Do you know who she was?" asked Hilman quizzically.

"We are assuming that's who it is. DMV pictures aren't great, and the condition of the body isn't good enough for us to go knocking on her parents' door until we have confirmed the identification. I was hoping you guys could do it, but maybe the fingerprints will help."

O'Malley rejoined the group.

"Well?" asked Reardon.

"My sister is such a company woman. It's against the rules to disclose who has registered at the hotel without a warrant or the guest's permission."

"Nice try. I guess we're back to waiting on the Orlando P.D. to wander down."

"Not exactly. Sheila was able to tell me that there was a convention of manufacturer's reps at the hotel, but it ended two days ago."

"Plenty of time to fly to Albany, pick up your car at the airport and get up to Bolton Landing and kill Maura Sullivan," observed Reardon.

"Try not to look so upset," said Kevin to Danny. "At least they don't think we did it!"

CHAPTER TWENTY

Smythe drove the rental car from the parking lot behind Annie King's Fine Wines and Spirits as if he did not have a care in the world and was in no hurry. The last thing he wanted to do was to draw attention to himself.

He had a few spots of Mookie's blood on his shirt, but, fortunately, his pants and shoes had avoided the spray from Mookie's neck. He drove until he found a small residential side street. He kept driving and watching the GPS, which suggested by the lack of roads ahead that he would shortly be reaching an unpopulated wooded area.

When he found the wooded area, he saw a dirt road into the woods that he turned down and drove for about fifty yards. Convinced that he was out of range of security cameras and nosy neighbors, he got out of the car and began rummaging through a bag he had in the trunk.

He rummaged around for his spare shirt. He stripped off the soiled shirt and, using his cigar lighter, set it ablaze. He held the burning shirt out as long as he could, but when the fire got too hot, he let the shirt flutter to the ground, where it continued to burn. Pulling a new polo over his head, he tucked it in and made sure that the burning shirt was nothing but ashes to be blown away by the wind before he got back into the car.

Smythe checked his wristwatch and was alarmed to see how late it had gotten. The robber was an unforeseen distraction that had consumed a lot of time. He was annoyed with himself for even going to the wine store rather than staying focused on his mission. It was a stupid and unnecessary risk to have taken. He would have to hurry to get back to Crandall Park in time to do any pre-meeting surveillance.

Smythe arrived and took up his position with five minutes to spare. He watched closely for any sign of Kenny Ames. He watched four septuagenarians lumber through the slowest game of tennis he ever saw. He saw a pretty young mother pushing her baby on a swing. He saw a young man throwing a Frisbee to an extremely quick and agile Labrador Retriever, but he saw no one who matched the description of Kenny Ames.

He waited fifteen minutes after the appointed time. He saw a police car and ambulance heading in the direction of Annie King's store. But, never in all that time did he put together the cause and effect relationship that the police action might be tied to the failure of Kenny Ames to show.

*   *   *

Kenny's heart rate had returned to nearly normal by the time he was south of Saratoga Springs. By the time he reached Latham, he had resolved to never again leave Albany. By the time he reached his exit on I-87, he had decided he needed an alibi, since Mookie's girlfriend saw him drive Mookie away. What he did not need were some Crips coming after him in revenge for abandoning Mookie.

Kenny pulled over to the side of the road and fumbled with his phone, searching for Mookie's girlfriend's number. The horrible woman from that morning answered.

"'Sup," said Kenny, trying to sound relaxed. "Is Mookie there?"

"No, he ain't. I have no idea where that mother . . ."

Kenny interrupted her because he wanted to be sure to get his story out before she disconnected the call, which seemed imminent.

"This is Kenny. I gave Mookie a ride this morning and he never showed up when I went back to get him. I thought maybe he finished early and got a ride home."

"Well, he ain't here, and you can tell him from me, he

better not be comin' back here all liquored up. I am through with his slack ass ways, and you can tell him I said so."

"For sure I'll tell him," said Kenny. "I'll go look for him and tell him right away."

"Wait, wait, wait. Where'd you say you dropped him off?" she asked with a suspicious tone.

"Ah, uuh, um . . ." It occurred to Kenny that he should have given this part of the story a bit more thought.

"I bet I knows where you dropped him off. He back cattin' around with that 'ho Shinequa, ain't he?"

"No, no. Sorry, I need to get going," replied Kenny.

"That's all I need to know, you be a liar just like him!"

"No, I really don't know who he was seeing," said Kenny.

Kenny heard a drawn out, knowing, "Ah huh," and then nothing.

It had not been much of a story, but it was the best he could do in such a short time. He needed to be able to convince people that he had no idea where Mookie went after he dropped him off, and, most importantly, that he did not know what he had been doing. He decided he needed to pick a drop-off spot so if he were questioned more closely about it, he could give details.

*   *   *

Sadiki Okoro's father believed that a child's name could be the child's destiny, so he named his fourth child Sadiki, or faithful. If that were true, Fahran Zadran would agree that the child's destiny had been fulfilled. He considered Okoro his most loyal and faithful soldier, so it was he that was sent to America to find Keenadiid Amiin Kuciil and do whatever was necessary to retrieve Zadran's diamonds now that Jambo had been taken care of.

Okoro had been to America before on missions for Zadran. He was tired as he walked into the terminal at Albany International Airport. He had left Cairo late on the day before and flown to Paris. From Paris he flew to John F. Kennedy

International Airport, where he then hopped a commuter flight on a cramped propjet to Albany. Jambo would have taken the same itinerary if his meeting with Zadran had gone better. As the meeting had gone very, very badly for Jambo, Okoro flew out under Jambo's name with a hastily counterfeited passport. He had not slept except for brief segments during the past nineteen hours.

He traveled with just two pieces of carry-on luggage, one of which rolled behind him and the other draped over his left shoulder as he passed the Italian Kitchen restaurant on his way out of the terminal. He was too tired to care who else was in the terminal. He did not take note of the young black man in baggage handler overalls, nor did he see the lovely young woman in a neatly tailored business suit with a crisp white shirt as they each sat in the Italian Kitchen eating a slice of pizza, seemingly oblivious to each other. Even if he had seen Edgard and Nubia, it would have made no impression on him, since he only had Keenadiid Amiin Kuciil's name and address, no photo.

There are many weapons in life and sleep is an important one. It keeps your mind sharp and able to make sound decisions. Sleep insures that your reactions are at their peak of effectiveness. Sadiki knew that a true warrior could go longer without food than he could without sleep. He also knew that he was not able to perform at his best in his current, exhausted, jet-lagged condition. He was going to get a car and find a hotel in which to sleep. When he awoke, he would deal with finding this Kuciil.

He would also secure a gun.

*   *   *

The transfer went just as planned. Nubia sat with her back to Edgard and her carry-on open on the floor next to her on her right side. In a well-choreographed maneuver, she bent over to the left to retrieve the napkin she had deliberately dropped while Edgard, all the while looking forward and with his movements hidden by Nubia's body, slipped the small box out from under his jacket, reached back with his left hand, and easily dropped the package into her open bag.

Edgard quickly finished his slice of pizza and then got up. Like any good and conscientious patron would do, he dropped the debris from his meal into the trash container, placed the tray on top of the container, and sauntered off to go back to work. Edgard was desperate to look back but remembered Nubia's words of caution, and so he did not.

Nubia did not get up right away. She fiddled with her smart phone and tried as best she could to look like a busy executive. She was more nervous than she imagined she would be. She saw a large group of deplaning passengers heading her way. This was her moment. She got up, smoothed out the front of her skirt, picked up her carry-on and started to walk - not to the terminal as planned, but toward the gates. She had a ticket to Syracuse and she intended to use it.

CHAPTER TWENTY ONE

Saturday was a day of contrasts. The sun was up and bright, the coolness of the morning air caused a breeze to rustle the leaves in the trees outside Matt's window. It all seemed too perfect, yet Matt was troubled by something as he lay in bed in a twilight sleep, not really awake, and not really asleep.

He suddenly was no longer in the Hilman house. He was standing in a garage and a lot of people were standing around laughing and joking. Someone he did not know, but for some reason recognized, was standing over what appeared to be a body with a sheet over it, beckoning O'Malley to come over. Matt was paralyzed. He could not walk over to the strange man, because he knew if he did the strange man would pull back the sheet and show Matt what was underneath. Matt knew that he would not be able to endure the sight. The man shrugged and bent over to pull off the sheet anyway.

Matt sat bolt upright in the bed, fully awake. In spite of the cool morning air, he was covered in sweat. The horror of the previous night came rushing back at him. He swung his legs over the side of the bed; with his elbows on his knees, he held his head in both hands. He was exhausted from not being able to sleep the night before. He stood and shook his head, trying to clear the cobwebs. He picked up his iPhone and pressed the only button on the front. The screen came to life with a photo of his two daughters and the time, which read, 5:13. That was a little early, even for an early riser like Matt.

He lay back on the narrow bed and started to go through his emails. It was the usual mix of ads for Canadian drug stores; jokes from friends; LinkedIn and Facebook updates; opportunities to buy four Jos. A. Banks suits for the price of one; and mail from work, most of which required follow-up telephone calls on the few mediations he had conducted that had not yet settled.

Most of his cases settled, but he considered the follow-up on those that did not settle to be very important to the success of his practice. He had cultivated a reputation for never giving up on a case, which was good for repeat business, since most lawyers really wanted their cases to settle. It bothered him that he had not returned the calls yesterday when he was finally back in an area with cell service, but from the time he arrived back at Danny's house, he had been consumed by the death of Maura Owens Sullivan.

It troubled him that when he referred to her it was always with her full name, as if using only Maura or only her last name would personalize her, and make her death even more horrific in his mind. This was not the first time he had seen a dead body, or even the first time he had seen someone who had died a violent death. Still, this was the youngest such body he had seen, and the utter waste of it all left him feeling hollow.

Something else was troubling Matt. He had found the body on the bateau. If it had not been him, then someone else would have found it at the popular dive site. It was pure random happenstance. Days later Maura Owens Sullivan was murdered, and her bloody corpse left not one hundred feet from where he presently lie in bed. It is a sad fact of life that such crimes occur, and frequently are crimes of opportunity, or of chance. Sometimes the victim is merely the wrong person, at the wrong place, at the wrong time. Happenstance. Fate.

Matt could accept that either of these events and his involvement were just chance encounters. Two such events in the course of a few days seemed to move these events out of the realm of happenstance and into something different, something more sinister, however. Yet, he could not make the synapses fire in such a way as to make the connection between these two events that would reveal the hidden truth. He could not even begin to ask the questions until they had some identification of the body from the bateau. Maybe then, he would be able to see a connection between these two seemingly random events. However, now, fixated as he was, and with few facts to work with, Matt could make no sense of it at all.

Shaking his head, as if doing so would make this troubling puzzle go away and allow him to focus, Matt forced himself to go through the messages on his phone.

Placing the phone back on the nightstand, Matt tried to close his eyes and get some rest, but as soon as he would drift off, he would be back in that garage. He was bedeviled by the idea that he knew something that would help in solving the murder of Maura Owens Sullivan, and that, somehow, it was related to the dead man from the bateau, but he could not imagine what it was that he thought he knew.

Finally, he decided four things. First, that he probably was so fixated on the murder because the young woman was so close in age to his own daughters; second, that he wasn't going to get any more rest; third, that he was hungry; and, finally, that he couldn't go banging around the kitchen waking up everyone else so early. *"Time for a road trip,"* he thought.

Matt took the long way down to town. He enjoyed driving the winding Potter Hill Road with its canopy of tree branches filtering the sun. The pleasantness of the drive and the cool morning air let him forget for a moment about the dead girl. Also, it dropped him off right at Donny's Market, a little deli, bakery and newsstand located under a big tree in the parking lot of the Grand Union. He loved Donny's because it was convenient, and had some of his favorite things in the morning: doughnuts, bagels and newspapers.

After securing the daily paper, next stop was the Railroad Car Diner on Lakeshore. He pulled into the gravel lot and parked by the wooden stairs leading to a dining patio. That suited him just fine. A little al fresco dining on a cool morning would wake him up and clear his head.

"Morning, Matt," called out Sally, who had been working at the diner for as long as anyone could remember. "Grab a seat anywhere," she said, as she ducked into the converted railcar that served as the main portion of the restaurant. Matt settled into a plastic chair at a round picnic table. Before he knew it, Sally was back with a large plastic glass filled with Diet Coke.

"You never forget," said Matt with a smile, eagerly

reaching for the only form of caffeine he could tolerate.

"How could anyone forget something so disgusting? Diet Coke at 6:30 in the morning!" she punctuated the sentence by scrunching up her face.

"The usual?" she asked.

"Perfect," replied Matt, putting the menu back in the holder, not bothering to even look at it.

"One order of sourdough French toast and a side of bacon coming up," she said, turning away to place the order.

Matt was not a big fan of change, and one of the things he loved about Lake George, and this diner, was that they were perfect as they were, and no one needed to worry about how to change them to make them better. Any change would just make them different, not better.

Matt was halfway through the first section of the New York Times when breakfast arrived, and with it came Chief Michael Reardon, plopping himself down at Matt's table.

"You look like crap," O'Malley said to Reardon.

"I feel that way, too. I've been up all night."

"How 'bout some coffee, Chief?" said Sally.

"That sounds great. And how about a double egg white veggie omelet and some whole wheat toast, no butter. Put it on his tab to make up for that last crack," said Reardon.

"You bet," said Sally, hustling off to put in the order.

"Why were you up all night?" asked Matt.

"Do you have any idea when the last time was that we had two murder investigations going on around here?"

"No."

"Never! That's when," replied Reardon.

"Anything going on to keep you up?" asked O'Malley.

"The Highway Patrol spotted Anniston's Jag in a motel parking lot in Saratoga a little after midnight. They checked with the night clerk and found out the dope had registered under his own name, using a credit card no less."

"Quite the master criminal there! I presume they were able to pick him up?" asked Matt.

"Of course. The night clerk didn't want to give them the room key until the State Police brought out their battering ram.

He changed his mind amazingly quickly. When they went in, Anniston was stretched out on the bed, sobbing like a baby."

"Did he have the murder weapon?"

"No."

"Was there any blood on him?"

"A little, but he had a story."

"You got to question him?" said O'Malley, a little surprised.

"It was tough to get him to shut up. We read him his rights. He even signed a waiver," said Reardon.

"Wow! That seems odd. The rich ones always want their lawyer present," said O'Malley.

"Not this guy. I think he thought he could talk himself out of this with a cockamamie story. He kept begging us not to tell his wife. She must be a prize. He's more afraid of her than he is of twenty-five to life in Attica!" said Reardon.

"So, what's his story?" asked O'Malley.

"He claims that Maura Sullivan worked for him and he had no idea what she was doing at his lake house. He had this convention to go to in Orlando, and it seemed like the perfect time to get a little extra time on the lake with his new fishing boat. He says he told his wife he was staying over a few days in Orlando to take clients golfing, but instead he had a long weekend planned by himself. He claims his wife hates the place and doesn't like how much time he spends there. "

"Oh, what a tangled web we weave when first we practice to deceive," said O'Malley.

"Tennyson?" asked Reardon.

"Nah, I think it's Robert Burns."

"In any event, his story is that he flew into Albany, picked up his car, and drove right up to the lake house. He went into the garage and saw her lying there. At first, he assumed she must have fallen, so he went over to check on her and try to help her up. He was going to give her 'what for' for being in his house. He thinks she must have stolen the key from the desk in his office."

"That would explain the blood on him," said O'Malley.

"It might, but so would slitting her throat," replied

Reardon.

"He says when he saw she was dead he panicked. He and the wife have been having a rough spot, and he's afraid that she'll jump to the wrong conclusion, divorce him, and he'll lose everything when she finds out there was another woman at the house."

"Okay, so what does he say about being in the motel in Saratoga?" asked O'Malley.

"He claims he was too freaked out to stay in the house, too panicked to call the police, and too afraid to go home to his wife, since he didn't know how to explain why he wasn't in Florida."

"His is not such an unbelievable story," said O'Malley.

"It's a terrible story, but I'll check it out. In my mind, it's just as easy to believe he was having an affair with Maura Sullivan and she wanted to be more than a mistress. Maybe she was putting pressure on him to dump the wife and marry her and he didn't want to give up the kids, the house with the white picket fence, the lake house, and all the other goodies. Maybe they argued and he just lost it and killed her in a fit of anger, or he killed her when she threatened to expose him."

"I like his story better," said Matt.

"Why?" asked Reardon, letting his weariness show through.

"Because, right now he's going to lose all that stuff anyway because he left a body in the garage. He's a smart guy. He's a salesman. He's used to fast talking his way in and out of things. He would have made promises and strung her along, trying to talk his way out of it, or he would have planned to kill her somewhere other than his own garage, on a weekend that he had lied to his wife about where he was going to be."

"He still had three days. Maybe he was going to get cleaning supplies and figure out a way to dump the body."

"Maybe. But, if they were having an affair why didn't he just take her to Florida? She would have loved Universal Studios. Just the right age."

"Who knows, maybe he thought it would be suspicious if they were both out of the office at the same time. Plus, he didn't know who he would run into at the convention who might actually know that this Mrs. Anniston-de-jour was not his real wife."

"He sounds like too much of a planner to have committed this crime in such a clumsy way. I'm not buying your theory."

"Always the defense lawyer," said Reardon, as he mopped the last of his eggs up with a crust of wheat toast.

"To change topics, maybe, have you ever received anything from Interpol on Bateau Boy?" asked O'Malley, trying to sound casual.

"No, and what do you mean by maybe?" asked Reardon.

"Oh, nothing really," said O'Malley, "it's just that I'm not a big fan of coincidences, and these two murders somehow feel related to me."

"How so?" asked Reardon.

"Chief, if I knew that I'd have your job!" said O'Malley. "It's just a feeling I can't seem to get past, but I have no evidence to support it."

"Well, if you get any, be sure to let me know."

"You'll be the first person I call," said O'Malley.

CHAPTER TWENTY TWO

Matt O'Malley was not the only one who had experienced a fitful night's sleep. Edgard Onobanjo was also restless. The plan had gone perfectly. He was sure that he and Nubia had positioned themselves in a way that had avoided the security cameras, and he had been able to retrieve the package from the restroom without incident.

He had felt such a sense of relief in the moments after he had dropped the package into Nubia's carry-on. He had fully expected someone to come rushing over to arrest them, but nothing had happened.

Edgard, according to the plan, had continued to act normally and worked the rest of his shift. He felt very relaxed, and no one had seemed to have any suspicions about his activities. He had laughed and joked with his co-workers as he normally did. There had been extra flights for the weekend so his shift had seemed to fly by.

The only thing that had been out of place was that Kenny had called in sick, but he had given that little thought. He had been so relieved to have the package safely out of the airport. He had spent the shift waiting to reunite with his beloved, Nubia, so they would be able to relive how they had worked together just like in a James Bond movie.

Nubia had insisted that he wait until his shift was over and he be alone in his car before he call her. She had said she was afraid his end of the conversation might be overheard and could have made people suspicious. After work, he had eagerly placed his call to her. There was no answer, which had disappointed him a little, but gave him even more incentive to get home as quickly as possible. The thrill of what they had done had elated him.

His apartment had been empty when he arrived home. Nubia had a key and was supposed to meet him so they could celebrate, and then they were supposed to complete the plan.

He had come up with the perfect hiding place. He had been sure that by placing their faith in God all would be well. He had already asked his American family if he could borrow their boat to take Nubia on a tour of Lake George. They had been excited to finally be meeting the girl they had heard so much about.

Edgard had called Nubia's phone repeatedly. At first, he would hang up when the message came on. After driving by her apartment and finding it dark, he had called some more and began to leave messages on her phone, each one just a bit more frantic than the one before. He had no idea what had happened. He was concerned for her safety. He had called the area hospitals, but they had claimed not to have a patient by her name. In desperation, he even called the police, but they did not have a record of her being arrested.

He had imagined all kinds of scenarios to explain her absence, but none of them had involved her betraying him.

As evening turned into night, and night turned into early morning, he began driving aimlessly, hoping to find her. He clung to the hope that she somehow was delayed, but okay. He drove by all her friends' houses that he could remember, hoping to find her.

Finally, he found himself driving down the Albany Shaker Road. It was not a conscious decision to go to the airport. He was not even sure why he was doing it, until he saw her car, parked on the ground level of short-term parking. He began to shake uncontrollably. *"Nubia never left the airport. She must have taken her flight!"*

He had never before felt so betrayed and so bereft of hope.

*   *   *

The wake-up call came right at 10:00 AM. Okoro came

instantly awake. He wanted to do this job and get home as quickly as he could, with Zadran's package in the diplomatic pouch he was carrying. He had always been able to travel on a diplomatic passport, arranged by Zadran through some well-placed bribes.

He was already forming a checklist in his mind. He needed a shave and a shower, and then he wanted some breakfast. He had directions to a pawnshop, where Zadran had promised that he would arrange for weapons. There was much to be accomplished.

Okoro needed to drive by Keenadiid Amiin Kuciil's residence to get a lay of the land. He needed to be sure that the basement of the pawnshop where he planned to take Kuciil to question him was suitable for his purposes, and there would be no interference.

Okoro also needed to have an exit strategy that would include a place to hide one or more bodies if that became necessary. He had orders to kill Myles Smythe, who Zadran no longer trusted. Men who do not respond to his phone calls quickly were perceived of as enemies. The other one he would kill or not kill depending on how he responded to his demand for the package.

It was going to be a busy day. He planned on having everything in place by nightfall. Once it was dark, he would strike.

*   *   *

Myles Smythe would never see a similarity between himself and Fahran Zadran, yet his response to the shortcomings of others was remarkably the same. Allies were easily converted to enemies in his book.

Smythe was not a man to be trifled with, and Kenny Ames had committed an unforgiveable offense when he had failed to arrive at an appointment that Smythe had considered essential.

As Smythe drove north on 9N, along the western shore of Lake George, the sun was out, the lake was sparkling with reflected sunlight and the canopy of trees dappled the light on the road; yet, he was not enjoying this tranquil tableau. He was too furious at Kenny Ames, and too busy planning what he would do next.

Also troubling Smythe was that Ames's no-show had set his timetable back. Time was running out and he knew that Zadran would be furious with him by now. Twice he had ignored calls from Zadran on his burner phone. Twice he had ignored the demand for a return call. He did not have the diamonds, so he had nothing to report; and even if he did have them, he did not intend to give them to that Third World thug. He had begun thinking of them as his diamonds. Tomorrow, he would find Kenny Ames and he would beat him until he gave him the package.

* * *

Nubia had spent Saturday morning in much the same way that Edgard had spent the hours after getting off work - making phone calls that were never answered. The difference was she was not calling Edgard; she was calling Jambo.

It was she who was in, what she hoped, an exclusive relationship with Jambo. It was she who had learned of Edgard's access to the baggage at Albany International Airport, and it was she who had been with an extremely intoxicated Jambo when he was going on and on about the king's ransom in diamonds that was going to be coming through the airport.

Later, when Jambo sobered up, it was she who convinced him that the diamonds could be theirs, and they could live together in luxury. At first, Jambo had hesitated, trying to explain that there were multiple levels of players involved, from his superiors back in Africa to dangerous men in Afghanistan, and it would be too dangerous to attempt to steal the diamonds.

It was Nubia who kept pushing Jambo to try to learn how the transfer would take place. Jambo had never met the one his African superiors simply referred to as the Chechen, but he knew that this man had couriered diamonds for his bosses before. Jambo knew him to be a very dangerous man, and he did not want to cross him.

But that is when fate, in the form of Myles Smythe, took a hand in matters. Smythe had approached Jambo, claiming that he had been sent by Zadran to take delivery of the stones in place of the Chechen. Smythe promised a great reward to Jambo for his cooperation. He did not want to take delivery from the Chechen, though. Smythe wanted to get the package directly from the plane. He said Zadran did not trust the Chechen.

When Jambo shared all this information with Nubia, she saw an opportunity. She convinced Jambo that Smythe would steal the diamonds for himself, and blame the Chechen and Jambo. The only reward Jambo would see would be an early grave.

It was Nubia who devised a plan that seemed to solve all their problems. Jambo was to negotiate with Smythe on what his reward was to be, and then he would provide information on how to locate the Chechen.

He would tell Smythe that the Chechen and the diamonds had arrived early but there was a problem. The Chechen had a contact that was supposed to arrange transport to Zurich, but he had been jailed, so there was a delay in moving the package out of the country. Jambo was to tell Smythe that the Chechen had hid the package in Lake George until he could finalize new arrangements.

With Smythe thus diverted, kidnapping the Chechen and torturing him to reveal a location that did not exist, Nubia would have the time necessary to convince Edgard Onobanjo that it was too dangerous to leave the package unprotected in the airport.

Since Edgard was blindly in love with Nubia, they were certain he could be manipulated into doing their will, just as they were certain that, once Nubia had the package, Edgard would never be seen again, and Jambo and Nubia would disappear and lead a life of luxury someplace warm and safe.

All had worked out better than they ever hoped, but now Nubia had a package filled with blood diamonds, no clue what to do with them, and Jambo was missing.

Jambo had been extremely nervous about the sudden

trip to Cairo, and had warned her that he might not come back alive. If all went well, he guaranteed that he would be back by Friday. She was to arrange to smuggle the diamonds out by then and meet him in Syracuse. From there, they would sneak into Canada and then, once they had made arrangements to sell the diamonds, they would be off to get lost in the South Pacific.

Nubia had a very bad feeling about Jambo's fate. She knew he would not fail to answer her calls. She knew he would be eaten up with curiosity to know if the diamonds were safe.

Poor, hapless Edgard was calling and pleading for her to call back.

"I need a new plan!" Nubia thought to herself.

CHAPTER TWENTY THREE

The sunshine had yielded to a low and threatening layer of grey clouds during O'Malley's breakfast at the Railroad Car Diner. He was wearing a light polartec jacket that he zipped up to ward off the increasingly cold temperature. This was typical Adirondack weather. Any given summer day could feel like a winter day - maybe not an Adirondack winter day, but certainly a Florida winter day.

After breakfast Matt decided a drive was just what he needed to help clear his mind. It was still early and he was sure that Danny and the others would sleep late on such a grey morning. He said his farewells to Reardon, paid his check, and briefly chatted with Sally prior to his departure. He was sitting in his car in the parking lot when a light rain began to fall. *"This is not going to be a lake day,"* he thought, looking up at a sodden sky.

O'Malley plugged his iPod into the car and started his favorite Wolfe Tones album. In short order, he was listening to fine Irish music, the perfect accompaniment to the cold, rainy day that his friends in Ireland would describe as a "grand soft day." The pace of the intermittent wiper picked up as he was waiting for a break in the traffic to turn north on Lakeshore Drive.

O'Malley had no plan other than he did not want to go back to the house where he would still have to be tiptoeing around so he would not disturb the others. He decided if he could not be on the lake, at least he could be near it. Lake George has a different persona on a rainy day. Patches of fog gave an eerie appearance to vistas that are so beautiful on a sunny day that they elevate the spirit.

The opportunity he was waiting for appeared. He gunned the engine, slipped into the brief gap in traffic, and made a quick left turn onto the narrow street. It did not register at first, but on some not quite conscious level he had a moment of recognition. He knew he had seen something, but he was not quite sure what. By the time he reached Sagamore Road to go to Green Island, he was able to piece it together. He thought he had seen that peculiar Englishman from Dunham's Bay. It seemed like another odd coincidence in a week filled with too many coincidences.

There was something about the Englishman's demeanor that bothered O'Malley. At Dunham's Bay, he gave the appearance of an affable "everyman." Nothing stood out about him. He was nice enough; he was sociable, but not in a way that made you want to later seek him out. He had told a story about his dead rich auntie and his teaching career, but it was done with so little detail it seemed almost banal.

However, in the instant Smythe had sped by in his car, a starkly different image was conjured up – of a man of strong will and determination who was seeking to control an unspeakable rage.

The intensity of the man was so markedly different from his presentation at the Dunham's Bay store that O'Malley began to think that his mind was playing tricks on him, and that it had to be a totally different man.

O'Malley crossed the picturesque bridge leading to Green Island and parked in the first lot on the left after entering the Sagamore property. Grabbing a camera, he walked back to the bridge to get a photo of the Boathouse Bed & Breakfast. The large structure was one of the more famous and frequently photographed structures on the lake.

The grey clapboard B&B was built over a large boathouse that, for a time, had housed one of the fastest wooden boats in the world, *El Lagarto*. Currently it houses the sleek, mahogany Hackercraft christened, *Miss Boathouse*.

The B&B had a beautiful Bavarian flair to it. In the summer, it was decked out with colorful hanging baskets of geraniums and impatiens. Guests could be seen sitting on the second story balcony enjoying their morning coffee and an incomparable view of the lake – Green and Dome Islands, and the mountains on the far side of the lake. The rain had eased up and O'Malley was able to get a photo, not only of the B&B, but also of the reflection of the B&B in the still waters in front of it.

O'Malley was walking back to his car when the Englishman's name popped into his head. Myles Smythe. That is how he introduced himself. He said he was a teacher in London. *"I wonder if he really is a teacher,"* thought O'Malley.

He would call his legal assistant. Mary was a wizard on the Internet, and a fact checker without equal. It was Mary to whom he would always turn when he needed research, verification or investigation. If it was on the Internet, she could find it and make sense of it.

Disregarding the hour and the day, O'Malley took out his phone and dialed Mary's number. Even though it was early on a Saturday, there was just as good a chance she was at the office. The phone rang three times before he heard Mary's voice.

"Good morning, Matt,"

"How'd you know it was me?" asked Matt, just to get a rise out of her.

"How many times do I have to tell you, on modern phones your name pops up on the caller ID, and the phone captures your number! Besides, there is no one else crazy enough to call me this early on a Saturday."

"Mary, I have a project for you."

"Surprise, surprise. What is it and how soon do you need it?" asked Mary.

Decades of working together had rubbed off all the rough edges between them. O'Malley knew he could not practice law without her, and she knew it as well but never took advantage of that fact, because she also knew that *"could not practice"* just meant he would not want to practice without her. This familiarity allowed communications without all the folderol of social convention.

"I want to know everything you can get me on a guy named Myles Smythe."

"Matt, I'm going to need more than that. There are

probably hundreds of Myles Smythes in the world."

"Okay," said Matt, reviewing in his mind all that he thought he knew about Smythe. "He is British; says he lives in London."

"That helps narrow it down," said Mary. "What else do you have on this guy?"

"He's white, about six feet tall, dark hair, about forty-five years old. He says he is touring the United States on an extended sabbatical."

"Did he say when he got here?"

"Uh, no, I don't think so," said O'Malley. "Why?"

"Immigration keeps records," said Mary.

"You can access Immigration records?" said O'Malley, incredulously. "How?"

"Don't ask a question you don't want to know the answer to," cautioned Mary. "You said he was on sabbatical. What kind of work does he do?"

"He said he was a teacher," replied O'Malley.

"Of what? . . . Where?"

"Let me think," mused O'Malley. "Oh yeah, he said he taught in London, something about religion."

"Okay, good. Did he give you the name of the school?" asked Mary.

"Yes," replied O'Malley.

Mary waited for more, and when no more was forthcoming she asked, "Are you going to tell me what school?"

"No, I can't remember," said Matt, "but it was in London. It was a short name, I think, and it started with a *B*, or maybe a *P*."

"Anything else about this guy that might help me narrow my search parameters?"

"Not that I can think of," said O'Malley.

"I'll get right on this and get back to you in a few hours."

"You're the best!" said O'Malley.

CHAPTER TWENTY FOUR

The rain had increased in intensity as the morning wore on. Touring around the lake lost some of its charm as the rain fell harder and harder, and getting out of the car to take pictures became less and less appealing. Matt headed back to Mohican Heights, arriving around ten thirty. The house was bustling with activity as Danny cooked breakfast, Kevin was engrossed in the New York Times, and Oak was watching ESPN.

"Matt!" exclaimed Danny, stretching out the name as a greeting that invariably made the target of it seem welcome, and even important. Instead of just a name it sounded as if he was saying, *"Matt, what a wonderful and delightful surprise you are here."*

"Catch me up," said Matt. "I know you must have a plan by now, and please tell me it doesn't involve going out on the boat."

Danny was unusually adept at coming up with alternative activities. Normally he would announce he had a plan and that it was going to be interesting, but no other details would be divulged until the group was so thoroughly committed to the plan that it was impossible to change it.

Danny's interests were eclectic, and he loved to interrogate people who knew about the things that interested him. Sometimes, the plan might involve a trip to an exotic taxidermy store to talk with the owner, but never to invest in his product line. Perhaps, it would be a short trip to a church that had been converted to a homemade ice cream parlor, filled with oddities and antiquities to entertain the eye as well as the palate. Occasionally, it was a long journey to Lake Placid to watch ski jumpers take off, soar frightening distances, and then land – all on artificial turf. Another time, it could be to a unique outdoor museum in Vermont, or a special restaurant with a salad bar set up in an antique wooden boat. The only consistent theme was that this area of the world was stocked with a seemingly unending supply of interesting nooks and crannies just waiting to be discovered and explored.

The other consistent theme was that it was best to go along with the plan, because risking the occasional dud rewarded you with dozens of offbeat, eccentric and fascinating little trips. Danny was the person who could not help but exit at a sign that promised the world's largest roll of twine, or something similar – and he would make it interesting.

"In fact, there is a plan," said Danny. Kevin looked up from his newspaper with a curious expression. Obviously, this was the first time he was hearing of a plan. "It will be fantastic," Danny continued, as if this was the only explanation needed.

"Could you be a bit more specific?" asked O'Malley.

"I could, but the anticipation is half the fun," he replied.

"Sometimes the anticipation is the only fun," said Oak. "Remember when he had us drive two and a half hours to see a collection of miniature lead soldiers?"

"Good point!" said Kevin. "It's too rainy to drive all over upstate New York."

"No worries. I can't believe that my people seem to be in open rebellion. I tell you this will be the most fantastic thing you have ever seen. Trust me!"

"Uh, oh," said Oak, "nothing good ever happens after the words, 'trust me.'"

"Alright, I'll give you a hint. It involved one of the major advances in science in the last three centuries."

"That's pretty vague," said O'Malley.

"Another hint. I checked the weather and a front is moving through. It's going to rain all day, and my plan involves indoor activities."

"Okay," said Kevin, "I'm in, but this better involve the new *Star Wars* movie."

"Even better," assured Danny. "Get ready. We need to

be on the road in fifteen minutes."

*   *   *

Myles Smythe was a man on a mission. Kenny Ames was his mission. Smythe drove south on 9N toward Lake George Village. He had read in the morning Post-Star that the body of Maura Owens Sullivan had been discovered, that she had been brutally murdered, and that the authorities had a *"person of interest"* in custody. Smythe figured that had to be Robert Anniston. *"The dumb bugger must have found the body and took off running,"* thought Smythe. *"He's screwed, but he surely didn't get the screwing he was expecting!"*

The article in the paper was good news. The cops had their suspect, and it was not him. This would give him a bit more time to locate the package, a task he believed was going to be much easier once he grabbed up Kenny Ames.

He was not surprised at his good fortune. Smythe had long believed that he was special, unique in a way, and that things would always work out to his advantage. He had reason to believe so. There were many times during his career with MI-5 when lesser men would have been brought up short in situations where he had prevailed, usually by cheating, but that wasn't the point, was it. He had prevailed. Even after being cashiered by that bastard, Jonathon Evans, he landed on his feet. Sure, it was by working for the "lowlifes" he used to pursue, but soon all that would be over. Once he had the diamonds, he would have more money than he would ever need.

These thoughts occupied him for the entire trip down to Albany, so much so that he almost missed his exit. He had to swerve from the middle lane when he barely had enough room to get to the exit ramp. Horns were blaring in his ears as he just managed to get off I-87.

The near accident on the Thruway served to focus his attention. Smythe realized that he was not being true to his core biblical philosophy. As a child, he had read the story of *David and Goliath*. The other children in his Sunday school class came away with a message about how God so loved and protected the Israelites that he allowed them to prevail over the giant.

But not Myles Smythe. He saw the story as a primer on how to attack an enemy. While he gave little credence to the notion of an all-powerful force in the universe, he still drew lessons from this Bible story. The first lesson was how David analyzed and developed his skills when he protected his sheep from the lions before deciding to even think of taking on Goliath. From that, Smythe drew that he had to be realistic and to only fight the fights he was confident that he would win.

The second lesson was that before David committed to battling Goliath, he demanded to know what his reward would be. From this, Smythe learned that only fools get involved in altruistic endeavors. He would fight only if the reward was great enough.

Smythe's problems with authority while an MI-5 agent arose out of the third lesson he took from the story. Just as David refused armor and weapons that did not fit and had not been tested, so Smythe refused to allow others to tell him how to do a job. He was regarded as a lone wolf, who could not be trusted as a team player.

The fourth lesson he drew from the story was that, just as David was careful to select five smooth stones from the brook, he had to be careful in his selection of weapons, and not be lured into allowing the enemy to force the selection of weapons. While Goliath was armed with a shield, a spear and a sword, David armed himself with a stick, smooth stone from the riverbed, and a sling. The first two were hidden in his shepherd's bag. This allowed him to approach Goliath when his guard was down and he did not perceive a threat, and then to initiate the fight with the weapons best suited to David.

The fifth lesson was critical. Goliath challenged David to come down to him to fight. Never fight the enemy on his own terms was the lesson learned by Smythe. David turned and ran. Goliath gave pursuit. When the battlefield suited him, David stopped, whipped out the sling, and sent a stone sailing deep into Goliath's forehead, causing him to drop to the ground.

The final lesson learned by Smythe was the most important to his twisted personal philosophy of life and living.

That lesson was, finish the job with merciless efficiency, for when Goliath had fallen, David grabbed Goliath's sword and struck a mighty blow, severing the giant's head.

It was time to put these lessons into practice. Smythe parked his car in front of the tiny, one story house where Kenny Ames lived. Smythe studied the house from his car as he went through his checklist. He was confident that he could defeat Ames, even if there were one or two others in the house. It seemed quiet and there was only one car parked in front of this sad, little house on this lonely dirt road. The reward was not an issue. He felt sure that Ames would lead him to the diamonds. The battle would be on Ames's field, but at a time and manner of Smythe's choosing. The scales tilted in Smyth's favor and he decided that it was *"Go"* time.

Smythe turned the engine off and walked in a gentle rain to a window on the west side. He peered into a room bare of furnishings, except for a weight bench and some dusty and worn-out looking exercise equipment. Moving down the side of the house he came to another room with a frosted window, obviously a bathroom. He could hear no one inside.

Going to the back of the house he could not see in the curtained window, but he could hear a television softly playing. Smythe surmised that this was a bedroom since the curtain was drawn. Moving to the next window he saw a small kitchen in a terrible state of disarray, with dirty dishes everywhere. Smythe hope this meant that there was no Mrs. Kenny, and that he lived alone. The next window gave a nearly unobstructed view of an empty living room.

Smythe was satisfied that Kenny was alone in the house. The home had a small stoop in front that could be reached by climbing the two steps leading to the door. Standing on the porch, he tested the doorknob. It was locked. He examined the Quickset knob and pulled a key ring from his pocket. Selecting what he thought would be the correct bump key, he inserted it all the way, and then pulled it out about the distance of one driver pin. Exerting a continuous, twisting pressure on the head of the key, he hit it sharply with a rock he had picked off the ground. The vibration of the pins created a shear line for just the split second he needed for the cylinder to turn. He was in. Smythe pulled the Glock 17 from the holster snuggled into the small of his back as he gently pushed the door open. No signs of forced entry, and not enough noise to be heard over the television.

It was enough noise, however, to wake the sleeping Doberman that had been dozing, unobserved, in the shadow beneath the living room window. The dog leaped up and positioned himself between Smythe and the bedroom. The black and tan dog appeared to be made completely of taut muscle, sinew, and teeth. His ears stuck straight up, and had turned so the cup faced Smythe. The dog was on high alert. He growled at Smythe as he stepped into the darkened living room. Smythe froze in place at the sound of the low rumbling growl emanating from the dog. The dog sprang forward, his lips pulled back, revealing a daunting set of razor sharp teeth. Smythe was not expecting the attack, and his heart rate soared.

As quickly as the dog sprang at him, Smythe was able to swing his Glock 17 to the right and shoot across his body, hitting the dog in its broad, tan and black chest. The Doberman dropped to the ground instantly and let out a small whimper before it breathed its last. Smythe's heart was beating even faster now, as he heard a sound coming from his left.

"What the hell!" You shot my dog!" screamed Kenny Ames. "You mother fu . . .," was all that Kenny was able to get out. While Kenny stood in one place screaming at Smythe, the canny Englishman was moving at the first syllable. Neither thought nor fear was involved in Smythe's action, just an overpowering instinct for survival.

Smythe spun, and with amazing speed was across the room in just two large strides. Without warning, without remorse, Smythe struck Kenny on the side of his head with the butt of the Glock. Kenny dropped as if he had been shot with the gun rather than just walloped in the head by it.

David's final lesson had been applied to both the dog and to Kenny - merciless efficiency.

CHAPTER TWENTY FIVE

Nubia was trying to calm herself, but she was getting more and more anxious as every hour passed with Jambo not returning her calls. The plan had worked so well, and now she had in her possession a king's ransom in diamonds, which were worthless to her without Jambo. He had the connections, and he knew how to sell them.

Nubia called his phone and once again the call was diverted to his message center. Jambo had been summoned to a meeting. He would not say with whom, but she knew it was in Cairo, with some very scary men, and he was clearly upset at having to go. He was afraid to go, and he was afraid not to go. Based on the stories he had told her, the men he dealt with were ruthless. He had even warned her he might not come back.

At this point she really did not care if he was dead or alive. She just had to know. She had the diamonds, but Jambo was as ruthless as his associates. She could not afford to double cross him. If he were alive, they would sell the diamonds and she would live well the rest of her days. If he were dead, well then, so be it. She would hide the diamonds until she found someone else who could sell them for her. She just had to know one way or the other if he were alive.

Nubia decided to call Utumbo Washington, Jambo's most trusted aide. If anyone would know what was going on, he would.

Utumbo had grown up in the projects in the Bed-Sty section of New York City. He had gotten involved with gangs, and his parents had been very worried about him. They both worked for the State of New York; and when a position opened in Albany for his father, they were able to negotiate a transfer for his mother as well. Moving the family out of the City, they hoped, would disrupt the pattern of conduct, activities, and associations they believed were sending their beautiful son down the wrong path.

Sadly, the change did not help. Within weeks of arriving in Albany, Utumbo was selling crack on corners, and was befriended by Jambo. That friendship was repaid with absolute loyalty, and as Jambo rose through the ranks, he brought Utumbo along with him.

Nubia was never sure whether Utumbo approved of her, but he would never say a word to Jambo against her, so she thought it safe to call him. He picked up the call after a few rings.

"'Sup?" he answered.

"Hi, it's Nubia," she said.

"What you want?" It sounded to Nubia as if he were trying to hold back his emotions.

"I want to talk to Jambo," she said, trying to sound casual.

"That ain't going to happen," he said.

"Why not?" she asked.

"Jambo ain't here," he said.

"Where is he?" asked Nubia, feeling as if her suspicions were about to be confirmed.

"I don't know, and I expect he ain't never goin' to be here," said Utumbo.

"Why not?" she asked.

"Why you be axing so many questions?" replied an increasingly hostile Utumbo.

"Jambo was supposed to call me when he got back yesterday," she said.

"Well, he was supposed to call me if there be any change of plans, and he didn' call me neither. I went out to the airport to get him. No Jambo."

"Maybe he just forgot," offered Nubia.

"Dis' was bidness. Jambo don't forget no bidness. More like he maybe got a cap put in his head."

"Oh, no," said Nubia, feigning horror, "don't say that! We

have to find him!"

"You want to find him, fool, go find him. Me, I'm collecting up all whats I can, and I'm getting' out of here before dey shows up to clean up the rest of his troops. I'd advise you to do the same," he said, as he disconnected the call.

"Hmmm, I guess I really do need a Plan B," Nubia said softly to herself.

*   *   *

Danny's excursion for the day took the men to Potterville and the model train museum. Despite the initial skepticism, it turned out to be a great way to spend a rainy afternoon. The museum billed itself as *RAILROADS ON PARADE—THE MODEL RAILROAD EXTRAVAGANZA,* and it actually lived up to the billing, with five thousand square feet of model train dioramas. There were five fascinating, intricately detailed exhibits, with over fifty operating trains, and nearly a mile of model train tracks. Everywhere you looked there was some minutely rigged version of the real world, including children on swings, carpenters raising a framed wall, hobos roasting hot dogs over an open fire and a fallen skier taking advantage of his predicament by making a snow angel.

After gazing at the tiny drive-in movie screen in the Station Exhibit that re-creates a train trip along the Hudson from New York City to the Catskills and finally to the Adirondacks, the guys were taken in by the intricacy of the sets. Oak preferred the western themed set, while Kevin spent a lot of time at the set recreating the 1939 World's Fair. Danny got hooked by the working harbor and surrounding community of the Prince Edward Island Exhibit.

O'Malley was temporarily diverted by the amazing collection of trains and the tiny world they lived in, but could not keep the two murders and the odd Englishman from his mind. He kept turning it over and over, and could make no sense of it. His gut told him that they were somehow connected, yet, when he would try to connect the dots, he found there were no dots to connect. He was near the peak of frustration when he felt his phone vibrating in his pocket. The caller ID said it was Mary.

"Hello, Mary! Hold on a second." The clatter of fifty model trains and the murmur of the guests were not conducive to hone conversations. O'Malley headed for an exit.

"Okay, I should be able to hear you now," he said into the phone, standing outside in the bright glare of an overcast day.

"What the hell was all the noise?" asked Mary.

"Model trains," said O'Malley.

"Model trains? What are you, twelve?" said Mary.

"What can I tell you? It's a rainy day. What have you got for me?" asked O'Malley.

"Matt, I don't have much. In fact, I don't have anything," sighed Mary. "I went through every school in London – public, private and religious affiliated, and found zilch. None of the schools have a teacher named Myles Smythe. I widened the search to surrounding communities and still no Myles Smythe. I checked a national registry of teachers for England, Scotland and Wales and there were two Myles Smythes, but one was dead and the other turned out to be a Mrs. Myles Smythe and she was nearly eighty-five years old."

"I don't think she's who I'm looking for," O'Malley laughed.

"You said you thought the school's name was short and started with a *B* or a *P*. I didn't find any short named ones that started with a *P*, but I did find a place called Blyth Academy."

"Hmmm, maybe? What did you find out?" asked O'Malley.

"Nothing. I spoke to the Headmaster – a real chatty sort of guy. He has worked at Blyth as a teacher, assistant administrator, and now as Headmaster. This is over a twenty-eight year period, and he swears that there has never been a teacher there named Myles Smythe."

"Okay, that's helpful," mused O'Malley.

"How is a big empty bucket of nothing helpful?" asked Mary.

"Because now I know someone has lied to me. People who tell lies have a reason to do so. I just need to figure out this guy's reason."

"Who has lied to you?" asked Danny as he exited the

museum.

"Mary, do you have anything else for me?" asked O'Malley.

"Sorry, Matt. That's it."

"Okay, thanks. I've got to go. I'll call you later," said O'Malley as he disconnected the call without waiting for a farewell.

"Who is lying to you, and it better not be me, because this train museum was very interesting, just like I said," asserted Danny defensively.

"Well, not to put too fine a point on it, but I think you said it was going to be the most fantastic thing I've ever seen. And it's not you who lied. It's that Smythe guy."

"Are you telling me that this wasn't fantastic?" asked Hilman.

"Danny, I've seen my children being born. I've seen the look in my wife's eye when I was waking up from surgery. I've seen the Trevi Fountain, and I've seen the sun come up over the Painted Desert. This was good, but not the most fantastic thing ever."

"Uh, who's Smythe?" asked Hilman, ignoring the slight directed at his hyperbolic description.

"That Englishman we met at Dunham's Bay," said O'Malley.

"You're nuts! Why would he even bother to lie to you?" asked Danny.

"I don't know," said O'Malley, still not finding a lot of dots to connect.

Kevin came ambling out the door, squinting in the harsh light of day. "That was fun," he said.

"Fun," said Oak, scrunching his face and tilting his head as if he were considering all the possible ramifications of the word. "It was fun," he concluded. "It was family fun. Now I'm ready for some manly fun!"

"What do you have in mind?" asked Kevin.

"Red meat, cold beer, and pretty waitresses with large breasts - and not necessarily in that order," replied Oak without hesitation.

"And where do you propose we find such an unbeatable

combination?" asked O'Malley.

"Where's the nearest Hooters?" asked Oak.

"It's all the way back in Albany, near the airport; and there's no way I am driving all the way down there just so you can harass some waitress," said Danny.

"Harass?" said Oak, indignantly.

"Careful how you say that, or you will convict yourself," warned Kevin.

"You guys wouldn't know charm if it hit you in the head," said Oak.

"How about The Boathouse?" offered O'Malley. "Good food, and maybe Katie is working and we can get some buy-backs."

"We are already pretty far north. We could go to King's Inn, or Fire and Ice," suggested Danny.

"Are you kidding? It would be quicker to drive to Albany," said O'Malley.

"Hooters it is, then," said Oak, slapping his thigh as if the decision was not clear.

"No," said Danny. "Let's go to The Boathouse. At least when we're done there, it will be a short drive home."

It would have been a short drive home. Although they did not know it yet, they were not going to get home that night.

CHAPTER TWENTY SIX

Exhausted from a night spent searching for Nubia, Edgard lay in a fitful sleep on his sofa. He wanted to flee Albany, if he only had the will. Nothing seemed to matter anymore, since he did not have either the package or Nubia. Eventually he would be called upon to turn over the package, and when he failed to do so, he knew he would not like the consequences.

He was awakened when the phone in his pocket began to ring. Paralyzed by fear, he slowly pulled the phone out, terrified that it would be the Chechen looking for his package at last. The number on the screen, however, was that of his beloved, Nubia.

"Nubia! Is it you?" he yelled into the phone.

"Of course, my love," she replied.

"Where are you? I have been so worried!" said Edgard, as a warm sensation of relief rushed through his body. *"She has not betrayed me!"* he thought.

"I am in Syracuse," she said, feigning breathlessness.

"Syracuse! Why? That was not the plan! You were supposed to be here at my apartment until I got off work!" he said.

"I know, my love, but things changed," she said.

"What changed? What things?" asked Edgard.

"After you left, I waited a while for a crowd of arriving passengers that I could blend in with to leave the airport.

A big group was coming up from the gates and I blended in with them. As I approached the exit, I thought I saw Jambo!" She lied, but by now, she was convinced that Jambo was dead and would not be coming back from his trip, so it seemed like a safe lie.

"I was in a panic. I thought he must have known I was carrying the package."

"Are you sure it was him?" asked Edgard.

It seemed best to keep the story vague here. "Yes, I think. He was pretty far away, but I did not want to take any chances. I was afraid to leave the airport, and I was afraid to stay, so I decided to take the flight I had the ticket for."

"Why did you not call me? I was so worried about you!"

Nubia really had no sufficient answer for this question, but she knew it would come up, and she had a plan – to accuse the accuser.

"Oh, you were worried, were you? Were you worried about me, or were you worried about the diamonds?"

"Diamonds? What Diamonds?" asked Edgard.

"That package you gave me was full of diamonds; and do not pretend you do not know what was in the package!"

"I swear, I had no idea," pleaded Edgard.

"Okay, do not worry, my dear, I believe you. The only thing that is important is that I get back to you as soon as possible," she said, in such a way that Edgard actually fooled himself into believing that he was more important to her than the diamonds.

"Yes, yes, that is what is most important – us being together for the rest of our lives."

"I did not want to be mean, but I had to be sure that you cared about me and not the diamonds," said Nubia.

"When are you coming back?"

"Now! Today!" she said, with urgency, "as soon as I can rent a car, my dear. But, I cannot come back to Albany. What if Jambo were to find me?" she said, and then, after an appropriately dramatic pause, "Or worse, what if he comes after you?"

Ten minutes earlier, Edgard would have welcomed a visit from Jambo, since he had no reason to live. But now, with this phone call, everything had changed.

"You are right. It is too dangerous for either of us to be here. I will meet you in Saratoga. Then we can hide the package as we discussed until we figure out what to do with it."

"Yes, my love, I agree," said Nubia. "That is the thing to do. We must be safe. All we have now is each other."

"Do not fear," said Edgard. "I am yours forever."

"I know, my love," said Nubia, as she disconnected the call. Had Edgard been in the room with her he would have seen an ironic sort of a smile on her face as she thought, *"But, forever for you shall not be long."*

Nubia needed Edgard to place the diamonds in a secure hiding spot, but when that was accomplished, Edgard had none of the other traits and abilities that she valued in a man. He would have to go, and she did not intend to share the diamonds with him.

*　　　*　　　*

Restaurateurs in resort communities love rainy days. Tourists locked up all day in hotel rooms and rented houses get "cabin fever," and just want to get out and do something on their vacations. By early evening, going out to a restaurant seems like an irresistible idea, even for those who have a full kitchen in their rental. So it was this day when O'Malley and his group arrived at The Boathouse Restaurant. The pretty hostess smiled her most sympathetic smile as she told them it would be a forty-five to sixty minute wait to get a table.

"What, is today 'Free Food Day?'" asked Danny.

"It just gets so busy when it's rainy; then no one wants to leave; so things just back up," said the hostess.

"Maybe we should go somewhere else?" said Oak. "How far are we from Hooters now?"

"I fail to see the problem," said Kevin. "The management has prudently provided a bar, and furnished it with draft beer and a television. The Yankee game will be on soon. I think the solution to our dilemma is evident. We need to drink beer and be patient."

Kevin started to amble toward the bar and the group followed.

"KAAYTEE!" was Danny's enthusiastic greeting when he

saw the bartender, "I am so glad you're working tonight!"

Katie Lufwick was the daughter of Danny's good friend, Timmy. She was an independent spirit; and, although her parents could afford to give her all she needed, she wanted to pay at least some of her own way. Katie was a great kid, who had found this job as a way to be both at Lake George during the summer, and earn money for school.

Katie gave a huge smile to the group, and came from behind the bar to give Danny a hug.

"What brings you guys in here?"

"We just wanted to see your beautiful, smiling face," said Danny.

"But I bet you wouldn't say 'no' to a beer!" she said, looking at the whole group.

"You are not just another pretty face! You are an insightful young woman," said Kevin. "Gennys all around!"

Katie, showing the speed and agility she had developed on the lacrosse field, resumed her position behind the bar, and in short order had four frosty mugs of Genesee beer sitting in front of them.

"Do you know why this is such a great beer?" asked Kevin as he savored this first gulp.

"Because it's cold," answered O'Malley.

Kevin shook his head.

"Because it's on you?" suggested Oak. Kevin scowled and then shook his head.

"Because of the company we're with?" offered Danny. Kevin smiled, but again shook his head.

"No, but good answers all," said Kevin. "The real reason is that the combination of New York's best spring water and hops from Washington State's Yakima Valley make for a truly amazing beer!"

They all solemnly nodded at the wisdom shared by Kevin and took big slugs from their glasses.

The bar was L-shaped and the men had climbed onto the four stools at the corner so they could talk easily and watch the television at that end of the bar.

"How are you guys doing?" asked Katie as she returned

from the far end of the bar.

"I think it would be prudent to invest in another round of beers," said Kevin, "and I'm afraid you have confused us with the type of people who care about what is going on in the world."

"What?" asked Katie as she started to pull the drafts.

"He's trying to tell you that he would rather watch the Yankee game than the local news," said Oak. "Can you change the channel?"

"Way ahead of you," said Katie. "The game will be on right after the news on this channel," she said, as she placed a fresh mug of beer before each man and began to collect the dirty ones.

"Holy crap!" said O'Malley. "Quick! Turn it up! Turn it up!"

" . . . and we will be back with Eyewitness News at the top of the hour with our lead story, and an amazing store video, right after these very important messages," said Heather Singer, the pretty young communications major from Manhattanville College, enjoying her first job as an anchor. She was wearing the small market anchor uniform: a constant big smile, a string of pearls, and hair so stiff it would not move in a hurricane. She was still not over the shock of moving up to the 57th largest TV market in the country after spending two years in Fargo as a field reporter.

"What's the big emergency?" asked Danny.

"Didn't you see that clip?" said O'Malley.

"No, what clip?" asked Danny.

Meanwhile, the "important message" was being shared with the viewing audience and the people sitting around the bar: *"Are you sick of sharing a house with that cheating louse you call a spouse? It's time you let the Divorce Law Firm start fighting for you . . ."*

"It was that Smythe guy! He was involved in a robbery or something. It went by too quickly. I couldn't make it out," said O'Malley.

"You're crazy!" said Danny. "You've got that guy on the brain!"

On the television, the important messages kept pouring out: *" . . . we have our whole inventory on sale, at prices you won't believe. Nobody, but nobody sells Ford trucks cheaper than your buddy in the car business, Buddy Abramowitz, on Wolfe Road in beautiful . . ."*

"We'll see who's crazy! Just wait for the news to come back on," said O'Malley, defiantly.

The selling was relentless: *" . . . for the finest training that will let you graduate and take your place in this exciting and high paying world of medical transcription or court reporting, you need to call now. Your future is just a phone call away . . . "*

"Hey, Katie, any chance you've got some nuts or pretzels or anything back there?" asked Oak.

"Where is this station based out of?" asked Kevin.

"I dunno," said Katie. "I think maybe Albany or Saratoga," she said, as she placed a bowl of Goldfish crackers in front of Oak.

"What makes you think it was Smythe?" asked Kevin.

"It was just a flash on the last teaser; but, I swear to you, it looked just like him."

"You only saw him that one time at Dunham's Bay, right?" asked Kevin.

"Yes, but I saw what I saw. Quiet! The news is back on," said O'Malley. "Katie, turn it up just a little more, please," said O'Malley.

"There was a shocking daylight robbery attempt in Glens Falls yesterday that did not work out well for the robber, whose final moments were captured on an in-store video surveillance camera," said the pretty young newscaster with an incongruous smile.

"A word of caution, in case there are children in the room," she went on, losing the smile for the first time as she tried to display all the gravitas she possessed.

"The video we are about to show is very graphic, and may be difficult for some to view. Now we go to our reporter in the field, Jennifer Cockrell, outside of Annie King's Fine Wine and Spirits store, near downtown Glens Falls."

"Good evening, Heather. *The shockingly violent story*

played out yesterday afternoon in the liquor store right behind me on Main Street in Glens Falls. Police report that an African-American male by the name of Tyrone Jones, who goes by the street name of Mookie, entered the store in the early afternoon hours, brandishing a gun, and threatening the ninety-year old owner, a Mrs. Annie King, " she paused for dramatic effect.

"According to Mrs. King, Jones entered the store and walked to the back, looking kind of nervous and jumpy. She thought he was checking the aisles for other customers since he didn't go down any aisle, or look at any merchandise. When he came back to the front of the store, he took out a gun and announced that this was a hold up, and demanded she open the cash drawer. He threatened to kill her. That's when she refused his demand and took out her baseball bat." Again, a dramatic pause for the image of this senior citizen with a baseball bat versus a young man with a gun to sink in for the viewers.

"This is where the standoff between them takes an amazing twist, and a tragedy was avoided. It was all caught on the store's surveillance cameras. This video is quite graphic, so you might want to turn away." Jennifer knew that she had the audience hooked, and no one was going to turn away.

Her station manager lived by the credo, *"If it bleeds, it leads,"* and she knew that people were glued to their televisions in anticipation of the guilty pleasure this video offered. It never occurred to her that the death of a young African-American male was also a tragedy.

The narration continued over the video that was now playing on the screen. *"As Mr. Jones was screaming profanities at the owner and threatening to kill her, a customer, who he evidently had not observed when he had canvassed the store, approached rapidly from behind. It goes very quickly on the video, but you can see the customer step into the frame. As he does, it appears that he reaches around Mr. Jones' neck from behind, and then Mr. Jones appears to try to take a step to the door, but just falls down. Police say that Mr. Jones died from massive blood loss, as a result of his throat being slashed."*

"The store owner calls the man who killed Jones a hero. She offered him some wine as a reward and he picked out two bottles before he left. She cannot identify him, and the unknown

man quickly left the scene, saying he did not want to talk to the authorities. This is Jennifer Cockrell, reporting live from Glens Falls for WTEN. Back to you in the studio, Heather."

"That truly was a terrifying situation that the store owner was in. What did the police say about her courage in standing up to the robber?" asked Heather.

"The police are relieved that she was not harmed, but caution others that she was just lucky, and that store owners should not confront robbers in such a manner. It is better to cooperate than to risk your life over money. If that brave, unknown customer had not been there, this all could have turned out quite differently. Back to you."

"Thank you, Jennifer. In other news, the Washington County Board of Commissioners . . ."

"Turn it off," said O'Malley. "So, you still think I'm crazy?"

"I don't know," said Danny. "I never saw the guy, remember? I was out on my boat when you were talking to him."

"Maybe. It could have been him, but I only saw him in profile," said Kevin. "That video was pretty grainy, and it went by quickly. Maybe if I could see it again . . .?"

"How could you *not* see it? The guy in the video was wearing the same clothes that Smythe was wearing when we saw him at Dunham's Bay. He was the same build and body type. I am sure it was him!"

"We've got to go find Reardon," said Oak.

"Why? Do you think that was Smythe?" asked Kevin.

"I can't say, based on that short clip, but we need to tell Reardon what we know. Whoever that was on the video was a highly trained, cold-blooded killer with the same M.O. as whoever killed Maura Sullivan. It's hard for me to believe that there are two such people up here with that same set of skills."

CHAPTER TWENTY SEVEN

Two men who lived within miles of each other were having two very unexpected sorts of nights. Both were very anxious, but for different reasons.

Edgard did not know where he was going, but he knew he was not coming back to his rented studio apartment and his old furniture. He packed his few belongings and stood in the middle of the place he had called home for almost two years. Except for the bathroom, he could see the entire dingy unit from where he stood.

He felt no attachment to the place; nor regrets at leaving. It was a different continent, but he felt the same as he did when he left his African village the day he found his murdered family. He felt a determination to survive.

He had made very few close friends in America, but Kenny Ames was one of them. They were both emigrants who had worked hard together in all types of harsh weather at the airport, and that helped forge a bond between them that only exists between people who share common suffering and experiences. They had played hard together as well, and it was Kenny who had introduced him to the love of his life, his beautiful Nubia. Edgard could not just leave without saying goodbye to Kenny.

Kenny, on the other hand, was dealing with much more pressing issues. He had a huge lump on the side of his head that was the size of a hen's egg and looked blue and purple and angry. He wanted to touch it, see it, or at least explore it with his fingers so he could soothe it and understand it better. However, when he tried to do so, he found that his arms and legs were zip tied to a sturdy wooden kitchen chair.

"Well, well, it appears Sleeping Beauty has returned from the Land of Nod," said Smythe as he entered the kitchen.

"Who are you? What do you want?" demanded Kenny. The question drew an immediate response from Smythe. He viciously slapped Kenny across the face with the back of his hand. Kenny's head snapped back and he could taste blood on his lips.

Smythe drew up another kitchen chair so that he was seated right in front of Ames, knees to knees. He leaned in and spoke in a very quiet voice, designed to make Kenny concentrate on what he was saying.

"You need to understand something. I *own* your ass. I will ask questions and you will answer them politely and truthfully. Should you fail at either of those requirements, I will deal with you harshly."

Kenny was enraged at his predicament. He strained mightily, trying to break the zip ties binding his limbs, but succeeded only in causing himself a lot of pain. His only thought was to break free and get his hands around his tormentor's throat.

"I have bound many a man with zip ties just like those. If you are able to break them, it will be the first time. Make it easy on yourself; just tell me what I want to know and I will leave you to get on with your life."

Kenny, remembering his dead dog, screamed a wordless, guttural sound that expressed his anger and frustration on a most primal level. The scream was rewarded with another powerful slap.

"Your house is on a very lonely road, so I doubt anyone can hear you, but just in case . . ." Smythe walked over and turned on the television sitting on the counter next to an ancient refrigerator.

"If you do not tell me what I want to know, I guarantee you - that will not be the last time you scream tonight!"

The smugness of the man served only to further infuriate Kenny. Smythe was sure he could break Kenny quickly. His captive's fear of what he may do to him would be more powerful than any actual pain he might choose to inflict.

Smythe started to rummage through the kitchen cabinets until he found a large pot. He filled the pot with water, put it on the stove, and turned it on. He hummed as he went about his work. Every time he looked at Kenny the young man's eyes were wider and wider, and he appeared transfixed by the preparations he was witnessing.

"So, tell me. What is your name?"

Kenny again strained against the ties and yelled, "What do you want from me?"

Smythe smiled as he realized how quickly Kenny had come to a near total psychological collapse, brought on by fear. *"This was going to be easy."*

"Right now all I want is for you to tell me your name," said Smythe, in an irritatingly calm voice, and as if he were speaking to a five year old.

Kenny began to sob uncontrollably as he blurted out, "My name is Kenny Ames."

Smythe went back to his chair and sat facing Kenny. He left out a big sigh, as if he had just experienced a terrible disappointment. Smythe pulled out his Kershaw Blur knife and slowly opened it.

"I require absolute honesty, and you just lied to me. Remember, I told you there would be consequences if you were not absolutely honest with me. I'll be honest with you. This is going to hurt you much more than it hurts me," said Smythe, almost gleefully.

If possible, Kenny's eyes got wider and he began shaking his head back and forth as he stared at the knife in Smythe's hands.

"Don't compound your sins now by trying to deny it. Your name is Keenadiid Amiin Kuciil. You just like to pretend you are an American, with an American name."

Smythe inserted the blade at the bottom of the v-neckline of Kenny's tee shirt and sliced the shirt open down to his belt.

"Do not lie to me," said Smythe, menacingly, as he drew the blade gently across the left side of Kenny's chest, just above his heart. The Crucible blade was so sharp that Kenny barely felt the shallow wound, but he was horror-stricken when he looked down and saw the smooth red line oozing blood.

Returning to the pot on the stove, he listened to Kenny trying desperately to get his sobbing under control.

"Do you know that water boils at one hundred degrees Celsius? Of course you do. You grew up in African schools where they teach the metric system, not like these backward Yanks, clinging to miles and Fahrenheit like their lives depended on it."

Kenny's sobbing began anew.

"Where's your salt?" asked Smythe. Not expecting an answer, he plundered through the cabinets, knocking things to the floor as he searched for salt.

"I have a great trick to show you. Do you know that you can get water hotter than its boiling point by adding salt?"

Kenny just stared and made no response, just as Smythe had been hoping. He immediately stood in front of Kenny, bending over nearly nose-to-nose and screamed, "I asked you a question! Do you know that you can get water hotter than its boiling point by adding salt?"

Kenny's sobbing continued as he shook his head back and forth, indicating he did not know that.

"That is better. See, you are learning things today. You always need to answer when I ask questions."

Smythe paused as if he were trying to think of his next question, but really he was just allowing Kenny to let his mind reach that level of insanity that only unspeakable terror can bring to a person.

"Oh, here is another question. Have you ever been to a burn unit in a hospital?"

Kenny violently shook his head back and forth.

"More's the pity. It is an amazing experience, really. You see and hear things there that you can never get out of your head. Some people can't ever sleep at night after they have seen a patient in a burn unit getting their dressing changed. They scream and scream and beg to be killed. Of course, the staff would never do that. In a few months, the worst of it is over, if they do not die from infections, and they are released. However, they are so badly scarred that they hide from their friends and families. Can you imagine some have no lips or eyelids?"

Smythe shrugged his shoulders and pretended to shutter as if he had empathy for the burn victims. He took a ladle from a drawer and began to stir the pot of water.

"This is coming along nicely. It should be ready in just a few moments," he said, with a cheery smile.

"I ... will tell ...you ...anything you want," said Kenny between sobs. "Just...please... do not scald me with that wa .. wa ..water."

"Now, that's a good lad. All I want is some information."

"Please, just tell me what..." Kenny did not get to finish that sentence.

"Shut up!" yelled Smythe, who now stood transfixed in front of the television.

"The video we are about to show is very graphic, and may be difficult for some to view. Now we go to our reporter in the field, Jennifer Cockrell, outside of Annie King's Fine Wine and Spirits store, near downtown Glens Falls..."

Smythe watched the entire story in stony silence. His life had just gotten a little more complicated. He was angry at himself for not thinking about the possibility of a surveillance camera. The store and the owner were so old, whoever would have thought she would have a surveillance system. He recognized himself in profile on the tape, and wondered who else might recognize him.

"Focus!" Smythe knew he needed to focus on the problem at hand - getting Kenny to tell him where the diamonds are hidden.

"Well, mate, it's time. You know why I am here, so tell me, where is the package you took off the plane and hid for Jambo?"

Panic flashed in Kenny's eyes. He had no idea what this lunatic was talking about.

"I don't know anything about a package."

"Are you telling me you do not know Jambo?"

"No, everyone knows Jambo," said Kenny, "but he never

told me to get a package for him off any plane."

This was a setback that Smythe had not anticipated. Kenny was too frightened to lie. Had Jambo once again sent him on a wild goose chase? He had to think.

All of Smythe's sources had confirmed that the diamonds had left Africa and were heading to Albany. Once they passed through customs at JFK in a diplomatic pouch, they were placed as cargo on a flight to Albany, where it was believed that Jambo and the Chechen would be able to secure them until they could move them through Canada to Zurich. The Chechen did not have the diamonds, and he was dead.

"What the bloody hell had happened to that package?" thought Smythe. He was convinced that Kenny did not know, but he was going to question him until he told him where it was, or died in the process, just to be sure.

"I have no idea what you are talking about. I just take the baggage off the planes and I put baggage on the planes. I do not take any of it or hide any of it." Kenny was pleading now, "If I knew anything, I would tell you."

Smythe picked up a ladle of boiling salt water and slowly poured it on the back of Kenny's left hand. The skin almost immediately blistered. Kenny screamed in agony.

"Let's try again, mate. Where . . . Are . . . My . . . Diamonds?"

Kenny was so hysterical he was unable to respond. When he tried to respond, he fainted from the intense pain emanating from his left hand.

"I really don't think he knows," thought Smythe. *"I am wasting my time here. I need to find Jambo and get the truth out of him."*

Perhaps if Kenny had not been screaming so loudly, Smythe would have heard a car pull up to the driveway. Perhaps if Kenny had not been sobbing so insistently, he would have heard the front door open.

Now that Kenny had passed out, the room had grown silent. Now Smythe was deep in thought, pondering what to do about Jambo, who unbeknownst to Smythe was still floating face down in the Nile.

Smythe's concentration faltered as he heard a sound that should not have been. He and Kenny were not alone. He looked at the shiny chrome toaster on the counter and he saw a man. A man with a gun.

Sadiki Okoro.

CHAPTER TWENTY EIGHT

Michael Reardon and his wife lived in a modest home on Cross Street, between Goodman and Stewart Avenue in Bolton Landing. He was close enough to the police station that he was able to walk to work, and he usually did. He had long ago decided that he liked living in a small town, and that the hamlet of Bolton Landing was the ideal place for him - nice people, easy access to the most beautiful body of water in the country, good restaurants, and movie theaters and mall shopping only seventeen miles away. All in all, a quiet and peaceful lifestyle. Usually. Lately, not so much.

Reardon stared at the file on his lap. He had read through it at least five times, but while the facts were straightforward and easy to understand, the connections and the significance of the information still eluded him.

He had two murders. One victim was Rizan Zakayev and the other Maura Sullivan. One died from a high-tech disappearing bullet and the other from having her throat slashed. The only thing they had in common was that there was no forensic evidence found at either murder site. They seemed like random acts; but, like O'Malley, Reardon was skeptical of coincidence.

Reardon looked up from the dining room table, where he had been reading the file, when he heard the sound of a car coming into his gravel driveway. Recognizing Hilman's car, he went to open the door.

"To what do I owe the honor of this visit?" he said with a smile.

"Did you see the news tonight?" demanded O'Malley.

"Hello, it's good to see you as well," said Reardon.

"Sorry," said O'Malley, "but we think we have a break in the Sullivan murder for you."

"Talk to me," said Reardon.

"Yesterday we went down to Dunham's Bay to get some work done on Danny's boat. While we were there this English guy comes up to us with a *cockamamie* story about wanting advice about buying a boat."

"Okay . . . ," said Reardon, not knowing where all this was heading.

"Just wait," said O'Malley, "and I will tie it all up for you. He said his name was Myles Smythe and he seemed to know a lot about us and kept pushing the conversation toward that body I found on the bateau. Claimed he recognized us from the newspaper."

"That's possible. You boys certainly garnered a lot of attention on the front page. But, I don't see what that has to do with the Sullivan murder."

"I'm getting to that. Today I had my paralegal check him out, and he lied to me about where he worked."

"So . . . lots of people fake a resume. You checked him out?" asked Reardon incredulously. "Why?"

"Just a gut feeling. There just is something odd, not right about this guy, and I was suspicious. But the lie is not the important part. Tonight we were down at The Boathouse having a beer, and we saw the news on the television. They ran a story about a robbery in Glens Falls. Some guy was holding up the store when a customer steps out of nowhere; and, in the blink of an eye, slits the robber's throat. Then he just takes off, says he doesn't want to talk to the authorities. Plus, he picks out two bottles of wine as a tip from the owner. Man, that's cold. How many people have the stones to do something like that?"

"Not many," said Reardon, thoughtfully.

"There was videotape of the whole thing," offered Kevin.

"Were you able to make out this guy's face on the video?"

"No," admitted O'Malley.

"But," suggested Kevin, "we only saw what they aired. I'll bet the cops have the whole tape, and maybe this guy's face shows up at an earlier time while he is wandering around the store."

"Oak, did you see it?" asked Reardon. Oak nodded his head in the affirmative. "Well, what do you think?"

"I think it looked like the guy from the marina's ship store, but we have to get a better look at it to be sure. If it is him, I'd say he'd be looking good to take the bust on Sullivan."

Reardon picked up a phone and hit speed dial.

"Lurman, this is the Chief," he said, without further greeting. "I have something I need you to do, right now."

"Sure, Chief. What is it?"

"I want you to go down to Glens Falls and meet with their chief. I'll call and let him know you're coming. I want you to go through the store video from a robbery yesterday at . . . ," Reardon put his hand over the speaker and asked, "Where was the robbery?"

"Place called Annie King's," said Oak.

"The robbery was at Annie King's. I want you to go through the video and get me a clear picture of the customer who cut the throat of the robber."

"Oh, yeah," said Lurman. "I saw that on the news tonight. It was fricking awesome."

"I'm glad you enjoyed it. Did it cross your mind that we have a vic here who died of a slashed throat?"

"Uhmmm," stammered Lurman.

"What station were you watching?"

"WTEN"

"Good! Send Bobby down to Albany to WTEN and tell him to find Mike Schweitzer. He's a friend of mine and the GM at the station. I'll call him and have him make us a copy of all his raw footage on the story. Have Bobby pick it up and get it back here to me as soon as possible. Get someone else to start checking with all the realtors to see if anyone has rented to any Brit anywhere around Lake George, especially if the name given on the rental contract was Myles Smythe."

"Got it," said Lurman. "Myles Smythe. The real estate offices will be closed now. Should we wait until the morning to check with them?"

"Hell, no," yelled Reardon. "I don't care what you have to do. Find them tonight. I want to know where every Brit in the area is staying. Check the hotels and motels as well. There can't be that many Brits in town," he barked into the phone.

"Chief, I can help," said Danny, who owned the largest real estate office on the lake. "If he's not in our files I have a directory with the home numbers of every real estate broker and sales agent in the county."

"Great!" said Reardon to Danny.

"I've got Danny Hilman here. He will help. He has a directory."

"Finally, a break," said Reardon, as he hung up the telephone.

"Chief?" asked Kevin. "There was something else odd about this guy, I think," said Kevin. "I don't remember seeing in the papers or hearing on the news that the victim on the bateau had been shot."

"No, we never released that information," said Reardon.

"Isn't that standard practice, to hold back information only the actual killer would know?" asked O'Malley.

"Yes, of course," said Oak.

"Well," said Kevin, "this Smythe character commented that his interest was piqued because they don't have many *shootings* where he comes from."

O'Malley slapped the dining room table. "That's right! That's exactly what he said. I knew it! There is a connection. One guy killed both victims. Probably Smythe!"

"Maybe, but that doesn't explain Rizan Zakayev," said Reardon.

"Who is Rizan Zakayev?" asked O'Malley.

"The victim you found. Zakayev is a very nasty boy, as least he was before someone shot him in the head," said Reardon. "We sent his picture out and our friends at Homeland Security got a hit on him using their photo recognition software."

"Was he a terrorist?" asked Danny.

"Not really," said Reardon. "His dossier makes him sound more like a criminal capitalist than anything. He was a gun for hire. If it was illegal, and if there was money to be made, he was in. He was very secretive about his activities and was known in his professional circles simply as the Chechen, but he wasn't involved in separatist activities in Chechnya, nor was he an Islamic fundamentalist. He did what he did purely for money. He's being investigated for a number of contract murders, but mostly he seemed to be like a high-end bagman. He would broker deals with drug lords and rebel groups and arms dealers, and then make sure the barter payments got delivered to the right people, after he took a cut for himself."

"That sounds like an unholy trinity," said O'Malley.

"You have no idea," said Reardon.

"The Chechen," said Oak, turning the name over and over in his mind. "Cool *nom de guerre*, but I've never heard of him."

"If you had heard of him, he wouldn't have been doing his job very well," said Reardon.

"How would something like that even work?" asked Hilman.

"Do you remember the Triangle Trade from your American History course in elementary school?" asked Kevin.

"Of course not," said Hilman.

"No matter," said Kevin. "This works in a similar fashion. The best examples of how this market works can be seen in Africa and the Middle East right now. African rebels, like the Lord's Resistance Army, need guns, but they usually have no money. What they do have is access to conflict, or blood diamonds."

He further explained, "Arms dealers want to sell their weapons, but they want to be paid in cash, since many of them try to maintain a front as legitimate businesses. Middle Eastern drug dealers have warehouses full of cash in the countries where they pedal their poison, but it does them no good because it's too bulky to transport, and no bank will touch it for fear of the Patriot Act."

"Great, so all the bad guys have problems. Boo Hoo!" said Hilman.

"When there are problems, there are solutions," said Kevin. "Guys like Rizan Zakayev come along and broker deals.

The rebels get their arms; the drug dealers pay the arms dealers and get to offload tons of cash; and, in return, they fill up safety deposit boxes in Switzerland with easily transportable conflict diamonds."

"What a great world we live in," said Hilman.

"But, I thought that there no longer was a market for blood diamonds," said Reardon.

"I wish that were only true," said Kevin. "We represent DeBeers and a few of the other big legitimate sellers, and they abide strictly by the Kimberley Process Certification system, but there are holes in the system large enough to drive an earthmover through."

"The Kimberley what?" asked Hilman.

"It's a system put in place around 2003 that is supposed to guard against conflict diamonds being able to enter the legitimate diamond supply chain," said Kevin.

"The problem is the system is only as good as the people, the companies, the governments, and the NGOs that supervise it. Today every diamond is to be checked all the way from production to distribution, and the conflict-free diamonds are placed in tamper-proof containers, each with a unique serial number."

Kevin continued, "But, there are seventy-four Kimberley process countries that can certify the diamonds. Places like the Ivory Coast, Botswana, Angola, Belarus, Guyana, and a host of other countries that are poor and full of corrupt officials. The certificates are easily purchased for a pittance, and immediately transform a worthless rock that can't be sold into something that Tiffany's will sell for a small fortune."

"This sounds like something right in the wheelhouse of the late, and little mourned, Rizan Zakayev," said Oak. "That guy had to be a truly one-of-a-kind bastard. The conflict diamonds are produced using slave labor, women, children, and captured enemies – all under the most brutal conditions imaginable. Let's find out who killed him and put a medal on his chest."

"I'd hold off on the medal if I were you," said O'Malley. "If it was Smythe that killed him, he was after something, and he was probably cut from the same cloth as Zakayev. And, let's not forget, he also probably killed that poor young girl in Anniston's garage."

"Yeah," said Reardon. "I'm having a hard time with that. I realize this is a very shadowy world we're dealing with, but how does she fit in the pattern? She was probably just a kid with a crush on her boss, not an international criminal. And, what would Smythe be doing in Anniston's house anyway?"

"You've got me," said O'Malley, "but since he seems to have an unnatural interest in us, I intend to find out. I want to go with Dave Lurman, to look at that store video."

"Okay by me," said Reardon.

Kevin and Oak looked at each other and shrugged their shoulders.

"It looks like Kev and I will be going too," said Oak.

"Take my car," said Hilman. I'll have Mike bring me back to the house after we make the calls to the realtors."

CHAPTER TWENTY NINE

Smythe was astounded at the presence of a third person in the room. The how and the who were questions for later. Right now he had to decide what to do about it. Tactically, the stranger had the advantage. Smythe's back was to him, and the stranger had his gun out. But, Smythe had an advantage that the intruder did not have, a level of situational awareness that might give him the upper hand.

Unbeknownst to the intruder, Smythe was aware of the man's presence. The intruder was observing; he was not taking action. Smythe still had the element of surprise working for him. He remembered David against Goliath. He could choose the timing and the tactics of the confrontation that was to come. He liked his odds.

The intruder had a gun, but a handgun is a very inaccurate weapon, and the greater the distance, the worse the accuracy. Unfortunately for Smythe, this was a very small area.

Smythe tried to go about his business, but turning around would spark a conflict for which he was not ready.

"What would David have done with this armed Goliath?" he thought.

Getting his own gun out would be too slow. The intruder would surely shoot, and could get two or three shots off before Smythe could turn around and get off one. The intruder might miss once, even twice, but not three times. *"Don't let your enemy pick your weapon . . ."*

Smythe casually leaned against the counter while talking out loud to the still unconscious Kenny.

"Come on, mate, wake up, so you can tell me where the diamonds are," he said, as he placed his hand, palm down, on the counter – covering his ever-faithful Kershaw knife.

The intruder could still be seen in the reflection from the toaster, and he stood as still as a statue in a park. *"Maybe he thinks he will let me get the answer from the bound man,"* thought Smythe.

Smythe regretted turning off the television. When he wasn't talking to the unconscious Kenny, the silence was so pervasive it seemed like a warm, wet towel over his face. He was afraid that the intruder would make a noise, or otherwise be spooked into action before Smythe was ready.

Then the sound came. It was loud; it was piercing; it was unexpected; and it galvanized Smythe into action. He was like a racehorse springing out of the gate as the starting bell rings. The sound so startled Sadiki Okoro that he jumped a little, and turned toward the ringing wall phone.

The break in his concentration was not long, but it was fatal. Before the first ring was done Smythe had, simultaneously, spun toward the intruder, raised his right hand, and flipped the knife around, positioning it to be thrown.

Okoro instantly realized the mistake he had made. Smythe had turned not toward the sound, but toward him! Okoro swung his gun toward Smythe and fired a shot.

The noise in the confined area of Kenny's tiny house was deafening. However, Smythe didn't hear it. He was too focused on the task at hand. He would have only one chance. He had to bury the blade deep into the intruder's chest, preferably into his heart.

The bullet whizzed harmlessly past Smythe, who had already sent his knife on a trajectory designed to pierce his enemy's heart. Before Okoro could get off another shot, he felt the knife strike him just to the left of his sternum, right below where the ribs attached. He dropped the gun and grabbed at the handle sticking out of his chest. He tried to tug it out, but he fell, face first, before he could move the blade.

Smythe drew his Glock and was across the room in a heartbeat. He kicked the intruder's gun, sending it sliding across the floor. He flipped the body over and, hoped to get whatever information he could before he killed the man.

He could see that the man was alive, but beyond questioning. His eyes had already completely dilated, and he stared up with an emptiness that only death could bring.

"Who the bloody hell are you?" he snarled at the lifeless body.

"And you!" he said, turning back to Kenny. "Really? A landline? What is this, your grandmother's place?"

If Kenny was insulted by this dig at his technological lack of sophistication, he did not let on. Of course, since Okoro's bullet missed Smythe but hit Kenny and tore through his head, removing a large section of the rear of his skull, he was quite beyond caring or responding.

"Bloody hell," said Smythe, as he realized that Kenny was now a dead end.

The phone rang again. Smythe could just taste the bitterness of defeat. Sure, he was alive, but Kenny was dead, and he had been his best connection to finding the diamonds. Now all he had was Jambo.

Again the ring; its discordant sound awakening in Smythe a burst of rage. In the depths of this rage-fueled frustration he took out his gun and, with a primal scream, discharged the weapon, sending a bullet into the dead Okoro's skull. Shooting him was a senseless act, born of anger, frustration, and despair. He had been so close, and now the diamonds seemed as if they had slipped completely and irretrievably from his grasp.

The telephone rang again, but this time the ring was cut short by the answering machine picking up the call. Smythe just wanted to put a bullet though the telephone, but he was feeling so completely defeated that he did not have the energy to do so.

"*This is Kenny. Sorry I am not here to take your call . . .*" Smythe began to laugh at how absurdly true that statement was. "*. . . Please leave a message and I will get back to you, unless you are a bill collector, in which case, don't ever call me again!*"

Smythe could hear the machine click and whirl just before it made the obligatory "beep."

"*Hi, Kenny. This is Edgard. Listen, I have screwed up really bad and I am in big trouble. I never should have listened to Jambo. I did things for him I never should have done, and now I don't even know who, but someone, will be coming after me. Nubia and I have to leave town, but I couldn't go without saying goodbye. You have been a very good friend, and I don't know that I will ever see you again. You can reach me at the Winkelman's place on Lake George for a day or so; but, after that, who knows. Please don't tell anyone anything about this. I just need to disappear. If I ever can, I will call you and explain all this to you."*

Smythe's luck had not yet run out, and he was suddenly again confident it never would. Grabbing a small pad and a pen he found on the kitchen counter, he examined the answering machine. He wanted to be sure he knew how to operate it before he touched any of the buttons. Finding the replay button, he pressed it and listened carefully. On the pad he wrote five words: "Jambo", "Nubia", "Winkelman" and "Lake George."

The message ended, but suddenly Miles Smythe had a whole new lease on life. Walking over to Okoro, he retrieved his knife, wiping the gore off on Okoro's shirt. Turning, he stepped across the room and cut open Kenny's trouser pockets. They were empty. Standing up he looked around the kitchen and did not see what he was looking for.

"I know you have one. Where is it?"

Smythe's search was rewarded when he found what he was looking for on the nightstand. He scooped up the charger and the phone, and went back into the kitchen. He opened the phone's contact list and started to scroll through them. There was one Edgard, an Edgard Onobanjo, there was a Nubia Mayardit, and there was one Winkelman. He would go to Edgar's place first, and if he could not find him there, he would try Nubia's address. Failing that, he knew he could find him in Lake George.

It was just a matter of time. He was excited that soon he would have the diamonds. He was so excited he bolted from the house, ran to his car, and headed out without wasting a second.

He should have wasted a second.

CHAPTER THIRTY

Officer Lurman had a head start and a blue light on his vehicle that allowed him to get to Glens Falls police department before O'Malley. Oak had a Retired New Jersey State Trooper identification card in his wallet that allowed him to get to the station just a brief time afterward. Everyone agreed Oak should drive for two reasons. After putting in his twenty years, at the ripe old age of forty-three, he had retired from the Troopers and had been teaching security driving and kidnap avoidance techniques. Also, as long as he had his retired trooper identification in his wallet, he viewed speed limit signs not as regulatory, but as mere suggestions.

Lurman had the security video cued up, and was getting ready to start it, when O'Malley, Kevin and Oak walked into the room. The Glens Falls Police Chief was worried about proving the chain of custody on the surveillance, so after conferring with the Assistant District Attorney, he insisted that one of his own officers, Gary Planck, be present, and be the only one to handle the DVD or operate the player. The officer was not happy to have three new faces entering the interrogation room where he had set up the video.

"Who are these guys?" he asked, making no effort to disguise his annoyance.

"It's okay. They are friends of my chief. They're here to help," replied Lurman.

"How can a bunch of civilians help?" This is going to turn into a major screw-up," said the Glens Falls officer, shaking his head.

"Watch who you're calling a civilian," said Oak, flipping out his ID card.

The officer looked at the card with contempt. "Great. Well, I got two things to say to you. First, things might have changed since you were on the job, what about, a hundred years ago? And, second, this ain't New Jersey!"

Provoked, Oak was getting ready to escalate the confrontation when Kevin stepped in.

"Don't be such a jerk," he said to the young officer. "We are ass deep in bodies, and our chief will not be too pleased if another body turns up while you hold us up, pretending to be Robocop. Just show us the damn video."

The young officer stared at Kevin, not sure what to do next. Deciding that prudence was the better part of valor, and not wanting a powwow between the chiefs to focus on him, he hit the Play button and slouched back in his seat, affecting a disinterested mien.

The video was stored in a digital format on a hard drive now attached to the department's computer. Consequently, while not broadcast quality, the image was much clearer than the old VHS format surveillance videos, and without the stop action herky-jerky motion.

"It must have been a slow day," said O'Malley, after staring at the screen for several minutes, watching nothing but aisles of wine bottles, and no movement of any kind in the store.

"Any chance we can fast forward to when someone is actually in the store?" asked O'Malley.

"Sure," said the young officer, as he held up a remote in his fully extended arm and pointed it at the player. Shadows started to jump around rapidly as the sun came in and out, changing the lighting in the store, but still no customers.

"That's better," said O'Malley. "Just keep it moving until you get to about twenty seconds before the robber comes into the store."

"Okay," said the officer, clearly communicating that he felt his time and talents were being wasted showing video to this bunch of amateurs.

"There! There! There he is!" said O'Malley. "Freeze it!"

The Glens Falls officer stopped the video, but not quick

enough to catch the man that O'Malley had seen.

"Back it up, frame by frame if you can," said O'Malley. Planck did as requested until finally, O'Malley told him to stop.

"Can you enlarge the face?" asked O'Malley.

The others gathered in closer to the screen to get a better view. The computer hummed for a moment as it worked on the pixilated image, bringing it into focus.

"I'll be dipped in shit," said Oak, as he gazed into the eyes of the Englishman he had met in Dunham's Bay.

"Wow!" agreed Kevin.

"Can you print that image for me?" asked O'Malley.

"Sure," said Planck, now more keenly interested. "Do you guys know him? My chief will want him brought in for an interview."

"We have met him, but we don't know him. He claims his name is Myles Smythe and that he's from England. That's all I know," said O'Malley. "But, I can't be sure that is even a real name."

The officer was scribbling notes as O'Malley spoke.

"I actually don't know how to print from this computer, but the tech officer will be here for the morning shift. I'll get it to you then," said the young officer, pushing Oak over the edge.

"Are you frickin' kidding me? You are sitting around here busting our balls and giving us attitude, and you don't even know how to use your own equipment!" yelled Oak.

The young officer stood up and looked as if he wanted to fight Oak, but rapidly changed his mind as Oak stood up to his full six feet six inches, appearing to welcome the opportunity to teach him some respect for old-school cops.

"Never mind; it doesn't matter," said O'Malley, as he snapped a picture of the screen on his iPhone. "I have it," he said, as he turned the phone around to show the image on the screen.

"Settle down, boys, this isn't helping anyone. We need to see the rest of the video," said Kevin.

The officer sat back down and pointed the remote at the computer. O'Malley half watched the screen while he texted the photo of Smythe to Reardon with the following message: *"U*

R looking at Smythe. Run it through photo rec. Maybe we will get a hit."

Oak was concentrating on the video. The camera was positioned at the back of the store, cattycorner from the front door. Oak watched as Smythe ducked down in the aisle.

"Did you see that?" he asked.

"Yeah," said O'Malley. "What's up with that? There isn't anyone else in the store yet."

"Back it up," ordered Oak. The officer complied.

Oak focused like a laser on the video as the same bit replayed. "There is a flash of light outside that seems to catch his attention," said Oak, "then it looks like he is looking outside, and whatever he sees causes him to duck down so he can't be seen. Shortly afterward, the video shows the door open and our very hopped-up looking bad guy comes strolling in."

The young officer volunteered, "That's the perp. He's on a slab in the morgue at the hospital now."

The three men continued to concentrate on the screen where the video was playing out the final moments of a tragic life.

"There's Smythe again," said Kevin, as the camera again picked him up. "It looks to me like he is moving around deliberately, hiding himself from the black kid."

"That's exactly what he's doing," said O'Malley. "Before anything happened, he knew something was up, and he was reacting to a dangerous situation."

"Maybe he knew the kid," said Kevin, "and knew he was up to no good."

"I doubt it," said Oak. "How would he have gotten to know some skell from Albany? Unlikely. I think he's a guy who is exceptionally well trained, plus has cop instincts. When this kid got out of the car, the window must have caught the sun and made the flash that caught his attention. Smythe knew from the perp's dress, or his demeanor, or his mannerism, or something, that a robbery was about to go down."

"So, you think he is, or at least, was, a cop?" asked O'Malley.

"No, not the way he slit the subject's throat. Cops are

trained to handle dangerous and volatile situations; and our first reaction is not to kill the subject, but to disarm him and make him submit to our control. With the level of training I think Smythe had, there was no need for him to kill that robber. He had complete control over the situation because the robber didn't know he was even there. No, his actions were more like a commando, or a spy."

"Or a psychopath," offered O'Malley.

"Whatever he is," said Kevin, "he is one stone-cold killer."

"We need to find him and take him down so he can be questioned," said O'Malley.

"That would be ideal," said Oak, "but this guy is not your average street thug. He's got some skills," said Oak, with grudging admiration. "He's not going to be taken down easily, or without a fight. I think we need to be guided by two old-cop principles."

"Okay," said Kevin, "what are they?"

"There are old cops and there are bold cops, but there are no old, bold cops," said Oak, turning toward the Glens Falls officer and pointedly saying, "That's one you should learn!"

"I agree," said O'Malley. "We will have to be very cautious with Smythe. What else?"

"It is better to be judged by twelve of your peers than to be carried by six of your friends!"

The other men greeted that adage with solemn silence as they contemplated its simple profundity.

CHAPTER THIRTY ONE

The quiet thinking created by Oak's aphorisms was shattered by the ringtone on O'Malley's phone. Wearily, O'Malley took out his phone and saw that it was Reardon.

"Hi, Mike, did you get the text with Smythe's picture?" asked O'Malley.

"Yeah, I did," replied Reardon. "I sent it over to Homeland Security, to your old buddy, J.P. Truak."

"Oh, hell, no!" said O'Malley, who had, several years before, been doggedly pursued by Truak when he believed that O'Malley was involved with a terrorist group. Even though the confusion was cleared up, there was still no love lost between the two men.

"I hope you didn't mention my name!"

"In fact, your name did come up. J.P. asked about you and sends his best regards," laughed Reardon.

"I bet he did," said O'Malley, derisively.

Truak had turned over O'Malley's investigation file, he claims against his will, to the State Department. They, in turn, gave it to officials in the Saudi government, who were subsequently unable to explain how it fell into the hands of the terrorist group who blamed O'Malley for the failure of their plan, the death of their operatives, and the imprisonment of one of their Imams. The group did what terrorist groups do – they set out to seek revenge, which was made easier after they learned chapter and verse about O'Malley's life, habits and usual routines – thanks to the very thorough investigative reports prepared by Truak. O'Malley had yet to forgive him for allowing that ball to get rolling.

"So, any hits from the facial recognition software yet?"

asked O'Malley.

"No, but they have only had the picture a little while. Give it a chance," said Reardon.

"Listen, Matt, I know it's late and you're probably beat, but I have a favor to ask."

"Anything you want, Mike. You know if I can help I will," replied O'Malley.

"I went back to the station after you left, and an alert bulletin popped up on the computer from the Albany P.D."

"Yeah, so?"

"They just discovered a double homicide in a little house on a dirt road in a rural area of the city. The Albany P.D. is still working the scene right now."

"I still don't get it," said O'Malley. "Maybe I don't think as clearly at 1:30 in the damn morning, but what does this double homicide have to do with anything?"

"Maybe nothing, but one of the dead guys had his chest sliced with a knife, and the other took a blade just under the sternum."

"So, these guys were in a knife fight and killed each other," concluded O'Malley.

"It's not going to be that simple. The guy with the cut chest was zip tied, arms and legs, to a chair and one of his hands had been scalded with boiling water. The other guy, in addition to the knife wound to the chest, had a bullet wound to the head that appears to be a large caliber bullet, shot at close range, with an entry wound – but, get this – no exit wound."

There was a third person there, the shooter," exclaimed O'Malley. "It must be Smythe. He would have been questioning the guy in the chair when he was interrupted by the other guy, and then he killed them both. Whatever he's looking for, he hasn't found it yet."

"That's a lot of conjecture with not much by way of facts," replied Reardon.

"So, what do you want me to do?" asked O'Malley, suddenly energized by this new information.

"As of right now, you three are officially consultants to the Bolton Landing Police Department. Lurman is a great guy, and good at being a small town cop, but this isn't a stolen bicycle report he would be taking. He would be over his head.

You guys are the closest people I have to get to Albany quick, and you have more insight into this case than anyone. You and Kevin are lawyers and the smartest S.O.B.s I've ever run into, plus Oak is a damn fine cop. He's forgotten more than most of the boys I have will ever know."

"You don't have to sell me. We'll go."

"Great," said Reardon. "Have Lurman take you, lights and siren all the way. I'll radio the contact information and clear it with the detectives down there. Report back to me as soon as you can."

*   *   *

Smythe was nothing if not thorough. But why not, if he could find Onobanjo in Albany things would be less complicated, and if he happened to miss him, he knew just where to look in Lake George thanks to the ill-considered voicemail he had heard on Kenny Ames's phone.

His bang key was not needed once he found Edgard's apartment. The front door was open. Smythe cautiously let himself in, the memory of the *hound from hell* at Ames's place still fresh in his mind. This time there was no snarling dog; there was no Edgard; there was no sign of life at all.

Searching the studio apartment did not take much time. It was sparsely furnished. There seemed to be nothing personal to Edgard to be found in the unit. There was clutter on the floor, dirty dishes in the sink, and even unopened mail addressed to Edgard Onobanjo, so it looked lived in. Yet, it was strange that there were no personal mementos around, and even stranger still that there were no clothes in any of the drawers or the small closet.

"So, you have left," thought Smythe, *"and do you think I will let you leave with my diamonds?"*

Smythe's next stop was the home of Nubia Mayardit. It was larger, it was better decorated and better cared for, yet, it too was unoccupied. Nubia had not bothered to pack all her personal items.

"*I wonder why,*" thought Smythe. "*Maybe she hasn't left, or maybe she thinks she is coming back,*" he speculated.

His search of the apartment proved to be a bit more productive than the search of Edgard's place. Buried deep in the back of the closet he found an album with photographs of what he assumed to be Nubia and Jambo. They appeared to be quite good friends - or more.

"*I wonder if young Edgard knows he has a tiger by the tail,*" thought Smythe.

Smythe was just about to leave Nubia's apartment when his phone began to ring. This was the London phone assigned to the undercover identity of his Miles Smythe persona. He never used this phone for outgoing calls, and he never expected an incoming call. The caller ID displayed "Blythe Academy."

Somehow, a Tripwire in the security system had set in motion this call, which was to alert him that his cover had been compromised. Smythe's senses once again were on full alert.

"Good morning," said Smythe as he struggled to remember the exact protocol for the exchange of signs and countersigns. "At least it is in the south of France."

"The south of France is desperate this time of the year, too much rain and humidity," came the preprogrammed response from a caller that Smythe had never met.

"That is why the smart crowd goes to Sardinia," replied Smythe, relieved that he seemed to be recalling the correct countersign.

"My family prefers the Canary Islands for holiday," said the very proper gentleman on the other end of the line.

"Why are you calling me?" demanded Smythe.

"Is this Smythe?" asked the man from London.

"You have the bloody signs and countersigns. Of course it is. Why are you calling me?" barked Smythe.

"Just being sure, to be sure," replied the man from London. "Whomsoever you told that you taught at Blythe Academy called here to ask about you."

"Interesting," said Smythe, as he pondered the ramifications. People like the Headmaster of Blythe Academy were called Tripwires. MI-5 built Tripwires into all the double blind, deep cover identities that they created as a safeguard.

The people who act as the Tripwires were never MI-5 employees; they weren't professionals; rather, they were loyal subjects of the Queen who volunteered to be listeners, and were never told the exact nature of their work, just that they were providing a patriotic service to their country. They never knew who they were calling, only the deep cover name.

Any time the undercover agent wanted to test his identity, or suspected that his identity had been compromised, he would find a way to drop enough information, without being obvious, that would allow the listener to identify and contact the Tripwire. If the Tripwire was then contacted, the agent knew that someone was getting suspicious enough of him to check out the story, and the agent would act accordingly.

The only time he had ever been concerned enough to utilize the Tripwire on this mission was when he disclosed Blythe Academy to O'Malley and his friends at Dunham Bay.

"Did the caller identify himself as Matt O'Malley?" asked Smythe.

"Actually, the caller was a lady named Mary, I believe," said the headmaster. "But now that you mention it, I do believe that is whom she claimed employed her."

Smythe was startled at how quickly O'Malley had acted. He may have underestimated him.

"What did you tell the woman?" asked Smythe.

"I told her that we never had anyone by that name working here," said the headmaster, nervously.

"You idiot!" exploded Smythe. "Your job was to confirm my employment and report the enquiry to me!"

"Are you quite certain?" asked the headmaster.

"Of course I am," said Smythe, struggling to control his anger. "The whole point of this exercise it to allay the suspicions of the caller, and alert us to the fact that there is someone suspicious of our back story. How can you not understand that?"

"Oh, yes, of course, now I remember. My training was only a few hours and it was years ago. The really should offer refreshers," said the headmaster.

"Did you at least get a call back number? May be you can say you made a mistake."

"That would have been a good idea; but, sorry, no call back number."

"Great!" said Smythe.

"A point of order here, if I might . . .," said the headmaster. "Now that I have alerted you about this enquiry regarding your employment, do I also call anyone at MI-5? My instructions, I have said, were a long time ago. I am a bit unclear about what to do next."

"No!" was the emphatic reply. "Your job is over now. Well done, old man," replied Smythe acerbically. "I am afraid it was nothing but a false alarm to test your preparedness."

"Thank goodness," said the headmaster. "I was fearful I had buggered up something important."

"I'll take care to inform MI-5 of your request for retraining," said Smythe. The last thing in the world he wanted was for his former employers to know that he had stolen one of their precious double blind deep cover identities before he left.

"Alright then," said the headmaster. "Right is might. I am delighted I was able to help. Cheerio. I must away. Morning tea awaits."

"Right, thanks," said Smythe, as he disconnected the call. His "To Do" list had just lengthened. He would have to do something about O'Malley before he left. It would not be tidy otherwise, and he was intent on leaving things tidy.

Smythe was careful not to disturb too much of the apartment, and he locked the door behind him. *"Can't be too careful these days,"* he thought. It had been a long roller coaster ride of a night for Smythe.

As he stepped out of the apartment, the glimmering of the dawn could be seen in the east. *"Today is the day I get my diamonds,"* he told himself, *"But not until I tie up a few loose ends."*

The message had said that Edgard was going to stay with his parents for a day or two. That would give him all the time he needed to get rid of the only people he feared had a reasonable chance of recalling and identifying him. Once he got the diamonds from Edgard he was off to Canada, and then to the most tropical place he could find without extradition treaties.

*   *   *

Hilman's career path had led him to a place of leadership in his professional community. Fortunately for him, being president of the Warren County Realtor's Association was a "one and done" proposition. He did not like the unpaid work, or the unrelenting politics that went with the *honor* of being president.

After spending the night calling realtors, in an effort to locate a property that may have been rented to an Englishman, he was confident that, even if he wanted to be re-elected, there was little or no chance of that happening. Based on the angry threats he received, which grew even angrier as the night progressed, he felt that he would be lucky to be allowed to remain as a member.

He was a bit amused that, overwhelmingly, the most popular response to his call was to ask him if he knew what time of the morning it was. He had learned something about his colleagues that he had not known before. They were extremely creative in ways to string together Anglo-Saxon profanities in a wide variety of combinations all designed to deliver the same message – you should not be calling me.

It was worth all the abuse. He had been able to identify a realtor that had rented a cabin in the woods below Juniper Hills to an Englishman who had identified himself as Myles Smythe.

Reardon was excited to receive the information about the rental and promised to get a search warrant as soon as he could find a judge. Reardon sent his patrolman home and took Hilman back to his house in Mohican Heights.

"You want to come in?" asked Hilman. "I can get you a beer or make you some coffee – your choice."

"Thanks, but I have a lot of work to do getting this

search warrant application ready for the judge."

The men said good night to each other, and Danny stood on his driveway facing west, arched his back and tried to stretch the night's tension out of it. He raised his hands over his head, yawning and stretching as he craned his neck to look up at the last of the night sky. The Milky Way filled the sky with an unimaginable number of bright white dots. He felt as if he could just reach out and grab a handful of them to put in his pocket.

Turning, Hilman decided to forgo the garage entrance and walked up the steps leading to his rear deck. Pausing at the top he looked down at the lake. The inky darkness of the water was just beginning to separate from the light green of the hillsides as the eastern sky began to brighten.

"Lake George is beautiful no matter when you look at it!" he thought, as the realization hit him yet again that he was lucky to have this part of the globe to call his own. *"It's a special place."*

Fearing that he would fall asleep on the deck if he dare sit in one of the Adirondack chairs, he reluctantly opened the door and went inside. Too keyed up to go to bed, he turned on Sports Center to help him calm down and plopped onto his couch.

CHAPTER THIRTY TWO

Matt O'Malley loved his country, and was grateful to the Department of Defense for many things. He was grateful for the soldiers who vigilantly protected the country and guarded the liberty of its citizens. He was grateful for the tradition of the military staying out of politics and allowing elected civilians to exercise control over the government. However, at this particular moment he was most grateful to Ivan Getting and the D.O.D. for placing in geosynchronous orbit all the satellites necessary to make the Garmin GPS hanging from the patrol car window function.

By some magic that O'Malley had never bothered to try to understand, the little unit was comparing notes with a bunch of satellites about where they were located, and how long it took their messages to arrive. Then, through some digital alchemy, the little box on the windshield calculated where it was in time and space, and how fast it was moving. O'Malley knew there was no way he would understand the science behind the GPS, but all he really cared about was that it had unerringly brought him down this dirt road to the home of Kenny Ames.

"What a dump," said Oak, as he surveyed the home from the front seat of Lurman's Ford Explorer, rigged for duty as a marked police vehicle.

"In Miami, they would call this a charming fixer-upper with privacy only obtainable in a true country estate setting," said Kevin. "And they would list it for a mil' or more."

"I'm guessing, given the number of flashing red and blue lights, that we have found the right place," said O'Malley.

"I've never understood why people love dawn,"

complained Lurman. "Let's go introduce ourselves. We can't leave until we go in and talk to them."

The four men got out and approached the yellow crime scene tape that surrounded the perimeter of the home. A young, uniformed officer stopped them, just before the tape, and demanded their identification. Once satisfied as to their bona fides, he then directed them to the detective in charge, Hall Whitworth.

Whitworth was a grizzled, veteran detective whose sensibilities had been deadened by repeated exposure to the horrific tableau that made up most murder scenes. He looked like he had been sent down by central casting to play the part of the hard-boiled detective. His hair and full beard were speckled with grey; he wore blue jeans with his gold shield clipped to his belt; a black shirt opened at the neck; and a tweed sports coat. His demeanor suggested he did not suffer fools gladly. He was standing outside sipping a cup of coffee, and keeping close watch on his crime scene as evidence techs and photographers were going about their business. Occasionally, someone would come up to him with a bit of information that he would scribble into the field notebook that he kept in his back pants pocket.

"What the hell is a consultant?" he demanded to know, after the men introduced themselves.

Lurman shrugged his shoulders and said, "My chief says we need their help. These two are lawyers," he said, pointing at Matt and Kevin, "and this one used to be a New Jersey State Trooper." Whitworth looked at them as if they were gum he had just discovered on the sole of his shoe. He took another sip of his coffee.

"So, how can I help you boys?" asked Whitworth, still not sure he had any intention of helping them.

"I think the real question is how we can help each other," said Oak.

"You just roll up to my crime scene, don't even look inside, and you think you can help me," remarked a critical Whitworth. "You must be quite a soothsayer or something."

"Well, let me try," said Oak. "You've got your M.E. in there examining the bodies, I bet."

"Of course," said Whitworth. "So far you're not much of a fortune teller."

"I also bet you think that you're going to dig a bullet out of one of the victims that you think you'll be able to send to forensics to help solve this crime."

"There's an entry wound and no exit wound; so, yeah, we'll get forensics off the bullet," said Whitworth.

"No, you won't," said Oak. "There's no bullet. Your shooter used a Fiocchi EMB round."

"Holy hell! I hope you're wrong!" said Whitworth. "Stay right here. There's coffee on the back seat. Help yourself. I'll be right back."

"Where's he going?" asked Lurman.

"To have the M.E. probe the wound and see if he can tap a bullet," replied Kevin, as if the answer was clearly obvious.

The four men sipped their coffee, and, as they did so, the dawn had transformed itself into a beautiful and bright day. The trees threw long shadows over the green fields, and birds could be heard merrily going about their morning routine. The sun had chased away the darkness and was pretending nothing had changed, yet for the two dead men inside the house, everything had changed.

"Okay, I want to know everything you know about this," said Whitworth, as he walked out the front door and toward them.

"M.E. couldn't find a bullet, could he?" asked O'Malley.

"No, but who knows where it went. He'll know more after he x-rays the body. So, how did you know there would be no bullet?"

"Just so we know that we're working on the same page here . . . We are working together . . . and sharing is a two way street, right?" said Oak.

"Yeah, yeah," said Whitworth, dismissively. "What have you got?"

"We have a bunch of bodies. We found a guy underwater in Lake George. He had been killed with a Fiocchi round. A few days later we found a young girl from Albany killed in Bolton Landing. Her neck had been slashed with one very professional looking stroke," said O'Malley.

"I don't see the connection – either with each other, or with my vics inside," said Whitworth.

"Yesterday a young man tried to rob a liquor store in Glens Falls. A customer was present who stepped in, and, without hesitation, took out the robber by slashing his throat with one fell swoop."

"You think it was the same guy?" asked Whitworth.

"I do," said O'Malley. "Not only that. I think it's a guy by the name of Myles Smythe."

"How does he fit in all this?" asked Whitworth.

"I'm not sure," O'Malley was forced to admit, "but there's something off about this guy."

"How so?" asked Whitworth.

"We've checked him out and he's not who he says he is. Plus, the body found in the lake has been identified as an international bad guy named Rizan Zakayev, who is also known as the Chechen. He's a killer, an arms and diamond smuggler, and who knows what else."

"Nothing is ever simple," said Whitworth. "Our two victims are the renter of this house, who we've positively identified as Keenadiid Amiin Kuciil and someone we're still checking out. Kuciil works as a baggage handler at the airport under the name Kenny Ames. He emigrated from Africa about thirteen years ago; no rap sheet; never been on our radar. The guy looks like a solid citizen. He was cut on his chest, but the M.E. says that the wound was superficial and would have bled some, but was not the cause of death. A G.S.W. to the head took him out. It looked like he suffered a bit before he died. In addition to the chest wound, one of his hands had been scalded."

"Someone wanted some information and they didn't care what they had to do to get it," said O'Malley.

"Looks that way," said Whitworth. "We were assuming this was a drug deal gone bad, but we have some problems with that."

"What problems?" asked Oak.

"First was you guys showing up with information that

seems to link all these cases together. None of our local bangers have figured out Fiocchi rounds yet, so we're dealing with some kind of pro. Second, is we can't find any drugs, cash, paraphernalia or anything else we usually see at a drug deal gone wrong. Third, our second victim has no ID except for an Egyptian passport we found in what we think is his car. It's his photo, but the name on it is a local hood who calls himself Jambo – who is on our radar. I know Jambo, and that's not Jambo lying on the floor in there."

"So, what's your current operating theory?" asked Kevin.

Whitworth took a deep breath and slowly blew it out through his lips.

"We don't have one," he replied, shaking his dead. "We're in the middle of an investigation."

"Well," said O'Malley, "if I were smuggling something through an airport, I'd want someone on the inside. And, if someone else wanted what I was smuggling, they might capture and torture my inside man."

"So, let me get this clear in my mind . . .," said Whitworth. "You think this Chechen was a smuggler and Smythe wants what he was smuggling. Smythe couldn't get it from the Chechen so he killed him and went after the inside guy."

"It's a theory," said O'Malley.

"It's a theory that doesn't explain the dead girl or the fake Jambo," said Whitworth. "Come back when you have some proof."

"Yeah, I never said it was a perfect theory," admitted O'Malley.

"Can we go in and look around a bit before we leave?" asked Oak.

"What for?" asked Whitworth.

"Just to see what we can see. New eyes on the problem, you know. Who knows what we'll find. Besides, O'Malley has this new iPhone, and he just learned how to take pictures, so I'm sure that he'll want to take pictures of the victims' faces for our chief."

"Put on booties and gloves. You can look but don't touch," said Whitworth.

The interior of the house was hellish. Portable lights on tripods made the room brighter than daylight. The bodies were eerily pale as the blood seeped out of them. The odor of drying blood and evacuated bowels assaulted their nostrils as soon as they entered the house. Officers, dressed in disposable paper suits, hoods, and gloves designed to prevent the cross-contamination of evidence, hovered over the bodies like silent guardians.

Oak, being careful not to interfere with the techs, made mental notes of the room's layout and furnishings. He examined, without touching, the bodies of the victims as he tried to reconstruct in his mind their last few moments on earth. O'Malley took iPhone pictures of the victims' faces and then wider range shots of the layout.

Kevin stood quietly, taking everything in. "The light is flashing on the phone," he observed. "Has anyone bothered to listen to the message?"

The techs all straightened up and looked at each other. The paper suits and masks hid the blushing that must have been going on as they each realized that no one had noticed the light, or listened to the tape.

"I am just saying," continued Kevin, "that we should probably listen. There might be something on it."

Whitworth was fuming at the front door that no one was moving. "Ferchristssake!" he said under his breath. "If you want anything done, you've got to do it yourself!"

He strode into the room and, using the barrel of his ballpoint pen, pushed the message button on the answering machine.

The room went silent except for the voice of Edgard: *"Hi, Kenny. This is Edgard. Listen, I have screwed up really bad and I am in big trouble. I never should have listened to Jambo. I did things for him I never should have done, and now I don't even know who, but someone, will be coming after me. Nubia and I have to leave town, but I couldn't go without saying goodbye. You have been a very good friend, and I don't know that I will ever see you again. You can reach me at the Winkelman's place*

on Lake George for a day or so; but, after that, who knows.
Please don't tell anyone anything about this. I just need to
disappear. If I ever can, I will call you and explain all this to you."

The message ended and the room remained silent for a
moment as the men absorbed what they had just heard, and
tried to make sense of it.

"Play it again," said O'Malley.

Whitworth replayed the message as he and Oak took
notes.

"Whit," announced Oak, trying out what he hoped would
be a nickname that would stick, "We've got to go. Bag and tag
that answering machine."

"Don't forget about the two-way street," yelled
Whitworth after them. "I'll want copies of all your reports . . . ,
and my name is *Detective* Whitworth!"

"You'll get them," said Lurman.

CHAPTER THIRTY THREE

Nubia and Edgard agreed that it was too dangerous for him to stay in Albany, or for her to return there. She had rented a car from Hertz at the airport in Syracuse, and the plan was for them to meet at the Gideon Putnam Resort in the Saratoga Springs Park. Edgard felt sure she would be able to return the car there, or they would go to a Hertz city office to drop it off. If anyone were following her, the trail would end in Saratoga.

Her trip was a fairly easy drive that would take about three hours. Until she reached Amsterdam, she would travel on I-90. At Amsterdam, she would cut north on MY-30 for a scenic trip to Saratoga. The racing season had not started, so the town would be relatively quiet.

Edgard's trip was shorter, just straight north on I-87, so he would arrive earlier, but he didn't mind. He loved to drive around this storybook-looking town, filled with beautiful Victorian homes covered in gingerbread trim. He had been there many times with the Winkelmans.

He drove by the racetrack to see the park-like picnic area in front of the grandstand. He peeked up at the steep slate roof over that historic grandstand. He stopped to watch the city workers installing the new flowers that spelled out the day's date. He parked and went to one of the public wells in the park and watched as people filled their water jugs. When they were done, he could not resist going over to slurp the delicious, cool, sweet spring water. He could not imagine that any water anywhere was ever better.

Acting like a tourist taking in the sights soothed his mind. He drove through town admiring the many decorated horses that artists had created for the local businesses. He drove through Congress Park, which he thought of as the most beautiful park in the world.

He travelled south to the beautiful Avenue of the Pines, the canopied road that leads into the heart of the Saratoga Spa State Park. Even though it was early, he could see the golfers out on the course that ran along this portion of the road.

His first sight of the Gideon Putnam Resort brought back a flood of memories to Edgard. When he first arrived at the Winkelman's home, he was shy and suspicious of them. Life with his own family on their subsistence farm had been hard. No one, except the priests back in Africa and Mr. Skip Mackey from Catholic Relief Services had ever shown him any kindness. When the Winkelman's gave him fine clothes and a clean place to sleep, he was not sure how to react, how long it might last, or what they expected in return. Nothing good ever seemed permanent to him.

The Winkelman home was old and modest by American standards, but it was right on the waters of Lake George, and seemed like a palace to Edgard. One day, shortly after his arrival, he was sitting on the dock when Mr. Winkelman called to him and asked him to get in the car for a surprise. A terrible feeling of foreboding overtook Edgard, and he was sure he was being taken away and would not get to return with the Winkelmans.

Instead, they took him to Blessed Sacrament Catholic Church in Bolton Landing. It was there he first began to learn of Blessed Kateri Tekakwitha, the Lily of the Mohawks. He believed it was through her intercession that he began to feel comfortable in the strange surroundings in which he found himself. After Mass, they went for his surprise to something wondrous called "brunch." It was at the Gideon Putnam brunch that for the first time Edgard began to believe that he had a new, safe home, and that the Winkelmans would lovingly care for him.

In the years that followed, that belief and that hope became the new reality of his life. To his disbelief, and his great joy and relief, these people loved him, selflessly cared for him, and made him part of their family.

Every time he came back to the Gideon Putnam and saw

the sturdy red brick colonial style building, that feeling of being safe would surge through him and lift his spirits. Today was no different. He parked his car and walked up to the outdoor café in the front of the building to sit under the broadly striped green and white awnings and wait for Nubia. He ordered tea and a scone while he waited.

Edgard loved Nubia with all his heart. He felt closer to her than to anyone else he knew. Yet, there was a part of him that did not fully understand her. She seemed to have clothes that were more expensive than her job would allow. He loved how smart she was, but it made him uneasy about how that mind of hers worked, and how quickly she could come up with a plan – such as she did for getting the package out of the airport. It troubled him that she had taken it upon herself to open the package, and he still wondered why she had waited so long to call him.

Shaking off all doubts, he smiled and thought of how they would have a whole life together to sort out these mysteries.

"Guess who?" said Nubia, as she covered Edgard's eyes with her hands from behind.

"Is it someone I love?" asked Edgard, delighted that they were finally together.

"I hope so," she said coyly.

"Is it someone who is very talented?" he asked.

"Some might say so," she responded.

"Is it someone very beautiful?" he asked her.

"Only if you say so," she responded.

"I know who it must be!"

"Who?" demanded Nubia.

"It must be Lupita Nyong'o," said Edgard, laughing as he did so. His laugh was rewarded with a playful slap to the back of his head.

"As if Lupita Nyong'o would give you the time of day," pouted Nubia.

"I was wrong. It is Nubia. I have never been so happy to be wrong!" he said, standing and taking her into his arms. He kissed her gently on her lips, but after a moment she pulled away.

"Edgard!" she scolded. "There are people watching us!"

"Let them watch. They may never see such love as ours again in their lives," he said, as they both sat down at his table.

"Did you know that was a true story, and Solomon Northrup was kidnapped by slavers not two miles from where we sit?"

"Who?" asked Nubia.

"Solomon Northrup from the book and movie, *Twelve Years a Slave.*"

"Oh, that Solomon Northrup," said Nubia. "You must forgive me. It has been a long drive and I am distracted. I will not feel safe until we have hidden the package!"

"Then you shall feel safe soon enough. We will go to the Winkelmans. They are very eager to meet you, and while you get to know them, I will go and hide the package."

Nubia's smile faded a touch before she forced it back into place.

"But I thought we were going to go together."

"Yes, but I started thinking about it. This is the perfect time for you to meet my American family. I have thought of the perfect spot to keep the package safe, but once I am out on the water, there is nothing I can do to protect you if we are attacked. No, I think it is better that I go alone."

"I will never feel safe unless I am with you. I cannot bear the thought of us being separated, even for a brief time," said Nubia, determined not to be separated from the diamonds.

"There is strength in numbers. We will protect each other," she continued.

"I love you so much," said Edgard. "I just want to protect you, but I will be happy to show you the beautiful lake if you insist on coming with me."

Edgard had a hiding place that he had decided was foolproof and untraceable. He knew Nubia would want the diamonds there.

His plan was to leave them there until the Chechen came for them and then finally he would be free of this burden.

Her plan was a bit different.

CHAPTER THIRTY FOUR

Hilman had fallen sound asleep on the couch in front of the television. Neither the grating pre-cooked basketball debate between Stephen A. Smith and Skip Bayless, nor the bright sunlight streaming through the two story windows of the A-frame disturbed his slumber. However, the touch of the cold, steel barrel of Smythe's Glock to his temple brought Hilman from REM sleep to full alert status in an instant.

Hilman was startled by the unexpected presence in his home. He attempted to jump up, but Smythe, anticipated the reaction, and struck him with the butt of the gun. Danny saw the proverbial stars and sank back into the couch.

"Who the hell are you?" asked Hilman, as he tried to clear his head.

"You'll figure that out soon enough," said Smythe. Danny knew immediately by the accent that it must be the Englishman the others had met in Dunham's Bay.

"So, where are your mates?" asked Smythe.

"You'll figure that out soon enough," said Hilman, earning yet another blow to the head.

"Don't be a bloody blighter!" advised Smythe. "It isn't good for your health. Now, I'll ask again. Where are your mates?"

"They should be home soon," said Hilman, "probably with the police, so you might want to think about leaving soon."

"I don't think so. It's kind of homey here, and I have a few more questions for you," said Smythe.

"Really? Like what?" asked Hilman.

"Like what were you and your friends doing diving on the bateau?"

"What bateau?" asked Hilman, to stall while he tried to clear his head.

"Wouldn't be that you were searching for a king's ransom in diamonds - my diamonds, by the way - would it, mate?"

"Diamonds! What diamonds? I don't know anything about any diamonds," said Hilman. "And if you think I do, then I'd like a little bit of whatever you're smoking."

"Ah, so that is how it is going to be," said Smythe.

"That's the way it has to be if you keep asking me about things I know nothing about."

"I suppose you know nothing about the Chechen either?" asked Smythe.

"Here's what I know," said Hilman, surprised to hear a second reference to the Chechen in one night. "The cops want to talk to you, and I expect them here at any time, so this might be a great time for you to get the hell out of my house!" yelled Hilman.

"Smashing idea," said Smythe. "Let's go. I have the perfect place for us to sit down and have a nice long chat," said Smythe, pleasantly, "until you tell me what I want to know," he continued, the tone decidedly more threatening. "Stand up and put your hands behind your back," he ordered harshly.

"I don't think so," said Hilman. "I've been up all night. I think I'll stay here and go to bed."

"Going to bed is not one of your options," said Smythe.

"Oh, good, I have options," said Hilman. "What are they?"

"Cooperating with me and getting out of this alive, or dying where you sit on that couch in about three seconds," said Smythe, as he backed away from Hilman while reaching out his arm and aiming the Glock at Hilman's face.

"I think I'll go with the cooperation option," said Hilman, as he slowly stood up from the couch, turned around, and put his hands behind his back. Hilman had no illusions that he was going to get out of this alive. He just wanted to get the gun out of his face for a moment to create an opportunity to act. To do something, anything, was his goal. He realized his odds of success were pretty low, but it was better to die fighting than to be herded like a sheep to slaughter.

As soon as he felt the first brush of the plastic handcuffs against his wrists, he leaned back, dipped his knees, and launched himself backward into Smythe's body, hoping the gun would not be in a position to fire.

The maneuver caught Smythe by surprise. He tried to step out of the way but lost his balance, and fell over a stuffed bear that was used as a footstool, landing hard on his back. Years of CYO basketball had made Hilman an extremely effective street fighter.

Rage, sparked by having a gun pointed at him in his own home, had triumphed over reason. Now, Hilman's goal was less to save his own life than it was to take Smythe's life. Hilman's thrust backward caused him to fall backward as well, and he landed on Smythe. He could hear the wind being knocked out of Smythe, and he saw the Glock slide across the floor toward the door and out to the deck.

Hilman sprang up and prepared to deliver a mighty series of kicks to Smythe's ribs. The first kick landed with a sickening thud. Hilman was certain that he had broken some ribs with the blow. Remembering the gun, he turned to go for it, but Smythe was quicker. Rolling onto his side, he grabbed for and caught Hilman by the ankle. Hilman tried to spin to get in another kick, but his efforts resulted in his falling to the floor, banging his head on the piano bench on the way down.

Wasting no time, Smythe was on top of the prone and dazed Hilman. He began striking him with his fists about the head and face. Smythe's knee was on top of the bicep of Hilman's left arm, pinning it to the floor. The pain was intense, but did not prevent Hilman from reaching up with his right hand and grabbing Smythe by the throat.

The blows to Hilman's face stopped as Smythe moved both his hands to Hilman's wrist, in a desperate effort to try to pull the other man's hand from his throat. Hilman clung to Smythe's throat with a grim determination, tightening his grasp on the Englishman's windpipe, knowing that if he let go, he would lose the fight - something he was not about to do. Smythe could feel himself getting light-headed, and knew he would soon pass out.

Smythe gave up trying to remove Hilman's grip on his throat. Instead, he grasped Hilman's wrist with his left hand and let go with his right. Reaching out with his right hand, he was just able to grab onto a cast iron statue of a grinning bear posed on his back, limbs up, in order to cradle a wine bottle. The bear, sans wine bottle, was sitting on the end table next to where the two men were struggling. Smythe raised the statue up and smashed it down on Hilman's head before Danny realized what was happening.

Smythe felt immediate relief when Hilman's hand dropped from his neck. Exhausted, Smythe, as he struggled to catch his breath, dropped the cast iron bear and rolled off Hilman.

Lying on the floor next to Hilman, he looked over at him. Hilman was laying perfectly still, blood seeping out of a wound on his forehead, just at the hairline.

*   *   *

"I can't tell whether I am too tired to eat or too hungry to sleep," said Oak, as he drove north on 9N through Diamond Point.

"I say let's stop at Donny's and grab some bagels to eat on the way back to the house so we can go right to bed," suggested Kevin.

"What's the sense of going to bed now? It's 10:00 in the morning. Danny probably slept all night and is ready to go out on the boat," offered O'Malley.

"That ain't happening!" said Oak. "I have guns in my trunk and I know how to use them!"

The three men drove on in sleepy silence for a while until they heard a distinctive *whoop whoop* and turned to see a police vehicle behind them with its blue lights blazing.

"Are you kidding me?" asked Kevin, plaintively.

"It's all right. It's Reardon," said O'Malley as Oak pulled his car into the parking lot of Chic's marina,. Once the car stopped, all three got out to greet the chief.

"Morning, boys! Don't you all look fresh as daisies!" said Reardon with a smile.

"You try being up all night," said O'Malley.

"I was," said Reardon, who actually did look well rested and energetic. "I guess it is just a matter of clean living and lots of exercise, not that you fellows would know anything about that."

"I hope you have a better reason for pulling us over than busting our balls," said Oak.

"Actually, I do. I have a bunch of news to share with you."

"Does it have anything to do with recommendations for breakfast?" asked Kevin, "Because all I want to do is eat breakfast and go to sleep for a couple of days."

"If you do that you'll miss all the information I have for you," said Reardon.

"Oh, yeah," said O'Malley, "What've you got for us?"

"First off, thanks for going to Albany to check out the double homicides, and for reporting back to me so quickly. It really helped. I'm starting to think that the murders there are connected to the murders here," said Reardon.

"Really? Why?" asked O'Malley, immediately warming to the topic.

"I got a call from Detective Whitworth right after I talked to you guys. He still has no idea who the victim with the phony passport is; but, as you know, the other guy is an African who came to this country years ago and he works as a baggage handler at the Albany airport. They're talking to all the baggage handlers down there right now to see what they can turn up."

"It makes a certain amount of sense," said O'Malley. "As I said to Whitworth, if Rizan Zakayev is some kind of international smuggler, he would want someone on the inside at the airport to either intercept his goods before they went through security or customs, or to get them on a plane bypassing customs."

"But why kill him if they needed him?" asked Kevin.

"Too many reasons to even speculate now," said Oak.

"What about the names in the message from the

answering machine?" asked Kevin. "Were you able to figure out who they were?"

"The Albany P.D. questioned the shift supervisors at the airport where the victim worked. They say there is an Edgard Onobanjo who works there and who they think was friends with the victim. Edgard is not a common name, so they went to check him out. The cops went by his apartment, but it had been cleared out. No idea who this Nubia is yet, but Jambo is a bit more than just the local thug Whitworth described."

"How so?" asked Kevin.

"Well, he has a well traveled passport, and seems to have a lot of money and connections. According to Truak . . ."

"I hate that guy!" said O'Malley.

"Yeah, I know, but get over it," said Reardon. "He was able to give me some background that might be helpful, and he feels bad about what happened to you. The Homeland Security guys have been keeping a close watch on Jambo. He has some very nasty friends that he visits in Africa – a lot. They seem to think that he has ties to rebel groups, terrorists, human traffickers, and arms dealers. Mainly, he brokers deals; but, our government and the governments we are working with want his bosses, and so far they have not been able to make the connections necessary to make a case. They lost him a few days ago when he flew, they think, to Egypt, but our CIA agents on the ground there either didn't get the message, or didn't care to do anything, but we have no idea where he is now, or what he might be doing."

"Any idea how he connects with that Chechen guy, Rizan Zakayev?" asked Oak.

"No," said Reardon, "but we have identified some people named Winkelman in the area. They live down in Diamond Point."

"That's good," said O'Malley. "If we can find this Edgard, maybe we can start getting some answers."

"There's more," said Reardon. "Thanks to Danny's efforts we know where your Brit buddy has been hanging his hat up here, and I'm on my way to get a search warrant."

"That's great," said Matt. "Where's he staying?"

"He's in a small log cabin on the road below Juniper Hills," said Reardon, "a place called Thousand Winds."

"That's pretty ballsy, hiding in plain sight," said O'Malley.

"It is, and it gets better, but way scarier," said Reardon. "After I dropped Danny off at his house, I got a call from Homeland Security.   From Matt's photo and their facial recognition program they were able to figure out who Myles Smythe really is," said Reardon, pausing to heighten the drama of the announcement.

"Don't keep us hanging, Chief!" said Kevin.

"The guy's real name is Ian Booth Parkington."

The three men looked at each other with blank stares, and finally, Oak spoke up.   "Is that name supposed to mean anything to us?"

"No, not really," said Reardon.   "Parkington was trained as a field operative by the British for MI-5.   He did a lot of deep cover work.   According to the guy I spoke to at Thames House, either Parkington was not psychologically suited for the work and they missed it during their vetting process, or, he was okay when they trained him, but he snapped while undercover."

"What is Thames House?" asked O'Malley.

"It's what they call the headquarters for MI-5," replied Reardon.   "Try to stay focused, will you.   I know you're tired, but what I'm about to tell you is important, and I need to know you fully understand it."

"Don't worry, I'm with you. Go on," said O'Malley.

"Parkington was well regarded for a while and he was highly trained in all types of weaponry – hand to hand, explosives, investigative techniques, etc.   They sent him on what they called 'wet work' . . ."

"You mean they trained him to be an assassin," said Oak.

"Bingo.   But they got nervous when he went off the reservation.   He was always kind of a lone wolf, but he was refusing assignments in order to work on his own projects.   He would disappear for months at a time, and often had no explanation for where he had been or what he had been doing.

He was refusing to account for money he was disbursing, other than to say it was for confidential informants, and he was suspected of killing some bad guys that they were watching, but didn't want dead."

"So, what's he doing here?" asked Kevin.

"They have no clue, or at least that's what they claim. They kept watch over him for a while after they fired him," replied Reardon, "but, eventually, they lost track of him. They're sending an agent over now to assist in his apprehension."

"I still don't get it," said O'Malley. "If Parkington is our guy here, who is Myles Smythe?"

"They were shocked when I asked them the same question. MI-5 has a department that creates false identities. Myles Smythe is one of those identities, but their records show it was never authorized for use in any of their operations."

He continued, "What they do is cook up a back-story and then they create real documents like bank accounts, driver's licenses, credit cards, passports, and more – basically, whole life histories and addresses with occasional moves. As the years go by, they keep them active, and they continue to add layer upon layer of information into public records that can easily be found by anyone who cares to look. It gives the undercover agent's false identity real authenticity. Then, when they are ready to put someone out in the field, they have a ready-made, longstanding identity and personal history for the agent to learn and then assume as his own."

"That's pretty amazing," said Kevin.

"What's truly amazing is that somehow Parkington expropriated the Myles Smythe cover before he left, without them even knowing it had been stolen. They had no idea that the cover was activated. According to them, it is an impregnable cover story because it's so rich in details."

"Pretty arrogant of the Brits to think they could create a perfect cover," said O'Malley. "Did you tell them we checked with the school in London he was supposed to work at and they had no idea who he was? Doesn't seem so impregnable!"

"I did," said Reardon. "They claim they build in what

they call Tripwires in every story. If an undercover agent begins to suspect that someone doubts his story, he drops some information that, if followed up, will lead to a Tripwire, which is just a civilian who has agreed to help MI-5. When contacted, the civilian, who knows very little beyond the false name and the false story as it would relate to them, are supposed to verify the story and then call a phone number that only the agent has, to let him know than an inquiry has been made."

"Oh, this is bad," said Kevin.

"How so?" asked Oak.

"In this case, the Tripwire screwed up and he put the lie to the cover story. If he then called Smythe, or Parkington, or whatever we call him, he probably told him that he said he had never heard of Smythe, so now Smythe knows that we know he's not a schoolteacher. "

"Oh, crap," said O'Malley.

"That's exactly what the guys at MI-5 thought," said Reardon. "They think we should assume that Parkington knows his cover is blown, and that we need to be very cautious in dealing with him. We are to assume he is armed, and we know he is dangerous. They predict that, given his past history and skill set, he will try to hunt you guys down."

"There's good news," said O'Malley.

"Oh, it gets worse," said Reardon. "During the exit interview process, the shrink who examined him concluded that he was a sociopath. Months later the shrink's office was broken into, and the only thing they could figure was missing was his file on Parkington. Two days later the shrink was found dead, wearing a jester's cap, drifting past Thames House in a rowing shell, and Parkington went missing."

"Wow," said O'Malley, softly.

"I don't have either the manpower or the qualified people to put an around-the-clock guard on you," said Reardon, "so I want you to go back to Hilman's and stay locked down until we can sort all this out."

"Mike, the locks on Hilman's house won't keep a guy like Parkington out," said Oak.

"No," agreed Reardon, "but at least you know now that

he might be coming, and that you have to take steps to protect yourself. Oak, I do take some comfort in the knowledge that you know how to protect yourself."

"Are you saying what I think you're saying?" asked Kevin.

"Counselor, you're not in Florida now, and we don't have a Stand Your Ground law in New York; but, even so, I bet you're familiar with your common law rights under the Castle Doctrine, isn't that right?"

"Yes," said Kevin, clearly not happy at the prospect of either being killed or killing someone else.

"Well, that's all I'm saying. You have rights. Use them. Protect yourself and you have nothing to worry about. Just be sure it is Parkington and not some hunter walking through the woods, or some UPS guy."

"Mike, you better get going. You don't want to keep the judge waiting," said Oak. "And we have to get going so I can explain the Second Amendment to my lawyer buddies here."

"Good idea," said Reardon as he got back into his vehicle. The three men stood silently, each with his own thoughts, as Reardon's vehicle disappeared down the road.

"Time to get back to the house and to my car," said Oak.

"Why to your car?" asked Kevin.

"So, I can show you how to exercise your Second Amendment rights!" said Oak.

CHAPTER THIRTY FIVE

The biblical David made it a point to choose his own battlefield when he went up against Goliath. Smythe intended to do the same thing as he decided that Hilman's A-frame, with its open floor plan, multiple doors, and giant windows, was indefensible if the other three men were to return.

He checked Hilman's breathing, which was shallow but steady. The bleeding had slowed from the forehead wound. Alive, he was a burden, but he might be a useful bargaining chip; and, at the least, should he ever awaken, he might even provide useful information. Smythe decided the only course of action was to leave, and to take Hilman with him.

Danny, had he been able to stand, would be about six foot two inches tall and solidly built, so he proved to be a bit of a task to move. The job was made easier because Smythe had no concern about either further injuring his hostage or in covering up his crime. He backed his rental car partly into the garage to obscure his activities from view.

Grabbing Danny by the ankles, he spun the body around and dragged him through the living room and dining room areas, through a sliding door to a breezeway, and then down a set of steps leading to the garage. Hilman's head banged against each tread on the way down.

Smythe had to struggle to get the body off the floor and into the trunk of the car, where it was unceremoniously dumped. He was in pain from the struggle with Hilman. He rubbed the ribs on his left side, which, he concluded, were not fractured because he was still breathing fairly normally. He bent into the trunk and punched Hilman in the stomach.

"That's payback for kicking me!" he said to the

unconscious Hilman, as he placed zip ties on Hilman's wrists.

It was dangerous to travel around in a car with a captive in the trunk. Too many things could go wrong. The victim could scream for help; or he could find the emergency trunk release; he could kick in the back seat. The last thing Smythe wanted was a public confrontation with his prisoner. There was little time, but Hilman had to be dumped somewhere so he could pay a visit to the Winkelmans.

Close by to the cabin Smythe had rented was another whose owner had chosen the name Live Free, after the motto on his New Hampshire license plate. It appeared that it had not been occupied for a while. Smythe, always thinking ahead, had realized he might someday need a second cabin.

Using the pretext that he was visiting a neighbor when he had spotted Live Free, and was charmed by its rustic trappings, Smythe had called a realtor and tried to rent it. He was quite pleased to learn that it was owned by someone the realtor described dismissively as an "old coot" from New Hampshire who refused to rent it, and rarely used it. That was enough for Smythe. He had moved in and kept a watchful eye on his own rental, Thousand Winds, just in case he ever received unwanted visitors. The realtor, who had many other cabins, was disappointed that the caller had no interest in anything but the Live Free cabin. When he asked why, the caller had laughed and remarked, "What is it you chaps say are the first three rules of real estate? Location, location, location."

Smythe was certain that by now the authorities, or at least that O'Malley chap and his crowd, had probably discovered that he had rented the cabin called Thousand Winds, and that they intended to surprise him there. There would be a surprise alright, but it would not be on Smythe.

*   *   *

Peter and Mary Ann Winkelman were excited from the moment Edgard had called and said he was bringing Nubia with him for a visit. He had dated before, but this was the first time he had brought a girl home, and Mary Ann could tell from the sound of his voice that this was someone special.

She immediately want into high gear, cleaning, baking and ordering Peter to do a hundred tasks. Peter was excited as well, but not enough to stop reading his newspaper in his home, and he certainly did not intend to begin to wash windows. He felt the house was fine just as it was.

When Nubia and Edgard arrived, both Peter and Mary Ann rushed out to greet him. Edgard felt as though she were squeezing the life out of him as she tightened her hug and complained that he had gotten too skinny. Nubia received the same type of hug, but she was simply told how lovely she was, and how delighted they were to meet her.

Edgard left his bag with his clothes and few possessions in his car. He was carrying only a small box. Mary Ann could not contain her curiosity.

"Have you brought me a present?" she asked. "You know that's not necessary. Just your coming to see us is present enough."

Edgard looked embarrassed and did not know what to say. He now realized that he should have brought a small gift for the woman who had given him so much care, and whom he so seldom had time to visit anymore. He looked at the warm smile on Mary Ann's face and he felt lost. He knew she wanted him to call her "Mom," but he had never been able to bring himself to do it. The memories of his own mother and her tragic death were still too vivid for him.

Finally, he was able to stammer out softly, "No, it's not for you. It's kind of a secret."

"Oh, I love secrets," said Mary Ann, as she squeezed Nubia's arm while looking in her eyes and saying, "Don't you?"

Nubia had smiled her own dazzling smile, but said nothing.

"Leave the boy alone," said Peter. "He's all grown now and entitled to keep secrets if he wants."

"Let's go inside," he said to Edgard. "Mary Ann has made all your favorite foods, which also happen to be my favorite foods!"

"I love your cooking," said Edgard, "but I have told Nubia of how beautiful the lake is early in the day. Can I please use the boat for a little while? When we come back, we can eat all the wonderful things you made, and spend some time together, I promise."

"I suppose that would be alright," said Mary Ann, trying to disguise her disappointment.

Then she brightened and said, "I think we would all enjoy a cruise to whet our appetites!"

"Actually, I was hoping that Nubia and I could take the first cruise on the lake together, by ourselves," said Edgard.

"Oh," said Mary Ann, now making no effort to hide the hurt she felt.

"Come on, don't be like that," said Peter. "Don't you remember when we were young?"

Mary Ann smiled and nodded a wan smile as her mind erased the years, and transported her back to a time before marriage and children, to when she and Peter would always engineer time to themselves. Life, family responsibilities, and all their other duties made that seem like such a long time ago.

"Have fun," she said. "Besides, I still need to go to Hannaford's, and I need Peter to do the heavy lifting. We should be back in a few hours. Will that work for you?"

"Perfect," said Edgard.

"How did this turn so bad, so fast, for me?" muttered Peter. "I don't want to go to the grocery store!"

"But, I need your help to carry the groceries," said Mary Ann, "and we may as well go now while Edgard is out on the lake."

*   *   *

The morning sun was high in the sky by the time Oak pulled into the driveway at the house in Mohican Heights. The stop at Donny's Market had been productive. The supplies secured included an assortment of bagels, cream cheeses, bear claws, doughnuts, fudge fancy cookies and newspapers. In other words, they had acquired all the ingredients necessary for a meal plan that would have been approved of by no one over the age of five.

Too hungry to wait and too eager to get to sleep, the men tore into the supplies as they drove up from town. Now there was little left except the newspapers, a gluten-free bagel purchased by accident in their haste, and a few crumbs.

"I just want to sleep for three days," said Oak as he headed for the back deck.

"We're getting too old to be skipping dinner and then staying up all night," said Kevin.

O'Malley stood on the driveway and looked at the house, feeling that there was a great mystery before him, but he just couldn't put his finger on what was wrong. Then it hit him.

"Guys!" he called out. "The garage is open! Why would the garage be open? We have Danny's car."

He stood there sleepily waiting for an answer that he really did not expect to come.

"Holy crap!" screamed Kevin. "There's a lot of blood!"

Both Oak and O'Malley ran inside. There they saw Kevin standing near the couch, staring at the floor. Furniture was knocked from its normal location and a lamp was lying on the floor. A grinning bear stared up at them, incongruously, given the condition of the room. Clearly, there had been a struggle.

"Danny!" yelled O'Malley, and then he paused, waiting for a response that did not come.

"Danny!" Again, no response.

"He's not here," said Oak grimly as he pointed to the blood smear leading to the garage.

He walked out of the room following the trail.

"What do you think happened?" asked Kevin.

"There was a struggle, and whoever lost was dragged out to the garage. Since the blood trail ends there, my guess is that the loser was loaded into a vehicle and taken away. My guess is that Smythe has Danny."

"Why?" asked Kevin.

"Because," replied Matt, "if Danny were the winner, he would have left Smythe where he fell and called the police. The question is whether Danny is alive or not."

"I'm sure he is," said Kevin. "If this was Smythe, he

made no effort to take that girl from the garage to cover up his crime. If he took Danny, it's because he is alive, and he has some use for him."

"I agree," said Oak. "Let's get going."

"Going? Where are we going to go?" asked Kevin. "Shouldn't we call the police?"

"Absolutely, we should," said Oak. "We can call from the car," he said, as he opened the trunk of his car.

O'Malley and Kevin immediately followed him. Oak handed each of them a handgun and a couple of ammo clips.

"You'll need these."

"Do you have a plan?" asked O'Malley.

"Yeah, I'm going to Juniper Hills and find that cabin. What did he call it?" said Oak.

"Thousand Winds," filled in Kevin.

"Yeah, Thousand Winds. If we find the cabin, my guess is we will find Danny."

"What about the cops?" asked Kevin.

"We'll call them, but we can't wait on them," said O'Malley. "They have too many rules, too many procedures. Danny could be dead by the time they're ready to act."

"He's right," said Oak. "Besides, we are the police, remember? Or, at least we are official consultants. What could go wrong?"

CHAPTER THIRTY SIX

The teakettle was just coming to a full boil, the comforting sound of the whistle alerting Smythe that the water was ready. He was prepared to endure many hardships, but he was not willing to compromise on some things, such as a proper cup of tea. Filling his grandmother's sterling silver tea ball infuser with Taylors of Harrogate Pure Assam Estate Loose Leaf Tea, which was the only brand he would drink at this time of day, he carefully placed it into a cup and poured the boiling water over it. Smythe was very particular about his tea. He would reluctantly use individual sachets if loose tea was unavailable, but he considered it a poor substitute, and that it showed a dreadful lack of breeding.

Hilman was prone and unconscious on the floor, softly groaning.

"I don't suppose you would be interested in a spot of tea?" said Smythe to the non-responsive Hilman. "Probably not," he said, shrugging.

The Live Free cabin that Smythe had appropriated was on the hill below the Juniper Hills condominiums. It was positioned in such a way as to provide both a view of the road and a view of the cabin he had actually rented. The road leading down to the cabins was narrow, steep, and full of potholes.

Oak put his car into its lowest gear in order to spare the brakes. The roar of the engine downshifting was the first notice that Smythe had that visitors were approaching.

Peering through a gap in the curtains, Smythe immediately recognized the car as one of the vehicles that had been parked outside of Hilman's house. The car was moving slowly, as the occupants were craning their necks to read the tiny signs announcing the names of the cabins, that acted a substitutes for more normal addresses.

"Your mates are stout lads to be coming after you so quickly," said Smythe to the still unconscious Hilman, "but not too bright," he noted as they drove past the driveway leading to the Thousand Winds cabin. As they disappeared out of sight, Smythe muttered, "What are they up to?"

*   *   *

"Good God, could your car make any more noise?" complained Kevin, as the car's engine roared in first gear, in an effort to slow the car's descent down the steep hill.

"I could put it into neutral and roll down silently," said Oak, "at least until I burn out the brakes and we make a big splash in the lake!"

"There it is!" said O'Malley, pointing at the small, unvarnished sign with the crude lettering spelling out Thousand Winds.

"Shall I pull in?" asked Oak.

"No, keep going," said O'Malley. "There's a cul-de-sac at the end by the docks. Let's check it out first and then decide what to do."

"I agree," said Kevin, as they drove past the entrance. "Someone is there. There's a car parked outside."

The drive the rest of the way to the docks was very short. There were a number of boats bobbing at their moorings, and a few at the dock. There were a few cars parked by the docks, owned by the fisherman who treasured an early start, but there were no people around. Oak swung the car around the cul-de-sac, but stopped before beginning to go back up the hill.

"What's the plan here?" asked O'Malley.

"I can't believe that Reardon doesn't have someone posted to watch this place," said Oak.

"He doesn't have a lot of experienced people in his department," said O'Malley.

"So what? Call in the Sheriff, or the State Police, but get some help. He's out getting a warrant to search the place. He should be taking measures to be sure nothing is disturbed until he gets his warrant," said Oak.

"Maybe we should wait until he gets here," said Kevin. "If we go busting in without a warrant and get incriminating evidence, we could blow the whole investigation. You know, everything excluded under the Fruit of the Poisonous Tree Doctrine, and this guy walks on a technicality."

"We can't wait for Reardon," said O'Malley. "If Danny is in there, he is in danger, and we need to act now!"

"I agree," said Oak, grimly, "and given what we know about this English guy, the last thing we need to worry about is his trial. If he is in there with Danny, he isn't just going to give up. He ain't walking on anything. This ends here, and it ends now."

"Okay, then," said Kevin. "I'll ask again. Do you have a plan?"

Oak grinned widely, "Of course I do!"

"Great," said a relieved Kevin, "what is it?"

Oak cocked his head to the side with the same quizzical look a dog gives when confronted with a command they fail to comprehend.

"We're going to make it up as we go along, aren't we?" said O'Malley.

*   *   *

"What are they up to?" muttered Smythe, as he patted his pocket to insure he had his Kershaw Blur knife. Walking across the living room, he lifted the Glock from the kitchen counter, released the clip, and snapped a new fully loaded clip into place.

Striding purposefully toward the front door, he looked at Hilman long enough to confirm he was still out. He tucked the Glock into the waistband of his trousers and stepped out onto the porch. For a large man, Smythe moved gracefully and silently through the underbrush as he positioned himself to see the south and front sides of Thousand Winds.

By his estimation, the men would either drive back up the road and pull into the driveway, or they would park their car below at the dock and hike up through the woods. Either way, he was positioned to observe their movements.

Smythe listened intently for any sound of their approach. He had amazing powers of concentration and he was able to filter out the inconsequential sounds of the pleasure boaters and the birds as he tried to discern footfalls and unnatural rustling coming from the hill below him.

"It truly is an advantage to be defending the high ground," he thought, as he saw the first of the men coming up the hill. It was the tall one they called Oak. He had calculated that this one would be the most difficult of the four to kill, but he was about to make it so easy for himself that it hardly seemed fair.

Next, and about twenty yards to Oak's left, he saw O'Malley. He was staying low to the ground, but every once in a while he would pop his head up above the underbrush to get his bearings. He was on a course that would bring him directly to Smythe. He had calculated that O'Malley would take less than thirty seconds to kill, but he did not want to kill just one of them. Smythe wanted to kill them all, so he was forced to alter his position and move closer to the cabin that contained Hilman.

He did not see Kevin, but was confident that he would be coming up the hill slightly behind Oak and to his right. There was nothing to do now but to wait. He positioned himself so he could again see the front of the cabin. Oak was the first to cross the clearing from the underbrush to the cabin. Smythe watched as Oak peeked in through the window and into the living room.

Smythe knew what he would see. A carefully staged tableau with food on the table, a television playing, and lump on the couch that appeared to be a man covered in a blanket who had fallen asleep, allowing his newspaper to cover his head and torso. It looked all so homey and lived in.

When Oak waived the other two men onto the porch, Smythe knew they would all be dead in minutes. He took out his phone and punched in the number for the triggering device. The charges had been placed to blow the walls out, and cause the roof to collapse, thereby inflicting the maximum number of casualties on those who were in the cabin, as well as those who were approaching the cabin. He did not have to wait for them to enter the cabin to kill them. He looked down at the phone and calmly pressed, "SEND."

*   *   *

The Volvo Penta engine on the Winkelman's yellow Four Winns F244 turned over immediately, and puffed out just a tiny cloud of white-blue smoke as the engine engaged with a low, throaty, muffled rumble. Edgard had been well schooled in the operation of this boat, and he was familiar with all the old boat's idiosyncrasies. He let the boat idle as he helped Nubia aboard.

Peter helped with the lines and passed some cash over to Edgard, saying, "I don't know how far you're going, but do me a favor and stop for fuel along the way. I'll be using the boat this weekend, and if it's warm the stations will be packed. So fill 'er up!"

Edgard smiled and promised he would as he was undoing the mooring lines from the cleats on the dock. Peter put a foot on the gunwale and gave the boat a push away from the dock as Edgard put the boat into reverse. After clearing the dock sufficiently, he put the boat into forward and patiently swung the bow around to head north on the lake. Once positioned properly, he pushed down on the throttle and the boat leaped forward and quickly came up on plane.

Peter and Mary Ann stood on the dock watching until the boat was nearly out of sight.

"They make a handsome couple, don't they?"

"Yes, they do, but let's not get too far ahead of ourselves," said Peter.

*   *   *

Smythe stared in amazement at the still standing Thousand Winds cabin. There had been no explosion! *"Impossible!"* he thought. He looked down at his phone and saw the problem. Where there should have been signal strength bars, he saw a damnable two word message *"No Signal."*

When he looked up, the three men had dispersed, one to each side of the cabin; and Oak was still on the porch, apparently trying to pick the lock.

Smythe knew what he had to do. He always had a backup plan. He had been there long enough to know the vagaries of cell service around Lake George so he had taken the precaution of adding a backup detonator to the charges he had installed in Thousand Winds. The backup detonator was a low frequency receiver, simple, reliable - not unlike a garage door opener. However, it was currently out of his reach, and back in Live Free.

He began to move as quickly as he could back to the cabin. He was obligated to move further south, deeper into the woods, in order to avoid detection by O'Malley, who had positioned himself on the south side of Thousand Winds. This lengthened his journey back to get the transmitter and left him temporarily without a view of Thousand Winds.

When Smythe got closer to Live Free, he broke into a run, nearly flying up the steps and across the porch to enter the cabin. Coming in from the bright sun to the dimness of the small cabin, it took him a moment to adjust his vision and realize that Hilman was no longer on the floor where he had left him.

As his eyes adjusted to the dim light, Smythe saw the box with the transmitter he needed on the breakfast bar separating the kitchen from the living room. From the corner of his eye, he saw a movement. Turning to his right, Smythe saw Hilman with a steak knife pressed between his knees, trying to saw through the plastic ties that bound his wrists. Both men locked eyes and froze in place for an instant. Then all hell broke loose.

With a guttural roar of rage, Hilman jumped up, the steak knife clattering to the floor, and charged forward at Smythe. The distance was short and Hilman was at full speed after just a step. Lowering his shoulder, Hilman ran into Smythe and drove him across the room and into the log wall of the cabin.

The impact was not good for either man. A searing pain shot down Hilman's arm from his shoulder, causing his right hand to go numb. Smythe had the wind knocked out of him and the ribs that had been previously injured now caused a searing pain to circle his torso. The pain in Hilman's shoulder made him react by stepping back and shaking the shoulder, in a futile attempt to lessen the pain.

Despite the pain that had Smythe doubled over, his MI-5 training kicked in. Instantly and instinctually, Smythe analyzed his options. He had to get to the detonator before O'Malley and his group found that Thousand Winds was nothing but a Potemkin village and left it; but he also had to neutralize Hilman.

His gun would be effective at stopping Hilman if he shot him, but Smythe feared that Hilman would not be subdued by a mere display of the Glock. By now, he must have realized that he was not getting out of this alive. With nothing to lose, desperation might compel Hilman to reckless action. Shooting him was out of the question, since it would alert the other three men, and perhaps bring them to the Live Free cabin to investigate.

Grasping the Kershaw Blur knife, he straightened up only to see Hilman readying another attack. Hilman charged at him, the fury evident on his face. Smythe quickly stepped aside and slashed the knife toward Hilman's stomach, aiming to hit just inches below his sternum and then drive the knife upward toward his heart. Hilman saw the knife coming and awkwardly stepped to the right to avoid the blade, which missed his stomach, but did slash across the underside of his left forearm.

Smythe had put so much force into the thrust with the knife that his own momentum swung him around, long enough for Hilman to recover his footing and charge at him again. This time Danny struck Smythe in the back with his forearms and elbows, driving Smythe face first into the wall. Before Smythe could regain the advantage, Hilman raised his cuffed hands and grabbed all the hair he could, and repeatedly slammed

Smythe's face into the log walls, which quickly became slick with his blood.

Smythe was trained to fight dispassionately. Emotion, he was taught, would make him the victim. He would never allow himself the self-indulgence to become as enraged as Hilman was, which gave Smythe the advantage of clear thinking. Hilman had ignored the fact that Smythe still had his knife. Grasping the knife with all his strength, Smythe blindly reached back and plunged the knife into wherever he could reach.

The mark it hit was Hilman's ass, where the full length of the blade was embedded to the hilt into the side of Danny's right cheek. Roaring in pain, Hilman disengaged briefly from the assault on Smythe. Smythe immediately headed for the breakfast counter where he tore open the box with the transmitter.

Hilman had no idea what was in the box when he saw it. All he knew was that if Smythe wanted it, it must be important; and, he was going to stop him from getting it. Oblivious to the pain that each step caused him, Danny staggered toward the breakfast bar, the knife still embedded in his gluteus maximus.

Smythe held up the transmitter, and, with a demonic smile said to Hilman, "It is time you said goodbye to all your friends."

The cabin was filled with a blinding, unnatural yellow light for a brief moment, followed immediately by the ear-shattering noise of the explosion that tore Thousand Winds apart. The compression wave from the explosion caused the windows of Live Free to rattle violently. Dazed and confused, Hilman had spun around to look in the direction the sound and fury was coming from when his world went black.

CHAPTER THIRTY SEVEN

For the first time in weeks, Edgard felt wonderful and free. Out on Lake George, his troubles seemed to vanish. The woman he loved was next to him, and he felt that his future was limitless. The water sparked in the mid-morning sun more than any diamond could hope to do. The clean, sweet air, and the shimmering water made him believe again that everything would work out.

Heading further north on the lake the boat plowed through the waves and occasionally sent a cooling spray washing over the bow and splashing onto Edgard's face. The water seemed to cleanse him of all his soul-crushing worries.

Once the diamonds were hidden away, his problems would be over. No longer would he worry that the package would be discovered by accident, and either be stolen or found by the authorities. The former would result in his death when he was unable to produce the stones for the Chechen and Jambo, and the latter would cause him to be arrested and deported. Neither outcome was acceptable to Edgard.

This was the only way. When this man they called the Chechen finally came forward and demanded his diamonds, Edgard would be able to deliver them to him.

"How much further?" asked Nubia.

"To where?" asked Edgard.

"I don't know. You have always talked about the Eye of the Needle and the Little Chapel," said Nubia. "I thought it was your favorite place and you would hide the diamonds there."

"Ahh, you mean Hecker Island," said Edgard. "We will not be going there."

"Why," demanded Nubia. She had been so sure that was

where he was planning to go that she had already purchased a navigational chart for Lake George, and knew just where Hecker Island was so she could return there without Edgard.

"So where are we going to hide the package?" continued Nubia.

"In a place that has been safe for hundreds of years from all searchers."

"Why are you talking in riddles?" asked Nubia.

Edgard had been following the west shore of the lake ever since they left the Winkelman's Diamond Point home. Now, as he passed Three Brothers Island, he nosed the bow of the boat to the starboard and headed east, crossing the lake south of Dome Island. In the distance, the huge white clapboard cupola of the Sagamore sparkled in the bright sunshine.

"Because I know something that no other man knows," he said, smiling broadly.

"What do you know that no one else knows?" asked an increasingly suspicious and irritated Nubia.

"Do you know who Kateri Tekakwitha is?" he asked.

"No," she replied impatiently.

"Well, you would know her if you grew up around this lake."

"What is so special about her?" asked Nubia, fearful that Edgard may be dividing his loyalties between her and a former girlfriend. She did not need any competition until she had figured out how to sell the diamonds.

"She is now a saint. She was a Mohawk Indian who lived in the sixteen hundreds. She renounced the religion of her tribe and became a Catholic. She suffered greatly for her faith and was ostracized by her tribe, but she refused to renounce her new faith."

Nubia shrugged her shoulders as if to say "*so what,*" but she said nothing. She tried to hide her relief that there was not another woman in Edgard's life now. That would have made it so much more difficult to manipulate him.

"You don't understand. The Europeans had come to North America and were forcing the Indians out. Kateri

Tekakwitha was a hero. She was also a person of color, like me. When I was a boy, I learned all the stories and legends about Kateri."

"Why would you bother?" asked Nubia.

"I felt so out of place here for so long. You must know how it feels to be the only African in your school. All those dead European explorers we learned about meant nothing to me, but Kateri Tekakwitha, she was like me. She spoke to me. She was living among the Europeans and, even though they didn't fully accept her, she knew their God better than they did. She was better than they were, and now she is a saint and no one remembers most of them. She was the hero I needed. She let me know that I too could be so much better than the people around me assumed I would be."

"That's a lovely story, but I still don't understand how that helps us hide the diamonds," said Nubia.

"One of the legends surrounding her life is that Father Isaac Jogues had a small box containing a treasure of inestimable value. The Mohawks had killed him, and since Kateri's father was a chief, he came into possession of the box. Her father and mother died when she was quite young and an uncle took her in. The uncle was kind to her, even though she was becoming an outcast in her tribe for converting. When she ran away to a Mohawk tribe near Montreal that had all converted to Christianity, he gave her St. Isaac Jogue's treasure box to take with her."

Nubia was doing all she could to resist the urge to do an eye roll.

"Kateri kept the hand-carved box, which was shaped like a turtle. She never shared with anyone what was in the box, but she was never without it until she felt she was close to death. Then she entrusted it to a young English soldier who had recognized he had a vocation and had committed to going to a seminary if he survived the war. The soldier was sent to Lake George to battle the French at Fort William Henry. Before the battle, he hid the turtle box in a cave along the shores of Lake George to keep it safe. The young soldier was killed in the battle and the box was lost."

"I still don't see how any of this helps us. It's just a silly legend," said Nubia, dismissively.

"No! It is not! I have seen the turtle box!"

*　　　*　　　*

O'Malley had seen it once before, on Bass Island. He did not know how stable it was back then, nor did he fully understand just how powerful an explosion such a small block of C-4 could unleash when it was thrown to him. However, he fully understood now that, if this block of C-4 he was looking at ever detonated, it would flatten the cabin and kill everyone in a fifty-foot radius.

"Shit!" he said softly under his breath as he backed away from the window into which he had been peering. He ran to the front of Thousand Winds, looking for his friends.

"Stop what you're doing," he said in a stage whisper to Oak.

"What . . .?" began Oak.

"No questions. Just get away!" said O'Malley as he turned the corner and grabbed the back of Kevin's Hawaiian shirt and began tugging him away from the cabin.

"What are you doing?" demanded Kevin.

"No time, no time, just move!" urged O'Malley as he broke into a run. He saw Oak sauntering down the steps from the porch as if he had no cares in the world.

"Oak, for christssake, RUN!" he yelled at him.

Oak got the message that time and began to run from the house, catching up to the other two without any effort.

"Matt, you never could run to save your life," he said, as the three came to a stop under some trees about seventy-five yards from Thousand Winds.

"Saving my life is just what I was doing. Yours too!" puffed O'Malley.

"Say what?" said Oak.

"I think the cabin is rigged to explode! I saw a block of C-4 pressed into the wall in the side bedroom," said O'Malley.

"How would you know what C-4 is just by looking at it?" asked Kevin.

"I've seen it before. This was a grey block of clay-looking stuff."

"So what. How do you know it's not Silly Putty or Playdoh that some kid had left behind?" asked Kevin.

"Well, if it is Silly Putty, it has wires coming out of it, and it is attached to something that looks like a detonator," said O'Malley. "I'd rather be wrong and embarrassed than right and dead!"

"Good point," observed Oak, nodding his head sagely.

The three men jumped at the next sound.

"If you boys were deer, you would all be dead right now," said Dave Lurman.

"Holy crap! You scared me," said O'Malley. "What the hell are you doing here?"

Lurman could not help but laugh at the look on the faces of the three men.

"Reardon sent me here to keep an eye on the place while he secured the warrant. A better question is what are you guys doing here?"

"When we got back to the house, there was evidence of a struggle, blood on the floor, and Danny is missing. We think that Smythe is holding him in there."

"I'd better call this in to Reardon," said Lurman, lifting his shoulder radio.

"It gets worse," said O'Malley. "Tell him to get a bomb disposal unit out here too."

Lurman's eyes widened at the mention of the bomb disposal unit.

"You think that there a . . .?"

A tremendous pressure wave knocked the men to the ground and stole the breath that Lurman needed to finish his sentence. A fireball rose into the sky as the walls blew out, spraying the area with flaming shards of the log cabin. The roof initially rose into the air and then settled back neatly onto the footprint of what once was Thousand Winds, and burned intensely in the bright sunlight.

The men were lifted off their feet by the force of the explosion and thrown down the hill. When they landed, their bodies slammed into the ground since they had no ability to try to lessen the blow. Their bodies landed in bushes twenty feet from where they had been talking.

They were no longer talking. If they were, they would have commented on the grey rental car that was speeding up the hill from the cabin behind where Thousand Winds used to stand.

CHAPTER THIRTY EIGHT

No amount of cajoling or pleading on Nubia's part could change Edgard's mind. He was going to hide the package in the cave he had discovered so many years before. He considered it lucky and he considered it sacred. He believed that God had a purpose in mind when He had allowed only Edgard, out of the hundreds of seekers over three hundred years, to discover the cave.

Edgard had kept the secret. He never mentioned the cave to anyone until he disclosed it to Nubia this very day. He considered it his duty to St. Kateri Tekakwitha to preserve her treasure. She never let other eyes see it, and he would honor that principle.

"What if someone else knows of this cave?" she asked.

"No one knows," Edgard assured her.

"How can you know that?" she asked, getting desperate. She knew she could find her way back to Hecker Island and the hiding place. However, she knew nothing of boats or underwater caves; she could not even swim.

"I know because the others who have sought out Kateri's treasure only wanted riches or fame. They would have exploited the turtle box for their own benefit, and the newspapers would have printed big stories. They were not pure of heart. They did not love Kateri as I do. They did not pray to her daily as I do. That is why only I have been allowed to discover the hiding place."

"This is not only for you to decide. We both own the diamonds. What if something should happen to you? How will I be able to get my diamonds?" she demanded.

Before he could answer, they both heard something

massive and distant, like a rolling clap of thunder, but the skies were completely cloud free. Edgard slowed the boat and looked back over his left shoulder. At first, he saw nothing, and then he saw the fireball somewhere beyond the Sagamore. The Sagamore's cupola flashed a bright orange color for an instant, nearly as quickly turned to red, and then, just as quickly, returned to its normal, gleaming white. In the distance, further than the Sagamore, he could see the enormous plume of grey and black smoke drifting into the sky.

For just an instant, he thought he saw the face of St. Kateri Tekakwitha looking down on him from the smoke plume. It made him shiver with fear that he had displeased Kateri somehow.

In that instant, he made up his mind. He could not betray the saint, and he was beginning not to trust Nubia.

"They are not our diamonds. They are not my diamonds. They are not your diamonds. I never wanted them, and I wish I never heard of them; but, since I do have them, I am going to give them to the only person I have ever been told has any right to them, the Chechen."

"You fool!" exploded Nubia, now overwhelmed with frustration, feeling that the diamonds were slipping away from her. "No one is coming for the diamonds or they would have been here already. Who lets millions of dollars of diamonds just sit around with some stupid, worthless, baggage handler?"

"I am not as stupid as you may think," said Edgard, as he tried to ignore the pain deep inside him that Nubia's insult had ignited. "I know you care for those diamonds more than you will ever care for me."

Nubia realized her error and tried to recover.

"I don't want the diamonds just for me. I want them for the life we could have together!"

She did her best to look chagrined and adoring at the same time. It was not working.

"I also know that you are willing to risk my life to steal the diamonds. What would I do if Jambo found out what I had done?"

"Jambo is not a problem. He is probably dead, anyway,"

said Nubia.

"Really?   He is probably dead?" said Edgard, incredulously. "And just how would you know that?"

"Utumbo told me."

"Utumbo?" bellowed Edgard.   "Why would you be taking to someone like Utumbo?" he demanded.

Nubia realized she had overplayed her hand.

"What does it matter? We do not have to worry about Jambo anymore, and we can be together always."

"No, I think Jambo is alive and you are just using me to get the diamonds so you and he can be together," said Edgard.

His tone was neither angry nor sad. It was just resigned to a truth that deep-down he had always suspected. A girl like Nubia, who claimed to be of royal heritage would not want to spend time with *"some stupid, worthless, baggage handler."* The romance had been too quick, too easy. He realized at that moment that he had been set up all along.

It was now shockingly apparent to him that he and Nubia were not meant to be together. It was also painfully clear that her definition of treasure would never be the same as his definition of treasure. He made a decision.

Edgard changed heading and set for Dome Island. Dome Island is known to all who ply the waters of Lake George, although few have ever been on the island. It is set aside as a bird and nature sanctuary and the law prohibits anyone from going on the island. It is the largest island on the lake with no docking facilities.

"Where are we going?" screamed Nubia.

"We are going nowhere," replied Edgard.   "You are going to Dome Island," he continued, as he pointed at the hulking, foreboding form heaving out of the water in front of them.

"No! I am staying with you!" she yelled, no longer able to contain her rage.

"You are going to Dome Island where you will stay until I hide the diamonds. I cannot trust you to know where St. Kateri's treasure is hidden."

"And what if I refuse?" asked Nubia.

"Then I shall throw you overboard," Edgard said, matter-of-factly.

The coldness of Edgard's response robbed her of all hope that she could change his mind. She had neither a weapon nor the physical strength to resist him. In desperation, she lunged for the package, but Edgard saw her movement and blocked the hatch leading to the storage space that held the package. He pushed her back onto the captain's chair.

"The water is one hundred and sixty-five feet deep where we are right now," said Edgard, squinting to see the depth gauge on the dashboard. "If you do not behave, I will throw the diamonds overboard and tell Jambo you stole them."

Nubia backed away from him, frustration so completely overwhelming her that she began insanely spewing vituperative invectives at him. Edgard was stung by her hateful words, but they only served to increase his resolve.

As Nubia insulted his intelligence, his heredity, his virility, and proclaimed her undying love for Jambo, he knew that he was doing what St. Kateri Tekakwitha wanted him to do – preserve her treasure. The diamonds were trash in comparison.

CHAPTER THIRTY NINE

O'Malley hurt all over, and he was confused about where he was and what had just happened. His ears were ringing, but all other sounds seemed muffled and distant. He could see Mike Reardon kneeling beside Dave Lurman, who was sprawled on his back on the ground and apparently saying something to him. Other than the ringing, O'Malley could not make out any sounds.

He rolled to his side, away from Reardon in order to try to stand. It was then that he saw Oak sitting on the ground, his back against a tree, banging the side of his head just above his ear with the heel of his hand.

All this made no sense to O'Malley. *"We had just been talking when . . ., when what?"*

Next he saw Kevin lying on his side in a fetal position, not moving. Panicked, he abandoned his failed efforts to stand and began to crawl over to Kevin. He had a difficult time coordinating his arms and legs to crawl, so he wound up face planting twice before reaching Kevin.

"Kevin! Kevin!" he screamed at his prone friend. Kevin moaned and swiped at his face with his right hand. His eyes fluttered open, but he seemed to be repelled by the light and closed his eyes again.

"Wow! That was quite a boom!"

The ringing in O'Malley's ears had begun to subside, but he was still having a hard time discerning speech. "What? What did you say?" O'Malley yelled.

Oak started to stand. "He said thanks," Oak yelled. "You saved our lives."

"Oh," said O'Malley, not sure what Oak meant.

"Oh," he said again, as he realized that Thousand Winds had blown up and he remembered pulling on Kevin to get him away from the cabin.

"Damn," he said softly.

Lurman was not up and walking around. After cursory review, each man came to the conclusion that, while everything hurt, nothing was broken; and they would feel fine in a few days.

"You guys okay?" asked Reardon as he walked over to them.

"We're fine," said O'Malley, "but I don't think you're going to need that search warrant anymore. This just turned into a crime scene."

O'Malley yawned and stretched his jaw, in an effort to clear his ears.

"I can't believe what you have done! Any evidence in there is gone now thanks to your meddling!" said Reardon. "On the other hand, if you had not gone poking your nose into things, I would have served the warrant and maybe gotten blown up. So, on balance, it's all good."

"No. No, it's not," said Kevin. "We were poking our noses into this because we think Smythe kidnapped Danny. The five men looked mournfully at the shattered remains of the cabin. In the distance they could hear the sounds of the fire engines approaching the scene.

"If Hilman was in that cabin . . .," began Reardon, his voice breaking and trailing off before he could finish the horrible conclusion.

"Danny is not dead until we know for sure Danny is dead," said O'Malley. "We've got to keep looking."

"No one is going to get in that cabin for hours," said Reardon, "and then we will just be sifting ashes."

"I know where to look," said Kevin.

They all turned and looked at Kevin, who was rubbing his neck and rolling his head to try to banish the pain he was feeling.

"Well, I don't know where to look but there is obviously a connection between Smythe and this guy, Edgard, who left a message on the telephone of our murder victim in Albany. It's reasonable to assume that Edgard is hiding from Smythe, and Smythe is trying to find Edgard."

"So, how does that help us?" asked Reardon.

"On the message, Edgard said he was coming to Lake George to hide out with someone called the Winkelmans."

"So?" asked Lurman.

"The Albany Medical Examiner put the time of death of the two victims at about the same time the message was time stamped on the answering machine."

The light went on for all of them at the same time.

"Smythe heard the message, and he's heading to the Winkelmans!" said Lurman.

"That's what I am betting on!" said O'Malley, as he started down the hill toward his car. "Reardon, you said you found some Winkelmans down in Diamond Point, right?"

"Let's go!" he yelled back at the group.

"Hold on for a minute," said Reardon, "none of you are in any condition to be confronting Smythe."

"You can come with us or you can stay here, but you'd better give us the address!" said Oak.

*   *   *

The members of the Bolton Volunteer Fire Department had responded immediately to the siren. Like thoroughbred racehorses responding to the bell as the gates open, the volunteer fire fighters had stopped whatever they were doing and bolted to the fire station.

The oversized garage doors were open as Smythe drove by the red brick building next to the athletic fields. He was a little amazed to see how quickly and professionally the volunteers had assembled and were donning their gear. Their conduct represented a selfless courage that was an enigma to Smythe, who had never experienced an altruistic moment in his life.

Smythe took some satisfaction from the knowledge that, no matter how fast they went, by the time they reached

Thousand Winds, the cabin would be reduced to a pile of flaming wood. There would be nothing left but a giant bonfire. The cabin sat in a small clearing, but the woods and underbrush nearby were quite dense. The real issue would be whether or not the volunteers could keep the fire from spreading and taking out the entire hillside of the Juniper Hills development.

Just past the firehouse, Smythe was stopped at one of Bolton's only three traffic lights, this one located at Sagamore Road. He glanced in the rearview mirror. What he saw was not a pretty sight. His nose seemed flatter than he remembered, and not quite lined up properly. He was peering through slits, as his eyes were swollen and blackened. He could see blood on his shirt collar. He smoothed his hair and squirted some water on his face from a bottle he found on the seat, in the hope of getting some of the blood off.

Ahead, he could see that Lakeshore Drive was teeming with summer tourists, shoppers, and traffic. A northbound wholesale food delivery truck had stopped to provision a restaurant, much to the frustration of a motorist coming from the opposite direction and towing a boat that was unable to make it past the truck.

Smythe had never been blessed with the virtue of patience, nor of very few other virtues if the truth be told. He could feel angry frustration rising in him. He knew he had to suppress it and maintain control of his emotions. He was so close now he could nearly feel the diamonds in his hand.

All the snooping around Hilman's house at Mohican Heights had given him a familiarity with the area. Not waiting for the light to turn green, he sped into the intersection. He was headed for the turn at Horicon, which he remembered would bring him eventually to Potter's Hill Road, where he could turn and go down Mohican Road to get to the south side of Bolton Landing and avoid the congestion in the hamlet.

Soon he was resuming his trip south on Lakeshore toward Diamond Point. The irony of the name was not lost on him, but he continued to focus on what he would do when he arrived. He did not like that he was going there with no pre-mission investigation except for locating the Winkelman home.

He did not know the land; he did not know the layout; he did not know how many people he would be confronting, or what their training or armaments might be. In other words, he was going in hot, blind, and reckless – something he rarely did. However, today the prize justified the risk. Besides, he was confident that he was a match for whomever he might encounter.

As he drew nearer Diamond Point, a northbound pumper truck passed him coming from Lake George Village. He smiled, assuming now that the fire had spread and they were calling for help. It suited his purposes that the fire would be the immediate concern of the local authorities, and would absorb all their resources.

Smythe turned left down a road marked "Private." Swinging from an arm extended from a slender pole was a series of wooden slats, each with a family name. Toward the bottom, he saw the name for which he was searching. Down the road, the asphalt soon turned into gravel. The homes were mostly older and seemed modest. The residents gave the impression that most were either vacation renters or enjoying their second home.

The Winkelman's house was at the end of the street, directly on the lake. Smythe stopped in the street to survey the property. The house was relatively small, a one-story affair that had the aura of a property that was loved and well cared for. Neat flowerbeds graced both sides of the driveway, and a large red elm shaded the front of the house. The lawn was neatly manicured, and there was no clutter anywhere to be seen. Near the street, a boulder standing about three feet high had been painted white and neatly lettered across the front was the family name, Winkelman. A pole, mounted at a forty-five degree angle, stuck out of the wall near the front door. From it hung a clean, bright American flag that hung straight down on this breezeless day.

Smythe was satisfied he had found the correct location. Everything seemed very quiet. He was trying to decide what to do next when a white man, appearing to be in his late fifties came out of the house and got into one of the two cars parked on the driveway. Smythe put his car in reverse and backed into the driveway of the house across the street from the Winkelmans. He still had a full view of the Winkelman property.

He saw a woman come out of the house. She was about the same age as the man, her hair was darker, and where the man had a sturdy build, she was more slender. She turned back toward the house and locked the front door. As she walked toward the car the man was in, Smythe could see she was carrying an armful of reusable grocery shopping bags. It seemed to Smythe that they were leaving and would be gone a long time to fill all those bags.

As the man backed the car out of the driveway the couple were engaged in an animated discussion and paid no attention at all to the strange car facing out of their neighbor's driveway. *"Two less problems to worry about,"* thought Smythe as he watched them drive away. Smythe took the small set of binoculars he had in the car and began to take a closer look at the property. He could only see the front and one side of the house. There did not appear to be a garage.

The only car left was an ancient looking Ford Taurus with an employee-parking permit on the rear bumper for Albany International Airport. *"Edgard, I've got you now!"* he thought to himself.

Probing his memory, Smythe tried to recall the names on the signs under the Private Road sign on 9N. Other than Winkelman only one name stood out in his memory, but that was all he needed. Taking a scrap of paper out of the drop he scrawled the words *Windsor – Diamond Point*. Now it was time to act the bemused tourist.

He would ring the bell at the Winkelmans and ask for help locating his lost friends, the Windsors. If the occupants were rude enough to ask about his appearance, he would claim he had been in a minor accident. It would give him the perfect opportunity to learn more about the lay of the land and to discover who was present. If his luck held, the only occupant would be Edgard Onobanjo.

CHAPTER FORTY

The three men sat in grim silence in the car, each preoccupied with what they feared was the fate of their friend, Danny Hilman. While it was all they could think about, no one was willing to broach the topic. Halfway up the hill they encountered the Fire Chief's Jeep coming down the hill. Each vehicle had to slow to squeeze past the other on the narrow road.

As they turned left out of Juniper Hills to go through the town, Oak was the first to speak.

"I know that Mike said he would dispatch officers as soon as he could, but when we get there, we have to be ready to do whatever is necessary to take Smythe down," he said grimly.

"Oak, we have no idea where Danny is, so we just can't 'take Smythe down,'" said Kevin. "We have to be able to question him. Besides, if we kill Smythe it will blow back on Reardon for giving us the information on how to find the Winkelmans. We've got to be smart about this!"

"I'm not talking about killing him. I'm talking about getting in fast and overwhelming him," replied Oak. "Believe me, I have every intention of conducting a thorough interrogation."

"Why not approach him from two directions?" asked O'Malley.

"What do you mean?" asked Kevin.

"We know that the Winkelman house is directly on the water. I think I can find it by boat while you two approach it by land. That way if Smythe bolts, one of us should be able to follow him," reasoned O'Malley.

"That makes sense, but you're not trained to take on a

guy like Smythe. It's too dangerous," said Oak. "I think we should stay together."

"I disagree," replied O'Malley. "It's too dangerous for us to take the chance of letting Smythe get away when he still might be holding Danny somewhere. I don't intend to go one-on-one with him. I'll just follow him if he leaves by boat."

"Matt's got a point," said Kevin. "This is the last lead we have on him. If we don't find him here, we are out of options to look for Danny. You said yourself we have to be ready to do whatever is necessary. This might not be ideal, but it's necessary!"

Oak looked ahead and saw how traffic was congested in town. Reluctantly, he agreed.

"Okay, it's your funeral. I'm going to circle around town. When I turn on Horicon, you jump out and run down to the Marina to get the boat."

"Got it," said O'Malley.

"You have your phone?" asked Kevin.

"I do," said O'Malley, taking it out of his pocket and waving it.

"Great!" said Oak. "Do you have any bars on it?"

"Uh, two."

"Wonderful cell service up here. Let's hope it works," said Kevin mockingly as O'Malley opened the car door.

"I'll see you at Winkelmans." He called to them as he crossed the street and started toward the Bell & Langston Marina.

"Hold on! Hold on!" yelled Oak.

O'Malley spun around and came back to the car. Oak pushed a small black 9mm SIG P 938 through the window.

"Don't you think this might come in handy?"

"I suppose," said O'Malley reluctantly, as he took the small weapon and slipped it into his pants pocket.

"Don't go crazy with it," said Oak. "You only get six shots with it."

"Let's hope I don't need any," replied O'Malley.

"You can hope for whatever you want, as long as you're ready to do whatever you need to," said Oak.

"Stanislaus," said O'Malley, knowing it would irritate Oak if he used his proper name, "you are always such a barrel of laughs."

*   *   *

Smythe could see his reflection in the storm door window. His appearance would certainly alarm anyone who answered the door, but he did not have the option to wait until his normal handsome features returned. He rang the doorbell and waited. No one came. He again rang the bell, this time holding it down even longer. He strained to hear any sounds – footsteps, barking dogs, radios or televisions. He heard nothing. Was it possible no one was home? He tested the doorknob. It was locked.

Smythe rang the bell for a third time and waited a respectable interval before peering into the living room window. He saw no one. Affecting a casual saunter, he walked to the rear of the house, where he also found no signs of any occupant. There was a set of five steps leading to a broad porch painted battleship grey. Perched on the porch was a hammock and several red Adirondack chairs. There was a narrow backyard leading to a dock and boathouse, but he could see no boat.

Smythe was becoming convinced that no one was home. This disappointed him, but he took solace in the idea that he was now in a position to be better prepared for when they did arrive. That had to be Onobanjo's car with the airport parking permit on the bumper.

"He will be back," thought Smythe, *"and when he returns, I'll be waiting for him!"*

Smythe slowly climbed the steps leading to the porch. Pulling open the screen door, he turned the knob on a door leading to the kitchen. He was delighted when it yielded under the pressure of his twist. He was in!

He pulled out his Glock, crossed the threshold, and stopped just inside the kitchen to listen carefully. Not a sound was heard in the old house except for the loud, rhythmic ticking of a wall clock in the kitchen. Smythe checked every room until he was satisfied that the house was clear.

Going through the house a second time, he examined the displayed minutiae of the residents more closely to get whatever insights he could. There was the usual collection of family photos. There was a framed article from the Post Star about how the family had taken in a refugee from Africa, and how they were raising him as their own child. In the kitchen, there was a cookbook opened up to Sudanese recipes. In what he assumed was the master bedroom, there was a display of military honors awarded to someone who had been in the United States Marine Corps. Over the bed hung a crucifix. A picture was developing in Smythe's mind about the kind of people with whom he was about to deal. Once a Marine, always a Marine. He would have to be careful with Mr. Winkelman.

There were two other bedrooms, one appeared to be the room of a female child, painted pink and well stocked with stuffed animals and posters of boy bands. The other was a more masculine space, with shelves filled with plastic toys, and a fielder's mitt with a baseball jammed in the pocket held together with thick rubber bands that were dried and cracked. This room also had a poster of a Native American woman, depicted with a halo. It seemed incongruously out of place. Both rooms felt lost in time, as if once occupied by beloved children, but deserted by the adults they had become. Obviously the remaining residents could not bring themselves to alter anything for fear that it would destroy the happy memories.

As he was returning to the kitchen, he heard a noise that he was very familiar with, the screaming of an angry woman. He walked to the kitchen sink in order to look out the window. There he saw a man he assumed to be Onobanjo and a woman who he was sure, based on the photographs he had seen in her apartment, was Nubia. Nubia was making no effort to hide her disgust with the man. She could be heard plainly as she lambasted him.

"You are not a man. You are nothing but a sniveling coward! A real man would have kept the diamonds! A real man would have made a new life with the diamonds. You will be loading baggage and dreaming about the trips other people go on until the day you die!"

Smythe's ears perked up at the mention of diamonds. He was right. This was the day!

Nubia's insults became even coarser as they got off the boat. Onobanjo made no response. It was as if he had inoculated himself from the woman and nothing she could say or do affected him in any way. Finally they reached the bottom of the steps and he turned to her and said in a soft voice, "Woman, you may plague me all of my days, but you will never know where the diamonds are. If you will just shut up, I will take you back to Albany and neither of us need see the other again."

Edgard's exceedingly calm demeanor served only to fuel her rage. Once again she began a profane denunciation of the young man standing before her.

Smythe was not about to allow them to return to Albany. Stepping through the kitchen door, he walked to the edge of the porch before either of them noticed he was there. Nubia fell silent and her eyes went wide as she stared at the barrel of the large silver Glock that was pointing at her.

"I don't know about him, but you are beginning to give me a headache," said Smythe.

Too dumbfounded to speak, the pair stared up at him, unable to comprehend where he had come from, or what he could possibly want.

"Ah, silence at last. The neighbors will be so grateful," said Smythe.

"Please join me inside," he said, gesturing toward the kitchen with his Glock.

Nubia bounced her stare between the gun, which terrified her, and Smythe's face, which repelled her.

Edgard started up the steps first and Nubia followed. She had spent so much time with Jambo and his gang that she was used to violent men and was starting to regain her confidence.

"What happened to you?" she asked, as she started up the steps.

"Nothing to be concerned with," said Smythe. "I cut

myself shaving this morning."

"What were you shaving with?" asked Nubia, "a lawnmower?"

"I like you. We are going to get along just fine," said Smythe.

Both Nubia and Edgard had to struggle to adjust their vision to the dim kitchen after being outside for so long. Nubia's toe caught on a piece of linoleum that had curled at the seam and she stumbled forward. The sudden movement surprised Smythe and he swung the gun directly at her, but did not fire, when she quickly regained her balance.

"Both of you," he ordered, "sit in those chairs," gesturing with the gun for them to occupy the kitchen chairs on the same side of the table. They both did as directed and Smythe efficiently zip tied their wrists to the arms of the chairs. He went and sat opposite them.

"It is not necessary for us to spend a lot of time together. I think you will find the more time you spend with me, the less you will enjoy it."

"Hummph," sniffed Nubia. "If that is true, I have already spent too much time with you."

"Cheeky," said Smythe. "I like that."

"Are you the Chechen?" asked Edgard, hopeful that his long ordeal might now be over and he could deliver the package.

"Do I sound like I am from Chechnya?"

Suddenly it dawned on Edgard that he did not know if the Winkelmans were safe.

"Where are the Winkelmans?" asked Edgard. "If you have hurt them, I swear . . .." The oath trailed off as Edgard realized the hopelessness of his situation.

Smythe smiled indulgently at the young man.

"I am glad you two have so much to say. It will make this go easier. I don't want much. I just want what is mine. You tell me where the diamonds are and I let you go, as soon as I have the diamonds in my possession, of course."

Edgard and Nubia remained silent, he to protect the location of Kateri's treasure, and she, still hoping that somehow this turn of events would help her secure the diamonds for herself.

"Not talking, eh? Cat got your tongues?" asked Smythe.

Edgard and Nubia stared silently at their captor until Edgard asked again, "Where are the Winkelmans?"

Smythe sighed and said, "So, you are not going to cooperate. I was afraid it might come to this. Here's what's going to happen. I figure Edgard here got the package for Jambo, and at some point his curiosity got the better of him and he peeked inside. I bet you peed yourself when you saw all those diamonds," laughed Smythe.

"You are too naïve to figure out how to sell them, and too stupid to keep your mouth shut, so you told this one . . .," pointing his gun at Nubia, " . . . hoping to impress her. She is fine, and there is no other way you could get a woman like her."

Nubia nodded and smiled a smile that modestly said, *"That's all true, thanks!"*

"Well, maybe she loves you, maybe she doesn't. Whoever really knows about these things? I figure you're smart enough to know that you have to keep the diamonds under your control if you want to hold onto the bitch. However, if you don't tell me what I need to know, I will have to start killing people; and, since I can't kill you I'll have to start with her."

"Hold on now, just a minute," said Nubia, "I can help you with this."

"You see," said Smythe with a sad smile, "you can't buy loyalty. Lucky for you, I don't think she can help me. Right! Now, so once she is dead, the Winkelmans will be home from their trip to the market. If you haven't helped me by then, they will be the next to die. You don't want that, do you? The Winkelmans saved you from a horrible life in Africa, at least that's what the newspaper article said. Now the Winkelmans, they have earned your loyalty. It's all on you, Edgard. You have the power of life or death for this bird here, and for the Winkelmans. Don't let them die."

"Don't waste your time talking with him. I can help you," said Nubia. "We can find the diamonds together. We can share them. We could share a lot of things, if you know what I mean," she said, seductively.

"Oh, I know exactly what you mean. Do you know where the diamonds are right now? Can you bring them to me or me to them?"

"Not exactly," said Nubia.

"Then what exactly do you know?" yelled Smythe.

"I know we were just out on the lake and he hid the package," blurted out Nubia, eager to please her captor.

"So, you know where they are?" said Smythe with a smile, his demeanor changing so quickly that it was frighteningly unnatural. "Now we are getting someplace!"

"I wasn't exactly with him when he hid the diamonds. He made me get off on some damn island filled with bird crap. But I do know, generally, where they are."

"So, you are just wasting my time then!" said Smythe.

Her eyes widened with fear as she realized what was about to happen. She opened her mouth to scream *"NO,"* but was unable to produce a sound before the weapon discharged.

Edgard, who had witnessed all kinds of savage treatment of one human being by another during the war in his homeland, could have been desensitized by those experiences to the killing of Nubia as just one more brutal act in a life filled with brutal acts. However, the years spent in America with the Winkelmans had renewed his soul and had given him a different outlook on life. He was horrified by what he saw, by the feel of her hot blood splashed on his skin, and by the sound of the shot still ringing in his ears. He loved Kateri Tekakwitha, but he realized that he loved the Winkelmans even more. He knew what he would have to do.

*   *   *

The sun was shining brightly and Lake George was filled with boaters, oblivious to the drama playing out around them, enjoying one of those spectacular summer days that Mother Nature served up in the north country of Upstate New York. These days seem so much better than summer days elsewhere, but it is hard to tell whether they are actually better, or just seem so compared to the challenging winters experienced by the locals.

O'Malley, however, was not enjoying what the day had to offer. Normally he would be admiring the homes along Millionaire's Row, and watching the unending variety of watercrafts that ply the waters of Lake George: dinghies cobbled together from old boards and canvas; elegant, antique, mahogany Chris-craft's; sleek cabin cruisers capable of crossing an ocean; and giant tour boats, some propelled by paddlewheel. Today he ignored all that. Today he was intently focused on just one goal – getting to the Winkelman home in Diamond Point.

O'Malley was so focused that he nearly failed to hear his phone ringing in his pocket. He had to put the boat into idle so he could hear.

"Matt, what's your twenty?" asked Oak without any other greeting.

"What's my what?" asked O'Malley.

"Sorry, cop talk. Where the hell are you?"

"Oh, yeah, I knew that," said O'Malley. "I'm just coming up on Basin Bay."

"Crap, what's taking you so long?" complained Oak.

"It's a great day so there was a lineup at the Marina to get out. To add to my luck, one of the forklifts wasn't working so it took a little longer than usual. Don't worry. I'll get there. What's your damn twenty?"

"Kevin and I have just turned into the subdivision, but we're parked and don't want to approach the house until you're in position," replied Oak.

"Okay, that makes sense. Get me oriented. Where is this place?"

"Do you know where the public dock is in Diamond Point?" asked Oak.

"Yeah, I think it's the one just across from the north end of Speaker Heck Island, near Gilchrist's."

"Exactly," said Oak. "Just beyond that you'll see a point of land on, like, a peninsula. The house should be right there if

I'm reading this GPS correctly."

"Got it. I'll give you a call after I pass the Yankee Boating Center. I'll be close then and we can coordinate our approach," said O'Malley as he shoved the throttle forward and ended the call.

*   *   *

Edgard stepped back onto the Winkelman's boat as he had a couple of hours before. Back then he was beginning to feel great about his life. Sure, he had problems, but he had a plan, and he had the love of a beautiful woman. What more could he want? He believed there was nothing he could not overcome with Nubia at his side.

Now, as he stepped onto the same boat, things had changed. He was humiliated at how blind he had been to Nubia's deceptions. He had put the Winkelmans in danger. He looked back longingly at the house he had spent so many happy days in, saddened by the conviction that he was not going to return to see it ever again. He did not expect to return alive from this voyage. He would be all right with that as long as the Winkelmans were safe, and as long as he could protect Kateri's treasure.

Edgard's reverie was ended as Smythe placed his foot on his shoulder and shoved.

"We don't have all day, mate," growled the Englishman.

Edgard lost his balance and fell to the deck between the seats in the bow, which, given his reaction, was one of the funnier things Smythe had ever seen.

"Stop playing around. We have diamonds to get," said Smythe. "Tell me again where they are."

"What difference does it make? If I told you a name, would it mean anything to you?"

Edgard had gotten himself up and had the engine running. As he spoke, he released the lines and threw them back onto the dock.

"I suppose not, but just humor me," replied Smythe.

"The place has no name that I know of, it is just an

underwater hole in a rock that I found years ago when I was a boy swimming off Mr. Winkelman's boat."

Edgard experienced a flash of regret that he had never called Mr. Winkelman "my father."

"I used to play pirate and hide my toys there."

Edgard kept the story as bland as possible. He did not want Smythe to know that the "hole" was actually an entryway into a cavernous room, only halfway filled with water.

Edgard had no idea how it had been created. Once he went in with a dive light to inspect it better. He imagined the space being created eons ago by a fortuitous piling up of boulders, creating this void as the ice sheets had retreated on their journey north.

Mr. Winkelman had told him stories of the great rock piles all over the area that he called moraines, just like the one that could be seen at the base of Deer's Leap. Edgard considered going in through the underwater entry and just staying in the room until this evil man would assume he drowned and just leave.

"Well, there's some real pirate booty in there now, lad, and I intend to make it mine," said Smythe, with an intensity that Edgard had never seen in any other human being. Sadly, he realized that Smythe would never give up. If he did not return quickly with the diamonds, he knew Smythe would come in after him and discover Kateri's hiding place. He could not allow that. This was a holy space, his to protect, and he could not permit its desecration by a man of such unadulterated evil.

Edgard pushed away from the dock and nudged the bow of the Four Winns north. He morosely sat in the captain's chair at the wheel of the boat while Smythe and his gun occupied the captain's chair next to him. Perhaps if he had not been so preoccupied with his impending death; or, perhaps if Smythe had not been so excited by the knowledge that he was finally just minutes away from possessing the diamonds, one or both of them would have noticed the green SeaRay Sundeck heading toward the cove.

*   *   *

"Talk to me," said Oak into his mobile phone.

"Alright. I have just gone by the Yankee Boating Center," said O'Malley, "and I think I see the point of land you were referring to."

"Great. We are up and rolling," said Oak. "I would estimate that we can be in position in the next few minutes."

"Okay, but I have to run by some shoals and warning buoys, so it will take me longer," said O'Malley.

"What the hell was that?" said an alarmed Kevin so loudly that O'Malley could hear him over Oak's phone.

"What was what?" asked a worried O'Malley. "I didn't hear anything."

"It sounded like a gunshot," said Oak. "We can't wait. Kev and I are going in," yelled Oak into the phone.

"Wait! Wait!" called out O'Malley, but he then realized that the call had been disconnected. Ignoring the danger, he sped the boat up, and aimed for the point of land in front of him.

Oak and Kevin arrived at the Winkelman residence within three minutes. Curious neighbors were coming out of their homes with looks that ran the gamut from dull confusion to outright fear.

Next door to the Winkelmans, on the lake, was a bungalow that, for the last twenty-five years, housed a rugged old woman named Marvel Fargo. Marvel was standing in the side yard of her house yelling for help. Oak ran to her and, too quickly for her to examine, flipped his retired trooper identification at her and said, "I am a Trooper, ma'am. What just happened here?"

"You're letting them get away! You're letting them get away!" she yelled. "I heard a shot!"

"Who is getting away?" asked Oak.

She pointed a gnarled hand at the dock and yelled,

"That man forced Edgard into the boat!"

Oak and Kevin looked up and saw the Four Winns speeding north on Lake George. Kevin immediately dialed O'Malley's number and just as quickly O'Malley answered.

"What's going on?" demanded O'Malley.

'It looks like we were too late. Smythe has a boat and he is going like a bat out of hell north on the lake. Do you see him?"

There was only one boat exiting the cove at a high rate of speed at the moment.

"I see him!"

The excitement was evident in O'Malley's voice. He spun the wheel hard and set a course to intercept Smythe. At this point Kevin could see the SeaRay, and he could see the radical course alteration.

"What are you doing? Come get us!" Kevin shouted, making no effort to hide his alarm.

"Sorry, buddy, if I come get you we will never find Smythe. I've got to follow him!"

"Matt! Are you nuts?" yelled Kevin.

"Probably, but you need to find your own boat," said O'Malley, just before he tapped the red circle and ended the call.

"Damn it!" said Kevin.

Stepping closer to Marvel and Oak, Kevin interrupted them and asked, "Lady, do you have a boat?"

"Of course I do! Who would live on this lake and not have a boat!"

"Sorry. Stupid question. We need to borrow it. Our friend is chasing the Winkelman's boat and is in great danger – and so is Edgard if we can't get to him."

"Oh, I don't know. I don't like to loan out my boat," replied Marvel.

"Sorry, but you have no choice," said Oak in his most commanding voice. "This is official police business."

"Couldn't you just shoot them?" asked Marvel.

"A pistol is not very accurate at this range, ma'am. I doubt I could hit them. I might hit your friend, Edgard, or I might hit someone completely innocent," said the Big Oak. "I'm afraid we must have your boat – and RIGHT NOW!"

"Well, I guess it will be okay then," said Marvel. "Come along while I get you the key. I bet Jim Rockford could have shot them."

CHAPTER FORTY ONE

Kevin ran to the dock as Oak and Marvel went to fetch the keys. In no time he had removed the canvas and found the switch to lower the cradle that was holding the boat into the water. The electric motor hummed as soon as he threw the switch, but the flywheel moved achingly slowly. He heard a screen door bang and he looked up to see Oak running toward the dock. Even at his age and size, Oak moved with remarkable grace and coordination.

What both men lacked was any particular skill at boat handling. They were proficient at boat riding, and expert at beer drinking onboard boats, but neither had ever felt the need to actually pilot one.

Oak jumped in the boat as it was still swinging in its cradle over the water and sat behind the wheel. Oak looked disgusted as he tried to make sense of the various switches and knobs as he searched for the ignition.

"Do you have any idea how to operate this thing?" asked Kevin.

"Sure, how hard could it be?" replied Oak, who usually assumed his superiority at any activity vaguely associated with masculinity. "You turn it on, this stick here makes it go. This is a steering wheel, just like a car. Bada bing, bada boom! No sweat! Fahgettaboudit! I'm just not sure where the brakes are!"

Oak found the ignition, inserted the key and gave it a twist. The engine roared to life. The motor was trimmed up and had yet to enter the water, so the sound was overwhelming - like a car without a muffler.

"That doesn't sound right," yelled Kevin over the roar.

"I think Danny does something and some electric thing tilts the engine down," Kevin continued to yell.

The boat was now fully in the water and floating free, but the water intakes still were not covered. Marvel stood next to the screen door, her hands covering her face.

Oak found the trim switch on the throttle and the engine settled into the water.

"See, I told you. Nothing to it!" said Oak, as he slowly moved the throttle backward, not completely engaging the gears and causing a grinding sound. He moved it back to neutral immediately.

"I think you just have to do that faster, with a bit more confidence," said Kevin.

Oak slammed the throttle backward and the boat lurched, struck the dock, knocked Kevin off balance, and resulted in Kevin's plopping onto the settee just as a wall of water washed over the transom.

Oak pulled hard on the throttle once again and the boat slipped into neutral and started to bob around on the lake.

"That did not go as well as I had hoped," said Kevin.

"Don't worry," said Oak, "I am much better going forward."

"You couldn't possibly be worse!" said Kevin.

"Yeah, yeah, just go ahead and dial up Reardon," replied Oak as he pushed the throttle forward and headed the boat north.

"We need him to get his patrol boat out, and to alert the Lake George Patrol boats. We need to have some cops looking for Matt and Smythe. Can you describe the boats to Reardon?"

"No! What do I know about boats?"

"Just call. It won't matter," concluded Oak. "Reardon knows what Danny's boat looks like, and if he finds Danny's boat he'll probably find Smythe's boat as well."

*　　　*　　　*

"Edgard, do you have any charts on board?" asked Smythe.

"There is a leather case with the charts," said Edgard, pointing to the hatch.

"Splendid!" Smythe threw open the door and got on his knees to reach in. As he did, he looked over at the glum Edgard.

"You seem sullen to me, Edgard. I do hope you don't mind if I call you Edgard. Do you, Edgard?" Smythe could not resist tormenting the young man.

"You have a gun. You can call me anything you want," replied Edgard, who was not even sure Smythe heard him, because by that time the Englishman was on his knees, with his head and shoulders in the tiny cabin, reaching for the chart case.

Finding it, he pulled it out and opened the case. Inside he found a chart, consisting of four sheets that covered the long, narrow lake. The sheets were difficult to manage in a moving boat, and Smythe did not immediately understand them. Frustrated, he shoved the chart pages at Edgard and ordered, "Stop the boat and show me where we are!"

As Edgard fumbled to straighten out the sheets in the wind, Smythe did a two hundred and seventy degree survey of the vessels off the stern, the port and the starboard sides. Nothing seemed out of place, except for one boat approaching aft, along his port side.

"Do you see that boat back there at about seven o'clock, about three hundred meters back?"

Edgard strained to see what he was talking about. "Yeah, I guess. What about it?"

"Do you recognize it?"

"No, I don't think so."

"Hmm, we'll see," mused Smythe. Turning toward the chart he asked, "So, where are we?"

Edgard pointed to their approximate location, south of Canoe Island.

"Alright then," said Smythe, "I want you to take us through here, between Assembly Point and Speaker Heck Island."

Edgard looked up at him and said, "That's not where you want to go. That's not where I hid your diamonds."

"That's where I want to go now!" said Smythe, "Just do it!"

"But, it is very dangerous," said Edgard. "It is very shallow and full of danger buoys."

"It is more dangerous not to do what I say," replied Smythe, still looking at the boat off his stern to the portside. He was convinced now that the boat had stopped. "Do it!"

Edgard made for the southerly tip of Speaker Heck Island as Smythe continued to stare at the mystery boat behind them, suspicious that it was shadowing their moves. "Are there binoculars aboard?" asked Smythe.

"I don't think so, but check in the glove box. If there are any, that's where they would be."

Smythe pawed through the glove box, thoughtlessly dumping the contents onto the floor. There were broken swimming goggles, old tubes of sunscreen, a flare gun, tissues, years of boat registrations, and dried out and moldy packages of peanut butter crackers. However, to Smythe's great frustration, amid the tide of debris that poured out of the glove box, no binoculars were to be found. "Damn," was all he said, as he stood and took two steps to get to the back of the boat, where he stared intently at the boat that had drawn his attention. It too was now moving and had altered its course to bring it closer to Assembly Point.

"I knew it!" he said, as he turned back toward Edgard.

What he saw was quite startling. There was Edgard, standing facing toward the stern, left hand on the wheel and in his right hand he was pointing the flare gun at Smythe.

"You'd better think about what you are doing," warned Smythe.

"Get off my boat," ordered Edgard defiantly.

*   *   *

O'Malley had never felt quite so alone. He was questioning the decision not to go in and pick up Oak and Kevin. Oak had experience and training at handling people like Myles Smythe, and he knew how to handle a gun. Kevin was always a valuable voice of reason, no matter how stressful the situation. The tiny 9mm SIG P 938 in his pocket was feeling like a cannon, and he dreaded the thought that he might actually have to fire the weapon. He thought he could if he had to, but he was not really sure.

He did a rough calculation in his mind about the time necessary to get into the Winkelman's dock, board two men and then get back into the chase. No, that would have been foolish. The speed of the boat he was chasing was so great that it would have disappeared, and they never would have found it in time on the vast lake.

The vibration in his pocket startled him. Relieved it was not the Sig, he pulled his phone out, saw it was Mike Reardon, and answered it. "Hi, Mike. I hope you're having a better day than I am."

"Matt, I want you to listen to me, and do exactly as I say," said an anxious police chief. "I just found out from Kevin that you are trying to intercept Smythe. Under *no* circumstances are you to engage with Smythe. He is a trained killer!"

"Well, what do you expect me to do? He's the only one who can tell us what happened to Danny!"

"I want you to keep in touch with me. I have a call in to the Lake George Patrol to render assistance, and I have Lurman going down to take the department's boat out after you. Just follow Smythe at a safe distance. Keep him in sight, but don't get too close!"

"Mike, it looks like he's stopping in the middle of the lake for no reason," reported Matt.

"Then you stop, too!"

"Okay, okay, I've stopped. Don't throw a clot!"

"Where are you right now," asked Reardon.

"I'm just south of the Golden Sands Resort," replied O'Malley.

"Okay, buddy, I'm sorry, but you're going to be on your own for a while. It will take Lurman at least forty minutes to get to our boat and make his way to you. All the Lake George Patrol Boats were deployed up around Hague doing some damn wolf pack enforcement detail. It will take them more than an hour to get to where you are."

"Maybe we'll get lucky and Smythe will continue to head north. That should close the gap and shorten the time."

"Let's hope," said Reardon. "Describe the boat for me."

"Okay, you know what Danny's boat looks like. I'm in that. Smythe is in an I/O bow rider, maybe twenty-two feet. It's yellow. There's no bimini up. That's all I've got, except, crap, it's moving again and it looks like it's heading toward Assembly Point."

"Okay, you can follow, but not too close. And keep this line open!"

"Sorry, Mike. I'll have to call you back. I'm down to twenty-three percent on my cell battery."

"No! Don't hang up!" yelled Reardon, but the call had already been disconnected.

*   *   *

"You don't know what you're doing!" said Smythe. "Just put down the gun. We can work through all this."

"I've seen how you work through things," came the sarcastic reply. Edgard never took his eyes off Smythe as he slowly tilted over to reach for the throttle and slipped it back into the neutral position. The boat quickly glided to a stop and rocked as its own wake hit it. "I'm sure you will be fine. Get off my boat and start swimming!"

"I don't think so, mate. I've come too far to leave without my diamonds, and you might call the police before I can get ashore. I'd tell them that you killed your lady friend, but who knows what they will believe. Besides, I don't think you have the goolies to pull the trigger."

"I swear, if you don't get in the lake right now I will shoot you," said Edgard, doing, at best, a fair job at sounding convincing.

The tour boat *Lac du Saint Sacrement* was steaming north along the west side of the lake and putting out a substantial wake, which struck the Winkelman's Four Winns, causing it to rock violently for a short time.

Edgard was knocked off balance and, as he grabbed for the top of the windshield to steady himself, he accidentally discharged the flare gun. The gun made a *zzzfffffpp* sound, as the red-hot ball shot out at Smythe.

Smythe was also struggling to keep his feet under him when he felt the searing heat of the flare zip past his left ear. The flare flew for about seventy-five yards, hit the water, and skipped like a flat stone for another few dozen yards. It shattered and then the hot fragments sank harmlessly into the lake.

Barely able to contain his anger, Smythe was quickly on Edgard and struck him firmly with the butt of his gun. "You are so lucky that I need you, or you would be in agony right now, begging for me to kill you," hissed Smythe through his clenched jaw. "I'll brook no more of this effrontery. The next time you give me cause, instead of me just getting my diamonds and disappearing, I'll get the diamonds and then I'll go back to your house and make you watch as I kill the Winkelmans. Do you understand?"

A desolate Edgard just stared at him with empty, hopeless eyes. "I asked you a question, boy," said Smythe, raising the gun again to threaten yet another blow. "Do you understand?"

"I understand," whispered Edgard.

"Good, then get back in your seat and let's get this boat moving." Smythe looked back at the boat he had been watching. At first he was relieved that he did not see it, but then he realized that the boat had come far enough north to have pulled even with them, but was keeping a respectable distance away. With his new heading, the trailing boat had moved into the six o'clock position.

When Edgard passed the warning buoy at the south end of Speaker Heck Island, Smythe ordered him to head north. The shadow boat was now out of view, blocked by the island. Edgard did as he was told, without question, and reduced his speed as they entered the No Wake Zone.

Smythe divided his attention between his young pilot, whom he did not trust, and the boat he was now sure was shadowing them. He was desperate to get possession of the diamonds, but he also knew that he could not outrun a cell phone.

He had no way of knowing whether the operator of the shadow boat was calling others to help, but it was a chance he was not willing to take. He would rather wait than lead others to his diamonds. However, he was also considering the possibility that he was being overly paranoid and that the shadow boat was nothing more than a family out exploring the lake. He had to be sure.

"Edgard, we need one more test." Edgard's heart sank even further as he thought he was about to endure some new torment at the hands of this evil man.

"I want you to take us between those two islands," said Smythe, pointing toward the tiny gap between Speaker Heck Island and Long Island.

Mr. Winkelman had always strictly forbade him from trying to navigate this hazardous route, so he hesitated.

"What's the matter, didn't you hear me? Turn this damn boat into the channel!"

Edgard did as he was instructed. The cat and mouse game was not on. Shortly after they entered the channel, the boat's bottom scraped an underwater rock outcropping and heaved a bit to the starboard.

"Careful!" cautioned Smythe.

The boat righted itself, and they continued on slowly. In a relatively short time, they cleared the channel and Smythe ordered him to stop. Edgard instantly put the boat into neutral and waited for further direction.

Smythe stood with his legs spread and knees braced against the settee for balance, as he strained to see back through the narrow channel, the Glock in his right hand at the ready. It was just as he suspected. As the shadow boat passed briefly through his field of vision, he knew for sure he was being chased. He saw O'Malley at the wheel of the shadow boat. He was talking on his phone as he darted his head all around, clearly searching for something.

"Go! Go!" urged Smythe under his breath. He had

always suspected that O'Malley and his buddies were hunting for his diamonds. He was not about to lead them to the treasure!

Smythe's boat was now in open water, the wind and current pushing it north. Long Island was sheltering it from O'Malley's view. Smythe had the boat run full throttle for about three minutes while he contemplated his options. Tapping Edgard on the shoulder, he made a slashing motion across his throat for him to cut the engine. The boat stopped just past the Ranger Station on Long Island.

"We have a change of plans," said Smythe. "You know this lake pretty well, don't you?"

"I guess. I spent a bunch of years living on it," Edgard said with a shrug.

"Smashing," said the Brit with the gun. "I want to ditch the boat, get off the lake, and I don't want anyone to notice us doing it. When we get off the lake, I want to find a car and get out of the area. How are you going to make that happen?"

Edgard just stared at him, trying to decide whether he wanted to help. He knew he did not want to go anywhere with this man, who eventually was going to kill him no matter what he did.

Smythe took his phone out of his pocket and waved it in Edgard's face. "Did I mention that, with one phone call, I can dispatch my associate to the Winkelman's house?" bluffed Smythe.

"I am thinking," said Edgard, picking up the navigational chart pages and leafing through them. He had an idea. Luck might truly be found where preparation, inspiration and opportunity intersect.

"I know the perfect spot," said Edgard with a broad, toothy smile. "I used to go there all the time when I was a kid. Right here," he said, as he placed his finger on the navigational chart.

*   *   *

O'Malley could feel the panic rising in his chest. *"How could this happen? This is a disaster!"* He turned his head in every direction as he passed the north end of Assembly Point, barely missing the danger buoy. It was time to fess up and beg for help.

"Reardon here," barked the Chief into his phone.

"Mike, this is Matt. I'm sorry, but I lost them," said O'Malley.

"How? Where did you lose them?" asked Reardon.

"I was keeping back, just like you said, and I thought they were heading over to Assembly Point to dock, but instead they went north between the islands and disappeared from my sight for just a couple of minutes. But, but the time I got there, they were nowhere to be seen."

"Go with your gut. What's your best guess as to where they went?"

"I don't know, Mike. Let me think. It's possible they went somewhere in Harris Bay. There are lots of boathouses and places to hide. Maybe even over to Cleverdale, and or even to Sand Bay, or what's that other bay over there . . .?"

"Warner Bay," filled in Reardon.

"Yeah, Warner Bay. That's it," said Matt.

"Pick one," said Reardon, "and start looking."

"None of them seem right. There are too many people. Whatever Smythe is up to, I doubt he wants witnesses," said O'Malley, as he continued to spin in the boat, hoping to get a glance of his quarry. "Let me ask you a dumb question. Can you get a boat through that channel at the south end of Long Island?"

"The one by Speaker Heck?" mused Reardon. "I guess, but you would be stupid to try. It's narrow, shallow, and full of rocks."

"That's why I didn't even look there. Damn, Smythe must have seen me following him. Mike, I'm heading north. I think the SOB slipped through that channel and is using Long Island for cover. I'll try to pick him up on the north end of Long Island."

"Go for it and keep me posted. I'll try to get the Warren

County Sheriff to get a copter up over the bays and the Lake George Village police to set up a roadblock at Assembly Point and Cleverdale, just in case. If Smythe tries to get off those peninsulas, we will get him."

O'Malley thrust the throttle forward, coaxing as much speed as he could from the MerCruiser engine. Picking up the phone, he went to his favorites list and tapped the line for Kevin.

"Hello, Matt," Kevin yelled into his phone.

"Did you get a boat?" yelled Matt over the thunder of the engine.

"Yes."

"Where are you?" asked O'Malley.

"We thought we saw you heading for that big island straight across so that's where we are headed," yelled Kevin into his phone.

"Don't bother. I lost him," admitted O'Malley. "I think he's on your side of Long Island. Just stay over there on the west side and go north. I'm doing the same thing on the east side. I'll meet you at the north end, unless one of us spots Smythe first."

"Okay," said Kevin, clicking off the call. He tapped Oak on the shoulder and pointed in the direction he wanted the boat to go. "Matt says to search for him on the west side of that big island."

"What do you mean? Search for him?" demanded Oak. "Doesn't Matt have him in sight?"

"He says he lost him."

"Crap!"

*   *   *

Smythe was very pleased with himself. He continued to search for the boat that had been shadowing him, but it was nowhere to be seen. However, he was worried that O'Malley might spot him again, or that he had passed off the chase to an ally. He plopped in the passenger side captain's chair. "Now, tell me, my young friend, just what is this perfect place you are taking us to?"

"It is quite secluded," replied Edgard, even though it is in a busy part of the lake. It is near the entrance of The Narrows. It's called Shelving Rock Bay. We can anchor there and go ashore to a nature trail."

"I am not sure I am liking this," said Smythe. "Why do we have to anchor?"

"You said you did not want anyone to notice us getting off the lake. Well, people anchor at Shelving Rock Bay all the time and hike the nature trail. If someone were to see us, we would look like ordinary hikers. Besides, it lies alongside the old Knapp Estate, so it is one of the few places along this shore that is undeveloped."

"Look at me, you twit. I am wearing black dress trousers and street shoes. Do I look like an ordinary tourist to you?"

"I have thought of that. If there is anyone around, you can change into one of Mr. Winkelman's bathing suits. There is always a spare in the hold. Problem solved."

"Okay, that might work, but what about this Knapp Estate? Won't there be a lot of people there?"

"No, it burned to the ground many years ago and nothing was ever built back. It is just empty land."

"I am looking at this chart and it does seem like this is a fairly isolated area, but it also looks like a long way to the road. You're not planning on trying to get me lost, are you?" asked Smythe.

"No, that's what makes this the perfect spot. The trail is well marked. You cannot see it on a navigational chart, but there is a little road called Hogstown Road, that leads to the trailhead. There is a parking lot not far from the lake for people who want to hike the trail, but do not have access to a boat. I promise you, there are always cars there. I am assuming you know how to steal one."

"As it happens, that is within my skill set. You find me a car and I guarantee we will have a ride out," said Smythe.

"Once you get a car you can head up the dirt road and work your way out to SR 149. From there, you can go to

Vermont or anywhere else you like."

"You are starting to hurt my feelings," said Smythe. "It's starting to sound like you do not want to continue on with this adventure. You don't think I am going to leave you behind, do you?"

"I suppose not," said Edgard, a bit sorrowfully.

"Buck up, my friend, you are being very helpful. Once I secure my diamonds, I will be leaving you, and you need never again concern yourself with me."

Edgard nodded his head, not knowing what to say, but being sure it would not serve his interest to say what he was thinking, and call the man what he was – a liar.

"So, how much further to this Shelving Rock Bay?" asked Smythe.

"Not too far," replied Edgard. "That is Huckleberry Island in front of us. We have to go past Hens and Chickens Island and then the bay is just past Fourteen Mile Island. It will not be long."

"Good, because I am in a bit of a hurry," said Smythe.

Edgard made no reply, but he thought, *I am in a hurry too, to get away from your sorry ass.*

CHAPTER FORTY TWO

Matt's head was turning and his eyes were darting as he cruised the entire length of Long Island in a frenzied effort to locate the yellow Four Winns containing Smythe. It was a futile effort. Not knowing what happened to Danny was eating at him, and he was anguished with enormous guilt at losing contact with their best hope of finding him. He positioned himself halfway between the north end of Long Island and Elizabeth Island to wait for Oak and Kevin, hoping they had better luck.

Standing in the bow of Danny's boat, he scanned the lake with binoculars. There were people and boats everywhere. The only yellow boat he saw was the one from Chic's towing the parasailing customers. Time was slipping by, and he felt a rising tide of hopelessness.

"Any luck?" called Kevin from the boat they had conned from Marvel Fargo.

Matt just shook his head and did not even bother to ask them, since their mere presence announced the failure of their efforts.

"We need a helicopter or a plane to do an aerial search," said Oak.

"Good luck with that! Reardon is trying to get the Sheriff's copter to do a search, but who knows if or when that will start," said O'Malley.

"So, what do you suggest we do?" Kevin asked Matt.

"The best use of our resources would be for you guys to search the west side of the lake and I'll continue up the east side," replied Matt.

"Nope, that's not going to happen," said Oak. "We stay

together!"

"Why?" asked Matt. "Separated we double our chances of finding Smythe."

"Maybe, but if you do find him by yourself, you will have quadrupled the chances that this wacked out MI-5 assassin will kill you. And then, where would we be?"

"I can take care of myself," said O'Malley defensively.

"Hold that thought," said Oak as he pulled out his ringing phone. "Mike! What've you got for us?"

"Good news, for a change. The fire department guys have the fire out and are checking out what's left of the cabin. So far there's no evidence that it was occupied."

"Thank God! That's great news!"

"What's great news?" asked Matt.

Oak signaled him to be quiet.

"There's more," said Reardon. "We just got a report from the Rangers that there is a yellow boat abandoned in Shelving Rock Bay."

"How is that good news?" asked Oak. "If it's Smythe, it sounds as if he's getting away!"

"There's only one road down to Shelving Rock Bay and it will be blocked in about five minutes. Anyone who tried to leave will have to be cleared by a deputy. I want you to go over there and keep an eye on the boat, just in case he realizes he is trapped and heads back to the boat."

"Okay, just a second," said Oak to Reardon. He then faced toward O'Malley's boat that was drifting a few yards away.

"Matt," he called out, "do you know how to get us to Shelving Rock Bay?"

"Sure, why?"

"I'll explain in a second," said Oak. "How long to get there?"

"Full out, maybe fifteen minutes," replied Matt.

"Mike, we can be there in about fifteen minutes."

"Okay, that's great. Understand, though, you are going as observers only. Take *no* action. You will be in support of Officer Lurman. He should be there ahead of you. Do whatever he says. Got it?"

"Of course," said Oak in a tone designed to express his amazement.

"Don't go all cowboy on me, Oak," said Reardon. "If I had any officer available for backup, you wouldn't even be getting this call."

"You can count on us, Mike!" said Oak as he ended the call.

"What did Mike say?" asked Kevin.

Oak spoke loud enough so that Matt could also hear the reply. "They searched what's left of the cabin. There was no body, so they think Danny is still alive. The Rangers spotted Smythe's boat over in Shelving Rock Bay, and Reardon wants us to get our asses over there as quickly as possible and grab up Smythe!"

*　　　*　　　*

Near the end of the nineteenth century George Knapp, the founder of Union Carbide, went for a boat ride on Lake George. He took one look at the Hundred Island House Hotel in Shelving Rock Bay and fell in love with the location. He bought it, tore down the hotel, and created a grand estate further up the mountain, complete with an electric tram that brought his few select visitors up the hill and directly into the main house.

The tram was quite a luxury in an era when much of the country was still not electrified; but, sadly, it proved to be his undoing. In 1917, the tram caught fire and the estate burned to the ground. He never rebuilt, and his heirs sold most of the land to the state of New York, who put it into a conservation trust.

"Forever Wild" is one of the great state level conservation programs in the country. It enabled a young boy from Africa to spend carefree days swimming in the bay, hiking the many trails around the Knapp Estate and exploring the beauties of nature, which gave his soul time to heal from the horrors he had witnessed in his own country.

Edgard's senses were overwhelmed each time he

approached the Falls, a wondrous black and white gem set in the lush green of the dense surrounding foliage. Sunlight filters through the canopy of trees and the water seems alive, as the reflected sparkles of the sunlight jump from place to place.

At the top, a very wide expanse of Shelving Rock Brook calmly spills over a uniform ridgeline, creating a ten-foot high curtain of white water. The disciplined display soon devolves to chaos as the water pours over more and more boulders and splits into the two main tributaries seen at the bottom before once again turning into a calm brook that meanders over the relatively flat land and eases its way into Lake George.

For Edgard and his friends, after a long school year nothing felt as liberating as running through these woods to Shelving Rock Falls. They would race to see who could get up the cold, crashing white water that came hurtling down this broad stair-stepped cascade. No one was better at the more than fifty-foot climb than Edgard. He had an uncanny ability to place his feet just right on the slippery rocks, and find the perfect handholds to get up the slippery face of the waterfall.

*   *   *

Edgard jumped from the swim platform, allowing his head to go three feet under the water. The cool embrace of the lake over his entire body felt wonderful; it felt energizing; it made him believe that his risky plan might even work. He stayed underwater as long as he could, allowing Lake George to soothe him. Finally, as his lungs began to burn, he gave one powerful kick and his head popped out of the water. He gulped down a huge gasp of clean, fresh air.

Spinning back toward the boat, he saw Smythe still standing on the swim platform in his trousers and dress shoes. He did not seem to be looking forward to the plunge. "Come in," urged Edgard, "the water is beautiful!"

Smythe gave Edgard a look that made his blood run cold. It was odd to have the embodiment of such evil sharing such an exceptionally perfect place. Wordlessly, Smythe took one large step off the boat and came up for air almost immediately. Edgard watched with satisfaction as the boat, complying with Newton's Third Law, started to drift away from the force of Smythe's pushing on it to step off. Edgard could only hope that the mushroom anchor he had tied on the bow cleat at a depth three feet from the lake's bottom, did not hook onto something before someone noticed the loose boat and called for help.

The two men swam to shore and climbed the slippery slope leading to a path near the edge of the bay. "You see," said Edgard, "a marked trail, just as I promised you."

"Yes, yes, very good. Brilliant. Now let's get going," said Smythe.

Five minutes into the hike Smythe was already beginning to have doubts about this decision. Edgard seemed just a little too enthusiastic, which made him suspicious; his John Lobb shoes, which had always been so comfortable, were wet and allowing his feet to slip about; he could feel a blister rising on his right heel; and he had been stung by a deer fly. He was not a fan of nature.

Edgard was made to walk two steps ahead of Smythe so that he could be closely watched. When he got to a fork in the trail, Edgard did not hesitate. He went to the right.

"Hold on," said Smythe.

Edgard stopped and looked over his shoulder at his captor.

"The little sign says the other trail is shorter. Let's go that way."

"It is shorter," said Edgard, but it is much steeper and it only leads to the Knapp Estate, where we cannot go. We would have to backtrack to here anyway. Besides, the lower parking lot is this way, not far from the Falls.

"What Falls?" asked Smythe.

"Come along and you will see," said Edgard, as he headed out again down the path he had previously selected. The two men walked along in silence for another few minutes.

Ahead of him on the path, Edgard could see the wooden bridge he had remembered from his days playing here as a child. It was just as he had recalled it - flat, wide, and with no side rails of any kind. It had been the perfect place to sit on a hot day and dangle your toes into the cool mountain brook. Today, it would serve a different purpose.

Normally, Edgard would never consider fighting Smythe; but the way he carried himself, as if he were in pain, and his swollen face were all the proof Edgard needed that Smythe had been in a violent confrontation. Edgard felt he had a chance to beat an injured Smythe.

"How much further?" asked Smythe.

Edgard looked over his shoulder to answer the question. He kept walking as he did so, and when he felt the moment was right, he deliberately tripped and fell to his hands and knees. This earned a laugh from Smythe and a snide comment, "Come on, Baryshnikov, you'll miss your curtain time at the ballet if we don't get going."

Edgard dug his right hand deep into the soft sand and gravel alongside the path. He stood quickly and muttered an apology as he stepped onto the bridge. He took a few steps and then, without warning, spun around and hurled the sand and gravel into the slits that Smythe's swollen eyes had become.

Smythe screamed in pain and rage. When he raised his hands to clear his eyes, Edgard went on the attack again, lowering his shoulder, running into Smythe like Jadeveon Clowney after Vincent Smith. The momentum drove Smythe to the side, and both men tumbled into the brook. Edgard landed on top of Smythe, who had landed hard in the shallow water, the rocks just beneath the surface pounding into his back and head. Sitting on top, Edgard smashed his fist into Smythe's face.

Wasting no time, he sprang out of the brook and began running down the path toward the sound of the waterfall. He was astonished at how quickly Smythe was able to regain his footing.

"Stop or I will shoot!" screamed Smythe.

Edgard did not stop or look back. He had one goal. He was going up the waterfall. He knew if he made it, he would be free from Smythe.

Despite his fury, Smythe knew that Edgard was his only connection to the diamonds. He could not kill him. It is much more difficult to shoot to wound a target than it is to shoot to kill that same target. The difficulty is compounded when the target is running, when there are trees that impair the line of sight, and when the shooter has sand in his swollen eyes. However, Myles Smythe was the best in his class when it came to shooting with a handgun.

On a peaceful summer day, in the quiet of the woods, his Glock sounded like a cannon going off.

*   *   *

As predicted, Lurman had arrived at Shelving Rock Bay first, in his center console Boston Whaler owned by the Bolton Landing P.D. He was trying to remain inconspicuous by floating just east and north of Fourteen Mile Island.

"Hi, Dave," said Matt, as he drew alongside the Whaler. "Where's Smythe's boat?"

"Over there," said Lurman, pointing toward an outcropping of land that formed the western edge of the bay. "It had been way up there," he retargeted his index finger toward a spot in the middle of the bay close to the shoreline.

"What's the plan? Are you just going to let it drift?"

Oak pulled up to the other side of the Whaler just in time to hear the exchange.

"My orders are to keep an eye on the boat, and to stay out of sight as much as possible," said Lurman.

"Of course," said Oak, "in that Police Boat, you might as well have a brass band and fireworks to announce your presence. Smythe will never come back if he sees you!"

"Here's what we should do," said Kevin. "Dave, you need to be close, but out of sight, so you need to hide behind Fourteen Mile Island. We need to reposition Smythe's boat so that, if he is driven back to the lake, he can get to it; but we need to somehow disable it."

"I agree," said Oak.

Matt took one of Danny's mooring lines off the bow cleat and held it up saying, "You guys tow the boat back and I'll get in and wrap this around the propeller. The boat will start but he won't be going very far."

"We're not doing anything until I clear it with Reardon!" said Lurman.

"Of course not," said Oak, as Kevin pushed them off. Oak engaged the engine and took off for Shelving Rock Bay.

"You get back here!" commanded Lurman.

Matt smiled at him and said, "Don't worry. I'll get them." Before Lurman could respond, Matt's SeaRay had lunged forward and was headed right for Shelving Rock Bay.

The two boats made it to the bay in no time. Kevin was in the process of getting a towline on the bow eye of Smythe's boat when Matt cruised up. "Boy, is he pissed!" said Matt.

"He'll get over it," said Oak.

"It's like I always say, *'It's easier to get forgiveness than it is to get permission,'*" offered Kevin.

"Wise words indeed," said Oak. "Words to live by."

"Maybe that's why you've been divorced so often," suggested O'Malley, as Oak began to move the boat back into position.

"No, that's because I couldn't get either forgiveness or permission," said Oak as he put the boat back into neutral. Matt jumped in the water to foul the propeller of Smythe's boat while Kevin undid the line from the bow eye.

Matt surfaced and gave the others a big "thumbs up" just as the sound of a shot, and then two more shots in rapid succession, echoed across Shelving Rock Bay.

"What the hell was that?" yelled O'Malley.

"Small arms fire," said Oak grimly. "Let's go!"

Matt, who was already in the water, made it to shore first and began running in the direction the gunfire came from, with Oak and Kevin just a short distance behind.

CHAPTER FORTY THREE

Smythe's first shot tore harmlessly into the side of the hill, sending up a tuft of moss and leaves. The second shot passed close enough to Edgard to tear a hole in his tee shirt, but did not strike his body. There was a small group of people at the Falls, and along the path, that were beginning to scream and run frantically, but they did not know where to run. There was a scrum of people, all trying to go in different directions that Smythe had to make his way through.

Smythe had climbed out of the brook and was now running on the path toward the waterfalls when he shot his third errant bullet. This one struck Barbara O'Toole, a visitor from Rome, New York, as she stepped between Edgard and Smythe in a panicked effort to seek safety. She dropped straight down, collapsing like the buffaloes when they were shot in old western movies, from the bullet that hit her thigh.

Edgard had reached the bottom of the Falls. It was just as he remembered it to be. He began to work his way up the right side of the Falls. Smythe pushed people aside in his rush to Shelving Rock Falls. He had a difficult time making progress, though, as he kept slipping on the loose gravel and wet rocks in his thoroughly drenched John Lobb Fencote loafers - stylish for a business meeting, but hardly the footwear of choice for a run through the woods, or a climb up a waterfall.

None of the shortcomings of his preparation for this effort dissuaded Smythe from his single-minded pursuit of the swift young man, now nearly out of sight, and quickly climbing the Falls. His passion to possess the diamonds dulled all his senses and clouded his judgment as he prepared to start his own assault on the Falls.

Smythe either overestimated his ability or underestimated the force of the water and the slipperiness of the rocks. His first attempt to jump to a rock resulted in a fall, and a wet landing in the pool at the base of the waterfall. Undaunted, and with more respect for the force of the water, he moved to the side, as Edgard had done before him, and attempted a more tactical climb, trying to stay out of the thigh-deep water and in the calf-deep water.

Once he was about a quarter of the way up, the going got tougher and the rocks bigger and even more slippery. However, he was encouraged because now he could see Edgard, and he was keeping pace with him. Had he not been so single-minded and preoccupied by thoughts of possessing the diamonds, he might have noticed Matt, Kevin and Oak arriving at the base of the Falls.

Smythe was screaming at Edgard to halt, while Matt was yelling up to Smythe to give up. All the commands were lost in the cacophonous roar of the water pouring down the face of Shelving Rock Falls.

"He can't hear you," Kevin yelled, to be heard over the rushing water.

Smythe had reached a plateau at about twenty-five feet up the Falls. He could see Edgard at about the forty-foot level. However, the people below could also see Smythe.

"Should I shoot him?" asked Oak.

"No, we need him alive if we are ever going to find Danny," said Matt. "We need to go up after him."

"Okay. You take the right side and I'll circle back and run up the path," replied Oak.

Kevin, always a sports fan, picked up a smooth river rock the approximate size and shape of a baseball, tossing it up and catching it in his right hand several times to get the heft of it. "I've got five bucks says I can hit him," said Kevin.

"I'll take that bet," replied Oak, as Kevin leaned back and threw the rock with all his might. The rock sailed up over the water and struck Smythe a glancing blow to his left calf.

"That doesn't count," said Oak. "We can't tell if it hit him or just brushed his pant leg."

O'Malley was starting up the outside route, about ten feet up, trying to keep in the shallow water, when Smythe, startled by being hit by the rock, spun around and looked to see where it had come from.

"Uh, oh," said Oak, "I think you pissed him off!"

Shocked to see Matt, Kevin and Oak, Smythe uttered a primal scream, raised his Glock, and shot down at Kevin - who had quickly jumped behind a large tree at the first sight of the rising gun.

"That counts!" yelled Matt. "You owe Kevin five bucks."

*   *   *

Edgard heard the shot and assumed it was directed at him. Fearing his plan had failed, he looked up to see how much further he had to go. He knew that, once he was at the top, the terrain and the woods would be familiar to him, and he was sure Smythe would not be able to track him. But – the last fifteen feet of the climb would leave him completely exposed to gunfire from Smythe, if Smythe was able to get up the Falls another ten feet or so.

When Edgard turned back to see where Smythe was, he was surprised to see Smythe directing his attention down the Falls. Although he could feel his resolve faltering under the pressure of Smythe's relentless pursuit, he looked up for his next handhold when he saw a young woman with dark skin, black hair in two tight braids, and a broad smooth face looking down at him and smiling. *"Go on! Don't stop! You can make it!"* she urged.

Suddenly reinvigorated, Edgard knew not only that he could make it, but that he *would* make it. He scrambled up the short remaining distance to the top and pulled himself over the ridgeline and onto the mossy rock alongside the brook. He was allowing himself only a moment to rest and exult in his escape before he would get up and dash across the small meadow to disappear into the dense forest.

He was not the only one with a plan for his immediate future. A man with a gun came up from behind him and barked orders. "Don't move! Put your hands behind your back!"

With the sun in his eyes, he could not make out who his new captor was; but he felt the snug embrace of the flex cuffs restraining his wrists, and the pain in his shoulders as he was lifted to his feet and shoved into a waiting car.

*   *   *

Smythe was frustrated that he had no shot at Kevin, who was behind a tree; or Oak, who was running toward the bridge to access the path on the left and was out of his range. Hearing Matt yell, Smythe moved to his right, toward the center of the Falls to get a better angle at his pursuer. Sighting down the barrel, he could not quite get a clear shot, so he moved even further right.

Oak could see what was happening so he stopped and pulled out his service revolver. At this distance, it was a one in a million shot, but he could not let Smythe kill Matt without at least trying. Oak held his service revolver with two hands and braced his forearms on a large boulder to steady his aim.

Smythe had moved too far into the main flow of the waterfall. Just as Oak was beginning to apply pressure to his trigger, the full force of the water took Smythe's legs out from under him. He disappeared for a second as he fell backward.

He reappeared almost instantaneously, moving with the swift current of falling water, and dropped feet first onto the next lower level of the waterfall.

Smythe tried to stand, but once again the powerful stream of water knocked him down. He struggled mightily to regain control of his body, but the force of the flowing water was just too intense. He succeeded in getting up on his knees, only to be knocked down again by the water when he tried to stand.

Matt and the others could see him struggle, but were helpless to render him aid. He tumbled down to the next level, his arms and legs akimbo.

Smythe was now in desperate trouble. He was on his back, the water streaming over his face. His right leg was shattered and his left leg was jammed between a fallen tree trunk and one of the many boulders that made up the waterfall. The weight of the water made it impossible for him to free his trapped leg.

Unable to breathe, with the water pouring over his face, he tried to sit up, gasping for air, but the intense pain from his legs and the force of the falling water quickly pushed him back down.

Matt immediately realized that whatever they had been doing was over, and this was now a rescue mission. Women were screaming, children were crying, and Kevin and Oak were racing toward Matt to see if they could render assistance.

Matt was closest to Smythe, but he faced the same problem that Smythe had – it was impossible to resist the unrelenting force of the water. O'Malley cautiously began to move toward the center of the Falls.

He could see Smythe again sit up and try to get air into his burning lungs. This time, all Smythe could do was cough up water uncontrollably, as he made a futile effort to grab at a low hanging tree branch that was just out of his reach.

Once again the water forced him back down. The flow of water over his face made it impossible to breathe, pushing him past the endurance his training had given him, to the edge of madness. The more he struggled, the more firmly his leg became wedged in place.

Matt knew he had to act quickly. At most, he figured Smythe had only one, or, at best, two attempts left in him to sit up. There was a rock sticking out of the water fairly close to Smythe, but the deep, rapidly flowing water between it and O'Malley's position made it impossible to traverse on foot.

Matt did the calculus in his head. He had only one choice left if he was going to save Smythe. To get to that rock he would have to jump, and hope to both land on the rock and not slip off it. He would have only one chance; and, if he failed, he would most likely share Smythe's fate and lose any hope of finding Danny.

O'Malley made the sign of the cross and jumped. Kevin screamed, "No! Don't do it!" but by then Matt was in the air. He landed firmly on both feet, but then they slid out from under him and he fell, straight down, butt first onto the hard rock.

That is where he stopped. He felt pain like an electric current passing up his spine into the top of his head. He closed his eyes, unable to believe that he could be so stupid and so lucky all at the same time.

O'Malley lay back and then he rolled over onto his belly and squirmed his way over to the edge of the rock. Smythe was still trapped between the fallen tree and the boulder, and Matt's rock was just out of his reach. Matt managed to slip his belt off and wrapped a section of it around his right hand. He watched, waited, and prayed for Smythe to sit up again.

As soon as Smythe reappeared, coughing and spitting out water, Matt tossed the loose end of the belt to him, screaming, "Grab the belt! Grab the belt!" Smythe lurched for the belt but missed it and went back under water, using what little breath he had gotten to scream his agony.

Matt pulled the belt in to get ready to toss it again when Smythe reappeared. The moments seemed like hours, and Matt knew that if he were not successful this time, this drama would soon be over.

Exerting what must have been near super human effort, Smythe popped up out of the water further than he had the last time, and when Matt threw him the loose end of the belt, he grabbed it. Matt felt a thrill of exultation that he had the man. Smythe looked at him, his eyes wide with panic like an animal caught in a trap, pain etched into his face.

Smythe pulled on the belt as hard as he could, bringing Matt a little closer to the water. Matt was surprised at the strength the man still had in him. "Hold on. Help is coming," said Matt, trying to encourage him, and hoping that someone had called the Fire Rescue team.

Smythe's face was contorted in pain and the belt began to slip through his fingers. He looked at Matt and just shook his head *no*.

Matt screamed, "Don't give up! You can do it!" Again, Smythe shook his head *no* and bit into his lower lip so hard that blood spurted out. His eyes rolled so far back in his head that Matt could see little but the sclera.

Matt knew that Smythe was reaching the end of his endurance and was experiencing a level of pain beyond human toleration, and he had borne it longer than any normal man could have.

"I have to know," screamed Matt. "Where is my friend, Danny?"

The response was half primal scream and half words. Matt thought he said, "live free." With that, Smythe lost consciousness, allowing the belt to slip from his hand. Once again, this time for the final time, the water forced Smythe to lie out on his back with tons of water flowing over him every minute, pounding his lifeless body against the rocks.

CHAPTER FORTY-FOUR

Physically, mentally and emotionally spent by the effort to save Smythe, Matt rolled over onto his back. The bright sun was blinding, so he clamped his eyes shut, placing his forearm over them for further protection. The ceaseless flow of water all around him drowned out all other sounds, so he was unaware of his friends calling out to him.

He had done all he could to save that bastard, Smythe. Tears of frustration and anger poured out of him. He had failed to save Smythe, and he realized that in so failing, he also failed to save Danny.

O'Malley had no way of comprehending such unmitigated evil. He had risked his life to save Smythe's, yet Smythe, who must have known he was not going to get out alive, refused to divulge the location of his friend. Only pure evil could drive a man to keep such a secret when he would get no benefit from it, and lost the possibility of some small act of redemption at the end of his life.

Instead, all he got for his efforts to save Smythe was a scream and some lame personal mantra, "live free." Matt wondered bitterly if that was on the Parkington family Coat of Arms. The son of a bitch was defiant to the end.

Even if Danny were dead, Matt had been determined to return him to his family so they could have closure. Now, everything was lost. He felt empty and cold stranded out on a rock in the middle of Shelving Rock Falls.

Matt had no idea how long he had been lying on that rock when he heard someone calling to him. "Hey, buddy! Wake up!"

Matt uncovered his eyes and blinked in the bright

sunlight. The firefighter was dangling from a rope that had been strung from one side of the Falls to the other.

"Stay seated, but put this on," said the firefighter as he dropped a SRT harness down to Matt.

"My name is Will. Will Kacheris. We're going to get you out of here."

Matt pulled the harness over his legs and then struggled to get his arms and shoulders through the top.

"You're doing great, pal," said the firefighter as calmly as if he were helping a child with his homework.

"Now, you need this too," he said as he lowered a bright orange helmet down to Matt. "Be sure the chin strap is really tight."

Will Kacheris was spinning a little on his rope but he tried never to lose eye contact with Matt. He lowered an automatically inflatable personal flotation device that Matt also put on.

"Okay, we are almost ready to get you out of here. I need you to locate the D-ring on the front of the harness and clip this rope to it. Give me a thumbs up when you've got it."

The rope with the carabineer was swaying in the wind, just out of Matt's reach. Standing, he shuffled over toward the edge of the rock to make a grab for it when his left foot slipped on the wet moss covering that portion of the rock. The people below screamed as Matt lurched toward the water, but he was able to catch himself and move back toward the center of the rock.

"Take it easy, buddy. Just stay put. I'll get the rope to you," said the young, unflappable Kacheris. The next two passes went wide; but, on the third attempt, Matt was able to grab the rope. He quickly snapped the carabineer into the D-ring, looked up, grinned at his rescuer, and stuck his thumb triumphantly in the air.

"You're doing great! You're a pro at this," yelled the firefighter. "Now, just grab onto the rope with both hands, right at face level."

Matt seized the rope.

"That's good. Now, just hold on. I'm going to lift you.

You don't have to do a thing but stay calm."

Matt nodded to indicate he understood the instructions. Will Kacheris tugged at a line that went through a pulley and Matt could feel the harness tighten on him as he slowly rose over the rock. He looked up and could see a rope attached to Will's waist go taut as other firefighters tugged on it. Both he and Kacheris began to slide toward dry land.

As the two men began to move, Matt could hear cheering from below. He looked down and saw a group of about twenty people gathered in a cluster, waving their arms and cheering their relief, as he got closer to the side.

He also saw Smythe, still trapped by the log and the boulders. It was surreal and overwhelming to feel the relief of knowing that he was going to be safe, while at the same time looking at the body of a man he did not even know, but whose fate he nearly shared.

Among the arms reaching up for him, to ease him to the ground, were all his friends, including Mike Reardon, who had rushed to the Falls as quickly as he could. One of the other firefighters wrapped Matt in a silver blanket and gave him hot, black coffee to drink. Matt did not like coffee, but he was so chilled from the spray coming off the Falls that he was grateful for the warmth. An EMT began to examine Matt.

"Matt, we could see you talking to him," said Oak. "Did he tell you where Danny is?"

Matt sighed and said, "No, he was a son of a bitch to the very end. I tried to get him to tell me, but all I got was some two-bit personal philosophy."

"What did he say?" asked Reardon.

"It was hard to make out, but I think he said, 'Live free' . . . live free! . . .," said Matt, turning the phrase over in his mind and trying to make some sense of it. "What the hell does that mean?"

"I don't know," said Oak, "but it seems like an odd thing to say given the circumstances. When exactly did he say it?"

"I don't know," said Matt. "It's all kind of confusing. I think it was right after I asked him to tell me where Danny is."

"Wait a minute! Let me get this straight!" said Kevin.

"You asked him where was Danny and the only thing he said was 'live free?'"

"Yeah, pretty much," said Matt, curious now about Kevin's excitement.

"Mike," said Kevin, "did you have anyone canvass the other cabins up at Juniper Hills?"

"Of course, but we didn't turn up much. Most of them were empty so there was no answer."

"Do you still have anyone up there?"

"Yeah, I left Billy to stay with the fire department. He should still be there."

"Great! I've got a favor to ask you. I was reading the signs as we were looking for Smythe's cabin. I'm sure I saw a place called "Live Free." Please, humor me and have Billy find that place and kick down the door if he has to. If I'm wrong, I'll pay for all the repairs," said Kevin.

"Holy crap! You're right! I went to that place myself! It's right behind the cabin that burned!" said Reardon, as he began barking orders into his Motorola.

After what seemed like hours, but what in reality was about five very tense minutes, Reardon's radio crackled to life.

"Chief, we got him! He's pretty busted up, but we got him!"

EPILOGUE

Matt was scheduled to stay in Lake George until near the end of August, but Oak and Kevin were supposed to go home just a couple of days after the events on Shelving Rock Falls. Once Danny was freed from the closet in "Live Free," he was taken to the Glens Falls Hospital where his diagnosis included a deep, penetrating puncture wound to the buttocks, multiple blunt force traumas, a separated shoulder with a torn labrum, a concussion, rib fractures, and a chipped front tooth. They kept him a week before releasing him.

Kevin and Oak extended their stay in order to visit him, and help him when he got home. Three days out of the hospital, he was ready for a big celebration on the deck overlooking his "million dollar view" of Lake George.

Oak was in the hot tub using his massive wingspan to occupy an entire side of the tub, his Genny Light perched on the edge. Danny's daughters were helping get the food ready. Danny was working the grill, basting the chicken with his "secret" barbeque sauce that was sold in every grocery store in the country. Timmy, Sybil, and all their children from Arcady Bay came to help celebrate his survival. Music was playing and everyone was in a great humor. Even J.P. Truak showed up, at the invitation of Mike Reardon.

"What's he doing here?" asked Matt, in less than a friendly tone.

"O'Malley, get over it," said Truak. "It wasn't my fault that the State Department turned your file over to the bad guys."

"I know," sighed Matt. "I just enjoy nursing a grudge," he said, as he handed Truak a beer. "But really, why are you here?"

"He's here because I asked him to come, to brief you on some background he has. Unofficially, of course."

"Of course," said O'Malley. "What've you got?" he asked, as he gestured for him to sit at the round, redwood picnic table with him and Kevin.

"I think I can fill in some blanks for you. "We, meaning the CIA and Homeland Security, have determined that the background on Parkington that MI-5 provided was accurate. He was a superstar agent who went rogue. They cut him loose and he went nuts. Before he left, he stole the Myles Smythe cover identity and probably killed one of their company shrinks."

"The story gets murky after that," Truak continued. "MI-5 tried to find him and bring him to ground, but he was too cagey. He had slipped into an underworld of drug and gun traffickers. He was the guy putting the deals together.

We're pretty sure he was here because he matched up a drug dealer with an arms merchant selling to the Boko Haram in Africa. The arms merchant wanted cash. The drug dealer, a guy named Fahran Zadran, was stuck with a ton of cash he was having a hard time storing here in the States. The arms merchant got the cash and Zadran, the drug dealer, was supposed to get a box of blood diamonds from the Boko Haram that would fit neatly into a Swiss bank safety deposit box."

"When we searched the cabin where we found Danny," interjected Reardon, "we found a valise stuffed with Kimberley Process Certificates to authenticate the diamonds and make them marketable as conflict-free diamonds."

"The only problem was that Zadran, the drug dealer, didn't trust the Chechen to pick up and deliver the diamonds so he sent Parkington to get them for him. What we think happened was that, after he set up the deal, Parkington got greedy and decided to keep the diamonds for himself. "

"So, that's why he killed the Chechen," filled in O'Malley.

"Maybe, but the autopsy showed that the Chechen had been tortured before he was shot, so we are speculating that Parkington either didn't know where the diamonds were, or he thought that the Chechen had already obtained them."

"I still don't get it. Why bring the diamonds to Albany of all places?" asked Kevin.

"The world where these deals go down is a very paranoid place," replied Truak. "If they haven't done business with you before, they sure aren't going to do business with you now. We think the Boko Haram people trusted the Chechen. Their man on the ground here, Jambo, a local emigrant thug, was found floating in the Nile. We have no idea why. But they didn't trust either very much."

Truak went on, "We think Zadran trusted Parkington as much as he trusts anyone, which is to say not at all. Anyway, we think that part of the reason they liked Albany is that it's only a few hours to Canada. It's an easy border to cross and then they could reship the diamonds to Switzerland."

"Mike, what about that kid you picked up at the waterfall?" asked Matt. "How does he fit into all this?"

"His name is Edgard Onobanjo. He has quite a story. After he found his family slaughtered by the local rebels back in Africa, he went by himself, on foot, hiding out from the rebels, to find an Irish Mission. Someone there arranged for him to emigrate to America. He used to live up here, with the Winkelmans."

"Wow, tough life," said Kevin.

"Yeah, but he did well here. He was a great kid, according to the neighbors, and the teachers at his school. He was supporting himself through college by working as a baggage handler at the airport."

"Uh, oh," said Matt, "I think I know how he gets involved."

"He claims he was duped by that woman who was killed at the Winkelman's house, Nubia, and coerced by Jambo and then by Parkington. Anything he did, he says, he did under duress."

"Do you believe him?" asked Kevin.

"I do; but, more importantly, we have a tough as nails prosecutor up here, Lawson Lamar. He's a by-the-books kind of guy, who is a fearless trial lawyer. He takes the toughest cases to trial rather than take a bad plea deal. He'd send his own mother to jail if he thought it was the right thing to do."

"He believes Onobanjo, and even if he didn't, there's no one left alive to challenge his story. Parkington's gone, Jambo's gone, his co-worker, Keenadiid Amiin Kuciil is gone; and his supposed girlfriend, Nubia was killed by Parkington, according to Edgard, to try to force him to tell where the diamonds were."

"Does Edgard know anything about where the diamonds are?" asked Matt.

"He says no. He says he never heard of any diamonds. He claims all he did was hold a package that Jambo told him was on a flight. He never opened it. He never gave it to anyone. He put it where he was told to put it and he has no idea where it went after that, or who took it from the airport."

"Do you think there ever were any diamonds?" asked Matt.

"Given the level of all the players, I'm guessing there were diamonds, but only God knows what happened to them. I doubt we will ever know."

*   *   *

It took several days of haranguing by Marvel Fargo, but the Rangers finally did tow her boat back to her dock. She was not happy about the condition it was in after the evidence technicians had gone over it, nor was she happy that it had been commandeered in the first place. She did remember the trooper's name that had taken her boat so she filed a formal complaint. She was shocked to find out that the New York State Troopers did not employ anyone by Oak's given name, Stanislaus Okonski.

The news story about the robbery at Annie King's Fine Wines and Spirits made it to YouTube and went viral. Annie King flew to New York City where she made an appearance on the Tonight Show. She autographed a baseball bat for Jimmy Fallon and played beer pong with him on the show. She beat him with no trouble. The clip of her at the end of the show dancing with Roots also made it to YouTube and it went viral as well.

Edgard was questioned and released. He went back to the Winkelmans, but the house was a crime scene, so the three of them went to stay at the home of a relative. While there Edgard asked if it would be okay if he called them "Mom" and "Dad." Both Winkelmans cried and hugged him as they told him that it was something they had prayed he would be able to do someday. They felt as if it meant that he had finally completed the healing from the mental wounds associated with finding his family slaughtered.

There was a second body found in the residence of Kenny Ames a/k/a Keenadiid Amiin Kuciil. The body was of Zadran's assassin, Sadiki Okoro. The police never did figure out who he was, or how he fit into the picture. His body wound up being buried as a John Doe by the county in a Potters Field.

Nearby, in the same Potter's Field was the body of Nubia Mayardit. She may have actually believed she was of royal blood, but none of her subjects claimed her body.

The story for Bob Anniston ended on a happier note. At first, everyone assumed it was obvious that he was a low-life philanderer who murdered his young mistress. He spent days on the front page of all the regional newspapers. Fortunately, his wife stood by his side and he was vindicated when a young man named Bobby O'Shaughnessy came forward and admitted that his girlfriend, Maura, had told him that she had stolen the key for her boss' lake house, knowing that he was going out of town, and they were going to spend the weekend there. When he heard she had been murdered, he never went to Bolton Landing, and his fear kept him silent for weeks. Maura's parents identified him as her boyfriend, and when the police went to talk to him, he blurted out the truth. The salacious stories were all page one, above the fold. The true story was buried on page four of the local section.

Edgard did not move back to Albany. Instead, he transferred to SUNY Adirondack in Queensbury. He completed his degree in Conservation Sciences and became a Ranger on Lake George. He married and raised his family in the old Winkelman place, which he eventually inherited. He lived a simple life, devoted to his family, his faith and his career. He never sought to profit from the diamonds he had placed in the underwater cave. Except for one, the diamonds remain there undisturbed.

Several years after these events, Edgard read in the paper that the National Shrine of North American Martyrs was in great financial trouble and in danger of closing. Edgard, being very cautious, went to Saratoga and rented a pickup truck. He traveled to Auriesville, New York to visit the Shrine. He never took off the wide-billed sunhat he was wearing pulled low over his eyes. He kept his head bowed, prayerfully and never looked up for fear that even a Shrine might have security cameras.

Waiting until he was alone, he strolled by the donation box, placing one hand on top as if to steady himself. He hoped that no one would notice his hand over the slot, or hear the large diamond drop into the box. He left immediately, returning the rental pickup to Saratoga, prepared to tell anyone who asked that he had needed it to carry some yard waste to the dump.

It brought Edgard great satisfaction to read in the Post Star a week later about how some totally anonymous donor had left a valuable diamond in the donation box and that it would save the Shrine.

Edgard maintained one other secret until the day he died. He believed, with all his heart and soul, that he would have died at the hand of Myles Smythe on Shelving Rock Falls that day had it not been for the intercession of the Lily of the Mohawks, Kateri Tekakwitha. Whenever he was in trouble thereafter, he would close his eyes and he would see her hair twisted in twin black braids, and her beautiful, dark, broad face smiling at him. He could hear her urging him, *"Go on! Don't stop! You can make it!"*

The End

Author's Note

I have a deep affection and respect for the area where these stories are set, and for the history surrounding them, so I try to portray them as accurately as I can, consistent with the needs of good storytelling. There are some times when I have to take liberties and fictionalize aspects of real places or real events. To anyone offended by that, I offer my apologies.

Things that are not fictional include places like Shelving Rock Falls. It is there, it is beautiful, and it makes for a wonderful hike. However, it is very dangerous, and no one should consider trying to climb it, even if a psychopath with a gun is chasing him or her.

St. Kateri Tekakwitha is also real, and Blessed Sacrament Catholic Church in Bolton Landing had a significant role to play in her canonization by Pope Benedict XVI as the first Native North American saint on October 12, 2012. She is considered the patroness of the environment and ecology. Her shrine is located near Exit 28 on the New York Thruway, near the village of Fonda. She is also honored at the National Shrine of North American Martyrs in the town or Auriesville, New York, near where she was born. It is well worth the trip, and if you happen to have an extra diamond on you, it would not hurt to drop it in the donation box.

The author hopes you have enjoyed this Matt O'Malley mystery, and he invites you to visit him at www.ThomasGKane.com to share your thoughts, questions, reviews, and opinions about this work of fiction.

At the website, you will have the opportunity to write directly to the author; and, if you wish, have your thoughts published on the website.

The author also welcomes photographs of you reading either

Desperate Hours, Desperate Days *or* **Kateri's Treasure**

for publication on the website.

At the website, you will also have the opportunity to purchase this and other books by the author.

Thank you for spending your precious time reading this book!